BREA
LITTLE
HEART

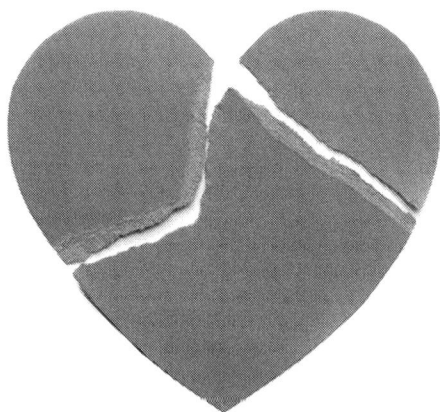

CHARLEIGH ROSE

Break Your Little Heart
Cover Designer: Amanda Simpson, Pixel Mischief Design
Interior Formatting: Stacey Ryan, Champagne Book Dessign

AUTHOR'S NOTE

Break Your Little Heart is book 2 in the Heartbreak Hill series and can be read as a standalone. Just be aware that you might read spoilers for book 1 if you read out of order. Hope you enjoy Holden & Valen!

CONTENT WARNINGS

Mentions of death/dying
Mentions of abuse (including SA, not on page)
Violence
Drug use
Graphic sex

For those who like them a little bit obsessed,
Holden's for you.

BREAK YOUR LITTLE HEART

ONE

Valen

One year ago

THIS WAS A BAD IDEA. I'VE HAD MY FAIR SHARE OF THEM IN THE past, but showing up unannounced to meet my boyfriend at a college party on a Friday night in my cheer uniform tops the list. He's in town this weekend, and since I had an away game, I wasn't going to be able to see him until tomorrow night. That was, until half the basketball team turned their bus ride into a puke fest thanks to bad sushi from last night's dinner. Needless to say, the game was canceled.

I reach into my cheer bag on the front seat, grabbing my sweatshirt and throwing it on over my uniform. Stepping out of my car, I rub my arms against the chilly night air. I hate the cold. Why couldn't my mom have gotten engaged to some rich man from somewhere with a more tropical climate? Massachusetts winters almost have me considering taking my dad up on his offer to spend the summer with his relatives in Spain. *Almost.* Not that he actually wants me to take him up on his offer.

Giggles that come from a group of drunk girls that I don't recognize snap me from my thoughts as I approach the white three-story apartment building. Two are blonde, one is a brunette, and all three are gorgeous and wearing the typical Massachusetts college girl uniform of black leather pants and black crop tops.

"Are you looking for the party?" Drunk Girl Number One says, clumsily throwing an arm over my shoulders, not waiting for an answer before she steers me inside with the other girls following behind. "It's this one," she explains needlessly, seeing as how the door she's pointing to practically shakes with the bass of the music coming from the other side. "Also, you're really pretty," she says, moving her mouth closer to my ear as the music grows louder.

"Thanks." I laugh under my breath, peeling her arm off of my shoulder.

I follow her inside the packed apartment, wondering how the hell they haven't gotten shut down due to the noise yet. Then again, I bet most of the tenants are other students since it's so close to the community college.

"Drink?" the girl tosses over her shoulder, leading me to the kitchen.

"I'm looking for my boyfriend," I shout over the noise. I see a few people I know—some from school, some who graduated before me—but it's dark and there are so many bodies here that it's hard to tell who anyone is. I spot Holden Ames, my best friend Shayne's stepbrother and perpetual pain in my ass, sitting in a chair while some girl dances and grinds on his lap. *Typical.*

"What's his name?"

"Liam."

She shrugs her shoulders, looking at her friends who have apparently adopted me for the time being. "Big dude? On the rowing team at Northeastern?" the brunette asks.

"That's him."

"Ooooh, he's hot. Congratulations," she remarks. "He's around here somewhere." She stands on her tiptoes, scanning the room.

An uneasy feeling settles in my stomach. I told Shayne just last week that I thought Liam and I were done. My first clue that things weren't quite right was the fact that I didn't miss him a single time after he left for college. He became busier. I became even less interested. We've slowly drifted apart, but any time I try to talk to him about it, he finds a way to avoid the conversation.

"He was with Tobin earlier," the other girl says. Tobin's the guy who lives here and I know he's friends with Liam, so that makes sense. "I think a few of them went to his room to smoke. They got in trouble for the smell last time they did it out front."

The first girl finds a bottle of vodka on the table cluttered with alcohol and Solo cups and beer cans. "Shot?" she asks, holding up the bottle in offering.

I shake my head. "No, thanks. I'm going to go find him," I say. After I say bye to my new friends, I push through the throng of bodies, making my way to where I think the bedrooms might be. I turn down the hallway, trying the first door I see. The room is bathed in a red glow from the LED lights lining the perimeter of the ceiling. The second thing I notice is a very un-rhythmic sound of skin slapping against skin. Jesus Christ.

Just as I start to close the door, I hear, "Fuck yes, baby."

I freeze, recognizing that voice all too well. I don't know how I imagined this night going, but walking in on my boyfriend balls deep inside someone who isn't me definitely wasn't it.

Neither of them seems to notice my presence. This is what shock must feel like. I should be raging right now. Screaming, yelling, storming out. Something. Yet, all I can do is frown, cocking my head to the side as I take in the scene playing out in front of me.

Liam thrusts into her from behind and the girl moans, whipping her head of blonde hair around, and that's when we lock eyes. That snaps me out of my trance. My heart starts pounding as my frozen shock melts and gives way to anger. The girl squeals, pulling away from Liam, and brings her knees up in front of her chest in a half-assed attempt at modesty.

"A little privacy?!" she shrieks as if she's the one being wronged—as if I'm the one intruding on a private moment between lovers—and well, apparently, I am.

Liam turns around, his smirk slipping when he realizes it's

me standing here. His eyes widen with pure panic as he scrambles off the bed, cupping his dick with both hands. The look on his face would be comical if the circumstances were different.

"Surprise." My voice is cold and hard, concealing the sting of betrayal I feel. I spin around before I'm hit with the onslaught of excuses that's sure to come.

"Valen, wait—"

"No, by all means, carry on." I slam the door shut and force my steps to keep a respectable pace as I head for the exit. I'm not going to make a scene, and I'm certainly not going to cry.

I knew something was up. Walking in on him in the act was a shock, but I'd be lying if I said I didn't see this thing coming to an end. I told myself I'd use this weekend to decide if I even wanted this anymore. Turns out, he's already moved on. He just didn't have the decency to tell me.

I push my way through the clusters of people gathered in the small living room, my eyes laser-focused on the front door. I just need to make it outside, and then I can lose my shit. I'm halfway there when I hear Liam call my name loud enough for everyone in Sawyer Point to hear, but I don't stop. I don't even pause.

"Valen, come on. We need to talk about this."

That has me pausing. I stop short and turn around, shaking my head, incredulous. Talk? His dick is still wet from another girl and he wants to *talk*? I want to scream at him, but I'm very aware of the fact that we've gained a rapt audience.

"I promise you, Liam, we have *nothing* to talk about."

He's wearing nothing but a pair of boxers as he scratches the back of his neck. He seems to consider his next move, beads of sweat rolling down his temples. As if this scene wasn't embarrassing enough, the music cuts out, allowing everyone the opportunity to hear us loud and clear. "Let's not be immature about this." He sounds exasperated, as if my being upset is inconveniencing him.

"That's what you get for dating high school girls," a bitter voice chimes in as the girl from his room appears behind him.

"Shut the fuck up, Tara."

Tara. So that's her name.

For once, I have no witty comeback or venomous retort on the tip of my tongue. I just…freeze. Humiliated. Stunned silent. And now every single person here is aware of exactly what just happened. I can *feel* their curious stares searing my skin. My ears get hot, either from anger or embarrassment or both, when suddenly, a warm, large hand captures mine, giving it a reassuring squeeze.

I frown, looking down at the hand that encases mine, then follow it up to the boy it belongs to.

"Well, this is awkward. You ready to get out of here, V?" Holden watches me expectantly, waiting for my response, casual as can be. It's the complete opposite of what I'm feeling. He's the last person I want to see right now.

"V?" Liam scoffs at the nickname that Holden has never once used for me—the nickname he just came up with on the spot for Liam's benefit—dragging my attention away from Holden. Liam's laser beam gaze is burning a hole through our locked hands as if he has any right to be upset. I snatch my hand out of Holden's, and Liam looks up to find me glaring at him before shifting his focus back to Holden.

"You been keeping my girl company while I've been gone?"

"Which one?" Holden quips with a pointed glance in his current companion's direction.

Outside. Fresh air. Only two feet away. *Cut it off.*

I turn for the door once more, and this time I don't look back. Once I'm outside, I hear the door to the apartment open again right behind me and I roll my eyes, hurrying my steps.

"I don't want to talk to you!" I yell over my shoulder without looking as I unzip my wristlet to find my keys.

"I don't want to talk to you either," comes a voice that

doesn't belong to Liam. I stop short, turning around as Holden approaches.

"Sorry," I mutter, not sounding sorry at all.

"It's all good. Rough night?"

I shrug in an attempt to play it cool. "I've had worse."

Holden's expression turns amused. "Told you that guy's a douchebag."

"Most are. Want a cookie for being right?" I don't know why I'm provoking him. He's not the one who cheated on me.

"Are you offering yours?"

I scoff, annoyed that he doesn't take the bait.

"Need a ride?"

"Nope."

"You sure about that?" he asks, quirking a brow.

"The last thing I want to do right now is to be in an enclosed space with—"

Flashing yellow lights illuminate the cocky expression on his face and I break off mid-sentence, looking over my shoulder to see what's caught his attention just in time to see my car... being towed.

"Hey!" I yell, throwing an arm in the air. But the tow truck driver is oblivious, already turning the corner. Super. Just fan-fucking-tastic. I squint at the parking space, seeing a sign partially obstructed by a tree branch that reads: *Resident Parking Only. VIOLATORS WILL BE TOWED.* When I turn back around, Holden looks smug.

"You couldn't have warned me sooner?" I snap, pulling my phone out of my purse and attempt to re-download the ride share app I used exactly one other time. Could this night possibly get any worse?

"Last chance for a ride," Holden says, dangling his keys.

"I'll Uber." I don't even look up from my phone that's loading at a snail's pace. Holden just witnessed my humiliation. The sooner he leaves, the sooner I can pretend this night never happened.

"Suit yourself."

To that, I don't respond, and I hear him walk away while I enter my destination address into the app. Being a Saturday night, there's no shortage of drivers in the area. But even the seven to ten-minute estimate feels like a century. I want to put as much distance between Liam and me as possible.

As if summoned by my thoughts, Liam jogs up from behind me, running his hand through his disheveled dirty blond hair.

Sex hair. From another girl.

His jeans are unbuttoned, and my stomach rolls at the sight. He says something—I know that because his lips are moving—but I don't hear what he says. I study him, knowing I should feel jealous or territorial. I should be heartbroken. I'm disappointed. Disrespected, for damn sure. I try to summon any of the appropriate reactions, but as I take in his stricken expression as the excuses spill from those pretty lips, I come to the realization that he doesn't feel like mine, and that's why I can't bring myself to care. He's just another boy doing what boys do. And I'm the idiot who thought he was different.

"Holden!" I shout abruptly, cutting off Liam who looks about as surprised as I feel. I whirl around to face Holden. He's standing in front of his Range Rover with a hard expression on his face. "Take me home?" The question sounds suggestive, and I don't bother to correct myself. A mean smile spreads across his face before he jerks his chin in invitation.

"You're not seriously leaving with *him,* are you?" Liam sneers at Holden in that condescending, arrogant way of his. It's ironic, considering Holden belongs to the Ames family—as in AmesAir—who happens to have more money than Liam's family could ever dream of. Money. Status. Power. It's all any of these people care about. Don't get me wrong. I enjoy the finer things in life. Most would probably describe me as spoiled—and they'd be right. But my self-worth isn't contingent on how much money Mommy and Daddy make. And it's that sense of self-importance that pushes me right into the figurative arms of Holden Ames.

Desperate. Times.

"I'm sorry," I say, my tone thick with sarcasm. "You lost the right to question me when you decided to stick your dick into another girl."

I hurry over to Holden, who's now sitting in the driver's seat. Through the windshield, I see him stretch across the middle console to open the door. I hesitate, one hand on the door, and Holden raises an eyebrow in response. My eyes flit back to where Liam stands with his hands fisted at his side, as if he's the one who's been burned tonight. My temper flares at the audacity, and I climb up, stick my middle finger in the air, and flip him off over the top of the car before sliding into the passenger seat and shutting the door.

"Where to?" he asks, amusement lacing his tone, but he doesn't comment.

"Anywhere but here."

He steps on the gas as I stare straight ahead, refusing to look in Liam's direction.

"You should see his face." Holden laughs.

"If I ever see it again, it'll be too soon," I mutter.

"So, uh…are you…alri—" Holden starts, but I shake my head, cutting him off before he can finish his question.

"Let's not speak."

"Oh, thank fuck," he says, the relief evident in his tone.

I snort out a laugh, leaning my head back against the headrest. "You're such an asshole."

"I was *attempting* to be nice."

"Did it hurt? Pretending to care about someone other than yourself?"

He shrugs his right shoulder, the same hand gripping the steering wheel. "I'd give it a solid four out of ten on the pain scale."

I lean forward and poke at the touch screen until I find

music. I crank the volume all the way up, making conversation impossible, and Holden doesn't seem to mind. I expect him to crack jokes at Liam's expense—or mine—but surprisingly, he keeps his mouth shut. Good to know he has *some* self-preservation instincts.

I don't know how long we drive, unspeaking. It's maybe thirty minutes before Holden pulls into a Dairy Queen drive-through and turns the music down.

"Really?"

"What?" he asks, defensive. "I'm hungry as fuck." He pulls up to the speaker, and a muffled voice greets him and asks for his order. "Let me get a chicken strip dinner, three cheeseburgers, a large fry, and two chocolate dipped cones. Oh, and a bottle of water, please."

"Will that complete your order?"

Holden faces me. "Want anything?"

"I don't know, is there anything left?" He ordered enough to feed a family of four, and yet, he still manages to look like a fucking Olympic athlete. "I'm good," I say when I realize he's waiting for a real answer. Even if I did want something, I doubt I could eat right now. Something about being publicly cheated on really kills a girl's appetite.

Holden finishes his order, and as we're pulling up to the window, my phone vibrates in my lap. I look down, knowing who it is before I see the screen. My suspicions are confirmed when I flip it over to silence it. I hear Holden pay and thank the woman at the window as a text immediately comes through.

Liam: Please call me. I'm sry.

Pro tip: if you want to appear genuinely remorseful, at least have the decency to spell the word out entirely.

I ignore the text, too, sliding my phone in between my thighs.

"Sir...your water?" a female voice says, prompting me to look up. When I do, I see that Holden's gaze is fixed on my thighs. I arch a brow, giving him a reproachful look as I tug my skirt down a little, but it's in vain because Holden has exactly zero shame.

Still looking at me, he holds his hand out his window until the bottle of water is placed in his grip, and then he's pulling out of the parking lot. The SUV smells like hot grease and salty fries, but surprisingly, it doesn't turn my stomach like I thought it would.

"Here," Holden says, passing me a cheeseburger. "Eat this."

"You sure? I wouldn't want you to wither away to nothing."

The corner of his lip tugs up into a smirk. "I'll survive. Eat the damn cheeseburger."

I make a show of peeling off the wrapper and biting into it. "Happy?"

"Hot."

I laugh under my breath. "Drive."

We both eat in silence while I ignore the barrage of text messages that vibrate between my thighs. Instead of looking at them, I keep my gaze focused on my window. It's too dark to see much of anything besides the streetlights whizzing by. I'm lost in my thoughts, so I don't realize that we're sitting in front of my house until Holden clears his throat.

"Thanks for the ride."

Fingers on the door handle, I glance back at my house, noticing the lights are on through the bay windows. Great. That means my mom and stepdad are still awake. I'm supposed to be spending the night at Shayne's after the away game. Coming home unexpectedly I could easily explain. Coming home without my car is something that requires a little more finessing, and tonight, I'm not in the mood for an interrogation. Before I can talk myself out of what is sure to be a terrible decision, I turn back to face Holden. "Can I come over?"

His eyebrows shoot up, a cocky expression taking over his face, and I'm quick to continue before he spits out some pervy remark.

"Don't get too excited. They're awake," I say, hitching my thumb toward my house. "And I don't feel like being home right now." Or ever, really. I try to stay as busy as possible, and between school, cheer, and their work schedules, it's not hard to accomplish. Except for Wednesday nights—the dreaded weekly family dinner that literally no one enjoys. But anything to keep up appearances, I guess.

TWO

Valen

"**W**AIT," I SAY, STOPPING SHORT A FEW FEET BEFORE the front door. "Is Thayer or Christian lurking around somewhere?" It's just now dawning on me that Holden was alone at the party earlier. There was a time when the Ames boys were never seen without each other, but when Daniel, the oldest, died, the fearsome foursome was down to three. Thayer, the middle brother, is sort of a lone wolf these days except when it comes to Shayne, but I've learned where there's one, the other is never far behind.

"Fuck if I know." He shrugs.

I hesitate.

"Problem?" Holden asks when he notices that I'm still standing in the same place.

"I can't be seen coming home with you."

"Why not?"

"Because we're not even friends. And I have a boyfriend. And it's definitely late enough to qualify for booty call hours." I tick each reason off. There are a million reasons I shouldn't be here right now, but for some reason, here I am. "And because you're...you."

"Had."

"What?"

"*Had* a boyfriend. I mean, unless you're planning on staying with him."

I fold my arms over my chest, feeling defensive. "And that's your business, how?"

Of course, I'm breaking up with Liam. As far as I'm concerned, it goes without saying. It's already done. But no one else knows that yet. I'm also not going to take judgment or relationship advice from Holden, of all people. He's easily the biggest player I've ever known.

He doesn't answer me. Instead, he pivots and starts walking in the other direction. I hang back, watching, waiting for him to say or do something. His dark form blends into the shadows as he gets farther and farther away, and I roll my eyes, contemplating leaving. Shayne lives on the other side of these woods. I could call her. But that would lead to a whole lot of questions I don't want to answer. Not tonight, anyway.

The steady sound of leaves crunching beneath his feet is suddenly gone, and I realize he's stopped, looking at me over his shoulder. "Coming?"

I let out a heavy sigh, arms dropping to my sides. "Why not," I deadpan. Keep the bad decisions rolling.

"You're the one who asked to come over," he reminds me.

I don't have a response for that. He's right, obviously.

I follow Holden, passing another structure next to the main house—a detached garage or a guest house, maybe? I don't know where he's taking me, but I'm too stubborn to ask, so I stay quiet. Finally, we come to another structure. Holden approaches the door before pushing it open. He doesn't wait for any sort of reaction. He heads straight inside, leaving me at the threshold. I peer inside, feeling the warmth all the way from here, and see that it's an indoor pool. Tall, vaulted ceiling, brick walls, and little sconces perched between each window casting a warm, orange glow against the dark water. The only windows are up high near the ceilings, giving it a private feel. I step inside, the humidity a welcomed sensation after being out in the cold.

"Shayne didn't tell me you guys had a pool."

"She didn't use it often. Drink?" he asks, making his way toward a wine fridge that's built into a counter. He bends over, opens the door, then pulls out two dark brown bottles, holding them up in offering.

Shutting the door behind me, I walk over to where Holden stands, coming to a stop in front of him. Instead of taking the proffered beer, I reach around his body for the tray of liquor that sits on the countertop. After a quick glance at my options, I decide on an expensive-looking white bottle with an intricate blue design. Plucking it from the tray, I hold it up, giving it a little shake in question.

"So it's *that* kind of night, huh?" He sets the bottles of beer down on the counter with a clang, and I take a step back, putting some space between us. "Even better."

Being alone with Holden isn't a good idea. Being alone with Holden and getting drunk off tequila is an even worse one. But tonight, I'm giving myself permission to make shitty choices.

He puts the bottle to his lips and tilts his head back, taking the first swig without preamble. When he's done, he pulls up the bottom of his shirt and swipes it across his mouth. *Why was that so attractive?*

When it's my turn, I'm not quite as skilled. The liquid burns my throat, warming my insides almost instantly. I make a sour face, wishing I had something to chase it with. Holden chuckles at my bitter expression and takes the bottle from me before setting it back down on the bar. He reaches over to a little basket with limes and sets it on the countertop before pulling a knife out of a wooden block.

That would've been helpful five seconds ago.

After he fills two shot glasses and cuts the lime, he holds one of the wedges in his hand. I pull back when he reaches his hand out for me. "Let me," he says. I relent, curious to see what he's going to do next. His fingertips graze my neck as he moves my ponytail off my shoulder, causing me to shiver at his touch. "Tilt your head."

I do as he says, exposing my neck to him. Holden brings the lime to my neck and squeezes, the juices running down to my collarbone. He rubs the lime against my flesh, then brings it to my lips. "Open."

I hesitate, knowing that this won't lead to anywhere good, but for some inexplicable reason, I find myself doing it anyway. He slides the lime halfway between my teeth and I bite down, holding it there. His teeth scrape across his bottom lip, his eyes glued to my mouth. He tears his gaze away, plucking a saltshaker off the counter and sprinkles some onto the liquid on my neck.

His palm flattens against the opposite side of my neck, holding me in place, then I feel his hot tongue against my skin. I suck in a breath, eyes falling shut at the sensation. All too soon, he releases me and pulls away. I watch, hypnotized, as he takes the shot before bringing his mouth to mine. Our lips brush as he takes the lime from me, then sucks all the juices from it.

I lick the flavor off my lips, wondering why the hell I'm so turned on from something as simple as a body shot.

"Your turn," he says in a way that sounds more like *I dare you* as he tosses the lime into the trash.

I grab another wedge, then squeeze it onto his neck like he did mine before sliding it up and down his skin. I hold the lime up to his mouth and he captures it with his teeth, holding it there while I shake the salt onto his neck. I take him by surprise when I wrap my fingers around his sharp jaw, quickly turning his head to the side to expose his neck. The muscles in his neck flex slightly, our chests brushing together as I push up onto my toes. I lick a path up his hot skin, feeling his pulse jump under my tongue. He lets out a sound that's somewhere between a grunt and a groan when I pull away. I take the shot and waste no time pulling Holden down to me by the back of his neck, taking the lime from his mouth with my own.

"Fuck," he says, sounding dazed as I swipe the remaining lime juice off the bottom of my lip and lick it off my thumb.

"Thanks," I say lightly, as if I'm not affected in the slightest.

His eyes narrow, looking at me intently, and I feel my defenses going up at whatever is sure to come.

"You don't seem surprised. About tonight, I mean," he points out.

"Look, I don't know what you *think* you saw—"

"What I think I saw?" he scoffs, cutting me off. "I saw enough."

Embarrassment burns through me. Being cheated on is humiliating enough. Being cheated on and having Holden witness the fallout is even worse.

"You're handling it well. That's all I meant," he amends, even though I know that wasn't his original point.

"You call this handling it well?" I ask, holding up the bottle. "I just licked you." I take the bottle with me and walk to the edge of the pool and sit down. Holden follows suit, sitting next to me with his forearms resting on bent knees. I peel off my white cheer shoes and socks before slowly dipping my feet into the water. It's surprisingly warm. I lean back, flattening my palms against the ground behind me.

"I've seen worse ways to cope."

"Cope." I snort. "You act like someone died." I regret the words the second they leave my mouth. Danny's death is a sore subject. The details surrounding it are still a mystery, and they think Shayne's brother, Grey, had something to do with it. "I didn't—"

It's his turn to roll his eyes at me. "It's fine."

"I just meant... it's not like it's the end of the world. A guy turned out to be an asshole. *What* a shocker."

I pull my phone out of the purse that dangles from

my wrist to find another text from the asshole himself, and Holden snatches it from my hand.

"Hey!" I object, lunging for it, but he holds his freakishly long arm in the air and out of reach. "Give it back."

"Ignore him," Holden says, setting my phone face-down on the stone floor between us.

"Fine. Let's talk about something else."

"Fine with me."

I swing my legs through the water, watching as the ripples move through the dark pool. "Why aren't you playing basketball anymore?" I ask, wanting to shift the focus off me. The season just started, and I was surprised that Holden wasn't there for the first game.

"Why, you miss cheering for me?"

I pin him with a look, waiting for a real answer.

He sighs. "It's not the same," he admits when he realizes I'm not letting him off the hook. "Without Danny, I mean. It doesn't feel right."

"What doesn't?"

"Fucking nothing," he says, huffing out a laugh. "Nothing at all feels right anymore."

I heard that Holden already had multiple college coaches expressing interest last year. If he doesn't play, he could lose that chance. "Do you think you'll regret it if you don't?"

My phone buzzes between us before he can respond.

"Is this guy serious?" Holden asks, ignoring my question. "He's texted you thirty-seven times, Valen. Thirty-seven." He looks over at me, picking my phone up. "He seems super stable."

"Ha-ha," I deadpan. "Give me my phone."

I see my phone light up in his hand again, and Holden's eyes find the screen once more. His eyebrows shoot up in question, but he doesn't look offended. If anything, he seems amused.

"What?" I ask, suspicion evident in my tone. He hands my phone back to me, showing me the text written on the screen.

If you fuck that piece of shit, I swear to God, we're done, Valen.

"God, he's an asshole," I mutter, shaking my head. "Sorry," I say awkwardly because I don't know what else to say.

Holden huffs out a laugh, reaching for the bottle between us. "He's jealous. Therefore, you're winning."

Now it's my turn to laugh. "The fact that he was balls deep in another chick says he is most definitely *winning*." Whatever that means.

"That's where you're wrong." Holden passes the bottle to me, and my pinky brushes against his hand when I wrap my fingers around the neck of it. "Are you jealous? Or are you pissed?"

I pause, the bottle lingering at my lips. The fact that he even asked me tells me he knows the answer. And that has me feeling a little unnerved.

"Both, I guess," I lie with a shrug.

"Bullshit." The accusation flies off his tongue without hesitation.

"I've seen jealous. I've seen heartbroken. I've seen vindictive. And right now? You're none of those things. It's actually kind of freaking me out," he muses. "Which leads me to believe one of two things." He pauses for dramatic effect, and I roll my eyes, waiting for him to continue.

"Enlighten me, oh wise one."

"First possibility—this is the calm before the storm. Whether it's shock or compartmentalizing, I don't know. But the meltdown is yet to come. The second possibility, and what I'm leaning toward, just so we're clear…you don't love the dude. You're just pissed and embarrassed."

"He was my boyfriend," I scoff. "That's a bold assessment."

"And yet, you still didn't deny it."

I go to take another drink, but Holden intercepts me.

"My turn," he explains, bringing the bottle to his lips before taking a long pull.

I glare at him, annoyed that he's psychoanalyzing me, and even more annoyed at the fact that he's right.

"So which is it?" he presses me for an answer.

I shrug. Both? Neither? I don't know how to explain my lack of emotional reaction to finding out my boyfriend was cheating on me. Maybe I just expected it, so it was only a question of when, not *if*. Maybe I'm just defective. "I'm bored of this topic," I announce. "Let's talk about something else. Or better yet, let's not talk at all."

Holden's teeth scrape over his bottom lip as he eyes me intently. "Then what do you propose we do?"

"Not that." I laugh. "We drink. In companionable silence."

Holden almost seems offended by the suggestion, or maybe just highly uncomfortable with the notion of spending time with someone without the possibility of hooking up.

"Drinking I can do. The silent part? No promises."

I narrow my eyes at him. "Try hard."

Holden mimics zipping his lips and throwing away an imaginary key. He won't last more than thirty seconds, tops.

"I'll take that," I say, reaching over his lap to grab the bottle. "Can't drink with your mouth sealed shut."

Holden leans back, bracing himself on his elbows. When I glance up at him, my chest pressed against his lap and arm outstretched, I see that he's giving me that look again.

"Perv," I say, pulling myself back up.

He opens his mouth to argue, but I shake my head, stopping him with a look. "Ah-ah," I tsk. "Silence, remember?"

To my surprise, he stays quiet long enough for me to take one final drink. I have to suck it up and go home eventually, and I probably shouldn't be shit-faced when I do. The liquid settles in my stomach, making me feel all warm and fuzzy. I lean back, propping myself up on my palms. I let my head fall back a little, looking up at the ceiling for a second before closing my eyes. Between the alcohol and the humidity sticking to my skin like a warm blanket, I'm feeling blissfully buzzed and relaxed.

But the feeling doesn't last long, because all of a sudden, Holden's ripping off his shirt, then pushing to his feet. "Quiet time's over," he announces, shoving his jeans down his legs. He kicks his shoes off, along with his pants, leaving him in only a black pair of boxers. Before I can get a word out, he's diving into the pool.

Holden swims toward me, his body barely visible in the glow of the dark blue water. Broad shoulders break through the surface as he comes up for air, and then he's whipping his head up, purposely splashing me with his hair.

"Holden!" I scream, scrambling away from the edge, but his hand grips my ankle, keeping me in place.

"Relax, it's only water," he says. One of my feet is planted on the deck of the pool, the other still in his hand. When he realizes that he's still holding on to me, he drops my ankle and pushes his dark, wet hair back off his forehead. Holden is gorgeous. Anyone with eyes would agree. But I have to admit that right now, all wet and shirtless, he's looking extra tempting. Or maybe that's just the combination of alcohol and a bruised ego talking.

He clears his throat, and I avert my eyes, trying to look anywhere else. "See something you like?"

I roll my eyes, but before I can respond, my phone lights up and buzzes with another text. I see Holden's eyes zero in on it, and at the same instant, he's lunging forward. I lunge at the same time, but he's quicker, his baseball mitt of a hand landing on my phone a nanosecond before mine.

"Give it back."

He holds my phone out of reach, backing farther away.

"Come and get it," he taunts.

I don't move an inch. "I'm not playing your little games," I say, aiming for nonchalant, as if my heart isn't beating a thousand miles an hour at the thought of him seeing more of Liam's texts.

As if on cue, another text comes through.

"Suit yourself," Holden says, finally looking at the screen.

"Fine!" I shout, unable to hide the slight hint of panic in my tone as I push myself to my feet. Deciding to take charge of the situation, I pull the hem of my uniform top up and over my head, effectively distracting him from whatever vile words are sure to be on the phone's screen.

I chance a quick glance at him to gauge his reaction, and the look in his eyes makes me hesitate. The mood shifts, his playful demeanor gone. His smile slips, his eyes filling with a mixture of surprise and something that looks a lot like desire. Before I can lose my nerve, I reach behind me to unzip my skirt, then shove it down my hips and let it fall to pool at my feet. Stepping out of the puddle of clothes, I nudge them to the side with my foot.

Of all the ways tonight could have ended, I'd have never guessed that I'd end up standing in front of Holden Ames' pool, wearing nothing but a baby blue bra and matching underwear. I really need to reevaluate my life choices. Taking a deep breath, I lift my chin and make my way toward the stairs that lead into the pool. Holden's eyes rake over my body appreciatively, but for once, he has nothing to say.

I'll consider that a win.

"Last chance." I try one more time, knowing it's in vain, holding my hand out.

"Or what? You're going to come in here and press those gorgeous tits against me?"

Spoke too soon.

"I was thinking more along the lines of putting my foot up your ass."

"Kinky." He wiggles his eyebrows, not missing a beat.

"You're gross."

"So you keep telling me."

Approaching the entrance of the pool, I curl my fingers around the cool metal handrail before stepping inside. The water is warm, but it still sends goosebumps fluttering up my body. I fight the urge to cover my nipples that I'm sure are making their presence known right about now. But to Holden's credit, he doesn't even look. That much. Okay, he's totally looking.

"Okay, I'm in. Happy?"

"*Tit*illated."

I force myself not to crack a smile at his pun and keep my annoyed expression in place. "My phone," I remind him.

"I said come and get it. So come…and get it."

Everything's an innuendo with this guy. I roll my eyes, and he gives a satisfied grin, knowing he's won.

As I wade toward him through the water, I know I'm going to regret this.

THREE

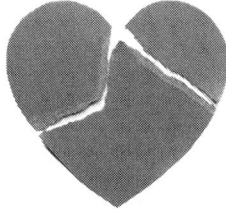

Holden

IMMEDIATELY REGRET THIS DECISION. I THOUGHT I WAS WINNING this battle of wills by getting her in the pool, but it turns out, the sight of Valen gliding through the water, her tits jiggling with each step, only serves to torture me. Thankfully, I kept my boxers on for her sake because my dick has been hard since the second she took me by surprise and pulled her shirt off. I didn't think she'd call my bluff, but fuck if I'm complaining. She's not bashful, not about her body at least. She's confident in that department. But there's a hint of shyness in her eyes. Or maybe it's hesitation that I'm sensing. But all that's gone the instant she gets within arm's reach.

Valen straightens her shoulders, pinning me with that take-no-bullshit gaze of hers, silently demanding I give the phone back. I almost do, but what fun would that be? When she realizes I'm not going to hand it over, she does a little jump, attempting to snatch it from my hand.

"Nu-uh," I say, lifting it out of reach. "I said come and get it, remember?"

For a second, I start to wonder if she's losing patience with our game, but once again, she manages to catch me off guard when she curls her hand around the back of my neck and hoists herself up. Water splashes up and around us as her knees lock on either side of my waist, leaving a safe distance between by stomach and the space between her thighs. My left arm instinctively bands around her waist to catch her. The movement causes her knees to slip past my waist, and then she's pressed against me in the next instant. I hear her breath hitch before her wide, brown eyes dart up to mine in surprise. I can feel the fucking heat of her pussy against my lower stomach, and it makes me even harder. If she moved just an inch or two lower, she'd be well acquainted with that fact.

I've never been this close to Valen, let alone had her pressed against me like this. In fact, I think the only physical contact we've had is when she slapped me upside the back of my head when I pissed her off by making fun of her boyfriend. Or that one time I had to restrain her from breaking Thayer's door down after he stomped off with Shayne thrown over his shoulder like a caveman.

Valen's mouth snaps shut, her eyes narrowing as she regains her composure, but it's too late. I already saw *the look*. I know it well. See it from girls every single day without fail. Valen may be immune to my irresistible charm and my status and my devastatingly good looks, but she can't hide the fact that she feels something. And I'm not talking about my cock that's dangerously close to making its presence known. If she shifts just a little lower…

"Don't look at me like that," I say.

"You did that on purpose," she accuses.

"You came at me like a koala. All I did was catch you. You're welcome, by the way."

"Yeah, you're *such* a gentleman," she deadpans.

"And you're still holding on to me."

"*You're* still holding on to my *phone*."

That, I am. In fact, it buzzes in my hand as if to taunt her of that fact.

"Let's see what Leonard has to say."

"It's Liam," she grits through clenched teeth while simultaneously lunging for—and missing—her phone.

"That's what I said." I laugh, stretching my neck backward in an attempt to read the message on the screen while Valen continues to climb her way up my body, the water sloshing around us. Joke's on me, because I can't even focus on the words with her slippery skin and soft tits rubbing against me. She smells like oranges and vanilla, like one of those fucking Creamsicles I used to eat as a kid. I want to know if she tastes like one, too.

"Please call me. I know I fucked up, but can you at least let me explain?" I read aloud before continuing to the one that comes immediately after. "Fine. If you're going to be a bitch about it, then fuck off. I don't know what you expected." I look over to Valen. "That escalated quickly."

I start to hand the phone back to Valen, but my eyes catch another text on the screen.

> **And if you're still with that loser, we're done for good.**
>
> **Are you fucking him?**
>
> **Maybe if you weren't such a frigid bitch, I wouldn't have had to fuck someone else.**

"How do we feel about a little bit of payback?" I ask her.

Valen regards me warily, her eyebrows cinching together. "What kind of payback?" I can hear the hesitance in her voice.

"Just go with it."

"Go with wh—"

I don't give her a chance to finish her question. I quickly open the camera on her phone while pulling Valen in even closer. She lets out a shocked yelp, her hands finding my shoulders as I dip my head to bring my lips closer to hers. Our mouths don't quite touch, but our noses do. I slide my free hand down the small of her back, dipping just the tips of my fingers beneath the waistband of her underwear. Her lips part, just a little, at the feeling. She tries to conceal it, but I can tell by the tiny gasp of surprise that she's affected.

I snap the photo from a high angle, showing nothing but

Valen's back and ass. And my hand, of course. Without giving her a chance to weigh in, I send the picture to Liam with the caption: *She's a little busy, bro.*

"And to add insult to injury…" I power her phone off before tossing it to join the pile of her clothes. She has no idea what I wrote, but she gets the gist, I'm sure. "The only thing worse than knowing your girl is hooking up with another guy is seeing your messages go undelivered and having your call go straight to voicemail."

"How'd you learn to be so toxic?" she asks, amusement flashing in her eyes.

"Years of practice. Stick around and you just might learn something."

"I'll keep that in mind in case I ever need tips on how to string girls along while giving as little of myself as humanly possible."

"Ah, so you're a fan of my work."

"Nope. But half of your victims are on my cheer team, so I have the honor of hearing all kinds of fun stories."

"Want to know what would be even better?"

"What's that?"

"If you went back with a story of your own."

"Not happening."

"Come on, Valen. Let's not pretend that you weren't even a little tempted to kiss me just now."

"I know it's hard for you to grasp that there's someone of the female variety who isn't interested in you, so I'm going to say this very slowly. I. Don't. Want. You."

"And yet, here you are in my pool, with your legs wrapped around my waist and your pussy lips practically hugging my dick."

Her lips purse, her nostrils flaring along with her temper as she unlocks her legs from my torso and pushes away from me, as if only just realizing she was still wrapped around me. "Trust me, Holden. If I wanted to kiss you, you'd know it."

"You sure about that?" I take a step toward her. "So you feel nothing when I do this?" I slide my hand behind her neck, pulling her closer. She glides through the water, only stopping when her body touches mine.

"Nope."

I grip the hair at the nape of her neck and tug, angling her face upward. Bending down, I bring my mouth close to her ear. "What about this?"

"Not a thing. Sorry to disappoint, but it takes more than some amateur fumbling around to make me melt into a puddle at your feet," she says, peering up at me with defiant eyes. She puts up a good front, but I see the way her throat moves when she swallows hard, the way her tongue peeks out to wet her lips, and the way her pulse flutters at the hollow of her neck.

Without thinking, I bend down even farther to ghost my lips across her jumping pulse, barely making contact. Slowly, I skim up the column of her neck, earning a shiver from Valen, then back down. Her chest is rising and falling quickly now. This game might backfire fast because she's not the only one affected. I'm torturing myself just as much, if not more than I am her. When I suck her wet, hot flesh into my mouth, her breath hitches, goosebumps dancing across her skin. Her nipples are hard as fuck, straining against the thin material of her soaked bra. I smooth my palms up her sides to wrap around her ribcage before flicking my thumbs against the hardened tips.

"And now?" I pull back to gauge her reaction.

"Nothing," she whispers, but her big brown eyes have gone soft, completely glazed over with lust. Lust for me, for what I'm doing to her. Not Liam.

"You can lie to yourself all you want, Valen, but I watched you pretend with that piece of shit for the better part of a year, and you never once looked at him the way you're looking at me right now." I circle her nipples with both thumbs, applying the faintest pressure. "He called you *frigid*, but you're fucking burning for me, aren't you?"

"Shut up," she says, even as she arches into my touch, her eyes falling shut.

"How does it feel?" I push. "To know that I've made you feel more than he ever did, and I've barely even touched you?"

Her eyes shoot open, any lingering softness in them gone in an instant. I smirk, knowing I've pissed her off. She shoves my shoulders again, but I catch her by the waist, pulling her against me. I think she might push me away, but instead, she stays where she is, her gaze dropping to my mouth. I lean in, and just before my lips touch hers, she draws back, leaving only a hair of space between us.

"Kiss me, Valen," I say against her parted lips.

She doesn't say anything, but she doesn't deny me either. We're so close that I feel her breath against my mouth, but I don't move in again.

"Show me how much you don't want me." I lick the seam of her lips.

Her nostrils flare, and for a second, I think she might slap me. Instead, she lunges for me, her mouth crashing against mine. I catch her by the waist easily, her legs wrapping around me, her hands on my face. Her kiss is hungry, bordering on desperate, and when her tongue slips into my mouth, I fucking groan. All too soon, she pulls back.

"Looks like I'm not the only one who's *feeling* something," she says pointedly. There's no point in denying it when she's sliding her pussy against the evidence. I run my teeth over my bottom lip as I watch her body move against me, trying to keep from tugging her underwear aside and fucking her right here in the pool. Not my favorite location, but she's making it seem more appealing by the second.

"What, no comeback?" she asks, her breathy voice betraying the unfazed façade she's trying to convey. "Cat got your tongue?"

"I'd rather use my tongue for other things right now." I back up to the edge of the submerged platform, bringing her along with me until I'm sitting on the step with her straddling me. I hold her stare as I slide her bra up slowly, exposing the swell of her tits inch by inch. When she doesn't stop me, I break eye contact to zero in on her chest, just in time to watch as two small, tan nipples peek out from the bottom of her bra. When I push it up the rest of the way, releasing her full tits with a bounce, my dick jerks against her. *Holy fuck, that was hot.* She squirms in my lap, telling me my reaction didn't go unnoticed.

Flattening my hands against her lower back, I hold her tight, ducking my head to take a nipple into my mouth. She gasps, sliding her fingers into my hair, gripping it hard. I suck on her once, and that's all it takes for her head to fall back, her long ponytail dipping into the water, her lips parting on a moan. When I give the other nipple the same attention, this time using my teeth a little, she rocks into me. I catch her hips with both hands, helping her rub herself on me as I bite, lick, and suck. My dick is begging to be freed, needing to feel her, and when she leans backward to rest her elbows on the ledge of the pool, giving me a glorious fucking view of her perfect tits as she grinds her panty-covered pussy against me, I almost lose control.

"He wasn't doing his job, was he?" I move her faster, pool water sloshing between us. "You're about to come just from this." I say it like an accusation. Like I'm not on the verge of doing the same.

She sits up, one arm circling my neck, the other hand covering my mouth. "God, Holden, shut up. You're *ruining* it." Her bare tits press against me as she continues to ride me.

I pull away from the hand covering my mouth. "Use me, Valen. Make yourself come."

"Oh, God," she breathes. "Holden…"

"Fuck this." I stand abruptly and she lets out a little yelp of surprise as I carry her out of the pool. I lay her on the deck, reach down to free myself from the fucking prison that is my boxers, and then I'm back between her legs, sliding against her wet heat. I fuck her without actually fucking her, my palms braced on either side of her head. Her eyes are soft again, almost vulnerable as she looks up at me like she can hardly believe this is happening. That makes two of us. Her fingers slide into my hair, our harsh breathing and the sound of her soft moans are the only sound.

"Are you going to come for me?"

Valen's eyes squeeze shut, her back bowing off the deck. "I can't, I need—"

I bend down, flattening my tongue to swipe across her nipple.

"Oh *God*, yes," she whispers. "More."

I suck hard, hard enough to leave a mark, and her whole body tenses up, her mouth falling open on a silent scream. I know she's seconds from coming, and I'm not far behind.

Suddenly, the telltale roar of Thayer's Hellcat coming up the driveway has Valen's eyes shooting open. She freezes beneath me, and I groan at the interruption. Usually, I can hear him coming from a mile away, but I was too caught up in Valen to be aware of anything else. I see the moment reality sets in and the panic hits. Her eyes are wide with what looks like a mixture of horror and regret as she scrambles out from underneath me, crawling away like she's the last one standing in a teen slasher movie, and I'm the guy with the knife.

"What the hell am I doing?" she says, more to herself than me, I assume.

"Relax. Thayer and Shayne are too busy pretending like they're not *special stepsiblings* to realize we're out here."

She doesn't seem surprised by that statement. So she knows about them, too. *Interesting*.

"I can't be here. This can't happen."

"A little late for that." I tuck my dick back into my boxers, wincing in discomfort.

She glares at me, and just like that, the moment is gone, as if the past hour never happened. "Tell anyone about this, and I'll kill you."

FOUR

Valen

"**D**O YOU USUALLY HANG OUT AT THE HOMES OF THE people you're trying to avoid?" Holden asks, coming to stand next to me. It's been a couple of weeks since the night I caught Liam cheating on me and had a temporary lapse in sanity that ended with me being half naked with Holden.

I stifle an eye roll. Barely. "Shayne invited—"

"Yeah, yeah," he cuts me off. "I know. You're not here for me. Keep telling yourself that."

"All these people," I say, gesturing to the crowded backyard with my untouched cup of beer, "and yet, you still choose to fuck with me."

"I'd love to fuck—"

I slap a hand over his mouth, realizing too late that I set myself up for that one. "Moving on," I say, not so subtly changing the subject.

"Have you seen my cousin around?" Holden asks, scanning the yard.

"I have not. Aren't you two supposed to be on security detail?" After the whole firebomb incident at Shayne's house, they've been on high alert. Honestly, even I've been a little spooked, and I'm not one for dramatics. Not that I'll admit it.

"Thayer's with her."

"Per usual."

"You gonna tell her about your boyfriend?"

I narrow my eyes in warning. "Not yet."

"And why's that? Because you're thinking about taking him back?"

"For one thing, that's none of your business. It's also not a big deal, and Shayne has enough on her plate right now. *You* have enough on your plate right now."

He lifts a shoulder, looking me up and down. "I could handle a little more."

I laugh, shaking my head. "You're relentless."

"Only when it comes to you."

"Only because I'm the only one who will tell you no."

"Is that what you think?"

"It's not exactly rocket science. You want what you can't have. You like the chase."

"So it's a game then? What, you want me to chase you? Is that what this is?"

"No. I'm just...not interested."

"See, that might be more believable if it wasn't for—"

"Is this why you're not answering my calls?" Liam's voice cuts through the air before Holden can finish his sentence. I'd be happy for the interruption if it were anyone, and I mean any-fucking-one other than my ex-boyfriend. By the look on his face, the *ex* part seems to be lost on him.

"What are you doing here?" I don't bother answering his question.

Liam opens his mouth to speak when something else occurs to me.

"Scratch that. How did you even know I was here?"

"I still have your location," he explains, holding up his phone. Sure enough, a little blue dot blinks on the map, giving me away.

"I never gave you my location."

"Answer the question, Valen." A hush falls over the crowded

yard, and I know without looking that we've gained an audience. Once again.

"You should go," I say, my voice low but firm. Red-rimmed eyes bore into mine as Liam takes a step toward me. I feel Holden closing in behind me, and I know I need to get Liam out of here soon if I want to avoid an even bigger scene than he's currently causing.

"Answer the question," he says again.

"I don't owe you anything. Go home, Liam."

"Are you fucking him?" he bellows, jabbing a finger over my shoulder, pointing at Holden.

"On that note," Holden quips, "I think it's time we wrap up this week's episode of *Days of Our Lives*. Time to go, Leonard."

"I'm not leaving without her."

I fold my arms over my chest and sigh. It's funny how he practically forgot I existed these past couple of weeks, but now he's here playing the part of a jilted lover.

"Come on. I'll even throw a to-go drink in as a special favor. I'm sure one of the girls has an extra White Claw. Are you a fan of the Claw? You look like a White Claw guy." Holden's smartass response garners laughs from the people who are no longer pretending to mind their own business.

Jesus, Holden, shut up. I don't doubt his strength, but I do know that the rowing team has kept Liam in top shape, and if I don't diffuse this situation fast, someone's going to get hurt.

Liam's hands fist at his sides and I see his jaw tighten, but his eyes stay focused on mine. "You didn't leave me much of a choice. I've been trying to apologize for weeks. Meanwhile, you've been, what? Ignoring me because you got some high school dick? I didn't take you for a slut."

Shock renders me momentarily speechless. Never once have I heard something so vile from him. I open my mouth to tell him to fuck off, but before I can get the words out, I see Holden's fist fly toward his face out of the corner of my eye. Liam doesn't even see it coming. One second he's glaring at me, the next he's laid out on the ground, holding his nose.

I slap my hands over my mouth as blood spills between his fingers.

"You motherfucker," Liam says, holding his hand out in front of his face with a perplexed look, as if he can't believe Holden had the audacity to make him bleed.

Holden advances toward him, throwing his arms out wide. "By the way, I fucked your girlfriend!"

"Holden!" I snap, shooting him a dirty look. *Why the hell would he say that?* The obvious answer is to push Liam's buttons. I rush toward Liam to help him up, not out of the kindness of my heart, but out of a desperate need to get him out of here before this gets any worse. However, when I attempt to pull him up, he shoves me away, and I stumble back before catching my footing.

"Touch her again, motherfucker," Holden warns in a tone that I don't recognize from him, closing in on Liam. It's low and deadly and menacing, all words I've never associated with him before. If I wasn't so pissed about his blatant lie in an attempt to provoke Liam, I might find this protective side a little endearing. And a lot alarming.

Thankfully, at that moment, Thayer steps in, holding him back. Liam pulls himself up before he spits out a mixture of blood and saliva and drags his sleeve-covered forearm across his nose to wipe away the excess. He glares at me, a mixture of anger, hurt, and maybe even a little regret shining in his bloodshot eyes. But he says nothing. Instead, he walks away without another word.

I lock eyes with Holden, caught in silent conversation, but then a very concerned, very confused Shayne is right in front of me.

"Are you okay?" she asks, eyes wild with questions.

I know I owe her an explanation, but I don't have it in me

tonight. If I stay, I have to face Holden and Shayne. If I leave, I can avoid them both and formally break things off with Liam.

"I need to talk to him," I say. "I promise I'll call you tomorrow." I give her a quick kiss on the cheek.

Shayne presses her lips together, conflicted, but ultimately, she nods, letting me off the hook. After all, she's been keeping secrets of her own. We're all allowed secrets every now and then.

As I'm walking away, Holden's voice has me hesitating. "Valen…"

I turn to look at him over my shoulder. His eyes bore into mine, as if they're willing me not to leave with Liam, but I know it's not for any reason other than the fact that this has become a pissing contest at this point. Nothing more. Nothing less.

An apology is on the tip of my tongue, but instead, I keep my mouth shut, deciding to deal with Holden later. Without the audience. His eyes go hard the moment he sees that I've made my decision. Gone are those deep dimples and playful smile. I frown, not expecting his reaction, but more than that, I didn't expect to feel my stomach swirling with guilt.

"Liam!" I practically growl, hurrying after him. It's not enough that he has to show up and cause a scene, but now I have to chase after him? He stops just short of the fountain in the circular driveway and turns to face me. "What the hell was that?" I demand.

"You tell me."

"You cheated on *me*," I point out the obvious. "You don't get to be mad."

Liam huffs out a sardonic laugh. "Don't act like we weren't over long before that."

I fold my arms across my chest. "I think that's the one thing we can agree on."

His jaw hardens. His bloody nose has slowed, and it's starting to dry on his skin. Once again, I'm struck by the thought that I should feel something. The guy I've been seeing for a year just took a blow to the face, but I feel…nothing. Mildly annoyed at how this whole thing played out, but overall, nothing.

He opens his mouth to say something, but the sound of gravel crunching under feet silences both of us. Holden's cousin Christian and his friend Baker are walking in our direction, although, *walking* probably isn't the right word to describe what they're doing. Christian is barely able to stand upright, his arm slung around Baker's neck. Baker has one hand holding Christian's wrist at his shoulder and the other wrapped around his waist, supporting his weight as they stagger to the front door. Christian seems to be too drunk to pay us any mind, and Baker's too focused on keeping him vertical.

Just another Friday night for the Ames boys.

"You'd rather be with people like this," Liam says, gesturing toward them as they stumble past me and through the front door, "than me. Since when are you so fucking close with Holden and Thayer, anyway?"

I turn my head to the side and stare at him, trying to remember what I ever saw in him in the first place. Liam's conventionally attractive. Nice smile. Blue eyes. Tall. Sandy blond hair. He's nice enough—barring recent events. A decent boyfriend—also barring recent events. He was there for me when Shayne left. But now, not even the superficial kind of attraction is there. Liam must mistake my silence for something other than it is because his eyes soften, and he takes a step toward me.

"Come home with me. We can talk this out." He reaches out a hand to touch my cheek, but I snap out of it, jerking away before he makes contact.

"No." I shake my head, taking a step back to put more distance between us. "I want you to stop calling me. Stop texting me. Just stop, Liam. You said it yourself; we've been over for a long time."

His nostrils flare and his head falls back, his face skyward as he sighs. "Fuck you, Valen," he mutters before walking toward his car. He slides into the driver's seat and slams the door shut before peeling out of the circular drive, his tires kicking up gravel on his way out.

I sigh, dropping down to sit on the front steps, resting my elbows on my knees. "Good talk."

I'm sitting in my car, still parked on the side of the circular drive-way when Christian and Baker burst through the front doors. I was too embarrassed to go inside after what happened with Liam, but I don't want to go home either. I can't hear what they're saying, but they're arguing about something. Baker seems upset, and Christian seems…resigned. And slightly more sober than he did when he stumbled up the driveway thirty minutes ago. They both get into Baker's car, and about five minutes after I watch their headlights fade away in the distance, the front door opens again. This time it's Holden, and he's prowling toward his Range Rover, keys in hand.

I jump out of the car before I can think better of it. "Holden!"

He slows his steps but doesn't turn to face me. I stop in front of him, anticipating a fight, fully intending to yell at him about lying to Liam and telling everyone at the party that he fucked me, but the look in his eyes stops me. Something is off. He looks haunted. Broken.

"Is everything…okay?" I ask lamely.

He arches a brow. "Dandy. Why do you ask?"

"Because you just punched Liam and now you're—"

"Yeah, I don't think your boyfriend was too happy about that. My bad," he says in a way that says he's not sorry at all.

"*Ex*-boyfriend," I correct, searching his eyes for any sign of the emotion I saw seconds ago, but they're completely blank. "And that's not what I meant."

"Your relationship status is none of my business."

"Since *when*? You had no problem inserting yourself less

than an hour ago. You were defending my honor and now you're treating me like—"

"Treating you like what, Valen?" he asks, cutting me off. "Not everything revolves around you. I've gotta go deal with something," he says dismissively before walking away from me. Before he gets to his car, he turns to face me, walking backward as he shouts, "But hey, if you're still interested in payback and need someone to bend you over later, I'm your guy."

"What the hell is wrong with you?" I yell. "For a second there, I almost thought there was more to you than the asshole you pretend to be."

He shrugs, a cruel smile on his face. "And for a second, I almost thought you were more than a stuck-up little cheer-leader with nice tits and an attitude problem. Guess we were both wrong."

FIVE

Valen
One Year Later

"I**T'S LIKE WATCHING** A**NIMAL** P**LANET**," I say to S**HAYNE**, who stands beside me, our shoulders touching. Both of us have our arms folded, watching intently as her boyfriend and her brother attempt to put aside their disdain for each other long enough to turn her bed into a loft bed to fit her desk underneath. "Which one will prove to be the alpha?"

Shayne elbows me. "As long as they're not fist-fighting, it's progress."

Grey still isn't thrilled about them, and it's been a year, so the fact that they're even in the same room together is kind of a big deal.

"Move over, rich boy. Working with your hands isn't your area of expertise," Grey says to Thayer.

"Why don't you ask your sister how good I am with my hands?"

"Oh, Jesus Christ," Shayne mutters before walking away.

"You guys see that little white thing with the words on it?" I ask, pointing to the forgotten pamphlet on the floor. "It actually tells you what to do. Literally spells it out for you. Crazy, right?"

"I don't need instructions," Grey grumbles.

"I'm going to order pizza," Shayne calls out from the kitchen. "Any requests?"

"I'm actually going to head out," Grey says, walking away from the pile of metal and screws littering Shayne's bedroom floor.

I turn for the kitchen in time to see Shayne's face fall. "Already?"

"Yeah." He scratches at the back of his neck. "I've got some shit to do. Call me if you need help with anything else."

"Okay. Thanks for coming over." She tries to conceal her disappointment with a smile, but I see it, and I'm sure Grey does, too. He pulls her in for a quick hug, ruffles her hair, and then he's gone.

She stares down at her phone, seemingly lost in her thoughts as I make my way over to where she stands.

"He'll come around," I assure her, hooking an arm around her waist, leaning my head on her shoulder. She rests her head on mine, hugging me back. I'm not the most affectionate person, especially of the physical variety, but Shayne is the exception to the rule.

"I thought he would have by now, but I think it's more about finding out Thayer's dad is his dad, too."

"That'll do it." I laugh. "If you can get past the fact that your brother is related to your boyfriend, they shouldn't have a problem with it."

"Don't say it like that." She cringes. "You make it sound so…"

"Incestuous? Illegal?"

"We aren't related!"

"I know. But it's so fun to give you shit."

"I hate you. Besides, that's not what I meant. I think his issue has less to do with our being together and more to do with Thayer and Holden specifically. He won't admit it, though. And Thayer and Holden aren't exactly welcoming their new brother with open arms. I think…" she lowers her voice and trails off, unhooking her arm and stepping back to peek into the room where Thayer's putting the finishing touches on her bed. "I think they really believe that if they treat Grey like a brother, they're somehow replacing Danny."

"Yeah, well, we both know the Ames brothers aren't exactly known for their emotional maturity. Guess that includes your brother." She gives me a flat stare, but I can see the smile she's trying to hold back.

"Enough about them. You know what I want to talk about?"

I raise a single brow, waiting for her to elaborate.

"The fact that I'm *finally* living with my best friend."

This was always the plan for as long as I can remember, but then Thayer happened, and I assumed she'd move into his apartment after we graduated, especially since it's not far from campus. She spends most of her time there, anyway.

Originally, she was offered a scholarship to a different school, but when we both got accepted to Hadley University, we couldn't pass up the chance to do college together. Unfortunately, things haven't exactly gone according to plan. Turns out, Hadley has a major housing crisis. Normally, we're required to live on campus as freshmen, but they made exceptions since they didn't have anywhere to put everyone. Almost two hundred students, including Shayne, were sent to a hotel for the majority of the first semester. I was able to secure a double on campus, and even though I would have preferred a single, I considered myself lucky that my roommate, Lauren, was quiet as a church mouse. That is, until she had her boyfriend come over every single night and fucked him—*loudly*—while I was in the bed next to them.

Between the unfortunate housing situation, cheer taking up all my time, and volleyball taking up Shayne's, we've barely gotten to see each other at all this semester.

When Shayne told me there was an opening for a double in Hawthorne Hall, the nicest, biggest, and newest building on campus, I jumped at the opportunity. They're more like tiny apartments than dorms and mostly reserved for upperclassmen and far more expensive than the regular dorms since they're fully furnished, have two separate bedrooms along with a kitchen, living room, and a full-sized fridge. The best part? No more communal bathrooms. If there wasn't a housing crisis, there's no way we'd have gotten so lucky. I still don't know how Shayne managed to get us in, and before the semester's end, no less.

"Definitely a cause for celebration. We need drinks. And extra pepperoni on that pizza," I say, pointing to the unfinished order on the screen of her phone.

Twenty minutes later, Shayne has a fully assembled loft bed, and she stands in her room with her arms folded across her chest, pinning Thayer with a disapproving look.

"What?" he asks, sounding defensive.

"You know what. Why do you have to push his buttons?"

"Because he makes it too fucking easy. And correct me if I'm wrong, but wasn't he the first one to start talking shit?"

"Really? You're going with *he started it*? What are you, seven?" She shakes her head, leaning back against the wall. "I've been patient. I've waited for you guys to figure it out on your own because I *know* it's…a lot. But is it too much to ask to just try? For me? When are you going to realize that your anger is misplaced? This isn't his fault any more than it is yours or Holden's. Your dad and my mom kept this from all of us. Blame them."

Thayer's jaw flexes as he considers her words, and then he's closing the space between them, gripping her hips to pull her closer. "I'm sorry, baby. I haven't made it easier on you."

Her arms are still crossed, but I see some of the tension leave her shoulders. "No, you haven't." She sighs. "It's not just you, though. Grey's just as bad, but I feel guilty because we have each other and he has…no one."

Thayer leans down, kissing her forehead. I should give them privacy, but I can't seem to peel my eyes away from the scene in front of me. I never thought I'd see Thayer Ames contrite or… *soft*. But that's exactly how he is with Shayne right now. He's still an asshole—will probably always *be* an asshole—but he's putty in her hands.

"I'll try harder."

She beams up at him, her smile victorious as she winds her arms around his neck. "Thank you."

The knock at the door rips my attention away just as they're about to start dry humping each other against the wall, I'm sure. "I got it!" I call out, all but running toward the door. I swing it open wide, fully expecting to see the pizza guy, but it's Holden who stands there, pizza boxes stacked on his palm. I'm momentarily frozen, completely caught off guard.

It shouldn't be surprising that he'd be here, seeing as how my best friend is essentially his sister, but I still wasn't expecting to see him so soon. It's not that I haven't seen him at all over the past year, but after the night he punched Liam, he was cold toward me. Angry. I later found out it was the same night he found out that his cousin, Christian, who doubled as his best friend, was responsible for killing Danny, and their uncle was covering it up.

I never quite understood what that had to do with me, but that anger eventually faded, and he went back to being his normal self, if not a little indifferent, like our night together never mattered at all. Like I never mattered at all. *Fine with me.*

I avoided him, mostly out of embarrassment, and he didn't exactly go out of his way to get into my pants anymore either. He was too busy drinking himself into oblivion and *entertaining* any girl with a pulse to bother with me. For the remainder of the school year, we reluctantly coexisted for our friends' sake, but since graduation, I can count how many times I've seen him on one hand. A party here and there, once on campus from a distance, and once with the basketball team in the gym during their practice. When basketball season started last month, I thought I'd have to face him, but he hasn't played a single game. I was confused on how or why he'd be practicing with the team if he wasn't actually playing, but I didn't let myself care enough to ask Shayne about it.

All in all, the night in Holden's pool house seems more like a fever dream than reality, and sometimes I wonder if it even happened at all. But as I stand here, face-to-face with him for the first time in months, I know it did.

I notice his hair first. It's shorter on the sides now, no sign of the wavy, messy brown hair I'm used to seeing on him. It makes his jawline seem even more pronounced and the rest of his features seem almost…severe. His light brown eyes don't hold the same warmth they used to either. Or maybe that warmth is just reserved for anyone who *isn't* me.

Suddenly, I'm all too aware of the fact that I'm only wearing a sports bra with a half-zipped hoodie, a pair of short black cheer spandex, and a freaking ankle brace over one of my white socks. I threw my hair into a ponytail earlier, so it was out of the way while we were moving stuff in, but I know without having to look that it's hanging limply. I don't attempt to smooth down the stray hairs that have escaped their elastic. That would mean I care about how I look in front of him. *Which I don't.* He's not exactly dressed up either in his gray sweatshirt, but somehow, he manages to make me feel underdressed. My eyes catch on the tattoo on his thigh that peeks out from beneath his black basketball shorts, but I can't make out what it is.

His gaze rakes over me, not leering, but…assessing? When his perusal makes its way back up to my face, I raise a brow, already feeling that familiar defense mode click back into place like it does whenever we're together. "Holden," I say his name like a four-letter word.

"You gonna let me in, Valentina?" I ignore the fact that he used my full name, refusing to give him a reaction. He knows I hate it. "Or are you just going to stare at me? I come bearing gifts." He holds up the pizza boxes and a paper grocery bag.

"Delivering pizzas now? Daddy Dearest finally cut the purse strings?"

"Nah, the delivery guy's allergic to bitch, so I told him I'd take care of it."

I give him a bratty smile before turning away, and he follows me inside, setting the pizzas on the countertop.

"How good of you to show up after we've done all the heavy lifting," Thayer says, walking over to open the pizza box, pulling out a slice before taking a seat at one of the barstools.

"I brought drinks," Holden offers, holding the grocery bag up, the contents clanking together inside.

"You're forgiven," Shayne says, making her way into the narrow kitchen.

Holden pulls her in for a hug, ruffling her hair as he releases her. "Congrats on the place, baby sister."

"Thanks for letting me know about it." She smiles, taking the bag from his fingertips. She sets it on the counter, digging through the contents before producing two six packs of beer.

Wait. Holden is the reason I no longer have to listen to moaning and skin slapping all hours of the night and risk athletes' foot every time I want to take a shower? Lovely.

"It's not fancy or anything, but my mom gave me this to celebrate, too," Shayne says, gesturing to a bottle of champagne next to the fridge. "I think I have cups in one of these boxes."

"I'll take a beer," Thayer says, leaning forward to grab one.

"Valen?" Shayne asks. "Beer or champagne?"

"She strikes me as more of a tequila girl," Holden says, making heat crawl up my neck. Shayne casts a curious look between the two of us, confused by his seemingly random statement.

"Champagne," I say, ignoring him and the memories of his mouth on me, once again. "We're celebrating."

Shayne hands them both a bottle of beer before grabbing the champagne from the fridge and handing it to me to open. I hold it out in front of me, squinting one eye shut as I start to push against the cork.

"Give it here before you take my eye out," Holden says, realizing he's in the line of fire. He doesn't wait for me to hand it over before he curls his fingers around the cold bottle, taking it from my grasp. God, even his stupid hands do it for me.

This inexplicable attraction to him is ridiculous, and I tell my-self that this tension, this *pull* to him is due to the fact that I'm still wondering what would've happened between us if Thayer never showed up that night. I was glad he did. Grateful that he saved me from making what was sure to be a huge mistake. Unfortunately, my brain and my body weren't on the same page.

The *pop* snaps me out of my thoughts. Holden hands the bottle to Shayne, who pours two glasses before handing me one. "To being roommates," she says, clinking the rim of her plastic cup to mine. "And a fresh start."

Twenty minutes later, we're full of pizza and champagne, all four of us squeezed onto the single couch as we watch some three-hour superhero movie that I have zero interest in. Thayer's on one end with Shayne cuddled into his side, his arm slung pos-sessively around her shoulders. Holden's on the other side of her, knees spread wide, and I'm on the far end with my knees up, sandwiched between him and the arm of the couch. I can feel Holden's eyes on me every now and then, but I keep my gaze pointed toward the screen, unseeing, my chin propped on my hand.

We really need more furniture.

"That reminds me." Shayne reaches for the remote next to Thayer and pauses the movie before adjusting her body to face me. "You're not going home for Christmas."

I blink at her, unsure of how we got here and what Christmas has to do with anything. "I mean, not that I'm complaining, but care to elaborate?"

She smiles, folding her legs into a crisscrossed position. "We're going on a trip instead."

"Where?"

"Vermont. Ski trip. Cozy cabin in the mountains. It'll be perfect. My mom's working, and these two aren't interested in spending Christmas with August, so we figured we'd put their cabin to use before I spend the rest of the break visiting my dad. Plus, now that you're off the hook with cheer, you have no reason to say no. Unless you'd rather spend the holidays with your mom."

I sprained my ankle during one of the last football games of the season doing a toe touch back tuck. Things I've done hundreds of times. I landed awkwardly and instantly knew something was wrong. I finished out the game, but by the time it was over, my ankle was purple and five times its normal size. The doctor made me wear a boot for two weeks, and when I went back for my follow-up after I got it off, he said I couldn't go back to cheer for another six weeks, or I'd end up needing surgery. Even though it's been a couple of weeks and I feel completely fine, my coach agrees with him and doesn't want me to risk further injury.

"Shitty reception, far away from civilization, no one to hear you scream…" Holden ticks off between us. "What's not to love?"

"Shut up." Shayne slaps his shoulder. "It's one of the biggest ski resorts in the country. It's hardly a ghost town."

I look over her shoulder at Thayer. "You agreed to this?" He's not exactly a social butterfly, although, he's no stranger to parties, so I guess it's sort of on brand for the Ames brothers.

"Let's just say she made me a deal I can't refuse."

Judging by the way Shayne's cheeks turn pink, I can guess said *deal* was sexual in nature. "So anyway, are you in?" she asks.

"I'll think about it," I say noncommittally.

Holden leans back into the couch, extending his arms out on the back of it as we go back and forth on either side of him. "Don't mind me sitting here."

We both ignore him.

"Come on, Valen," she pouts, sticking out her bottom lip, folding her hands together under her chin. "After the past year, we all need this."

I'm not sure how being holed up with Holden in an isolated cabin will lead to anything other than trouble, but I don't say that. As far as Shayne knows, Holden and I shared an alcohol-induced kiss to piss off Liam the night he cheated, and that was the end of it. Nothing more than a drunken mistake. Which isn't far from the truth. It *was* a mistake. But I wasn't very drunk at all. And it was more than just a kiss. As much as I want to deny it, the sad truth is that I felt more turned on with Holden than I did the entire year I spent with Liam. It's not that it was bad with Liam. It was nice. A release, somehow, even though I never actually managed to have an orgasm. With him or anyone else.

My phone vibrates on top of one of the cardboard moving boxes at my feet, saving me from having to answer. I jump up, a little too eager to answer, and Shayne narrows her eyes at me, knowingly.

"Hello?" I answer without looking at the screen. I'd entertain a spam call at this point.

"Tine?" a familiar yet slightly surprised voice says from the other line, using the nickname he's used for me for as long as I can remember. "I didn't think you'd answer."

"It's Valen," I correct, my tone a little sharper than I intended. "And I didn't know it was you, so."

"Right." He clears his throat. "I've been trying to get a hold of you. Decided to use my business phone."

"Well…here I am."

An awkward silence stretches over the line.

"How's the car?"

My laugh isn't one of humor. "You want to talk about my car? What do you actually want?" I walk into the kitchen, feeling three sets of eyes on me.

"Remember, I've given you everything you've asked for, daughter of mine. I can take it away just as easily. Including the extra housing expense that I just paid. I think you can entertain a phone call."

I almost laugh at how quickly his act crumbled. "How can I forget?" I deadpan. He loves to remind me. Less than five seconds into the phone call and he's already making threats.

"I'm calling you about Christmas."

"What about it?" I ask, suspicion lacing my tone. I haven't spent a Christmas with him in years.

"I'd like to spend it with you this year. I've already cleared it with your mother."

Somehow, I doubt that. My mother would sooner roll over and die before she'd agree to me spending the holidays with my dad, his new fiancée, and her daughter. I don't know which option sounds worse.

"Actually, I have plans."

"Plans," he repeats. "On Christmas?"

"With friends. Ski trip in Vermont."

Shayne beams up at me, doing a silent celebratory dance on the couch. Holden eyes me curiously, as if he's trying to put something together, and Thayer's thankfully already unpaused the movie, apparently done with the conversation.

"I suppose I can't force you. But I'd like to see you soon, Valen. And I'd much rather it be in person."

Curiosity mixes with dread and swirls in my stomach. What could be so important? "Are you sick?"

"Depends on who you ask."

"Are you dying?" I clarify.

He sighs, and I can picture him pinching the bridge of his nose. "No, I'm not sick or dying."

"Great. Then it can wait 'til after Christmas." I end the call without waiting for a response.

"So it's settled?" Shayne asks, hopeful.

"We'll see."

"She's coming," she tells Holden.

"We'll see," he repeats, but his meaning is entirely different. If Shayne picked up on his suggestive tone, she doesn't react.

"Hey, was that your dad?" she asks, switching gears, as if it just occurred to her.

"Yep."

"He wants to spend Christmas with you?"

"I'm just as surprised as you are." In the handful of years that I've known Shayne, she's seen my father a grand total of one time, which sadly, isn't much less than me. He spent the vast majority of my childhood working for the media company his family owns.

"Why is that weird?" Holden asks, folding his arms over his chest, leaning back into the couch.

Shayne and I exchange a look, but neither one of us responds.

"Ah. Daddy issues," he says knowingly.

I glare at him. "You're one to talk."

"Never claimed otherwise."

"Let's be real. Everyone in this room has Daddy issues," Shayne says with a laugh. She spent her whole life not even knowing who her dad is until recently. I haven't figured out if that's something to be jealous of or not.

"And Mommy issues." Holden smirks.

Shayne makes a face at the same time Thayer reaches around to smack the back of Holden's head. "Never say Mommy again," Shayne grimaces.

"What about Grey?" I ask. "Where's he going to be?"

Holden's smile stays in place, but it no longer reaches his eyes, and I can tell he's making an effort to keep it there. Thayer doesn't do as good a job at concealing his disdain for their half-brother, his jaw clenching and releasing at the sound of his name.

"He's invited," Shayne says, giving them both a pointed look.

"The fuck he is," Holden argues.

"You have to get over it eventually. It's been long enough," Shayne says stubbornly.

"Fine. Then he can come and get his ass beat. He's long overdue."

"Fine."

I arch a brow, feeling half-guilty for starting this conversation, but half-amused at their bickering.

"Fine?" Holden repeats, incredulous.

"If fighting like a bunch of idiots is what it'll take for all three of you to get your head out of your asses, then so be it."

"Deal. But if you're bringing him, I get to bring a friend," Holden says.

"It's your cabin, not mine," she says with a shrug.

"So…who needs another drink?" I ask, trying to lighten the tension.

Shayne raises her hand and stands, but Thayer is right behind her, scooping her up. "I think she's had enough."

"I think *you* can't tell me what to do." He leans down to whisper something in her ear, and whatever he says gives her an instant change of heart. "Okay, night, guys. Love you both!" She rushes out as she's being carried off to her room.

And now I'm left with Holden. Alone. He stands from the couch, stretching his arms above his head before turning to face me where I stand with my back to the counter, arms folded. He holds my stare, neither one of us speaking without the buffer of other people. A second later, music blares from Shayne's room, and Holden's lips quirk up at the corners, knowing exactly what that means.

He walks toward me, not stopping until he's right in front of me.

"You cut your hair." I don't know why it comes out so aggressively, like an accusation. I don't know why it comes out at all.

"Is that a problem?" he asks, bemused.

I shrug a shoulder. "Just an observation."

He leans in even closer, bracing his palms on the countertop, trapping me between two thick arms. "I can grow it back out for you. I know how much you liked holding on to it when I—"

"You're still an asshole."

"And you still smell like a fucking Creamsicle." His fingers twist around my ponytail and tug, then his nose is in my neck, inhaling deeply. I freeze, forcing myself not to melt into him, even as goosebumps immediately spread across my skin. Why does it have to be Holden, of all people, who has this effect on me? It just goes to show that you can't choose who you have chemistry with, because if I had even a little bit of a say in the matter, he'd be last on my list.

"You can't just go around sniffing people like a dog, Holden. It's uncivilized."

I feel his amusement as his smile spreads against my neck.

"No one's ever accused me of being civilized. That's especially true when it comes to you."

His words catch me off guard, considering our last real conversation was the fight we had the day after he punched Liam. He wins this round because I don't know how to respond to that other than to stare daggers at him.

"So…Christmas?"

"I don't know, are you going to try to fuck me the entire time?"

"Are you going to let me?"

I try to slide out from under his arms, but he moves with me, keeping me trapped. "I'm just fucking with you, Valen." At my pointed look, he corrects himself. "Poor choice of words."

"I haven't decided."

"If you're scared, just say that," he taunts.

I scoff, knowing his game, "What could I possibly be afraid of? *You*?"

"No. Not of me. You're afraid of what you'll do if you let yourself be alone with me."

"You cannot be that conceited." I laugh. "Or is it delusional?"

"Still lying to yourself, I see," he counters, unfazed. "Don't think it escaped my notice that you've gone out of your way to avoid me for the past year."

"Maybe because I don't like you. Did you ever think of that?"

He looks at the ceiling, pretending to think it over. "Yeah, that's not it. I think you liked me just fine in my pool house."

"Well, would you look at the time," I say, not having any

idea what time it actually is. He pulls away, taking his heat with him. "See you on Christmas, I guess," I say, ushering him out of the dorm and into the hall.

"Oh, I have a feeling it will be much sooner than that." The smirk is back in place, infuriating as ever. I go to close the door on him, but he throws out a hand, stopping it. "Aren't you going to make sure I get home safe?"

I look at him, confused, as he takes approximately two steps in the hall...and opens the door directly across from mine.

"Goodnight, *neighbor*."

SIX

Valen

HAVING HOLDEN ACROSS THE HALL ISN'T NEARLY AS BAD AS I thought. I assumed there would be loud music and parties, but the reality is, I barely ever see him. That could be due to the fact that I've been focusing on finals for the last two weeks, or the fact that Holden doesn't crawl out of bed until after noon most days according to Shayne. In fact, I've seen his roommate Ryan Thompson, a guy on the basketball team, more than Holden. That's not to say I haven't seen him at all, though. I've bumped into him a few times, mostly late at night with a girl or two on his arm, or on his way back from what I assume is training.

That's about to change, though, because exams are finally over, and we leave for our ski trip tomorrow. I caved. Of course, I caved. I had four options. Spend my Christmas with my passive-aggressive, self-absorbed mother, spend it with my flaky, newly engaged father, spend it alone in the dorms, or spend it with my best friend at the Ames' vacation cabin. My parents were out of the question, and even I have to admit that spending the holidays alone would be depressing as shit. Tempting, but depressing, nonetheless. Besides, it might be fun. Holden's bringing a girl to keep him company, so he'll be too busy to drive me insane, and after the stress of the past few weeks, I'm actually looking forward to it.

"Ready?" Shayne asks, wheeling her suitcase out into the living room. I look at the floor that is littered with our pillows and blankets and grocery bags of snacks and drinks, making sure we have everything we need.

"I feel like we're forgetting something."

Shayne pulls out the list she made on her phone. "Phone charger?"

"Got it."

"Face wash, shampoo and conditioner, lip balm, body wash, deodorant?"

"Check, check, check."

"Headphones, warm clothes for snowboarding, wallet, bathing suit…" She lists off.

"Bathing suit?"

"For the hot tub!"

"You didn't say anything about a hot tub. I might have agreed to this trip a lot sooner." On second thought, water, Holden, and I don't mix well if our history is anything to go by.

"Please, like you'd say no to me. You know you're excited."

"A little," I admit. I run to my room and grab the one bikini I brought from home, then stuff it into my backpack.

"Are you sure you can go snowboarding with your ankle?" Shayne asks when I walk back into the living area. "We can day drink by the fire at the lodge instead."

I shrug. "It feels fine now." Mostly. I'm not supposed to put extra strain on it, but snowboarding boots are literally *made* to support your ankles, and it's only for a day or two. "I don't care what we do, as long as I don't have to use my brain to do it."

"For real," Shayne groans. "I'm just glad it's over."

"Same." For another few weeks until we have to do it all over again, that is.

The door swings open, and we both turn to find Holden standing there looking half-asleep. He shoves a hand through his mess of hair, hair that I've noticed has gotten noticeably longer in the near month since we've been here, eyeing the chaos laid out in front of him. "Thayer's pulling my car around. Is all this going?"

"No. We just thought we'd trash the place for funsies before we left," I quip.

"You do realize we're leaving for five days, not five years, right?"

"Shut up and load the car," Shayne says with a laugh.

Holden takes both of our suitcases and lugs them down the hall. We follow him out into the cold with our backpacks and pillows in tow. We get outside just in time to see Thayer backing into the loading zone. He pops the lift gate, and after one more trip back to the dorm, we're ready to go.

"I'm going to pee," Shayne announces.

"Me, too. I just downed a gallon of coffee," Thayer says.

When they both take off for the bathroom, I'm left alone with Holden. I lean against the back of his Range Rover, pulling the sleeves of my sweatshirt down to cover my cold hands before crossing my arms against my chest.

"Looking good, Valen," he says, looking me up and down.

I snort. "Where's your date?"

"My date?" He smirks, flashing his dimples. "Oh, I'm sure my *date* will be here any second."

I narrow my eyes at him, wondering why he's being so weird.

"I think you two will really get along."

"Oh yeah?"

He nods. "My date is super chill. Funny as hell. Athletic. Not to mention, tall, dark, and gorgeous."

"Okay," I draw the word out. Why does he keep saying *my date* like that?

"Does that bother you?"

"Why would it bother me?" If he's bringing some supermodel along for Christmas, good for him. In fact, it's ideal. Seeing him with another girl is a surefire way to kill any lingering attraction.

"Well, speak of the devil. Here's my date now." He holds out his arms and I look up to see a very confused Ryan walking toward us, duffle bag slung over his shoulder.

"Ryan is your date?" I deadpan. The word has officially lost its meaning with how many times we've said it.

Holden takes Ryan's cheeks in his hands before pinching them. "Did I lie? Just look at this face."

Ryan smacks his hands away before adjusting his black beanie. "What the fuck is he talking about?" he asks me.

"About how you're tall, dark, and gorgeous." And he is. Dark eyes with full lashes. The pronounced hollows of his cheeks and a razor-sharp jawline are softened by full lips and an easy smile. Rich, brown skin. He towers over me, even more so than Holden. I'm used to seeing him on the basketball court, but he's even more attractive up close. It's easy to see why everyone wants him, my cheer team included.

He lifts a shoulder. "Can't disagree there."

And humble, too.

"Get your pretty ass in the car and let's go," Holden says.

"Change of plans."

"What do you mean, *change of plans*?" He eyes his duffel bag. "I thought you didn't have enough time to go all the way home for Christmas this year?"

"I don't. I was supposed to have a few days off, but now I don't even have that. Coach wants us to run some new plays since we play Stonewood two days after Christmas."

"So, you're not coming?"

"And miss out on the powder princesses? Fuck that. I just have to drive separately. You've got me for two days, sweet cheeks." He gives Holden's face a playful slap. "Consider yourself lucky."

"Powder princesses?" I snort out a laugh.

"Girls who dress up in those hot little ski outfits but don't actually know how to ski or snowboard. You know the type," Holden supplies.

I raise my eyebrows at his insinuation. Truth be told, my mind went in a completely different direction. One that involved a white, powdery substance. "You mean like Shayne and me?" I challenge.

"Fuck no," Holden says. "Powder princesses aren't…there for skiing. They're there to hook up."

"Maybe that's exactly why I'm going," I say just to mess with him for his shitty comment.

"In that case," Ryan says, slinging an arm around my shoulders, "want to ride with me?"

"No," Holden barks out the word so harshly that we both look at him, surprised. *What the hell is that about?*

Ryan's face breaks into a wide grin while I continue to look at Holden with confusion. Before the moment can get too awkward, Shayne and Thayer are back from using the bathroom. Shayne waves while Thayer extends his hand, pulling Ryan in for that handshake-hug thing that guys do. Their familiarity throws me for a second until I remember that Holden and Ryan have been roommates since August, so it makes sense that Thayer would be friends with him, too.

"Ready?" Shayne asks. "It's freezing."

"Sooner the better," Thayer agrees. "It's supposed to dump later."

SEVEN

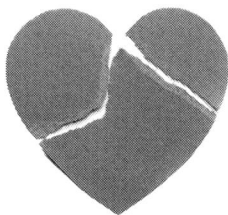

Holden

MY CAR SMELLS LIKE A FUCKING CREAMSICLE. AT FIRST, I thought I was imagining it, but every time Valen moves around or flips her hair while she and Shayne talk animatedly, I catch a whiff from where she sits behind me. Having her next door has been bad enough. I haven't been able to stop thinking about her since she stood in her doorway and uttered my name like an accusation, but having her in my car, and soon to be in a secluded cabin, is a different level of torture. Too bad I promised Thayer and Shayne I'd be on my best behavior where Valen is concerned.

I know she hated me after how I treated her last year. Admittedly, I was a dick. In my defense, I had to watch her choose her slimy ass boyfriend over me minutes before I found out that my cousin and best friend was responsible for my brother's death. Suffice it to say, I didn't handle it well. So sue me. But when I showed up at the door the first night they moved in across the hall, Valen didn't look at me with the usual disdain I've become accustomed to.

She was shocked—that much was clear. I was amused to find that Shayne clearly left out the fact that we were going to be neighbors. But it was more than just surprise I detected. Then when she assumed I was bringing a girl to the cabin, there was an edge to her voice. I know better than to call it jealousy, but if there's something between jealousy and cool ambivalence, that was it. She can pretend to hate me all she wants, but it was there.

After what seems like hours of twists and turns through the mountains, we finally pull into the long, snow-covered driveway. Valen's the first one out of the car before we even come to a complete stop.

"You good?" I ask, amused, as I step out of the driver's seat and into the snow. Snow that almost reaches Valen's knees. She has one hand pressed to her stomach and a scowl on her face. "You're looking a little green there."

"Yeah, thanks to you. You took those turns like a NASCAR driver."

"Thank you."

She shoots me a glare. "It wasn't a compliment."

I suck in a lungful of air, inhaling fresh pine trees and winter, a welcome reprieve from the scent of Creamsicles. I watch Valen for a reaction as she looks up at the house, snowflakes collecting on her dark hair. The log cabin is nestled between tall pine trees with a thick layer of snow lining the roof and floor-to-ceiling windows. Somehow, it looks smaller than I remember.

"So pretty," Shayne says, rounding the car. "I've never actually been here. The pictures don't do it justice."

"Like something out of a Christmas movie," Valen agrees.

"The key should be in the lockbox next to the door," Thayer says, pulling some of the bags out of the back of my car. Shayne and Valen follow his lead, grabbing their backpacks. I tilt my head to the side, admiring the way Valen's ass looks as she walks toward the house in her skintight black leggings when a snowball hits me in the back of the head.

"I thought you and this girl weren't even friends," Ryan says knowingly, coming up behind me, using my words from when he questioned me about Valen the day she moved in. I told him she was my stepsister's best friend, conveniently leaving out the part about almost hooking up with her.

"We're not."

"Then why did you look at me like you wanted my head on a fucking stick when I asked if she wanted to ride with me?" When I don't have a response for that, he laughs, clapping my shoulder. "That's what I thought. Don't worry, Ames. I won't go after your girl."

I might have promised to be on my best behavior, but the thing about promises? They're meant to be broken.

EIGHT

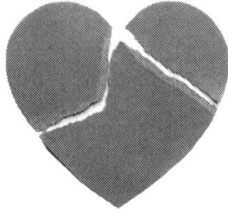

Valen

"**A**RE YOU SURE YOU DON'T WANT TO ROOM WITH ME?" Shayne asks for the third time.

"Yes, *please*, ditch your boyfriend and spend your romantic cabin getaway with me instead," I deadpan.

"It's not a romantic getaway," she argues. "It's more like…a family vacation."

The place has a rustic feel, all wood floors, exposed wooden beams in the high ceilings, and a stone fireplace. It's cozy, but the open floor plan makes it seem spacious at the same time. A narrow, wrought iron spiral staircase leads to a second floor with a long hallway and four doors. Probably bedrooms and not much else by the looks of it.

"You can have the big room," Thayer says, picking up Shayne's suitcase by the handle. I catch a glimpse of a smirk before he turns for the staircase.

"Why is he making that face? Is it haunted?"

Shayne laughs. "I have no idea. I told you I've never been here."

"It's Holden's room," Thayer throws over his shoulder. When he sees my *hell no* expression, he clarifies, "He'll room with Ryan. They have bunkbeds."

Annnd there it is.

Both Shayne and I laugh, following him upstairs. When he

shows us where Holden's sleeping, we laugh even more. The room itself is barely bigger than a shoebox, and the wooden bunkbed, complete with a log ladder, takes up the majority of the space. I cannot imagine Holden even *fitting* in that thing.

"Here's your room," he says when we get to the room at the far right side of the hall. "Bathroom's the door on the other side of Holden's and we're down there." He points to the left side of the hall.

Thankfully, this room has a queen bed (also made out of logs. Shocker.) and a little more space than the other room. I'm surprised at how clean everything looks since I was under the impression that they haven't been up here in a long time, but I'd guess they pay someone to maintain it throughout the year.

"How is this Holden's room? Isn't he the youngest?" I may be an only child, but even I know the rules of the sibling hierarchy. The oldest gets the bigger room.

"He was a baby when my parents bought the place, so my mom ended up staying in here with him half the time because he was such a bad sleeper. Kept everyone up. Danny and I had the bunkbeds."

I see a rare flash of emotion in his dark eyes, and I wonder if it has to do with his mom, Danny, this place, or maybe a combination of the three.

"Show me our room," Shayne says.

Once they leave, I toss my backpack onto the bed before sitting on the mattress. There's a little nightstand with a lamp that has bear cubs climbing each other on the stand. Just to be nosy, I pull open the drawer and see a couple pennies, a tube of Chapstick, a few other miscellaneous items, and a handful of condoms.

Must not have been that *long since they've been here.*

I slam the drawer shut when I hear the front door open downstairs followed by the sound of two sets of footsteps clanking against the metal steps. They head left, to the primary bedroom I presume. I can hear their deep voices reverberating through the walls as I shrug my jacket off and hang it from the hook on the back of my door, but I can't make out what they're saying. I walk back to sit on the edge of the bed and flop backward, stretching my arms over my head.

"Are you fucking kidding me?" I spring upright when Holden's loud voice echoes down the hallway. His footsteps pound down the hall until he's standing in my doorway. "This is my room." He points to where I'm sitting. *"That* is my bed."

"This bed?" I ask innocently, leaning backward as I smooth my palms along the thick patchwork quilt, making a show out of feeling out the mattress and testing its firmness. "Looks like it's mine for the week."

Ryan appears behind Holden and shakes his head, looking more amused than put out, before he heads to their room. Clearly, he isn't as bothered about his sleeping arrangements.

"I haven't fit in that bunkbed since I was seven years old." He throws his backpack onto the bed, and it lands right next to me with a bounce. "Move over."

"I'm not sharing a bed with you." The idea of sharing a room, let alone a bed, with anyone has my palms starting to sweat.

"Once again. *My* bed. Stay wherever the hell you want, but I'm sleeping here." He pins me with a heated gaze. "With or without you."

Aiming for nonchalance, I shrug a shoulder before rising to my feet. "Fine. I'm sure Ryan won't mind rooming with me," I say, hoping he doesn't call my bluff. I won't pretend to know why he had an issue with Ryan's harmless flirting earlier, but I'm banking on the assumption that his irrational objection extends to sharing a bunkbed with him, too.

The muscles in Holden's jaw tick, and I can tell he's trying to play it cool. When he doesn't say anything, I grab my bag off the bed and walk past him, heading for the hallway. I don't get more than three steps before he yanks me backward by the strap of my backpack.

"Fine," he bites out. "Take my bed."

The first day was a success. After we finished unloading the car, we all decided to make a grocery run for necessities before it got too late. We planned on having a couple drinks and then going to sleep early in order to be able to wake up at an ungodly hour for snowboarding. But it's now three o'clock in the morning and Shayne and I are still hanging out in her room upstairs, talking about everything and nothing, while Thayer, Holden, and Ryan play video games downstairs.

"Okay, I have to sleep or else there's zero chance I'm going snowboarding," Shayne announces, setting her beer bottle down on the bedside table before twisting her long hair up and securing it with a clip at the base of her neck. "Thayer says we'll have to leave by eight to get a parking spot."

"Ugh," I groan. "I thought the whole point of break was to *not* wake up early." I stand, swaying on my feet a little as I gather up an armful of empty bottles we've amassed over the past few hours.

"Leave them there." Shayne laughs, waving me off. "I'll get them in the morning."

The bottles clank together as I set them back down. We say good night before I set off for the bathroom. As I walk down the hall, I note that the guys are noticeably quieter than they were earlier, but the faint sounds of literal warfare coming from the TV downstairs tells me they're still playing video games.

Once I've grabbed my toiletry bag from my room, I grip the knob of the bathroom door and push it open and freeze at the sight in front of me. Holden. Shirtless. Standing in front of the toilet with his sweats pulled down and his considerable length in hand.

"You mind?" His voice snaps me out of it and I drag my wide eyes away from his crotch and up to his face. I recover quickly, schooling my reaction once I see his cocky expression. Pun not intended.

"Ever heard of locking the door?" I roll my eyes before turning my back to him and pulling the door shut behind me.

"Ever heard of *knocking*?" he throws back from the other side of the door. I hear the faucet run for a few seconds before the door swings open behind me. I start to step aside to let him out, but he stops me with a hand to my upper arm. "If you wanted a free show, all you had to do was ask."

I spin around, raising a brow. "I've seen your little show before, remember?" I lean in, keeping my voice low so no one can overhear. "I'm not interested in a repeat." I step around him and into the bathroom before placing my palm on his bare back and pushing him out into the hallway.

When he's across the threshold, he turns around to scowl at me, arms crossed. "Nothing about my show is *little*," he says, sounding wounded.

Of course, that's the part of my statement he latched onto.

"Sweet dreams," I say with a flick of my fingers. He's still scowling when I shut the door in his face. And lock it for good measure.

No. Nothing about Holden Ames is little. And I was one hundred percent lying to myself when I said I wasn't interested in a repeat. Fuck.

NINE

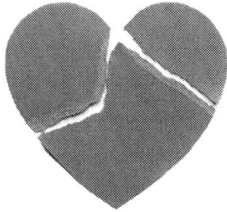

Valen

S HAYNE'S NEVER BEEN SNOWBOARDING, AND I HAVEN'T BEEN IN so many years that this may as well be my first time. Most people start with skiing, but Shayne insisted on snowboarding. "It's like riding a bike, right?" She tries to assure me as the ski lift takes us higher, our feet dangling beneath us, the left one strapped into the bindings and the right one free so we can step off the lift. Holden and Thayer are on the chairlift behind us, then Ryan and two girls I don't know are behind them. It took them less than five minutes to find some so-called *powder princesses*.

"Let's hope so," I mutter, and she laughs, unconcerned. The lift slows enough for us to exit, and I grab Shayne's gloved hand so we can hop off together. "Are you ready?"

Shayne nods as I angle myself sideways and push off the lift, dragging her with me. At first, I think she has it, but her board goes wiggly and she squeals, fisting the shoulders of my jacket with both hands to keep herself upright. Her weight throws me off balance and then she's falling face-first into the snow, bringing me on top of her.

We land in a tangle of limbs and equipment, laughing hysterically and blinded by our snow-covered goggles. Each attempt to get up ends in failure either from laughing too hard or slipping, which only causes us to laugh harder.

"Valen, hurry," Shayne rushes out between fits of laughter. "I think I'm going to pee!"

"I'm *trying*!" I manage to push myself up into a downward dog position with Shayne still underneath me. When she tries to army crawl away, I start laughing again. My board is slick against the snow and starts to slide, but before I collapse on top of her again, I hear Holden mutter a *Jesus Christ* as two large hands grip me underneath my arms, pulling me upright. We've drawn a crowd and the liftie has paused the chairlift, waiting for us to get our shit together. Thayer helps Shayne, and then they're carrying us out of the way like a couple of misbehaving toddlers so the lift can resume its operation.

Once we're off to the side, Holden brings his bare palm to my goggles, wiping away the remaining snow. "Hold on to my shoulders," he instructs.

"I can do it," I object, but he ignores my protest, dropping to a knee in front of me, grabbing the foot that isn't already strapped in. Trying to conceal my amusement with annoyance, I look over to Shayne, who's getting the same treatment from Thayer, and almost lose it all over again when we make eye contact.

The first time down the hill, Shayne falls a couple more times, but she gets the hang of it surprisingly quickly. And just like she said, it is like riding a bike for me. Even if I don't remember all the rules, my body does instinctively. I'm no professional by any means, but I can make it down the hill and stop without falling. Thayer, Holden, and Ryan, on the other hand? They make it look effortless, the way they glide down the mountain at warp speed. Naturally, Holden's the one to show off, jumping off every box and rail in our path, and to my complete and utter annoyance, I find myself appreciating the way he looks while doing so.

Turns out, Ryan knows his *powder princesses*. He went to high school with one of them, so our group went from five to seven. After sticking together for a few runs, our little group breaks apart, each of us doing our own thing. I end up getting stuck on the lift with the two girls that Ryan knows. They're both insanely beautiful. The one next to me has strawberry blonde hair, faint freckles across her fair skin, and piercing green eyes. The other has long, straight black hair and a flawless, naturally tan complexion.

"So," Green Eyes says, breaking the silence. "Which one is yours?"

"My bet's on Holden," the one with the dark hair says.

"None of them." I laugh.

"Really?" She scrutinizes me, her head cocked to the side. "I just thought—I mean, he hasn't stopped looking at you."

I look over at her, eyebrows pinched together. "Definitely not."

"So you're saying he's fair game? I don't want to step on any toes." This comes from Green Eyes.

"He's all yours," I quip as the lift nears the top. My stomach pitches, and I tell myself it's from the chair lift and not in protest to my words. She'd be doing me a favor, really. I quickly hop off the lift, finding Shayne, Holden, Thayer, and Ryan waiting. The guys have all ditched their jackets, wearing nothing but short-sleeved t-shirts and snowboard pants. And apparently, they're too cool for helmets because the only one actually wearing one is Shayne.

"I think it's time for a safety meeting," Holden says.

"What the hell is that?" Shayne asks.

Holden shakes his head, amusement sparkling in his eyes. "It's code for a smoke break, little sister."

I scrunch up my nose in disgust. "Who smokes cigarettes?"

"I'm not talking about cigarettes."

Oh. Duh.

"We're in," Green Eyes chirps from behind me.

"One more run. Then we can get lunch at the lodge after."

Everyone agrees, making quick work of pulling our goggles back down over our eyes and strapping our feet to our boards.

We're not even halfway down the mountain when someone plows into me from behind. I barely have time to react, belatedly throwing my hands out behind me to break my fall, but the effort is in vain. Before I know it, I'm flat on my back, all the air in my lungs forced from my chest with the impact. I'm gasping for air that doesn't come. I try to suck in breaths to no avail, my panic rising with each passing second.

I'm vaguely aware of a nearby commotion, but all I can do is lie here, stunned, feeling like I took a punch to the gut.

"Shit, you okay?" Holden's face comes into view as he leans over me, blocking the blue sky. He pulls my googles up to rest on my helmet, and he must notice my wide eyes because he quickly pulls me up to a sitting position, squatting down beside me. "You're okay. Just breathe."

Easy for you to say, I want to yell, but I still can't take in air, and I'm not wasting it on insults.

Shayne drops down at my side next, ripping her helmet off. "What the hell happened? Are you okay?"

Holden answers for me, cool as a fucking cucumber, while I fight for air. "She just got the wind knocked out of her. She'll be fine." He looks over to me. "It'll feel like you can't breathe, but it'll come. Sit here for a second and catch your breath."

I nod, feigning a calm exterior even though I feel anything but. After what feels like an eternity, I'm able to take in shallow breaths, but I still have that heavy feeling in my chest.

"Maybe we should get ski patrol to check her out?" Shayne suggests.

"God no." I shake my head. "I just needed a minute." I try to stand, ignoring the twinge of pain in my wrist and butt when I do. There's no way in hell I'm getting carried down a mountain on one of those rescue sleds.

"Are you sure?" She doesn't seem convinced.

"I've taken harder hits from cheer," I point out. "That was nothing."

She's about to argue, but Thayer skids to a stop behind us,

apparently having missed the action and had come back up the lift to find us. "Ryan's saving a table." Seeing us on the ground, his eyes immediately rove over Shayne, as if searching for any sign of injury. "What happened?"

"Relax, lover boy. She's fine." I laugh. Or try to. "Go eat," I tell Shayne. "I'm going to wait back at the house, if that's cool?" She starts to shake her head, and I can tell she's going to insist on coming with me, but Holden speaks first.

"I'll take her," he surprises me by saying.

"I'm good," I decline. Once again, he ignores me, dropping down to unclip my feet from the board. "What are you doing?"

"Helping you."

"I don't need your help."

"You plan on getting back down the mountain on your snowboard?"

It hadn't occurred to me, but I don't tell him that. My silence is answer enough because he continues to treat me like I'm incapable. When he has both feet out, he takes my board, handing it to Thayer. "Bring this back for me?"

Thayer nods, sticking it underneath his arm. Shayne's watchful eyes are bouncing between Holden and me, and I can practically hear her thoughts, but she doesn't voice her concerns. Yet.

"See you in an hour?"

I give her a reassuring nod, letting her know I can handle my own with Holden, and then they're heading for the restaurant. Before I can react, Holden rises to his feet and grips my waist.

Uh… "Can I help you?"

"Yeah, you can hold on."

"What?" I ask, confused.

Instead of answering, he lifts me, and my hands fly to his shoulders, my knees digging into his sides to keep some distance between us. The position is reminiscent of the night in the pool, and judging by his heated gaze and the way he clears his throat, he's thinking the same thing.

"Wrap your legs around me and hold on tight."

"Absolutely not."

"Suit yourself." Knees bent, he leans forward, shifting his weight to ride down the mountain. A squeal flies out of my mouth, and I immediately give in, locking my legs around his waist. I feel his chuckle more than hear it, his chest rumbling against mine.

"You couldn't have given me a piggyback ride?" I grumble loud enough for him to hear me.

He hoists me up a little higher by my thighs before adjusting his grip. One arm banding around my waist with his palm in the center of my back, the other under my butt. "Then I wouldn't be able to feel you wrapped around me again."

My stomach flips at his words, my mind once again recounting the night in his pool. The one he won't let me forget. We go over a mound of snow and the movement jostles me, forcing me to grind into him. It sends a bolt of lust straight between my legs, and I tense against him. Jesus Christ, getting turned on when I'm forced to cling to Holden for dear life is the last thing I need. "If you drop me, I'll punch you," I say, concealing my inconvenient arousal.

"Calm the fuck down, Sweet Valentine. You're not going anywhere." *Sweet Valentine*. I roll my eyes at the new nickname. He stretches the word, pronouncing it like my full name without the *a*. *Valenteen*. It's better than Valentina Ballerina, I'll give him that much.

The ride down seems to last an eternity, and eventually I give in and relax, sagging against him as I rest my head on his shoulder. We don't speak, and I close my eyes, weirdly comfortable in his arms as he glides through the snow. He's…sturdier than I thought, his movements effortlessly confident, even with an extra weight to support.

"Valen."

I open my eyes at the sound of his voice, stiffening when I realize we're at the bottom of the hill, surrounded by people. Oh, God, how long have I been clinging to him with my eyes closed like an idiot? I quickly release him, untangling my legs. Hands on my hips, he slowly lowers me to the ground.

"Better?" he asks as we both tear off our goggles.

"Hmm?" I ask, not meeting his eyes. I take my helmet off next and tuck my tangled bangs behind my ear.

"Are you okay?"

"Oh, yeah. Fine."

He drops down, unlatching himself from his board.

"Thanks…for that. If you give me the house key, I'll take one of the shuttles back." I hold my palm out in front of him.

He looks up at me, arching a brow and ignoring my outstretched hand. "Not happening." He stands, walking in the direction of the parking lot with his board under his arm, leaving me no choice but to follow.

"What, you don't trust me?" I ask, falling into stride next to him, ignoring the way my butt throbs with each step. That's definitely going to bruise.

"I'm done for the day. Maybe I'm ready to go back, too." He stops in front of the passenger side of his Range Rover.

"Somehow I don't believe you."

He opens the door, holding on to the frame as he waits for me to get in. "I don't give a fuck what you believe. Get in the car, Valen."

With a glare, I give in, sliding into the passenger seat. I clench my jaw to keep from visibly wincing as my butt makes contact with the seat. The door slams shut, then Holden walks around to the back, waiting for the powered liftgate to take its sweet time opening, then tosses his stuff inside.

TEN

Valen

"**I**'M GONNA GO CHANGE," I SAY ONCE WE'RE THROUGH THE door, hurrying to my temporary quarters. All I want is to get out of these clothes and bust out my trusty heating pad. I gingerly climb the stairs, then walk into the room, swinging the door shut behind me. I strip out of my heavy, wet layers until I'm down to my bra and underwear. Unzipping my suitcase, I pull out a change of clothes, then dig for my heating pad. I started using it for cramps when I was younger, then any time I was cold, and somehow, somewhere along the way, it became my emotional support heating pad. Never travel without it.

Except, it appears this time I have, because it's nowhere to be found.

"Ugh," I practically growl, flinging clothes out of my suitcase. I didn't use it last night because I was half-drunk and didn't feel like digging for it, but I swear I packed it.

The sound of someone clearing their throat has me turning to find Holden through the crack in the door, his eyes glued to my ass. I face him, hand on hips, not bothering to shield myself from his perusal. "Ever heard of knocking?" I ask, throwing his words from last night back at him.

He nudges the door open, stepping through the threshold.

In his hands are an ice pack, a bottle of water, and a white bottle of pills from the looks of it. "Give me your wrist."

I narrow my eyes, clutching my wrist with the other hand as he comes to a stop in front of me. "How do you know I hurt my wrist?" It didn't even hurt enough to mention—just tweaked it when I fell—but somehow, it didn't escape his notice.

"Because I'm not blind. Give me your wrist," he repeats.

Instead of giving in, I snatch the ice pack from him, noticing he has an extra. "Thanks," I mutter, turning around to give him my back. When I don't hear him leave, I look at him over my shoulder. "You can go now," I say, dismissing him.

He tosses the water and bottle of Ibuprofen onto the bed in front of me, but still, he doesn't leave. Instead, he moves in closer, his warmth radiating to my back before he even makes contact. I feel his finger slip underneath the bra strap that has fallen down my shoulder, and he gently guides it back into place. I force myself to keep my breathing even, mentally chastising myself for getting so worked up from a single touch. Keeping his finger under the strap, it burns a path down my shoulder blade. I shiver, my eyes falling shut. Holden moves in even closer, until his front is fully pressed against my back. A hand smooths down my side, stopping to clutch my bare hip. My heart slams against my chest. We haven't exchanged more than two words to each other in the last year, and now he's touching me as if it's the most natural thing in the world. As if I belong to him. And I'm *letting* him.

"One of Ryan's friends asked if we were together," I say, in an attempt to create some distance between us—of both the emotional and physical variety. "The redhead."

"And? What'd you tell her?"

"The truth."

"And what is the truth?"

"That you're single. I told her she should make her move."

"Is that what you want?" His grasp on my hip tightens.

"Why would I care either way?"

His hand flattens against my side before smoothing down my stomach, resting just above the band of my underwear. My breathing stops, heart pounding as the tip of his pinky slips beneath the elastic. I should tell him to stop. I should push him away and lock the door. But some stubborn part of me has me rooted to this spot.

"And if I want you instead?" His pinky slides back and forth, taunting. Goosebumps spread down my arms at his touch.

"Not an option."

He doesn't respond, and a second later, his palm meets the center of my back and pushes me forward. A gasp flies from my mouth as I hit the mattress, my ass on full display. Seconds feel like hours as I wait for his next move.

I yelp when he slaps the other ice pack against my sore ass before walking away and leaving me here feeling like an idiot.

"Fuck you."

"I would, but I believe you already volunteered someone else for the job."

Four hours later, the sun has set and we're at the lodge bar. It's packed full of people and the few beers I've had are doing their job, making my sore muscles feel loose and relaxed. Thayer, Holden, and Ryan are off playing pool while Shayne and I strategically stand right in front of the fire to keep from freezing our asses off.

"There are a lot of hot guys here tonight," she hedges, glancing around the room over the rim of her glass.

"Haven't noticed," I tease.

"Seriously. How long has it been? I thought you were going to put yourself out there."

I roll my eyes. I tried, but after two different hookups and getting absolutely nothing from them, I realized I need to be a bit more selective. "I tried, but they're all so…disappointing."

"What was wrong with that guy you met in the dining hall? He was cute."

I shrug. "He used way too many exclamation points in his texts."

"What about the guy who asked for your number in class?"

I scrunch my nose in disgust. "His fingernails were too long."

Shayne laughs, shaking her head. "And the guy from the hockey team?"

"I actually did hang out with him," I surprise her by saying.

"And?"

"And he took off his pants *before* his shirt and all I could think was, *he looks like Winnie the Pooh right now.* So I left before anything happened."

"Oh my God." She throws her head back with a laugh. "You didn't even get an orgasm out of the deal?"

"I've never had an orgasm from anyone other than myself," I say, correcting her.

"Not even Liam?" she asks, sounding horrified.

"Not even Liam," I confirm. "There were a couple times that I thought I might—"

I cut off my sentence quickly when I notice that Shayne is looking at someone over the top of my head. I know without turning around that Holden is the one standing there because the universe hates me.

"I could help you out with that," Holden says, confirming my suspicion. He comes into my line of sight, propping his forearm on the top of Shayne's head in true annoying big brother fashion.

"Please." I roll my eyes.

Shayne laughs, not taking his words as anything more than shameless flirting. She's used to our back and forth by now, and she knows better than anyone that Holden's a walking, talking sexual innuendo. But the look he's giving me tells me his offer is a serious one. One I won't be taking him up on.

"Besides, I thought you were going to be *helping* Alex tonight," I remind him, having since learned the girls' names. The one with green eyes is Alex. Dark hair is Jordan.

He shrugs. "The night is young. I think I can fit you in."

Shayne sends an elbow into his side, and he recoils. "Don't be gross," she says to him before turning to me. "What you need is one of *those* men." She gestures toward a group of guys standing in the kitchen near the back door.

"Who are they?" I ask, scanning each one appreciatively.

"Who cares?" She lifts a shoulder. "They're hot."

"Fair enough."

"Not your type," Holden chimes in, eyes narrowed in their direction.

"And what is her type?" Shayne asks, amused. "Please enlighten me."

"Preppy douchebags, if her previous boyfriend is anything to go by. Those guys look like they eat babies for fun."

I glance back at them again. They're all wearing short-sleeved t-shirts despite the freezing temperature, and two of them have tattoos crawling up their arms, extending all the way up to the neck on one of them. I don't know how I'd categorize them—some weird mix of snowboarder meets bank robber, but I can't lie, they're nice to look at. My mom would hate them, which only makes them more appealing.

"I disagree," Shayne responds. "Liam was never her type. Those guys are everyone's type."

"You wanna tell Thayer you think so, baby sister?"

She rolls her eyes. "We're not talking about me."

"Tell Thayer what?" Thayer asks, coming up behind her. He knocks Holden's arm away before he circles his own around her waist, resting his chin on her shoulder. With him are Ryan, Alex, and Jordan.

"Little sister's lusting over the local ski bums."

"Not true."

"Better not be."

"Or what?" she taunts. He doesn't get to answer because Alex cuts through our little circle, coming to stand right in front of Holden.

"Ryan said you guys have a hot tub?" she asks coyly. "The one here closed at ten. Think we could move this party to your place?"

"Knock yourselves out," Holden says.

Alex turns back around to face us, and I don't miss the way she strategically backs her ass up into Holden. "Anyone else up for some jacuzzi action?"

Holden eyes me over the top of her head, daring me to say yes. I'm not one to back down from a challenge, but if I don't stop this game we're playing now, things are bound to get messy. And messy is the last thing I need.

"I'll pass," I say, noticing the way his brows furrow, as if he's disappointed in me somehow.

"Same," Shayne says through a yawn. "I have to get up early to start our Christmas Eve feast."

"If you guys are going to sleep, we could hang out in our room instead, so we don't bother you," Jordan suggests.

"Fuck it. It's my last night here. Might as well." Ryan looks over to Holden, his eyebrows arched in question. "You coming?"

I grab our purses from the brown leather chair behind me and finish the last of my drink, purposely avoiding Holden's gaze.

"Yeah," I hear him finally say. "I'm in."

After we Uber back from the lodge, Shayne and Thayer go straight to bed. I try falling asleep, but it's cold, and my body hurts. Two things that wouldn't be an issue if I had my heating pad. I'm in a pissy mood, and I tell myself it has nothing to do with the fact that Holden went back to the room with those girls.

After half an hour of trying to get comfortable, I throw

on my bathing suit, grab my towel from earlier, and tiptoe downstairs.

I open the back door as quiet as possible and freeze when I see someone in there. Holden. What's he doing here? When did he get back? His back is to me, long arms stretched over the rim of the hot tub. He probably doesn't know I'm standing here. I could turn around and go back inside. If I were smart, I'd do just that.

"Come on in. The water's fine." Okay, so maybe he does know I'm here.

"It's not the water that has me hesitating. It's the giant meathead inside of it."

"Meathead?" he asks, looking over his shoulder, eyebrow raised. "You can do better than that." Not my finest work, I admit. My insults are usually more creative.

"It's late and I'm tired. I'll come up with something better tomorrow."

"Are you going to stand there until your nipples cut through your bathing suit, or are you going to come in?"

I blow out an exasperated sigh and give in. Holden's answering smile is cocky and so infuriating that I almost turn right back around. Almost. The hot tub does look inviting, though, and my ass cheek is sore as hell. With one last look over my shoulder to make sure we're alone, I step toward the hot tub. Holden tracks my movements through heavy-lidded eyes as I make my way over and up the steps, and when I drop my towel, the look in them is nothing short of predatory.

"Don't look at me like that," I snap. He jerks his gaze from my chest to my eyes.

"Don't *look* like *that*." There's not a trace of humor in his tone, and my stomach flips.

The water feels almost scalding against my chilled skin, and I welcome the burn. Slowly, I lower myself in, goosebumps breaking out across my entire body.

"What happened to your plans?" I ask, taking the elastic

off my wrist, gathering my hair off my neck, and pulling it up into a high ponytail.

"Wasn't feeling it. You're cute when you're jealous."

"I don't get jealous."

"Could have fooled me."

"You should know that better than anyone." Upon his confused expression, I elaborate. "I wasn't even jealous when I saw my boyfriend fucking someone else with my own eyes."

"That's different."

More like defective. "How so?"

"You never really liked him," he says casually, as if it's a simple matter of fact and not his opinion. "Besides, the guy couldn't even get you off. Why would you be jealous when you know firsthand that it was nothing to be envious of?"

"Fair point." I laugh, but it sounds forced. It still makes me uncomfortable that Holden seems to be so perceptive when it comes to me, even after all this time apart.

"I could, you know."

"Could what?"

"Get you off."

I raise a brow. "Is that an offer or just a little fun fact?"

"Both."

"Well, in that case, I decline your offer."

"I wouldn't even need to use my hands," he says, undeterred by my rejection.

"Jesus Christ, your ego is insane."

At that, he cracks a smile. "It's just a fact, Valen. I bet I could have you coming in less than two minutes. No touching. Suit stays on."

I scoff, "No way in hell is that possible."

He shrugs, leaning back into the built-in seat. "Come find out."

"Well, here I am. You said no touching, so," I wiggle my fingers at him, "work your magic from there."

He leans forward, hooking a finger into the front of my

bottoms, pulling me toward him. I glide easily in the water, landing between his spread legs. He stands to his full height, then moves around me, until my back is pressed against his solid chest. My eyes fall shut when his warm palms cup my shoulders before smoothing down my arms, and then his mouth is at my ear. "I meant I wouldn't have to touch your pussy."

I can't help the shiver that rolls through me at his touch, his words. I swallow hard, knowing this is usually the part where I say something shitty, but morbid curiosity renders me silent. I feel him lower himself into the water behind me.

"Lean into me."

I don't look at him. I *can't* look at him if I'm going to do this, so I'm grateful for the position choice. I sink down into the water, into him, until I'm cradled between his arms, my head resting against the top of his shoulder.

"Since I'm not allowed to touch you where I want to, you're going to have to help me out."

"That wasn't the deal."

"Fine. Permission to touch you in non-erogenous zones?"

I pretend to mull it over. "Granted."

"Close your eyes."

I do as he says, exhaling through my nose.

"Sometimes I think about you," he says, his lips still close to my ear. "I imagine you in your cheerleader uniform, with that stupid fucking ribbon in your hair."

I jerk my head around to give him a dirty look, but he grasps my chin between his thumb and forefinger, forcing my face forward.

"In my fantasy, you're in my bed and—"

"Against my will, obviously," I quip.

He squeezes my chin, making my lips mash together, and angles my head to the side before running his nose down the length of my neck. "You usually say something bitchy that only gets my dick harder…"

I snap my mouth shut, feeling his laughter as his exhale hits my flesh. "Back to what I was saying," he starts again. "You're in my bed, sitting against my headboard in that cheer uniform, and I pull the ribbon out of your hair, using it to tie your wrists together." I feel his fingertips on the underside of my upper arms, guiding me to hold on to the back of his neck.

"Keep them there." Swallowing hard, I lock my fingers together at the base of his neck. His hands smooth down my sides, stopping right above my bottoms. "You let me tie your wrists to the headboard, rendering you completely helpless to everything I want to do to you." His right hand moves down to grasp the back of my knee, and he plants my foot on the seat of the hot tub, then does the same with my left leg. Anticipation has my heart pounding. I don't know where this is going, but I'm too worked up to stop now.

"And like the little fucking brat you are, you bend your knees, spreading them just enough for me to see what's between those thighs, teasing me, tempting me…"

I feel my pulse between my legs, and I'm almost regretting this whole no-touching thing. Maybe letting Holden touch me wouldn't be such a bad thing.

"I want to taste you, Valen."

I almost say yes, but then I realize he's still talking about the fantasy.

"So that's what I do," he continues, oblivious to my traitorous thoughts. Or maybe he knows exactly what I'm thinking. Maybe that was his whole plan. Get me so hot and bothered that I beg him to do something about it. "I push your skirt up those smooth thighs, pull your panties to the side…" he trails off, leaving me practically panting.

I'm squirming against him, waiting for him to continue. When he doesn't, I finally cave. "And then?" I ask tightly, frustration lacing my tone.

"So impatient," he teases, his mouth moving back up to my ear. "And then I'd lick your little clit." I clench at his crude words and squeeze my thighs together to relieve the ache building there. He's good at turning me on with his words, but if he thinks he's going to do anything more than that, he's mistaken.

"Spread your legs for me," he instructs. "Good girl."

"Don't push it." I can only give up so much of my pride at once.

I feel his chest rumble with his laughter as he jostles around behind me. Before I realize what's happening, the jets are bubbling to life, and one of them is pointed right between my legs. I tense up when I realize what his plan is, but his hands find my hips again, holding me in place.

"I eat you like that, tied up, at my mercy. My head under your skirt, face between your thighs," he continues his fantasy to distract me, I'm sure, and it's working. The jet hits slightly higher than where I need it, but before I can adjust my position, Holden hooks his hands under both knees, lifting me into position.

"Oh *fuck*." My voice is something between a whisper and a moan, my back arching off Holden's chest. Briefly, I worry someone will walk out here and see us like this. Me holding on to his neck for dear life with my legs spread obscenely wide. But it feels too good to care. The orgasm is already building with a quickness, my nipples tightening almost painfully.

My head falls back onto his shoulder, and Holden makes a pained groan. "Tell me to touch you, Valen." His voice is full of lust, and I realize that he's not getting anything out of the deal.

Good.

"No."

His grip on me tightens in response, and I smile, knowing he won't cross the line if I don't ask him to. I want to push him, to tease him like he's been teasing me. Before I can overthink it, I unlatch my right hand from his neck, bringing it to the triangle of material that covers my chest. I can't see his reaction, but I feel him tense behind me, hear the hitch in his breath.

I slip my finger beneath the thin fabric and slowly pull it to the side, baring myself to him.

"The other side," he instructs. I slide that one over, too, the bubbles from the jets just barely concealing my chest, giving him brief glimpses of flesh. Holden hoists me up a little higher, so my tits are exposed to the cold air, giving him an unobstructed view.

"Fuck, I missed these tits. Tell me I can touch you, Valen," he says again, but this time, his tone is tortured. Almost begging. And so am I.

"No," I breathe, so close to breaking. "I think—"

"You're going to come for me?"

I nod my answer, no longer able to find my voice. I'm too focused on chasing this feeling. Holden drops one of my legs and I practically whine in protest, but then he's pulling my bottoms to the side, letting the stream of water hit my clit directly.

"Oh my God." My back bows, legs tensing.

"You want me to touch you now?"

"Please," I breathe out in a rush, too far gone.

"You want my hands or my mouth?"

"Your mouth." I don't hesitate. Keeping me supported with one arm, he moves to my side and leans over, licking my nipple once, twice, before taking it into his mouth. I cling to him, fisting his hair.

"I told you I'd grow it back out for you," he taunts.

"I'm coming," I breathe, holding him in place as he sucks on me, my legs starting to shake.

"You want my fingers?"

"Yes!"

Two fingers slide into me, and that's all it takes for me to break apart. Eyes squeezed shut, I clench around him, the force of my orgasm ripping through me, and his free hand covers my mouth to muffle my cry as his tongue and lips continue their assault on me.

His hands slip away and I open my eyes to a sea of stars above me, with nothing but the sound of our ragged breaths, floating weightlessly. Almost immediately, reality sets in and along with it, the embarrassment. *Did I really just let Holden touch me in a hot tub? And where anyone could see?*

I release my grip, pulling my bathing suit back into place. As I peel myself off him, I brush against him, feeling his hard length bobbing against my thigh. When I finally meet Holden's eyes, they're self-assured and full of lust.

I'm tempted to return the favor, to wrap my hand around him and make him feel half as good as he just made me feel, just to wipe that cocky look off his face. Instead, I stand up and immediately regret doing so. The air is so cold. I climb out on shaky legs, willing them to get me to my room before giving out, lightheaded from the jacuzzi or the orgasm, maybe both.

"You lost," I say, snatching my towel off the handrail, wrapping it around me. I wasn't planning on getting my hair wet, but that went to shit the moment I agreed to let Holden show me his little party trick.

"Come again?"

"You used your hands. You lost." I shrug. "Better luck next time."

"You asked me to," he argues. "Begged me to, really. If I'm not mistaken, there was even a *please* involved."

"Fuck off." *I did say please.* Embarrassing.

"Planning to," he says, with a pointed look at his crotch. "So you can stay and watch, or you can run away. Again." His challenge hangs in the air between us, but we've pushed our luck enough as it is.

"As tempting as that sounds, I think I'll pass." My tone is sarcastic, but there's truth in the statement. It is tempting, for reasons I'd rather not explore.

I step inside, shutting the door as quietly as I can, and when I turn around, I see a shirtless Thayer standing in the kitchen. He freezes, knife full of peanut butter poised above a slice of bread and another one with jelly sits on his plate. He looks over my shoulder, as if he knows someone else is out there. My heart pounds in my chest and my ears get hot. Did he see something?

Hear something? He looks just as surprised to see me, so maybe I'm in the clear. It's not weird to use the hot tub alone, in the middle of the night, right? That was my plan, after all.

Except Holden chooses this very moment to make an appearance. I hear the door slide open behind me. I feel him at my back, heat radiating from his overheated skin, but when his freezing wet shorts press into me from behind, I jolt forward.

"Late night snack?" he asks Thayer, appearing completely unfazed by the possibility of getting caught as he drips water all over the hardwood.

Thayer slaps the two slices of bread together before taking a bite and mumbling his answer around a mouthful of food. "Yeah." He bobs his head, chewing. "You?"

"Same."

I close my eyes, internally cringing at his implication. Jesus Christ, Holden. As subtle as a fucking sledgehammer, as per usual. When I open my eyes, Thayer is glaring at Holden, and I take that as my cue to leave. They're silent as I make my way up the stairs, waiting until they think I've gone in my room before they start talking. I stand quietly in the dark hallway to listen. I can only see the light of the kitchen from up here, but their voices carry clear as day.

"What the fuck are you doing?" I hear Thayer ask.

"Well, I was enjoying a soak in the hot tub. Now, I'm going to bed."

"You know what I mean. What are you doing with Valen?"

There's a pause, and I hold my breath, waiting for Holden's answer, hoping he doesn't throw me under the bus.

"Pissing her off, mostly. Why do you care?"

"Find someone else," Thayer says cryptically.

"To piss off?"

"To stick your dick in. If this shit gets ugly and somehow fucks shit up with Shayne and me—"

"Calm down. I was bored and she was the only one awake. Nothing happened. End of story."

I clench my jaw, refusing to acknowledge the sting of embarrassment at his words. I shouldn't be surprised. This *is* Holden we're talking about. He just fingered me in the jacuzzi, for Christ's sake.

"If you're bored, read a book," Thayer says. I don't stick around to hear the rest of the conversation.

I slink down the hall and into my room, resisting the urge to slam the door a little harder than necessary. I don't waste any time stripping off my wet bathing suit, letting the top and bottoms land on the carpeted floor with a wet thud. After getting dressed, I run into the bathroom to hang my suit. I consider showering. I need to wash the chlorine—and the Holden—off me, but I'm not risking running into anyone else again tonight.

ELEVEN

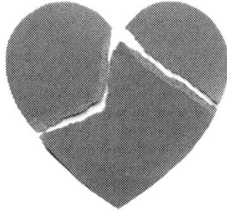

Holden

I DIDN'T GET A CHANCE TO TALK TO VALEN LAST NIGHT AFTER I gave her the orgasm of her life. Thayer's nosy ass held me up with his spiel while I stood there trying to conceal the raging hard-on in my shorts. By the time I got upstairs to talk to her, her—my—door was closed. I debated on stealing my bed back, but thought better of it, deciding that I prefer to keep my balls intact. Balls that were blue courtesy of Valentina Solorio for the second time in my life. I went back to my room both horny and frustrated—never a good combination.

Something about the way Thayer warned me away from her for the second time pissed me off, but I couldn't put my finger on why. It's not like I want to *date* her. But he should know that the second you tell me something is off-limits, I only want it more.

After replaying visions of Valen coming in my arms, I stared at the wooden beams in the ceiling until the early hours of the morning before I finally passed out. Soon after, Ryan came back, and judging by the smile on his face and the scratches down his back, I'd say he had a good time. He only stuck around long enough to pack up his stuff, and then he had to head back to campus. As much as I hate the fact that I'm not playing with the team yet, I'm glad I don't have to rush back for practice after a night of drinking and fucking. Better him than me.

By the time he left, and I managed to fall back asleep, it

was probably close to eight o'clock. The sound of dishes clanking around has me rolling over to check the time with a groan. Grabbing my phone from the bedside table, I see that it's 11:08. Knowing I won't be able to fall back asleep even if I tried, I swing my legs over the bed and reach for the gray sweats I left on the floor. I shove my feet in, then pull them up my legs, not bothering with a shirt. At the bottom of the stairs, I catch sight of snow falling outside the window. When I follow the noise to the kitchen, I stop short, rubbing my eyes to make sure I'm seeing this right.

Shayne's bending over to check something in the oven, Thayer seems to be chopping something up at the counter, and Valen's pouring what looks like champagne into a flute of orange juice while the sound of Christmas music floats from the portable speaker.

"Well, isn't this domestic as fuck," I grumble, moving farther into the room.

"Say one fucking word," my brother warns, pointing the knife at me.

Shayne shuts the oven door, but before she does, I catch a glimpse of the turkey inside. "Merry Christmas Eve!" she says, then frowns. "You look like shit."

"Couldn't sleep." I hazard a glance at Valen who avoids my gaze with a scowl on her pretty face as she studies the contents of her glass as if it holds the secrets to the universe. "What's all this?" Every single inch of the counters is covered in food and bowls and…chaos.

"Turns out, Christmas dinner takes a lot of preparation." Shayne uses the back of her hand to swipe a piece of hair away from her face.

"So you decided to start a day early? At eleven A.M.?"

"Technically, we're having Christmas *Eve* dinner."

"I didn't even know you could cook." I absently scratch my stomach, making my way over to where Valen stands. She stiffens when I approach, but she still won't look at me.

"I can't," Shayne says, oblivious to her best friend's discomfort. "And the service is shit here, so I barely have the help of Google."

"That's comforting. Got one for me?" I ask, nodding my chin toward the mimosas.

"Nope." Valen slides two of them in Shayne's direction for her and Thayer, keeping one for herself.

"Fine." I shrug before reaching over her to grab the champagne, chugging it straight from the bottle. There's not much left, so I polish it off, then drag my arm across my mouth and let out an exaggerated *ahhh*. "Refreshing." It's not exactly the breakfast of champions, but it'll do.

"Pig." Valen rolls her eyes before walking to the opposite end of the counter. I frown at her, wondering what crawled up her ass. Is she mad about last night? Does she regret it?

"Any word from your brother?" she asks Shayne. At the mention of Grey, my already shit mood takes a nosedive. I catch Thayer's eyes and he gives a slight shake of his head, silently telling me to let it go.

"He said he's going to try to make it, but I haven't heard from him today." She tries to sound unaffected, but I know she's hoping he'll show up and we'll all bury the hatchet and be best friends forever. But he won't show. He's been dicking her around for a year, giving her little pieces of hope but never actually following through. "Then again, I'm barely getting *any* calls or messages here."

"Same here. It's still early," Valen reassures Shayne. "Maybe he'll just show up even if he can't get a hold of you."

"Let's be honest. He's not coming."

"Fuck him," Thayer says what I'm thinking. Shayne shoots him a glare, and he pinches the waistband of her sweatpants, pulling her toward him.

"I just feel bad that he's going to be alone for Christmas."

"When does your mom get back?" Valen asks.

"The twenty-ninth, I think? She said she'd be back in time for New Year's. Apparently, August invited her to the gala himself."

Valen's eyebrows shoot up. "August and your mom? Is that not…weird?"

"It's not like that," Shayne clarifies. "They've been talking more since everything came out about Grey being his, but she swears there's nothing else going on."

"Better not be," my brother mutters.

"Sounds juicy," Valen says. "Report back with details."

"I never said *I* was going," Shayne points out.

"Why not?"

"Yeah, why not?" I ask. "We'll be there, too." There's a New Year's party every year, but the difference is this year, our uncle is the one hosting.

"Who is *we*? Because I sure the fuck won't be there," Thayer says.

"Then I'll go solo. We've let our dear old uncle live in peace for too long. This is his event. It's the perfect chance to make him sweat a little in front of his new friends. Let him know we're not going to forget what happened."

Thayer narrows his eyes at me. "What are you planning?"

"Nothing's set in stone." I shrug. "Rumor has it, the governor will be there. According to Dad, one of the current associate justices is set to retire, and Samuel has his eye on the position."

"What does that have to do with anything?" Shayne asks.

"In Massachusetts, associate justices are nominated by the governor. Samuel will want to be on his best behavior if he's going to be there."

"Things never go well when you go rogue," Shayne reminds me.

"Relax. I just thought we might be able to corner Rebecca. Maybe get some answers out of her. She *has* to know something about Christian, and I'm willing to bet she cares about him more than Samuel." Our dad has assured us that he'd handle it, but he's clearly not in any kind of hurry to get answers.

"Rebecca is Christian's mom," Shayne supplies for Valen who looks slightly confused.

"It's not a *bad* idea," Thayer concedes, crossing his arms over his chest. "Then we can put this shit behind us."

"What do you think happened that night?" Valen voices the question that all of us are thinking, but no one answers. We all exchange looks, silent for a beat.

"He pussied out. Probably got cold feet about spending time in prison and used my uncle to cover his tracks."

"That, or Samuel intercepted him before he could turn himself in."

I huff out a sardonic laugh. We all know he didn't plan on turning himself in. It was the guilt and alcohol talking. Once he sobered up, he had no intention of taking responsibility for what he did.

"Do you really think your uncle is capable—" Valen's voice cuts into my thoughts.

"Yes," Shayne answers, her tone resolute. "He's capable of whatever you're thinking and worse."

I'm sure she's thinking about the night she witnessed Christian getting the shit kicked out of him at the hands of his own father, and on the night of Danny's memorial to boot.

Before anyone can respond to that, a gust of wind blows so hard, whipping snow at the window, and the rustic chandelier flickers on and off above us.

"Branch probably hit a powerline," Thayer explains, looking up at the lights.

Shayne snaps into action, running to the oven to check to see if the turkey is still cooking.

"We're good," she informs us.

I eye the turkey, not quite trusting Shayne's culinary skills. I haven't seen her make anything more complex than a grilled cheese sandwich in all the time I've known her. "A meat thermometer might be helpful. Unless you're planning to give us all the gift of salmonella this Christmas."

"Hater," Shayne says even as she digs through the kitchen drawers, presumably for said thermometer. "It would be even more helpful if you actually *had* one."

"I have to go to the store before the weather gets worse," Thayer says. "I'll grab one."

"Oh good," Shayne says. "Can you also grab flour for the gravy?"

"Sure."

"Shit, I need tampons, too."

"Make a list," he says. I raise an eyebrow, amused at the fact that a year ago, he claimed to hate our ex-stepsister, and now he's not even batting an eye at buying her tampons. My, how the mighty have fallen.

"Oh, and we probably need more alcohol."

"Maybe you should just come with me," he suggests.

"Good idea."

Valen's eyes flash over to mine for a split second before she looks away, and I can tell she's thinking about the fact that we're going to be left alone together. It also doesn't escape my notice that she doesn't volunteer to go with them.

She can pretend to hate me all she wants. I do love a good challenge.

TWELVE

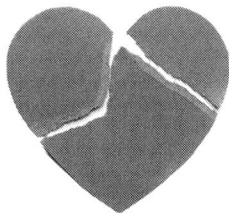

Valen

"**Y**OU HAVE GOT TO BE KIDDING ME," I MUTTER. I'M MID-shower when the lights go out again. Shayne and Thayer didn't end up going to the store until after three o'clock, and once they did, I went upstairs to get away from Holden, and I haven't seen him since. Even when we were in the same room together, I didn't so much as look in his direction. I knew he looked at me, though. I could feel the heat of his stare on my cheek every time he did.

I stare at the dark ceiling, impatiently waiting for the power to kick back on like it did earlier, but when a full minute ticks by, I know I won't be so lucky. *Of course*, the power would go out now when I'm wet, naked, and full of soap bubbles.

I move back under the spray of water to finish rinsing off in the dark before feeling for the faucet and turning the water off. I step out onto the bathmat, blindly feeling for the towel I hung before I got in, then wrap it around me. Stepping out into the hall, I listen for voices, for anything at all, but it's dead silent, save for the sound of wind howling outside. And pitch-black, even though it can't be much later than five o'clock.

"Shayne?" I call out, keeping close to the wall as I make my way down the hall, but silence is all I hear. How long have they been gone? At least a couple hours now. They should've been back. A bad feeling has my stomach twisting. What if something happened to them? I know Holden didn't go with them, so where is he? I need to find my phone, but I left it on the counter downstairs—the only place it gets service—and I can barely see my own hand two inches from my face.

I walk toward the stairs, holding my hands out in front of me so I don't walk into anything. Not being able to see is one thing, but not being able to see in a house you're not completely familiar with is another thing entirely. I bend over, flattening my hand near the base of the wall, feeling for an outlet, hoping to find one of the plug-in flashlights I've seen around the house. I can't remember if I've seen them up here, but I know for a fact there's one downstairs—also in the kitchen.

"Dammit."

When I straighten, my towel starts to slip. I refasten the knot, walking down the steps. "Shayne?" I call out again. "Holden?" I call out his name begrudgingly.

Nothing.

A tree branch scrapes against the window at the bottom of the stairs, causing me to jump. *Get it together, Valen.* I blow out a breath, annoyed at myself for being so jumpy as I hurry down the rest of the way, keeping my hand on the railing. I go as quickly as I can while still being careful not to slip on the cold, metal steps. Once I'm at the bottom of the staircase, I can vaguely make out the large outline of the couch in the living room and the chairs on either side of it. I stay in the space between the coffee table and the couch, sticking closer to the couch side so I don't hit the sharp corners of the table, but I second-guess myself when the tips of my bare toes meet resistance. I nudge it again, something hard and cold and unmovable in the way.

Frowning in the dark, I lean over, holding my palms out toward what I think is the couch. A second before I make contact with it, I hear movement, then a quiet, deep chuckle. I yelp, straightening my spine, just as a hand wraps around the back of my thigh and jerks me forward.

"Boo," Holden says barely above a whisper. I land in his lap, straddling him, scrambling to hold my towel together where my legs are parted. My bare skin is pressed against his rough jeans, his warm hand still gripping my thigh.

"You scared the shit out of me." I slap at his chest. "What the hell are you doing?"

I hear the unmistakable flick of a lighter a second before I see the flame between us, illuminating Holden's face. "Tell me why you're mad at me."

"I'm not mad at you," I say, bracing one hand on his shoulder and lifting my left leg to pull off his lap, but he holds me in place with his free hand curving around my waist.

"You're not going anywhere until you tell me."

"Right now? You want to talk about this *now*, during a power outage, when we don't know where our friends are?"

"That about sums it up, yeah."

"Let me go."

"Tell me what I did to piss you off."

"Nothing," I lie.

"You've been avoiding me for no reason?"

"No, there's a reason. I don't like you."

"I've heard that before." His hand moves down until he meets the outside of my bare thigh when he realizes I'm in a towel and *only* a towel. "So, are you going to explain what changed between last night and now?" His other hand abandons the lighter before landing on the opposite thigh. The tips of his fingers dip underneath my towel before gripping the sides of my ass. God, the sooner I leave this cabin, the better. It was so much easier to resist Holden when I wasn't forced to cohabitate with him. I just need to get through this trip, and everything will go back to normal.

He groans when I lean forward, my tits pressed against his chest, hands braced on the couch behind him. "Maybe I was just *bored*."

He tenses beneath me, and I can tell the pieces have clicked into place. "I hurt your feelings."

I laugh bitterly. "I don't have those." I spring off his lap before he can react. He says my name, but a buzzing sound has both our heads whipping toward the sound. I walk into the kitchen, following the dim light of my phone vibrating on the counter. I stumble over something—a slipper, I think—but I right myself before I fall. I breathe a sigh of relief when I see that it's Shayne's name that flashes across my screen.

"Where the hell are you?"

"Oh my God, I've tried to call you guys like one hundred times."

"Where are you? What's wrong?"

"Well…um," she hesitates.

"Shayne. Where are you?"

"The roads are closed. Cars are backed up for miles. They're making everyone turn around. Apparently, the storm is coming sooner than we thought."

"It's here," I say dryly. "We don't have power."

"Shit," she curses. I hear Thayer ask what I said, and she repeats it to him. "Where's Holden? Thayer wants to talk to him."

"Right here." I put the phone on speaker. "Go ahead."

"It's dumping. Supposed to get six feet in the next three days."

"Fuck. Didn't anyone think to check the weather before we came up?"

"Last week, it said we'd get a foot, max. This shit came out of nowhere. There should be enough food and water to last you guys a few days, then I'll drive back up to get you when it's clear."

"A few *days*?" I screech. A few days. Alone with Holden. Snowed in. Possibly without power? Holden snatches the phone from my hand.

"Don't worry about me. If I have to eat Valen to survive, then so be it," Holden says, appearing entirely too unfazed for my liking. "I'll start with her ass. I hear the meaty parts have the most flavor."

I take the phone back, holding the speaker close to my mouth. "You can't leave me here with him. I swear to God, Shayne, I'd rather take my chances with the elements."

I hear muffled laughter, like they're covering the speaker, but not good enough.

"I'm sorry. If there were any other option—"

"Yeah, you sound *super* sorry."

"We'll keep an eye on the weather and I'll come get you as soon as it's clear," she promises. "At least you have a delicious Christmas dinner to enjoy? Some of it, anyway. We're surviving on beef jerky and Pringles."

"Drive safe and call us when you get home. And just in case anything happens to you, I love you. But if it doesn't, then I hate you."

"You'll survive, Valen." Shayne laughs. "I love you. And Holden?"

"Yes?" He leans over me from behind, his chin nearly touching my shoulder.

"Be nice to my friend."

"Always." Then his lips are at my ear, his voice too low for her to hear. "In fact, just last night, I was *very* nice to her. Isn't that right?"

Holden and Thayer take over the conversation, talking about flashlights and firewood. Meanwhile, I'm trying not to have a panic attack. I don't hate the dark, but I don't love it either, and I'd feel a lot better about this whole situation if I didn't feel like I was in the middle of a horror movie wearing nothing but a towel.

"Don't you have a generator or something?" I ask when he ends the call.

"I'll check the garage, but I doubt it has any gas."

Figures. "Just know that if we get attacked by inbred canni-bals, I won't hesitate to leave your ass in the dust."

"Bold of you to assume you could run faster than me," he taunts. "Plus, we're in Vermont, not the fuckin' Appalachian Trail or wherever the hell that movie takes place. In the middle of a blizzard, I might add. No one's getting to us."

"That's even worse," I mutter, holding out my hand. "Give me my phone. I need to get dressed." It's getting colder by the second, my battery is low, and I can't begin to process this disaster until I have clothes on.

I narrow my eyes at him when he hands it over, waiting for some witty comment that never comes. Using the flashlight on my phone, I hurry back upstairs. I opt for the warmest outfit I packed—a white pair of sweatpants and a matching sweatshirt. It's still cold, even with a shirt underneath, but it'll have to do. After putting on a pair of socks, I write out a text to my mom, letting her know the situation. Maybe she can find a way to get me out of here. I'd even take a favor from my father at this point. But the red exclamation point next to my message tells me that I won't be so lucky. I try to call instead, but it doesn't even ring. Before I can try again, my screen goes black.

"Shit." Why didn't I charge it earlier when I had the chance? It's going to be a long couple of days.

THIRTEEN

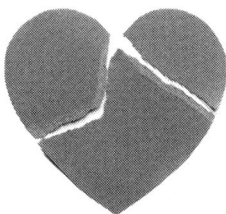

Valen

I THINK ABOUT YELLING FOR HOLDEN TO TURN ON HIS FLASHLIGHT to make it easier to get downstairs, but I made it down once. I can do it again. I don't have to ask, though, because when I step into the hall, I'm met with the scent of burning wood and an orange glow emanating from the fireplace below.

Thank God.

I fold my arms across my chest against the cold as I make my way down the stairs. Holden is knelt in front of the fireplace, crumpling up a page of newspaper before tossing it in.

"Well, I guess you're not totally useless."

"Was that your idea of a compliment?" he asks, turning his head to the side, the flames illuminating his disgustingly perfect profile. "If so, it could use some work. See, a good compliment would be, 'Wow, Holden. Not only are you a big, strong, insanely good-looking sex god that made me come so hard I saw stars, but you're also incredibly useful in emergency situations. I'm so lucky to have you here.'"

"As always, your modesty overwhelms me. And once again, may I remind you, the *jets* made me come so hard I saw stars. You were merely…a witness."

He lets out an amused sound, as if he didn't expect me to say that, but he recovers quickly. He stands to his full height, then turns to face me before eating up the distance between us.

"In that case, I'd like a do-over. One where I'm an active partic-ipant in making you come."

It's not just the words he says, but the tone of his voice and his nearness that has me feeling flustered. This is what Holden does. He flirts. He chases. He *catches*. And then he loses interest.

And that's a problem because? It's not like I'd want to actually be with Holden, but I don't want to be discarded like yesterday's trash once he's had his fill either.

"And I'd like to not be stuck in a blizzard without power, but here we are."

He smirks, flicks my nose ring, then heads to the kitchen. He lights enough candles that we can make out our surround-ings. The food from earlier still sits on the counter untouched and covered in aluminum foil. He peels back the foil on the tur-key. "Come on. Might as well eat this shit before it goes bad."

"How long do you think this is going to last?" I ask, leaning back on my palms, feet stretched out in front of me. I'm stuffed and finally warm, thanks to the food in my belly, the champagne running through my veins, and the fire warming my skin.

"Hard to say," Holden says. He's sprawled out on the floor across from me, his upper half propped up by one of the foot poufs. "Is your mom going to be pissed?"

I shrug. "She won't notice unless I fail to show up on New Year's Eve."

"And your dad?"

"My dad hasn't spent a Christmas with me in years," I say, apparently in a sharing mood. "He's probably busy with his new family, pretending I don't exist."

"I find that hard to believe," he says, nudging my hip with the side of his foot. He barely makes contact, but it's enough to make me wince. His eyes narrow at my reaction before he reaches forward to circle his fingers around my ankle. He tugs me toward him, my sweatshirt bunching up to expose my stomach as I slide down the rug.

"Show me."

"Show you what, you neanderthal?" I ask, kicking off his hold on my ankle. Instead of answering my question, he reaches for the waistband of my sweats. "Hey!" I smack his hand away.

"Let me see it."

With a dramatic huff and an eye roll for good measure, I push my pants down to the middle of my thigh.

"Jesus Christ," he curses, repositioning me onto my side, using the flames from the fire to get a better look. "Have you not been icing it?"

I frown, looking down to see what he sees. It's bigger and darker than it was this morning, a deep red, almost black in the middle, fading into shades of purple and blue that stretch from the side of my hip to my butt cheek. "Not since it happened," I confess. I know from years of cheer that you're supposed to ice injuries every few hours for the first couple of days, but it's a bruise. Not a sprained ankle. "It's not that serious."

He rolls me onto my stomach, moving closer to inspect the damage until he's face-to-face with my ass. I'm propped up on my elbows, ass on full display with nothing but a light blue thong to cover the important parts, my shirt still bunched up around my ribs. "Looks serious to me."

"Oh my God," I mutter, letting my head fall forward. "Are you done inspecting my ass?"

"Never." His fingertips ghost across my tender flesh and I shiver at his touch. "Hurt?"

"No," I croak, then clear the lust from my voice. Holden grips my thigh to turn me back over, which puts his face directly above my crotch. I can tell by the way his eyes drop to my underwear that this wasn't his intention, but he's not complaining either. His hands find my hips, his grip tightening as he looks up at me. His thumbs stroke my hipbones once, twice, three times.

Suddenly, the power flicks back on, bathing us in light. I hear something beep in the kitchen, the hum of the refrigerator. The interruption feels like a bucket of ice water. I should be thankful, but instead, I feel achy, needy, and wound too tight. Holden mutters a curse, dropping his head to my lower stomach. I can feel his breath through the thin material of my underwear, feel his hair tickling my skin. And then he's pulling my sweats back into place and backing away.

"*Finally*," I say, rising from the floor, doing my best to look anywhere but at Holden. Every light in the house is on, leaving me feeling exposed, and suddenly, I miss the darkness.

Holden stands, adjusting the bulge in his sweats without an ounce of shame before making his way over to the thermostat on the wall. I hear the heat kick on as I walk over to the counter where my phone is plugged in, waiting for it to get enough juice to turn on. The little battery icon appears, but my hopes are shattered when the power cuts out again.

I take it back. I don't miss the darkness.

"You've got to be shitting me." I drop my phone back to the counter.

"Stay here," Holden instructs. A small flashlight gleams from his direction. "I'll go get some pillows and blankets."

"We're going to die here, aren't we?" I grip the edge of the counter, the cold marble seeping into my skin and straight to my bones as I mentally talk myself off the ledge.

The storm can't last much longer. A day or two, tops. The power came back on once. That means someone is working on it, right? I'm sure it'll be fixed soon and I can get back to pretending Holden doesn't exist.

I take a few deep, calming breaths.

"Praying for a miracle?" Holden asks, a hint of amusement in his tone.

"Actually, I'm trying to put a curse on you, so stop distracting me." I turn my glare on him, watching him bound down the stairs with an arm full of pillows and blankets.

"I think someone beat you to it." He drops the blankets into a pile in front of the fireplace before he gets to work arranging them on the floor.

"What are you doing?" I ask after he lays down the fourth layer of blankets, suspicion lacing my tone.

"Making us a bed," he explains, not stopping to look at me as he pushes the couch and coffee table out of the way. "This shit has been stuffed away for about a century judging by the smell of it, but it's better than sleeping on the hard floor."

I cross my arms over my chest. "And why would we sleep on the floor when we have perfectly good beds?" In separate rooms.

He finally stops. "The power is out," he says, like that explains everything. "If you want to freeze your tits off—and I do mean that literally—then go for it. I, for one, will be nice and toasty in front of the fire."

I'm afraid my *tits* are already halfway there. The floor feels like ice cubes under my feet, even through my thick socks, and it doesn't help that my hair is still damp from my shower earlier.

"I'm never going to forgive Shayne for making me come here," I promise, walking back over toward the warmth. Instead of lying on the bed of blankets, I sit on the hearth of the fireplace itself, my back to the flames. I watch Holden unroll a black sleeping bag with a green plaid interior before spreading it out on the floor. He stands, holding a mini flashlight in his outstretched hand. I accept it, craning my neck to look up at him.

"In case you need to pee in the middle of the night or something."

"Thanks."

Holden rips off his shirt before he lies down on the makeshift bed, crossing his arms behind his head like he doesn't have a care in the world.

"Why are you so…unfazed by all of this?" I ask. "Aren't you upset that you're stuck here?"

I see him shrug, the flames highlighting the shadows of his muscular chest. *Stop looking at his chest, Valen.*

"Could be worse."

Once I've been sitting so long that the fire has warmed my back almost to the point of pain, I peel myself away from it, deciding to bite the bullet and lie on the "bed" Holden made. Almost immediately, the cold returns with a vengeance. I take the pillow next to his, moving it a few inches away. I see his lips twitch, but he doesn't comment on my not-so-subtle attempt at putting more space between us. Slipping under an old, colorful, crochet blanket, a white down comforter, and a dark blue quilt, I collapse back onto the pillow, bringing said blankets with me.

I shiver under the covers, my muscles tight from tensing against the cold. When I look over at Holden, he's scrolling through his phone, looking like he could be lying on a beach somewhere—not stuck in an arctic fucking tundra.

"I'm bored," I complain.

He doesn't take his eyes off his screen. "Wanna make out?"

"Pass. Don't you have any movies on your phone?"

This time, he meets my eyes. "Not unless you want to watch *The Little Spermaid*."

I laugh, shaking my head. "Why do you have that saved to your phone?"

"For emergency situations like this one, obviously."

I roll my eyes.

"Don't be jealous that you didn't think of it first."

"Some people know how to use their imagination and don't need visual aids."

"And what do you imagine? Besides me, of course."

"Hate to break it to you, but you're not starring in everyone's fantasies."

"False." His head falls to the side to look at me. "I told you my fantasy. It's only fair you tell me yours."

"At the moment? I'm fantasizing about getting rescued by a private jet. One that won't stop until I'm on a beach somewhere tropical." I pull the blankets up to my chin, blowing out a breath.

I can feel Holden's gaze burning into me, and then he's lifting his covers in invitation. "Get over here."

"I'm good here," I lie through my chattering teeth.

"Don't be stubborn, Valentina."

I cut him a dirty look at the use of my full first name. The faster I go to sleep, the faster this night is over, and the power will come back on. "No."

"You'd rather freeze than sleep next to me?"

"That is correct."

His eyes narrow as he seems to consider something. "You don't trust me," he declares. When I don't answer, he speaks again. "I might be an asshole, but I would never touch you without your permission. I think I proved that last night."

"Please stop talking," I groan, trying to think of anything but last night. Or five minutes ago. Or any time we get within a foot of each other and nearly end up ripping each other's clothes off. I don't trust easily, but the truth is, for some reason, I do trust Holden in that regard. It's myself that I don't have much faith in. Case in point: last night.

I roll onto my side, giving him my back, and pull my knees up to my chest. I cup my hands around my mouth and exhale in an attempt to warm my icy fingers. Holden doesn't say another word. After what feels like hours, I decide to trade in pride for comfort—and sanity at this point.

Sitting up, I gather the pillow he gave me and one of the blankets. The fire has dwindled, taking its light with it. I bite down on my lip, leaning forward to see if Holden's still awake. He's still on his back, eyes closed, right arm shoved behind his head under his pillow. "Holden?" I whisper into the dark.

Eyes still closed, he opens the blankets in invitation, like he knew I'd get desperate and cave eventually. I crawl over before I can talk myself out of it. I'd snuggle with a lion right about now if it meant I'd be warm. On second thought, a lion might be a safer bet. I slip underneath Holden's blankets, settling in next to him. He lets the blankets fall without a word. I face away from him, trying to leave a healthy distance between us. We're not touching, but I can already feel his heat. Still, I'm shivering. I'm cold to my bones, and I can't stop shaking. Holden must feel it because I hear him shifting behind me, then his arm hooks around my waist and pulls me into his bare chest.

"Holden, what—"

"Shut up, Valen."

"This isn't—"

"Go to sleep."

I want to argue. I don't even cuddle the people I do like. *This isn't cuddling. This is purely…survival.* And right now, Holden is my own personal furnace. His warmth seeps into me, stealing the objection from my lips. My eyelids grow heavy, and I feel myself drifting to sleep with his nose on the back of my neck and his heavy arm locked around my waist.

FOURTEEN

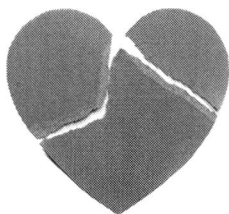

Holden

I FELL ASLEEP. I FELL ASLEEP WITH VALEN'S ASS NESTLED RIGHT against my dick, no less. I don't know what kind of magic the little devil used on me, but I don't remember the last time I crashed that hard. That quickly. And I wasn't the only one. She was stiff as a board when I pulled her against me, but within minutes, I felt the tension leave her body and her breathing even out.

It's still dark, and it takes me a minute to realize what woke me, but then I feel her. Her tits are pressed against my chest, her thigh slung over my hip. My right hand apparently found a nice home while I was out—right on Valen's ass. She's wrapped around me pretty tightly for someone who was so opposed to sleeping next to me.

She lets out a noise—something between a sigh and a moan. *Maybe I'm not the only one plagued with bad dreams.* When my eyes adjust to the dim light, I pull back slightly, taking in her parted lips and her flushed cheeks. Her eyebrows draw together as she shifts forward, unintentionally rubbing against my cock.

Oh, fuck.

I'm hard in an instant, my dick trapped between us. If she were to wake up, there's no way she wouldn't feel it. I try to slide out from under her, but she wiggles into me again. If I didn't know she was sleeping, I'd think she was doing it on purpose just to fuck with me. She still manages to torture me, even in her sleep. Figures.

"Valen," I say, squeezing her hip to still her movements. It doesn't help, though. The damage has been done. Even without her grinding against me, I'm so horny that it fucking *hurts*. It takes everything in me to stop my hips from thrusting forward of their own volition. "Valen," I say again, a little louder this time.

This time she hears me, her sleepy, brown eyes opening. Immediately, she pulls back, taking in our precarious position. "What is it?" she asks in her soft, sleep-laden voice, sounding confused.

"Think you had a nightmare," I tell her, waiting for her to notice my…predicament.

Valen's teeth sink into her lip as she looks down between us, then back up at me. "Sorry," she murmurs before she turns to face the other way. Her shirt rides up as she does, and my palm lands on her lower stomach with the movement. She wiggles her ass, pressing it against me. The tips of my fingers brush against the taut flesh of her lower stomach, back and forth. Her breath quickens, her stomach rising and falling under my hand. She pushes into me again, and I'm one more dry hump away from coming in my pants. Her skin is warm and soft, her sweet Creamsicle scent invading my senses.

"Stop," I manage to grind out.

"Stop?" she asks. "Why?" Her husky, sleepy voice only adds to my problem.

"Because if you don't stop, I'm going to explode." I expect her to jerk away. Maybe slap me and call me an asshole. What I don't expect is for her to wrap her delicate fingers around my wrist and guide my hand inside the waistband of her pants and underneath her underwear. She doesn't stop until I can feel the heat of her pussy, feel how wet she is with the tips of my fingers.

"Don't you want to?"

Oh, *fuck*.

"Are you sure you're awake?" That was an invitation if I've ever heard one, but I'm not taking any chances.

"You saw me explode," she explains. "Fair is fair."

Maybe I'm the one who's still asleep because I can't be hearing this right. *Unless…*

I narrow my eyes as something occurs to me. "You weren't having a nightmare. You were having a sex dream."

"No," she denies, but I know by the way she tenses in my arms that I hit the nail right on the head.

"Then what were you dreaming about?"

"I don't remember," she says, sounding more awake, more like her bratty, insolent self.

"How convenient." I smirk.

Valen tries to untangle herself from me with a scoff, but I flip her onto her back, rolling on top of her with my hands around her wrists. I can feel her anger rolling off her in waves. Or maybe it's the same pent-up sexual frustration I feel whenever we're together. Her chest heaves, her delicate jaw set hard.

"If you want to watch me make myself come, I'll do it. If you want me to touch you, too, even fucking better. But I am going to make sure you're fully conscious before we do something you'll regret tomorrow, and I'm going to make you ask for it. So if you'd make your decision, preferably in the next ten seconds, that'd be great."

Keeping that glare intact, she tilts her hips upward in answer, rocking into me. I groan, my head falling forward, but I manage to stop from rutting into her, keeping the bulk of my weight off her.

"Tell me what you want from me, Valen. Spell it out for me."

"I want you to make me feel good again."

It's not specific enough, but it'll fucking do because my self-control is hanging on by a thread. I slip my hand back into her pants, parting her pussy lips with my middle finger to rub her little clit.

"No sex," she clarifies, rocking into my touch.

"I can work with that." Sliding down her body, I push her sweatshirt up, taking the undershirt with it, exposing that warm, smooth skin of hers. When just the underside tits are on display, I take the flesh in between my teeth and pause, looking up at her, giving her one more chance to stop this. She holds my gaze as I slowly raise her shirt the rest of the way, uncovering her nipples. Fuck, they're even more perfect than I remember, small, hard and a shade darker than her skin. Prettiest tits I've ever seen.

As I kiss my way down her stomach, my fingers find the waistband of her sweats. She lifts her ass for me as I pull them off, taking her underwear with them. I barely get a glimpse of her bare pussy before her hand appears between her legs, blocking my view.

"Not that either," she instructs.

I laugh, leaning my face into the inside of her impossibly soft thigh. "I'm starting to understand how you've never been given an orgasm before." Summoning every ounce of willpower I have, I pull back until I'm kneeling in front of her. "Let me see you."

She removes the hand between her legs and opens her thighs, just enough for me to see what's between them. I palm my cock through my sweats, gripping it hard as I take in the sight beneath me. Shirt pushed up to her chin, knees bent and spread, pretty, wet pussy on display. I only wish I had more light to admire the view.

"I want to see you, too," she says, looking at where my hand has disappeared under my pants. I shove them down enough to free myself from the confines of my boxers. Valen's eyes are glued to my cock as I work my fist up and down.

"Here's how this is going to work, Sweet Valentine." I reach over to grab her abandoned pillow, then mine, before propping them up against the base of the fireplace. I make quick work of lighting a piece of newspaper and tossing it between the logs. I crumple up two more pieces and add them to the small fire, hoping it will be enough to last. I want to be able to see Valen for what I have planned.

I drop the lighter and turn back around to face her. She rises to her knees, brown eyes full of suspicion. She's pulled her sweatshirt down and it falls to the top of her thighs, covering up those perfect fucking tits, her pussy, and everything in between. I kick myself for not taking it off her completely. "You're going to sit on my lap, and you're going to make yourself come," I continue. She doesn't trust me. And if she can't trust me, she can't let her guard down. And if she can't let her guard down, she can't let herself come. And that's something I want to witness again.

"No," she huffs out a laugh of disbelief, shaking her head. "I am not."

I yank her to me, scoop her up, and settle back against the propped-up pillows. She sucks in a surprised breath, her hands catching my shoulders. Her knees are on either side of my hips, and I can feel her damp pussy through my pants.

"Use me."

FIFTEEN

Valen

"**U**se me."

I swallow hard, feeling my nipples tighten beneath my sweatshirt at Holden's blunt words. The same words he used that night in his pool a year ago. Suddenly, the fabric feels too rough against my sensitive skin. I'm itchy and needy and my heart is pounding so hard I think he must be able to hear it.

I can't believe I'm even considering it. If it were anyone else, I'd laugh in their face. But there's something about the way Holden talks to me, the way he touches me, the way he *looks* at me…he makes me feel things I've never felt before. Part of me wants to run in the opposite direction, but the bigger part wants to explore this. I couldn't stop now even if I wanted to. Logic is nowhere to be found, and in its place is something I can only explain as *need*. It's completely foreign to me. Intoxicating.

I roll my hips once, testing, seeking that much-needed friction. Holden doesn't react. Doesn't speak. Those hands don't move to touch me. I don't even think he's breathing. But I feel him twitch underneath me, and it's all the confirmation I need. He's affected, too. And suddenly, I want to make him just as crazy as I feel. I want to snap his self-control in half.

"I can do anything I want?" My fingers find the drawstring

on his sweats, twirling and toying with it between my open thighs. His eyes follow the movement, his stomach tensing.

"Anything you want," he confirms.

I walk my fingers up the front of his pants, stopping at the waistband before hooking them just inside. I hesitate, looking up at him.

"If you change your mind this time, I think I might actually die."

Fuck it.

I dip my hand inside his boxers, wrapping my palm around him. I squeeze, my grip gentle but firm, and he groans, eyes squeezing shut. He's hot and thick in my hand. His skin is soft as silk but hard as steel underneath, and I decide that I need to get a better look. I can barely make out the outline of him without the light of the fire. Using my free hand, I pull the waistband of his pants and boxers away, and he takes that as his cue to lift his hips and shove his pants down his thighs. His impressive length stands at attention between us, long and thick. I bring my hand to my mouth and lick the length of my palm. His mouth falls open as he watches me, and it gives me the confidence I need to continue. When I wrap my hand around him again, his eyes zero in on the movement, and mine follow suit, dropping down to watch. My hand slides up and down easily and he groans, his hips pushing up into my fist. His face is the picture of agonized pleasure, and it only makes me want this more. Holden's hands ball into fists at his sides as I pump his length, as if he's trying to give me all the control but struggling to keep himself from doing so.

"As good as this feels," he says, voice strangled, "this is supposed to be about you."

"Who says it isn't? Maybe I like seeing what I do to you." I like having the upper hand, the freedom to explore him at my own pace. There's power in being in control. There's safety in calling the shots.

I'm not sure which part did it, but his hand flies out to jerk me forward by my waist, bringing me closer. Our chests are touching, our lips nearly grazing. But all I can focus on is the fact that he's now dangerously close to being inside me. With one shift of my hips, he could be. His words from a minute ago echo in my mind. *Use me.*

My hands are flat against his chest while he clenches my waist. I give another tentative roll of my hips, this time sliding up his length.

"What are you doing?" he asks, his grip on my waist tightening, as if he thinks I'm going somewhere.

"What you asked me to do." I lean forward even more to brace my hand against the bench of the fireplace behind him. "Using you."

His teeth scrape across his lower lip as his eyes dip down to where our bodies meet before lifting back to my mouth. "Do your worst, Valentina." That one hand stays in place, but then he's slouching back to get more comfortable, bringing his other hand behind his head as if he's going to simply sit back and enjoy the show but can't bring himself to fully let me go.

If it's a show he wants, a show is what I'll give him.

I rock into him again, this time harder. Holden groans, but words seem to fail him as I press myself against him. I lean back, my ass seated on his thighs, palms braced on his legs behind me. Holden lifts my sweatshirt, watching my tits bounce as I ride him. I quickly pull it off altogether. His gaze lowers to where we're connected, and we both watch as I start to work my hips. I move slow at first, but it doesn't last long. I angle my pelvis down, trying to reach that friction where I need it and grind against him. I go from freezing cold to burning up in record time, thanks to the fire. Thanks to Holden. I feel a bead of sweat roll down my back, and then his other hand comes into play, finally. He uses his free hand to press his cock where I need it most, and the one on my waist starts to help guide my movements when they get a little sloppy. I can feel it building. My eyes squeeze shut, head falling back. My thighs and upper arms are tense, muscles burning. I'm right on the edge, and it takes me by surprise. Not just that it's happening so quickly, but that it's happening at all. Am I really about to have an orgasm from essentially dry humping a guy I don't even like?

"Look at how pretty your pussy looks with my cock between your lips," Holden says. "Spread your legs wider. Let me see it."

His words only add to the pleasure coursing through me. I do as he says, opening my thighs wide as I reach forward, curling my hand around the back of his neck for leverage.

"Fuck, you're going to make me come," he grinds out as his other hand flies to my hip, both of them working together now. Sweat rolls down his temple and his eyebrows tug together, bottom lip trapped between his teeth. He's fucking beautiful. And apparently, some sort of magician, because I feel my second orgasm in as many days start to tear through me.

I bite down on his shoulder to muffle my cry as I break apart in his lap, hips still grinding into him. Holden abruptly lifts me off him too soon, and lays me onto my back, using his hands to keep my knees spread. I can barely see him with his back to the fire, but I know he can see me—all of me—at this angle. But I'm past caring, still shuddering when I feel him spill onto my stomach.

"Fuck," he breathes. "I want to feel that from the inside." His meaning doesn't register until I feel his finger there, just barely inside me as I continue to contract around the tip of it. I bring my knees together in a belated attempt at modesty, but Holden stops me. He pulls his finger from me, spreading my wetness around before he brings it to his mouth and sucks it clean.

"Merry Christmas, Sweet Valentine."

SIXTEEN

Valen

H E COLLAPSES ONTO HIS BACK NEXT TO ME, AND WE BOTH LIE silent as we catch our breath. After a minute or two, Holden gets up without a word. I watch as he walks toward the downstairs bathroom, naked and illuminated by the fire. I hear a clatter, then a curse, telling me he knocked into something, thanks to the lack of light, followed by the sound of the faucet running. I cover my face with my hands, trying not to feel awkward as I wait for my turn to clean up.

I don't know what got into me. No, that's a lie. I know exactly what got into me. I was dreaming of Holden while sleeping next to him. I've had sex dreams before, but none that felt so real. I woke up feeling like I was on the brink of an orgasm, heart pounding,

"Having regrets already?" Holden quips, sounding much closer than I thought he was. I didn't even hear him return. I flinch when I feel a warm, wet cloth pressed between my legs before he drags it upward to my stomach. My hands fall away from my face, and I look down to see Holden inspecting me as he cleans me thoroughly.

"I can do that," I say—pressing my thighs together—but he ignores me, making sure he gets every drop. Once he's finished, he walks back over to the bathroom, presumably to dispose of the washcloth, and then he lies back down like nothing ever happened. I roll my eyes at his casual demeanor. Refusing to show the awkwardness I'm feeling, I sit up, patting the floor in search of my shirt. I tug it over my head, only to realize it's Holden's shirt when it falls to the middle of my thighs. Whatever. Better than nothing. I stand and make my way to the bathroom. I don't know why I do—it's not like I can do much without light—but I need a minute to myself.

A gasp flies from my lips as I step inside, the cold tiles a shock to my now overheated system. I leave the door cracked, needing the dwindling light from the fire to make out my surroundings. I use the bathroom and clean up as best as I can with my limited resources, then make the walk of shame back to our makeshift bed.

I try to avoid eye contact, but I can feel the weight of Holden's stare as I situate myself on the floor, leaving a few feet of distance between us. When I finally look up, it's to find him staring at me as if he's trying to figure something out.

"What?" I ask, sliding under a stack of three blankets. The adrenaline is fading fast, and the cold is already settling back in. *Where are my pants, anyway?* When Holden doesn't answer, I pull the covers up to my shoulders and turn away. Even with my back to him, I can sense him watching me still. What is going through his mind? What could have possibly happened within the two minutes it took to use the bathroom to warrant that scowl? As far as I'm aware, both of us should be very...sated.

I hear Holden shuffling around behind me, and then his arm is around me, scooping me up and pulling me firmly into his chest. He molds his body against mine, his forearm banded around my ribcage, my head tucked under his chin.

This isn't a good idea. Cuddling under the guise of keeping each other warm is one thing. Cuddling after earth-shattering orgasms when that pesky little oxytocin hormone is running rampant is another thing entirely. His bare chest is hot against my back even though the fire is almost non-existent at this point.

I know that without him, I'll inevitably wake up freezing in an hour or two.

"Stop thinking and go to sleep," Holden says into my hair, cutting off my internal warring. Deciding that falling asleep in his arms isn't the *worst* way to fall asleep, I give in, huffing out an exaggerated sigh. The last thing I hear before I slip into unconsciousness is something that sounds a lot like "stubborn as fuck," mumbled into my ear.

I don't know what wakes me or what time it is. It takes me a second to place my surroundings, but the steady rise and fall of Holden's warm chest under my cheek reminds me of what happened earlier. Or last night? I peel myself away from the comfort of his body heat, looking out the window for a clue of what time it is. My eyes widen, stomach sinking, as I take in the sight. I stand, slowly making my way toward the floor-to-ceiling windows, rubbing my eyes, convinced they must be playing tricks on me, but when my vision comes back into focus, it's confirmed. The snow is stacked at least a few feet high. It makes me feel trapped. Like the walls are closing in on me. Taking a deep, calming breath, I remind myself that it's temporary.

I glance back at Holden's sleeping form before I tiptoe upstairs. I'd rather not do the whole morning-after thing with him. Once I'm in my room, a sliver of light draws my attention to the closet. I pluck the dark red throw blanket from the end of my bed and wrap it around my shoulders before walking into the closet. I look up at the ceiling, finding one of those pull-down ladders, but it's slightly ajar, the sun just barely filtering through the crack. I didn't notice that before. My curiosity gets the best of me, and I tug on the string before my brain has made the conscious decision to do so.

I pull it open, pausing, my face screwing up into a wince when it creaks loudly. When I'm sure it didn't wake Holden, I pull it the rest of the way down. The room is dim, dust particles dancing in what little light there is. Holden must have grabbed all the blankets from up here and left the door open. The floor is cluttered with board games, cardboard boxes, and what appears to be old video game consoles. One entire wall is made up of built-in bookshelves packed full. Reading used to be my preferred form of escapism, but I don't think I've read anything that wasn't required since my freshman year of high school.

An emerald green tufted armchair with a small side table and lamp sits in the corner next to the shelves, but what really catches my interest is the wooden ladder leading up to a small, triangular loft. I step onto the third rung of the ladder, the wood cold and smooth beneath my bare feet, reminding me that I need to go get a pair of socks out of my suitcase—and a pair of pants while I'm at it.

I peek over the top, finding a few forgotten throw pillows and blankets. It's even smaller than I initially thought. The angled ceiling allows for just enough room to sit upright. I look out the window, unable to fully appreciate the view thanks to the white-out, but I bet it was the perfect reading spot. I'm tempted to crawl up there right now. I might if I thought those blankets have been washed in the past century. Instead, I step back down the ladder and make my way over to the bookshelf. I run my fingers over the dust-coated spines, stopping on a familiar cover. They say smell is the strongest trigger for memory, but the same can be said about books. They hold memories, for better or worse. For example, when I see this one—the dystopian novel about a girl who ends up leading a rebellion and falls in love with the boy with a number for a name—I'm transported back to hiding out in my walk-in closet with my music blasting to drown out the sound of my mom in a screaming match with her flavor of the week.

I shake off the memory, moving on. The more I snoop, the more I come to the conclusion that this eclectic collection most likely belonged to more than one person. There is everything from the classics to thrillers, romance, non-fiction, fantasy, children's books, and everything in between. It feels like something from a fairytale. All that's missing is a sliding ladder. I pluck a book off the shelf that looks interesting—a dark blue hardcover sans dust jacket with intricate gold detailing on the front. Fantasy, if I had to guess. Blowing off the dust, I walk over to the chair in the corner and curl up in it, making myself comfortable.

SEVENTEEN

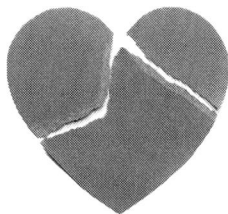

Holden

I WAKE UP COLD AS FUCK, AND I KNOW BEFORE OPENING MY EYES
that Valen has bailed. I'm not exactly surprised, but I can't
deny the inexplicable flash of disappointment when that
suspicion is confirmed. I stretch my arms over my head with a
yawn, feeling more rested than I have in a long time.

After taking a piss, I go in search of my phone in the pile of
blankets on the floor. I fish it out from under my pillow, dismissing the low battery notification. It's 10:44. Holy shit. I don't remember the last time I slept that many consecutive hours. And
not a single nightmare. I still don't have service, but I try to call
Thayer anyway. The call fails, as expected, and I toss my phone
back down. Heading into the kitchen, I flick the light switch on
and off like it's going to do anything. Power's still out. I half-expected it to come back on in the middle of the night. If it's not
fixed by tomorrow morning, I might have to start thinking about
digging us the fuck out of here.

I decide to wait Valen out. See how long it takes her to
face me. But after cleaning up the entire downstairs, including
the mess from Christmas dinner, all the while visions of Valen
coming beneath me play in my mind on repeat, I give up the
one-sided game. I check the room she'd been sleeping in first
but find it empty. I check Thayer and Shayne's room—no luck.
Same with the bunkbed room.

"Where the fuck is she?" I mutter to myself, leaning over the railing to see if I somehow missed her downstairs. Nothing. What if she left? I dismiss that as a possibility. She'd have to be suicidal. But then again, she did say she'd rather *take her chances with the elements* than be stuck here with me.

I'm about to go check for footprints in the snow when I realize I left one room unchecked. The attic. Or the secret room, as we called it when we were kids. We haven't used it in years. It's more of a storage room than anything now. I walk back into her room and notice the closet door open and the ladder is down. I don't know how I missed it the first time. I climb up and, sure enough, Valen's curled up on a chair in the corner. My chest feels tight as I take in the scene. She's fast asleep, an open book lying flat against her chest. Her feet are tucked underneath her, her cheek resting on the crook of her elbow that's propped on the arm of the chair. The position should be painful, but she makes it look like the most comfortable thing in the world.

I watch her as she wakes, stretching her foot out in front of her and rolling her ankle like it hurts from being in the same position for too long, oblivious to my presence. The blanket on her lap slips off with the motion. She's still only wearing my shirt, and I like the sight of her in it more than I'd like to admit. The hem rises on her thighs with the movement, exposing the fat bruise on the outside of her thigh. I should have shoved a ski pole up that fucker's ass for leaving a mark like that on her. Still unaware of the fact that I'm watching her like a creep in the doorway, she stretches her arms behind her head, her back arching enough for me to make out those pretty nipples straining through the thin, white fabric.

I clear my throat, and her eyes snap to mine.

"You read?" I ask, gesturing toward the book that's now in her lap with the flick of my chin.

"Only when I'm held hostage. Is the power back on yet?"

I make a show of flipping the light switch next to me.

"Nope. What's the matter? Not having any fun?" I give her a pointed look.

"I was until you interrupted."

"You were asleep," I point out. I stay by the door, making a point to keep my eyes trained on her and her alone. This room reminds me of a time when my mom actually gave a shit about being my mom, and the less time I spend in here the better.

Brown eyes narrow in my direction. "Exactly. Sleeping happens to be my favorite. In fact, my plan is to sleep through this whole thing until we can get the hell out of here and go home." I envy her. I can't so much as remember a time that I didn't dread sleep. Ironically, people assume the opposite since I'd pass out during class or sleep until noon, but that comes with the territory of insomnia. Last night, though? I slept better than I have in years. It was a fluke. Or maybe it was Valen and the way she slid her pussy up and down my cock like she was born to do it. I didn't even get to feel her from the inside, but it was still the best sex I've ever had.

"How long have you been standing there, exactly?" Valen asks, bringing my attention back to the conversation at hand.

"Long enough. Are you hungry, or are you going to hide in here all day?"

"I'm not hiding," she says quickly. Too quickly. She's one hundred percent avoiding me after last night. I'm sensing a pattern. The question is, is she ignoring me because she regrets it? Is she embarrassed for some reason? Or is she already dying for a repeat like me?

"Of course not." I smirk. "I've gotta get the fire going again before the pipes burst and do some other shit." Translation: busy myself with whatever else I can to distract my thoughts from straying to what she looked like with her legs spread, tits in my face as she ground herself against me. How she sounded when she came. How she *felt*. Valen's jaw is set hard, but she's looking at me the way she did last night. I grip the doorframe harder to keep from giving in to the impulse to do it all over again. I don't want to be up here longer than I have to, but I might just make an exception if she keeps looking at me like that.

"I'll be downstairs if you need me."

My words seem to cut through her thoughts and she blinks, as if ridding herself of the same images that are plaguing me, and I force myself to walk away before she can respond.

I start with the fire first, needing to take the chill out of the house, but knowing it won't be enough, then I throw some more layers on, grab a shovel from the garage, and head outside to clear the snow. When I open the front door, I'm faced with a wall of snow that comes up to my thighs. Fat, heavy flakes fall steadily, showing no sign of stopping any time soon.

"Awesome." I blow out a breath, the air so cold that I can see it. At least this'll keep me busy for a while. And it does. I shovel the entrance, walkway, and driveway. Who the fuck knows how long we'll be waiting for a plow to come by. We're not exactly a priority way out here, but I need to keep it clear for when Thayer's able to get to us. By the time I'm finished, I've ditched my coat, hoodie, and beanie, down to nothing but a t-shirt, my sweats, and boots. I'm sweating my ass off, even with the frigid temperature, and my muscles are sore as hell. The snow has slowed down some—thank fuck—and the sun is starting to break through the gray sky. With any luck, the power will be back on soon, and I'll be able to warm the hot tub up. Even better if I can get Valen to join me again.

I grab my discarded clothes and beanie on the way inside. I'm not even through the door yet when I start to peel off my shirt with my free hand, knowing the house is about to feel like a sauna after being in the cold for the past couple hours. Just as I grip the handle, the door is pulled open from the inside, and I nearly knock over a surprised Valen. I straighten to my full height and step inside as she backs up. I close the door behind me, looking down at her. She's eye level with my chest, starting straight ahead rather than looking me in the eye, a plate of food in one hand. Is she—is she *blushing*?

"That for me?" I ask, nodding toward the plate.

"Thought you might be hungry. The food in the fridge is still cold, so we might as well eat it before it goes to waste."

I shove my sweaty hair off my forehead, taking a step closer. "You made this for me?" I ask, inspecting the plate.

She rolls her eyes. "It's just a turkey sandwich. Take it or leave it."

"Did you poison it?"

"Nope. Lucky for you, you're fresh out of poison."

"Spit in it?"

"Is that a request?"

"Are you offering? Kinky, but I'm not opposed."

"God, you're gross."

"You didn't think I was gross last night."

She shoves the plate into my chest and I grab it, laughing as she spins around and heads for the kitchen.

I drop my shit to the floor and follow, unable to keep my eyes off the way her ass sways as she walks. Unfortunately for me, she's now wearing pants, but it doesn't stop me from appreciating the view. She stops at the island in the middle of the kitchen and picks up half of the sandwich she made for herself. Mayonnaise, a bag of bread, a jar of olives, and the whole ass turkey are scattered across the countertop. I make a mental note to pack the fridge with snow later if the power doesn't kick back on soon.

We eat in silence, her on one side of the counter and me on the other. She stands in some weird ass flamingo position with the flat of her foot braced on the inside of the opposite thigh, her hip propped against the counter. She sticks the tip of her thumb between her lips and sucks something off it—an innocent, thoughtless gesture on her part—but the sight goes straight to my dick. If I tried to kiss her right now, would she let me? If I were to lift her onto the counter, spread her smooth thighs and—

Fuck.

I need something else to do. *Quickly*. I scarf the second half of my sandwich down in two bites. Valen looks at me with a mixture of shock and disgust.

"What…is happening?" she asks.

"Thanks for the food," I mumble around a mouthful. She wrinkles her nose, watching in confusion as I hurriedly throw my plate into the sink and storm out of the kitchen.

I ran out of shit to do two hours ago. I haven't caught a glimpse of Valen since lunch, and I don't know who is avoiding who at this point. The sky is getting dark fast—still no power—so I head downstairs to start lighting the candles I collected in my attempt to stay busy. I even found an old lantern in the garage.

I stop short when I see Valen standing in front of the window. Her back is to me, but her posture is rigid. Her arms are folded across her chest, her fingers toying with the tiny butterfly charm of her necklace as she stares ahead.

"Valen." She doesn't seem to hear me, so I walk over to stand right behind her. It's snowing steadily again, but it's not dumping like it was for the last day and a half. "You good?" I ask, causing her to startle.

"How long do you think this will last?"

I shrug. "Could be weeks."

"Weeks?" she yells, her head whipping around, eyes wide. She's nervous. Maybe even on the verge of a panic attack.

"I'm fucking with you." I lay my palm on the nape of her neck in an attempt to calm her anxiety. "My phone still has some charge. If we don't get power soon, I'll hike until I find a signal." What I don't tell her is that we're going to be out of firewood by tomorrow.

She nods, some of the tension leaving her body as I rub my thumb up and down the back of her neck. The fact that she seems genuinely nervous takes me by surprise. Aside from the night in my pool, I've never seen her show even a hint of vulnerability.

"Do you know what my name means?"

She turns to face me, and I reluctantly let my hand fall away with the movement. Her crossed forearms brush against my chest as she looks at me. "What?" she asks, not following my sudden change in subject.

"My name. Got bored and looked up the meaning one day last year after the one-thousandth Holden Caulfield reference." I thought anything would be better than a character known for being a self-absorbed, whiny little shit. I was wrong.

"And?" she asks.

"It means hollow." I huff out a laugh. "My name literally means empty."

Her eyebrows pull together as she looks up at me. "And are you? Empty?" Her question catches me off guard. I only started this conversation as a way to distract her from our current situation.

"As a wasteland," I joke in an attempt to cover up the truth in my words, because *yes, I'm fucking empty*. And I've been that way for a long time. "Do you know what your name means?"

She shakes her head.

"It means strength."

"It does not," she says, rolling her eyes.

"It does. I looked it up."

Her eyes narrow at my slipup and she tilts her head to the side. "You looked up the meaning to my name?"

I stuff my hands into my pockets, aiming for nonchalance. "Like I said. I was bored."

"Mhm. Just how much time do you spend thinking about me?" she teases.

"Way too fucking much." Her playful smile slips at my admission. I can't quite place the look on her face as she closes the distance between us. I stay still as a fucking statue, hands still in my pockets as she pushes up on her tiptoes, flattening her hands on my chest. She presses her lips to the side of my neck. I swallow thickly. She does it again, kissing her way up the front of my throat, the side of my jaw, and finally landing on the corner of my lips.

"What are you doing?" I ask, my voice sounding hoarse. My heart thuds so hard she has to feel it.

"I want you to fuck me," she whispers, eyes zeroed in on my mouth. The words go straight to my dick.

I almost choke on my own spit. I mean, not that I'm complaining, but... "I think I missed a step." I know it wasn't discussing name origins that turned her on.

"I need...a distraction."

"A distraction, huh?" Fuck that. "That's the only reason?" I push.

Her tongue darts out to wet her lips as she pulls back a little. "What else would it be?"

It's my turn to close the distance between us, walking her backward until her back is against the window. I pull my hands from my pockets, placing them on the glass behind her. "I've wanted to get inside you for the past three years. I've let you call the shots. I've played your hot and cold games. But if you want this, you're going to say it. Not out of boredom. And sure as fuck not as a distraction. Admit it, Valen."

"Admit what?" she grinds out.

I slip a hand underneath the hem of her shirt, and she shivers as my thumb traces her hip. "That you want me just as much as I want you. That last night wasn't nearly enough, but you're too afraid to say it out loud." Afraid of what exactly, I don't know.

Her chest heaves as she scowls at me, but she still doesn't respond. Gliding my fingers to the waistband of her leggings, I slip them inside. She pushes into my touch, urging my hand lower.

"Am I wrong?" I ask, the tip of my middle finger just barely brushing her clit. She doesn't answer me as her head falls back against the wall, her eyes falling shut as I apply more pressure.

One hand still braced on the window behind her, I look

down, watching her writhe against my hand. She's so fucking wet already. There's nothing I want more than to take advantage of her offer and fuck her right up against this window. But I won't. Not until she tells me what I want to hear. Not until I get the truth.

"Tell me I'm right, and I'll give you what you need." I say the words against her pretty neck, feeling her pulse beat wildly against my lips, but still, she says nothing. I back away, pulling my hand from the warmth of her pussy, ignoring her whine of protest as I do so. "You're a lot of things, Valen, but I didn't think a coward was one of them."

Her eyes burn with anger, watching as I wipe my fingers on the front of my shirt. "Suit yourself." I shrug before turning away. I take one, two, three steps before her voice stops me.

"Fine."

I stop dead in my tracks and wait for her to continue, my back still to her.

"I want you," she whispers so quietly, I'm not sure I heard right.

"What was that?" I ask, turning to face her.

She rolls her eyes. "I *want* you," she says again through gritted teeth. "For some idiotic reason that I can't explain, I do. And I think the only way I can get over this..." she gestures between us, "*thing* is to give in to it and get it out of my system." She closes the distance between us, her big brown eyes looking up at me. "So I'm asking you to fuck me."

"Thank fuck."

EIGHTEEN

Valen

"THANK FUCK," HOLDEN SAYS, AND THEN HE'S ON ME. His hands circle my waist and lift at the same time his lips land on mine. My back hits the window, legs winding around his waist as his tongue pushes past my lips. It's desperate and full of need, his lips kissing away every last ounce of uncertainty with each passing second. My hands find the back of his head and thread through his hair as I pull him closer. He groans into my mouth and I squeeze my thighs tighter, needing to be closer, needing...more.

Without breaking our connection, he turns around and effortlessly carries me up the spiral staircase. When I realize we're heading for his room, I break the kiss, pulling back. "We're doing this now?"

"Were you thinking of scheduling in advance?" He drags his lips down the side of my neck, goosebumps pricking my skin. He pushes the hem of my shirt up and I lift my arms to help him in ridding me of it.

"Now's good," I breathe.

"Glad that's settled." He lets my shirt fall to the floor before kicking the door open and walking us into the dark room. A surprised squeal flies out of my mouth before I can stop it when he tosses me onto the bed. I bounce off the mattress and then his body comes down onto mine. His weight pins me to the bed, and my heart pounds wildly in my chest. My eyes haven't adjusted yet, leaving me on edge and blind to his next move. Why he chose to go up here, away from any light and the warmth of the fire, is beyond me. A million possibilities run through my mind. Maybe he wants to avoid the vulnerability of looking someone in the eye while he fucks them. Maybe he simply wanted the comfort of his bed. Either reason is fine with me.

His weight leaves me a second before a bite to my nipple has me sucking in a breath. Not painful, but a warning. "Stop thinking," Holden demands. "Especially if it's about anything other than me and what I'm about to do to you."

Warm fingers curl into the waistband of my leggings before tugging them down. I use my feet to work them off once they're at my shins, and then I feel his touch between my legs. He must have night vision because he finds his target immediately. My legs fall open, just slightly, as his finger softly circles my clit. "That's the problem. I can't think rationally when you're touching me like this," I admit in a rare moment of honesty. My voice comes out breathy and needy and completely unlike me and I hate myself for it.

"Good," he says, before taking his touch away completely.

"What are you doing?"

"Stay here," he says cryptically. I feel the bed move before I see his shadowy form leave the room, and I'm left here alone. I groan, not feeling particularly patient, and press my thighs together to ease the ache. Seconds later, I hear the floor creak, alerting me to his return.

"Where are you?" I call out into the dark, squinting as if that's going to help. No answer, but I know he's here. I can *feel* him. "I can hear you breathing, asshole," I tell him. I sit up in the middle of the bed, feeling like a prey animal who's moments away from being pounced on. My head whips around when I think I hear something behind me and I pause, listening for more clues to his whereabouts. "Okay, I'm bored now. I change my mind—"

My words break off into a yelp when Holden's hand wraps around my ankle and jerks me toward the edge of the bed. My head is near the middle of the bed, ass on the edge of the right side. Holden slides between my legs, one hand propped on the mattress next to my head. I hear a quiet click before a soft glow fills the room. A lantern dangles from his fingertips, inches above my face.

"What are you doing?" I squint against the light.

"Ensuring I get to see exactly what you look like when I slide inside you for the first time."

"First and only," I correct.

"Whatever you say."

My gaze flits from his eyes down to his lips, and then I lunge for him, my hands on his face as I kiss him hard. When my tongue slips into his mouth, he groans, pressing his hips into me. The feel of his sweatpants against my bare skin reminds me that he's still fully clothed. I practically claw at his shirt, pulling it up his torso. He takes the subtle hint, sitting back on his heels and setting the lantern on top of the nightstand before reaching into its drawer. He tosses a condom that lands next to my face and I arch a brow.

"Remind me to thank my past self for these," he says, answering my unspoken question. He stands, quickly ridding himself of his pants, and then he's back, his body covering mine, my thighs cradling his waist. When his hard length slips through my arousal, his eyes squeeze shut as if he's in pain. "You're fucking soaked," he grinds out, pumping his hips.

"This means nothing," I clarify.

"Keep telling yourself that," he says, his hand skimming down my stomach between us before two thick fingers curl inside me. I gasp at the sudden invasion. *Oh my God, yes.*

"I mean it, Holden." I rock into his hand. "This is a one-night thing. We tell no one. Then we go back to hating each other."

"Mhm." His lips find my neck, catching my skin between his teeth as he fucks me with his fingers. No longer able to form words or the will to argue, I give up the fight. Nothing but the wet sounds of his fingers pumping inside me and our ragged breaths fill the air. He moves lower, his hot mouth covering my nipple before sucking softly. My fingers slide into his hair as I arch into him.

"Holden, please."

He releases my nipple with a pop, his fingers sliding from me. I instantly feel their absence. "Please, what?" He starts to move lower again, and when I realize his intent, I tighten my hold on his hair. He pauses his descent, his chin on my chest as he looks up at me.

"I don't need that. I just need you to fuck me."

He captures my wrists in his hands, stretching my arms above my head. "It's about time you admit it," he says, adjusting his grip to hold both my wrists in one hand. His free hand reaches in between our bodies. I look down in time to see his palm wrap around his impressive length and drag the thick head of his dick between my lips. I squirm against his hold, unable to take any more of this teasing, but he tightens his grip on my wrists in silent warning. "Do you know how many times I've imagined this?"

"Don't get too excited. The fantasy is always better than reality." My words aren't meant to be anything more than a snappy retort, but the way he pauses for a minute and stares down at me has me wondering if he heard the underlying fear in them.

"I'll be the judge of that. Spread your legs for me, Sweet Valentine."

I do so without hesitation, and then he pushes forward, filling me slowly. He groans, sounding almost pained. My mouth falls open on a silent scream as I adjust to the feeling of Holden inside of me, stretching me inch by inch. Once he's fully inside, he holds himself there, looking down at me with the most intense expression I've ever seen him wear. I wonder if it matches my own. *Surreal* is the only word I can use to describe this feeling after years of back and forth.

My arms are still stretched above my head, the tips of my fingers numb under his tight grip. I wiggle my hips, needing him to *move*, and then his fingers are digging into my hip, anchoring me in place as he pulls out and thrusts back in. This time it's not gentle or careful. His movements aren't hurried but rough, almost desperate, and exactly what I need.

"Yes," I breathe. I should feel anxious trapped under him, rendered immobile like this. But it has the opposite effect. All I can do is lie here and take what he gives me. To give in to this inexplicable pull I feel toward him. He looks down at me, his jaw clenched tight as he pumps into me.

"You're fucking perfect," he says so quietly, I don't know if he meant to say it out loud. His flattery, along with the way he's fucking me, has me clenching around him. I know he can feel it because he lets out another curse, squeezing his eyes shut. "You're killing me," he says, pulling back. Not wanting him to sever our connection, I plant my feet on the mattress, my lower back lifting as I grind up into him. I slide along his length, up and down, my clit pressing into his lower stomach with each tilt of my hips. His mouth falls open, letting me fuck him from the bottom, his hand still securing my wrists, as if to give himself some semblance of maintaining the upper hand.

"Valen," Holden says, his voice strained. "Wait." He releases me abruptly, pulling out. I collapse against the mattress, heart pounding. I feel myself clenching and releasing around nothing, my impending orgasm throbbing like a heartbeat between my legs. When I look up at him with daggers in my eyes, he's rolling the forgotten condom down his length.

Shit. At least one of us is thinking straight.

Standing at the side of the bed, he leans forward, curling his hands around the tops of my thighs, yanking me to the edge. "Now where were we?" He fills me without hesitation, his fingers biting into my inner thighs. His thrusts are deep but slow, his gaze locked on to where we meet.

"Do you know how long I've waited for this? To see your pussy stretched around me like this?"

Words like that would usually make me feel hyper aware of my body, of my movements, like I have a fantasy to live up to. Like I need to *perform*. But I'm too caught up in the way he feels inside me to care about anything else. His grip moves from my thighs to my hips, lifting my ass off the mattress to meet him thrust for thrust. My breasts bounce with each punch of his hips, his top teeth raking over his bottom lip as his eyes zero in on the movement.

He drops one of my legs and leans forward, using his unoccupied hand to grip my jaw. "You feel so good." He rocks into me, slower now.

Wordlessly, I peel his hand off my thigh and guide him to where I need him. He doesn't need further instruction, his expert fingers immediately finding my clit. One of my legs is bent, my foot flat against the mattress as the other leg dangles off the edge of the bed as he fucks me and rubs me at the same time. *Oh God, that's it.* My fingers dig into his back, toes curling, as everything comes to a boil.

"I'm coming," I say, sounding as surprised as I feel. I wasn't sure it was possible for me this way.

"Fuck." He groans. "I can feel it." His movements become more frantic. My nails claw their way down his back on a moan as I start to break apart, and then he's kissing me hard, his tongue sweeping in to fuck my mouth as he holds my jaw. Hands, mouth, and cock all work in tandem, overloading my senses, and then I'm falling over the edge. Sparks light up the back of my eyes as Holden swallows my cries, burying himself inside me as deep as he can go.

He pulls his mouth from mine, his forehead creasing as he looks down at me with lust-glazed eyes. The veins in his neck are on display, his hair damp and hanging in his eyes as he fucks me, watching me tremble and shatter beneath him until my body goes limp. His eyes fall shut and then I feel him spill inside me.

I let my hands fall away from his back and flop down against the mattress as we both fight to catch our breath. Holden doesn't make a move to pull out, his hips still pressed firmly against me. I close my eyes, waiting for his next move, but then I feel the soft stroke of his thumb along the side of my jaw. I blink up at him, our eyes locking, unable to look away. My chest is still rising and falling as I try to regain my composure. Holden stares down at me with an unreadable expression. He almost seems… angry. Maybe even confused.

That makes two of us.

I open my mouth to say something—anything—when the room is suddenly bathed in bright light.

NINETEEN

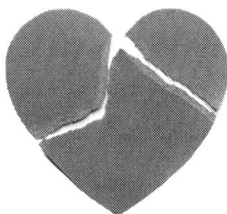

Holden

VALEN'S EYES SEARCH MINE, LOOKING AS CONFUSED AS I FEEL. Her pretty mouth opens to break the silence, but it's this very moment that the power kicks back on, the hum of appliances coming to life, filling the silence, and breaking our trance. Her eyes squeeze shut against the bright light, turning her face to the side so quickly that we nearly knock heads.

"Shit," I say, pulling out of the warmest, wettest fucking heaven I've ever felt. She brings her knees together as I pull the condom off my still-hard cock with a wince and tie the end. Taking mercy on her, I slide the dimmer on the light switch down to a more bearable level of brightness.

"Finally," Valen says, sitting up quickly to search for her clothes. Her cheeks turn pink, probably realizing that they're downstairs...and *on* the stairs. I stand in front of her, not bothering to cover myself up, my t-shirt dangling from my outstretched hand in offering. Her gaze lands on my dick before her eyes dart away, and I feel my lips tug into a smirk at her sudden bout of shyness.

"Thanks," she says, plucking the shirt out from my grasp and pulling it over her head. "I should check my phone. See if I can get a hold of Shayne." She's out the door in the next second.

Walking back to my room, I pull on a fresh pair of boxers before heading for the thermostat in the hallway. I crank the heat up extra high to take the chill out of the house then snatch my sweats off Valen's floor before meeting her downstairs.

"Anything?" I ask. She's standing at the counter with her phone plugged in, her eyes fixed on the screen with a frown marring her features. Her hair is still wild, her neck still wearing a faint red mark from my hand. I usually find myself feeling distant and detached after sex. Instead, I immediately want to take her back upstairs. *What the fuck is wrong with me?*

"Nothing."

She tenses when I walk up behind her, tossing my sweats over the back of one of the barstools before bracing my hands on the edge of the counter in front of her, trapping her in my arms.

"I'll go find service in the morning."

She spins around in my arms to face me, her chin tipped to meet my eyes. I back up, leaning against the stove, waiting for her to say whatever's on her mind. Her eyes trail down my chest, stopping at the tattoo on my thigh.

"Danny's number," she says knowingly. I nod in confirmation. Soft brown eyes meet mine again. "You're not playing?" she asks.

"I am. Will be," I correct. "Once the new semester starts."

"You can do that?" she asks, sounding skeptical.

I shrug. "Long story. But the head coach presented me with a loophole, and I took it."

"What does that even mean?"

That I spiraled after finding out Christian killed Danny and pissed my shot away senior year.

"It means I'm supposed to be using this time to get my shit together before officially joining the team."

"And are you? Getting your shit together?"

Another shrug. "Haven't decided yet. What about you? I haven't seen you at any of the recent games." I turn the focus on her, mostly because I don't have answers to the questions she's asking. I'm supposed to be training my ass off. I'm supposed to be thankful for the second chance I've been given with basketball, and I'm supposed to move on with my life. Everyone else has. So why the fuck do I feel so…stuck?

She arches a brow. "You've been keeping tabs on me?"

"Merely an observation."

She looks down at her feet and extends her ankle. "Sprained it a while ago. Taking a break for a bit to figure out what I want to do."

"And are you? Figuring it out?"

"Haven't decided yet," she quips, echoing my response.

"Guess we're both a couple of losers then."

"Guess so." She's quiet for a minute, contemplating her next words before she speaks. "You remember the night Liam came to your house?"

I cross my arms over my chest. How could I forget? That's the night everything changed.

"I didn't know what happened with Christian when we got into that argument. I didn't find out until the next day."

How could she have known? She wasn't there when Christian staggered in and confessed to killing my brother.

"I felt like an asshole for coming to you with…petty *bull-shit* when you were going through that. Anyway, I never said sorry. So. I'm sorry." She scratches behind her ear, as if the act of apologizing is uncomfortable or foreign for her. "About what I said to you, about Liam, about Christian and Danny. All of it."

"Who knew all it would take was a couple of orgasms for you to be sweet to me?" I tease, trying to lighten the mood.

"Fuck off," she says, but her words lack any venom.

"While we're apologizing, I'm sorry for calling you stuck-up."

She snorts out a laugh. "A stuck-up little cheerleader with nice tits and an attitude problem," she corrects. "I deserved it."

"Two out of three are still true," I say, walking over to where she stands. I brace my palms on the counter on either side of her then skim my nose down the side of her neck. When I kiss her there, she lets out something between a moan and a sigh as her head lolls to the side, allowing me better access. "But I want to make it up to you, anyway." Her fingers white-knuckle the ledge of the counter as mine leave their position to drag the hem of her shirt—my shirt—up her smooth thighs. When I slide my fingers toward her pussy, she arches a brow.

"One-time thing," she reminds me.

"Hmm. I could've sworn we said it would be one *night* only. And technically, the night isn't over." Bending slightly, I grab her behind the knees and lift her onto the countertop. She squeals when her bare cheeks hit the cold granite. "Besides," I say, squeezing the soft flesh of her ass, "I want you to let me taste your pussy."

She rolls her eyes. "I told you I'm not into that."

"You're not into it, or you haven't tried it?"

She glares at me. "Both," she answers reluctantly.

I arch a brow. "Never? Not even with Liam?"

"Not even with Liam. He tried once, I redirected him, and I guess he never cared to try again." She shrugs. "And any other time, I've been the one to…take control."

Redirected. She makes it sound like he was a toddler behaving badly, which might not be far from the truth. I'm starting to think that control is Valen's shield. If she's the one directing the show, she doesn't have to be vulnerable. And I bet the fucking losers who've been lucky enough to be with her were clueless. Clueless and undeserving.

I want all of her. In every way. And if I only have one night, I'm going to make it count.

"He's even more of a bitch than I thought. And that's saying a lot."

She laughs. "I don't know why you're so fixated on him. I think you think about him more than I ever did."

"The only thing I'm thinking about is getting my tongue on your pussy." Her grip on my shoulders tightens at my words. I slide my hands from her ass down to her knees and push them apart. She doesn't resist when my fingers circle her ankle and bring one foot to rest on the edge of the counter, opening her for me completely.

I swallow hard at the sight. She's glistening, still wet and swollen. She's perfect. "Is that a yes?" I ask, just to be sure I'm not misreading the very clear signs. I run a gentle finger up her slit, and it makes her hips jerk forward.

"Okay."

I'm on my knees before she finishes the word, kissing the inside of her thigh. Her hands fly to the lip of the counter, gripping the edge as I get closer. She smells so fucking good. Like her signature orange Creamsicle scent and sex. I'm just about to take my first taste when Valen's palm smacks against my forehead, stopping me. I practically growl at the interruption.

"Do you hear that?" she whispers in a panic.

"Yeah, it's the sound of all my blood rushing back to my—"

She mashes her hand over my mouth. "I'm serious."

Then I hear it. A car door slams, and then another, followed by the sound of faint voices.

Valen's shocked eyes shoot to mine. "Oh my God, *move*." Her hand drops from my mouth as she slides off the counter, her pussy narrowly avoiding my face as she does so. I stand, watching her with far less panic and a lot more irritation. They choose *now* to save the day? Less than an hour after I finally got Valen underneath me? I stand, grabbing my sweats off the back of the chair and pulling them on.

"My clothes," she hisses, referring to the ones scattered around as we both scan the room for evidence of our transgression.

"You're also not wearing pants," I point out helpfully.

Valen takes off for the stairs faster than I thought her capable of, snatching her bra off one of the steps just as I hear the beeping sound of the code being punched into the lock.

"Surprise!" Shayne yells, holding up two bags of what I'm really fucking hoping is food. Thayer is right behind her, shaking the snow out of his hair and closing the door. "Your rescue crew has—" Shayne stops short and looks around, taking in the state of the place. "Where's Valen?"

Thayer's eyes bounce from the pile of blankets in front of the fireplace to me before narrowing with suspicion.

"Fuck if I know. She's hiding around here somewhere."

"What'd you do to my best friend?" Shayne asks, her tone accusatory. She probably suspects I pissed her off somehow. Thayer probably suspects I fucked her. They'd both be right.

I hold up my hands in surrender. "I was a perfect gentleman."

Unconvinced, she walks past me and stands on the bottom step, peering up the staircase. "Valen! I'm here to rescue you!"

Avoiding Thayer's probing stare, I crane my neck to see up the stairs, half-expecting Valen to still be half-naked and guilty-faced. But she appears at the top of the steps clothed and collected.

"Oh thank God," she says dramatically. "I thought you were going to leave me here to die."

"We tried calling you guys," Shayne explains.

Valen bounces down the stairs and into Shayne's waiting arms. They hug like one of them just got back from war instead of being separated for a couple of days. Valen is the first to pull away, sticking her finger in the bag before peering into it. "Do I smell pancakes?"

"That depends. Do you forgive me for the worst Christmas ever?"

Quite the opposite if you ask me.

"Hand over the pancakes and we'll call it even." Valen plucks one of the bags from her grip and they both walk back into the kitchen. "Besides, it wasn't that bad, all things considered." She meets my eyes for a split second as she says it.

Shayne raises a brow. *"Wasn't that bad?"* She feels Valen's forehead with the back of her hand.

Valen realizes her mistake, but she recovers quickly. "Compared to spending the holidays with my mother? Even Holden can't be worse than that."

Shayne snorts out a laugh. "Aw, leave him alone." She wraps her arms around me before standing on her tiptoes to pat the top of my head. "He can't help it that he requires the attention of a six-week-old puppy."

"Valen gave me *lots* of attention," I tease, earning a glare that would have most men cowering in fear.

"Those might need to be warmed up," Shayne says, ignoring me. "We stopped at the bottom of the mountain like an hour ago. You guys eat. I have to get the rest of my stuff."

"I'll help," Thayer says, heading up the stairs behind her.

"What are you doing?" Valen hisses once they're out of earshot.

"What?"

"Don't act stupid. *Valen gave me lots of attention*," she mocks. "I thought we agreed not to say anything."

"Chill out and think for a minute," I say, moving closer. I slide my hand up the back of her thigh and under her shirt. "I always talk like that. You are the one who's acting differently. If anything, you'll be the one to give it away."

She scowls but doesn't say anything because she knows I'm right. This is our thing. I say shit to get under her skin, and she gives it right back. I move back to the other side of the counter, taking one of the plastic containers of pancakes out of the bag. I don't bother heating them up or adding butter. I just open the syrup package, fold my pancake in half, and dip it inside.

She looks shocked as she watches me eat the whole thing in one bite.

"What can I say? I'm starved. My meal was interrupted." I hear the toilet flush, and I know we only have a minute before Shayne's back. "By the way, your shirt's inside out. And backward." *Or should I say my shirt?*

Taking me by surprise, Valen holds my stare as she whips my shirt over her head, revealing those perfect tits I had my mouth on just minutes ago. She takes her time righting her shirt, allowing me to look my fill. I can't tear my eyes away from her chest, and I'm seconds away from taking one of those little hard nipples into my mouth when I hear the bathroom sink shut off.

Valen pulls the shirt back over her head the right way, smirking at my crotch when she notices the very inconvenient bulge in my sweats. Fuck, I'm pissed all over again. Pissed and hard.

"So," Shayne says, bouncing back into the room, completely oblivious to my torment. I step back behind the counter to hide the tent in my pants. "The weather is supposed to get bad again tomorrow around ten. We can either leave tonight or get some sleep and head out early."

"Morning," I answer at the same time Valen says, "Now's good."

Shayne looks between us, a smile on her lips. "The day you two agree on something is the day Hell freezes over."

Thayer comes down the stairs, carrying one of their suitcases.

"What do you think?" Shayne asks him. "Turn back around and go now or in the morning?"

"Sooner the better," he says predictably before turning his attention to me. "But you're driving so I can sleep on the way." He tosses me the keys and I catch them before stuffing them into my pocket.

"It's my car," I point out. "No shit, I'm driving."

Valen heats up her food in the microwave before taking a seat at one of the barstools. She starts to tear her pancakes into bite-sized pieces while she talks with Shayne. Meanwhile, Thayer and I take to loading up the trunk with our bags and discuss the best route home with most of the roads still being closed. I'm half-listening, in a foul mood, and it's getting worse by the second. I'll admit, I was stupid to think I'd feel the kind of cold ambivalence that comes after a casual fuck, but I thought I'd feel satisfied after hooking up with Valen. I'm nowhere fucking *near* satisfied.

I should've never touched her. Because now I want more.

TWENTY

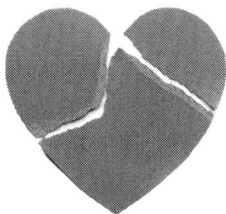

Valen

S OMEWHERE BETWEEN HOLDEN ALMOST EATING ME OUT ON
the kitchen counter and the hour spent packing up our
stuff, something shifted. The drive home is silent, and
Holden's even quieter. Shayne's next to me in the back seat, a
pillow wedged between her head and the window. She passed
out almost immediately. Thayer's up front, his seat reclined
and his feet on the dash. I'm pretty sure he's asleep, too,
considering a single word hasn't been spoken for the last forty
minutes or so. Then again, he's not the talkative brother.

The *talkative* one is anything but right now and hasn't so
much as spared me a glance since we left. I could lie to myself
and say that he's just focusing on the winding roads that are
pitch-black and slick with ice beneath thick layers of snow, but
the vibes are off and I can feel it. I see his fingers squeeze and
release the steering wheel—which, again, can be attributed to
driving in this shit—but I know something else is bothering
him. If there's one superpower I got from growing up with
unpredictable mother, it's my ability to read a situation on
nothing but vibes alone.

I almost take advantage of the fact that we're the only
ones awake to call him out on his sudden shift in behavior, but
what's the point? It wouldn't be the first time in history that
a guy turned into an asshole after getting what he wanted. I

assumed there was a mutual respect there, under all the hostility and bickering. Someone who could handle a casual hookup without getting weird afterwards. But then I remember his words to Thayer in the kitchen.

I was bored and she was the only one awake…

When we finally get out of the mountains, my phone lights up, and to my surprise, my screen is flooded with text after text from my mom and missed calls and voicemails galore. My stomach instantly fills with lead. This whole time I was desperate for a phone signal, and now I wish I were back at the cabin and completely out of reach.

When I open my messages, it's worse than I initially thought. It's not just my mom, but my dad, old cheer friends, and family members I haven't spoken to in years have messaged me, asking if I'm okay. I'm only confused until I see that my mom went to social media and immediately made a sympathy post.

What the fuck? I huff out a laugh, shaking my head. I shouldn't be surprised.

As if I summoned the drama queen herself, my screen lights up again with her name. I decide to answer her, only because I know she won't give up. I'd rather get it over with now.

"Hello?" I ask, trying to keep my voice low.

"Valentina!" my mother shrieks, and I hold my phone away from my ear. My eyes dart up to the rearview mirror to see Holden's reaction, but he either doesn't hear her or doesn't care because his expression never changes, his eyes never leaving the road. "Thank God. You have no idea what I've been going through."

"What you've been going through?" I repeat, confused.

"Yes! I was worried sick."

"You were," I say flatly, skepticism clear in my tone.

"Of course, I was," she admonishes. "When Shayne told

me you were stranded, I was afraid you'd be stuck there and miss New Year's Eve."

I roll my eyes, more at myself than her. I must be tired because I'm never so quick to believe that she might actually care about my well-being more than herself. "Don't worry, Mother. You'll have your perfect little family together for a picture."

"Don't be a child. I knew you were fine, and let's be honest, it would be just like you to use something like this to your advantage. Anything to get out of spending time with me."

"Yes. You caught me. I orchestrated this entire thing to avoid going home, actually." My words are meant to sound sarcastic, but it's not lost on me that it was, in fact, better than being home for the holidays.

"Well, your plan backfired because your father was so worried that he came in early." The pure glee in which she informs me of this fact tells me that this was part of *her* plan all along. Funny how the schemers are always the one accusing others of scheming. She may be engaged to someone else, but she'll never pass up an opportunity to get my father back into her clutches. She acts as if she's happier than she's ever been, but if given half a chance, I have no doubt that she'd drop her fiancé, Lawrence, in a heartbeat.

"Why would you do that?" I hiss into the phone. This time when I look into the rearview mirror, I find Holden's curious eyes on mine.

"I did nothing. I simply told him about your predicament. He was already on his way when Elena called to let me know they were going to get you. I let him know you'd be home late tonight."

She talked to Shayne's mom? "I'm not coming home tonight. We're heading back to campus." There's no way I want to face her or my father, but especially not in the same room. Then again, if I go back to the dorms, I'm going to be right across the hall from Holden. I don't know which one is worse.

"Unacceptable," she starts, but I put the phone down as she rants when Holden starts to speak.

"We're going to crash in Sawyer Point tonight. It's late and it's closer than Hadley." Oh, right. Normal people don't stay on campus during the holidays.

I give him a wordless nod, picking up the phone to cut off her spiel. "I'll be there in an hour."

TWENTY-ONE

Valen

LUCKILY, MY DAD IS SMARTER THAN I GIVE HIM CREDIT FOR AND booked a hotel room for the night instead of meeting me at the house, much to my mother's dismay, I'm sure.

When I finally get home, the house is dark and quiet, and my mother is standing at the entryway wearing a silk robe, her hair still blown out from when she was expecting company. Her fiancé is noticeably absent, and I have to wonder if that was strategic on her part. Lawrence is nice enough. He keeps to himself and hasn't tried to get me to call him *Dad*, so I take that as a win. He's some investment banker, ten years younger than my mother. Compared to the company she has been known to keep, the guy's a goddamn saint.

She holds out her arms for a hug and I reluctantly trudge over to her, dragging my suitcase behind me. I step into her arms and return her hug with limp arms. She pulls back, hands grasping my shoulders as she inspects me. "You look awful."

"Thanks so much," I say, unbothered by her remark. I could be red-carpet ready and she'd still have some critique. I'm surprised it took her this long to comment, to be honest. My baggy sweatpants and Holden's even baggier shirt that hangs beneath my ski jacket are probably the most offensive things she's seen in a long time.

She gives me a disapproving look, reaching out a hand to

tuck my hair behind my ear. "Why don't you go have a shower? Clean yourself up, and then—"

"It's been a long night. A long *week*," I correct. "I'm going to bed." I leave her standing there looking slightly offended as I lug my suitcase up the stairs before she can say another word. My mother takes control in every situation. Sometimes, I don't think she's even aware of it. Years and years of begrudgingly following her orders disguised as advice and desperately seeking her approval make it hard for her to handle it when I dare to go against her wishes. Even when it's something as simple as not wanting to shower on her schedule. I used to have a lot more tolerance for her. You'd think the distance would make things better—absence makes the heart grow fonder and all that—but the longer I'm away at school, the more my resentment grows, and I find it harder to be around her. Harder to forgive her.

Once I'm upstairs, I pull my suitcase into my room, kicking my door shut behind me. I could almost cry at the sight of my bed. This room is all my mother's design. Fit for a princess. But I'll give credit where credit is due. She spares no expense when it comes to furnishing a room. If there's one thing I miss about being home, it's my bed.

Before I can face-plant onto it, my mom opens my door and follows me into my room. "Don't you want to open your Christmas gift?"

I turn around to find her with a red box wrapped in a white ribbon. I raise an eyebrow as I toss my phone onto my bed before I take my jacket off, letting it fall to the floor. "Valentino?" I ask, recognizing the gift box.

She smiles, holding it out for me. I eye her with a healthy dose of suspicion as I take it from her outstretched hand. Gifts from my parents are usually one of two things: apologies or bribes. Usually, accepting them is not worth it, but I have a feeling that whatever is in this box is going to be really pretty.

When I pull off the lid, my mouth falls open. A gorgeous pair of transparent, six-inch platform pumps. "These cost like two thousand dollars," I tell her, as if she wasn't the one to buy them. Now I'm really suspicious. "What's the catch?"

"Nothing," she says with a hint of defensiveness in her tone. "I thought you'd like them, that's all. You can wear them to the New Year's Eve gala."

"The what?"

"The gala," she repeats. I don't even have to ask which one.

"Since when was that the plan?"

"Since you said you'd spend New Year's with us since you spent Christmas with your friends. That was the deal."

I shake my head, putting the lid back onto the box before holding it out for her to take back. "I didn't agree a gala." I don't want to spend my New Year's Eve at some old people party. Not to mention, Holden will be there.

"Don't be ridiculous." She doesn't take the shoebox, pushing it back toward me instead. "It's just a nice dinner and a silent auction followed by music and mingling. Your father's going to be there, too. There's no reason you shouldn't be with your family."

I set the box on the edge of my bed, then turn back around to face her. Narrowing my eyes at her, I wonder what her true motives for wanting me there are. Why does she all of a sudden care about spending time with me? She never gave two shits before. It's as if the more I pull away, the more she digs her claws in lately. "And if I don't go?"

She sighs, pinching the bridge of her nose. "Wear the shoes or don't, Valentina. I don't care. But it would mean a lot if you decided to show up without me having to make threats or strongarm you into going."

Dammit. Why I still let her make me feel guilty, I'll never understand. "Fine. I'll make an appearance."

"That's all I ask."

"And thanks. For the shoes." My words sound stiff to my own ears. It's not exactly a heartfelt thank you, but it's as good as I can do.

"You're welcome." She smiles. Just before she's gone, she

stops in my doorway and turns around to eye me up and down. "And Valentina? Try to look nice."

I roll my eyes, climbing into bed. I spend the next hour trying to fall asleep, cringing each time images of fucking Holden flash in my mind. Of all the stupid decisions I've made, that one is near the top of the list. Even knowing that, I can't deny that it was amazing. Just as I'm about to finally doze off, my phone vibrates on the mattress next to me, pulling me back from the edge of sleep.

It's a text from an unknown number, but instinctively, I know who it is before I read the words on the screen.

For what it's worth, reality was better than the fantasy.

TWENTY-TWO

Valen

"W E'RE GOING TO MISS THE—WHY AREN'T YOU dressed?" My mom's voice draws my attention away from the Funny Bunny polish on my toes. I look up to find her in my doorway, putting her earrings in. I have to admit, she looks beautiful in her pale gold satin floor-length gown. It's simple but elegant, and it clings to her slender figure like a second skin.

"I have plenty of time." I prop my chin on my knee, putting the finishing touches on my toes.

"You'll be late for the auction."

"It's a good thing I'm not planning on bidding on anything then."

She sighs, shaking her head. "Have you even showered? It's a black-tie event, Valentina. Nothing casual."

"I'll be right behind you," I assure her without giving her an answer. She narrows her eyes at me, knowing that this was my plan all along. There's no way in hell I'm riding with them. Having a getaway car is mandatory in situations like this. "Promise."

"One hour." She points a freshly manicured finger at me. "If you can get yourself presentable by then, it will be a miracle."

"I could always just…sit this one out?" I suggest.

She gives me a saccharine smile as she tilts her head to the side to put her other earring in. "Nice try. One hour."

"Fine."

"Thank you." She looks taken aback by how quickly I capitulate, as if she expected me to put up more of a fight. She turns to leave, and I turn my attention back to painting my toes. "Don't forget to take out the nose ring," she throws over her shoulder.

I roll my eyes. Any time I think we might get away with having a civil conversation, she has to get at least one dig in. "If you're lucky," I shout after her, hearing her heels click-clack down the stairs.

Once she's out the door, I twist the cap back onto my nail polish and walk over to my closet, careful not to smudge my toes. I set my phone down on the shelf next to a pair of shoes before pulling out the dress I picked out for tonight. It's cute enough. A black satin fitted slip dress with spaghetti straps. My phone lights up, so I pluck it off the shelf, not surprised in the slightest to see that it's my mom. Already.

> **Remember: black tie event. And try not to look like you're at a funeral. It wouldn't kill you to wear something festive.**

I glance around, half-expecting to find a hidden camera.

With a frustrated groan, I hang the black dress up and start flipping through my collection until I land on a very different dress. One that could never be mistaken as *casual*. It's a silver chainmail mini dress with slits up both thighs, a draped neckline, and a dangerously low back. The material is delicate and sparkles when the light hits it. In other words, it's perfect. She wants festive? I'll

show up looking like the damn mirror ball.

The event is in full swing when I show up fashionably late. I didn't make it in an hour like I was supposed to, but it's still early enough. I follow the sound of laughing and mingling down the halls and into the crowded ballroom. I knew Holden's family was well off, but where his estate in Heartbreak Hill is the understated, old money kind of rich, his uncle's place is the flashy, shiny, new kind. I scan the room, searching for a familiar face. It's your typical charity event. Old money, new money, politicians, businessmen, waitstaff, and, of course, a few photographers to document all the goodwill going on here tonight. All of whom are predictably well on their way to tipsy. A server with a tray full of glasses stops to offer drinks to a couple next to me. He says nothing when I pluck one of the bubbly beverages off his tray, looking me up and down, not bothering to conceal his leering.

It almost makes me regret my dress choice. Almost.

I walk away, taking a sip of the champagne cocktail. It's fizzy and sweet, thanks to the sugar cube on the bottom, and warms my insides. I'm hoping to find Shayne, but instead, it's my mother that I spot in the sea of tuxedos and floor-length gowns. She's mingling in a group of people next to the bar, putting on a show. She has perfected a flawless mixture of demure and classy, yet captivating and confident. Too bad it's all a façade. When she sees me making my way toward her, the mask slips, her eyes practically bulging out of her head before they narrow into slits. I smirk as she breaks away from the crowd to grab my elbow and steer me to a less populated area next to an empty table.

"What are you wearing?" she asks, sounding horrified. Being Claudia's daughter is a constant balancing act of being smart enough to make her look good, but never smarter than her. Having enough accomplishments to make her seem like mother of the year, but never surpassing her own achievements. Looking pretty enough so as not to embarrass her, but never more beautiful.

"The shoes go perfectly with the dress, don't you think?" I point my toes, admiring the transparent pumps. They really are perfect with this dress.

"The shoes aren't the problem."

"What?" I ask drily, smoothing my hand down the delicate material. "You don't like? You told me to dress nice."

"Please," she scoffs. "You don't look *nice*, Valentina. You look like a slutty baked potato. Wait until your father sees you."

I lift one shoulder in a shrug, letting her insult roll off my back. "I'm sure that won't stop you from trying to borrow it in a week or so." I used to walk on eggshells with her, filtering every word that came out of my mouth because no matter how innocuous they were, my mother knew how to twist anything into a reason to be insulted or offended. Which then led to days or even months of the silent treatment. Back then, it seemed like the worst possible punishment. Now, it seems like a vacation. With any luck, my latest infraction will earn me at least two months of peace.

She opens her mouth, preparing to spit some venom my way, but I'm saved from her vitriol when her fiancé Lawrence joins her side.

"Happy New Year, Valen," he says, leaning in—probably to kiss my cheek—before thinking better of it and giving my shoulder a squeeze instead when it's clear that it wouldn't be a welcomed gesture. I've never been the touchy-feely type, and he knows it. It was a slipup, a polite introduction that he's probably replicated thirty times tonight alone, I'm sure. *This one* doesn't try to force it. I appreciate him for it. I also appreciate the way his gaze stays at eye level, never venturing below my shoulders.

The bar really is in hell.

I smile at him, thankful for the interruption if nothing else.

"Your mother tells me you had quite the adventure. She worried herself into a frenzy."

"I bet she did," I mutter, taking a swig too big to be considered ladylike. I'm too busy polishing off the rest of my drink, champagne flute tilted to the ceiling, to notice the pair of men approaching. My mother and Lawrence greet them, and then she introduces me with a firm shove in the back in a not-so-subtle warning to get my shit together. I almost choke on the effervescent liquid, slapping a hand to my chest as I try not to sputter in front of whomever she so clearly wants me to impress.

When I look up, I see an older man with brown hair that's slightly graying around the temples. Next to him is the younger version of him but with sandy blond hair and familiar blue eyes that aren't yet hardened by life. *Liam*. His father looks at me with amusement, seemingly unbothered by my lack of decorum.

"Valen," Liam says in greeting before he leans down to kiss my cheek. I flinch away a second too late, still caught off guard by his presence. I guess I shouldn't be surprised that he's here. Massachusetts' elite run in the same circles, after all. "You remember my father."

"Of course," I say, forcing a smile. "It's good to see you, Conrad."

"Lawrence tells me you're at Hadley now," his father says. "You're only, what, an hour and a half away from Northeastern? I'm surprised you and Liam haven't reconnected yet."

"I'm sure Liam has his hands full." *Literally*. They all chuckle, thinking I'm joking, but Liam clears his throat, tugging at his collar.

"What are you majoring in?" Conrad asks. Why so many questions? I think this is the most consecutive words we've ever exchanged. "I hear their computer science program is pretty impressive."

"I'm still undecided, but I can promise you it will have nothing to do with computer science." The comment is meant to be self-deprecating, but it comes off bitchy instead. There's a moment where no one speaks, but I don't bother to clarify to save face. My mom lets out an awkward laugh that breaks the silence.

"Well then, it's a good thing you're pretty," Conrad quips.

My eyebrows shoot up, my mouth opening to respond, but my mom cuts in, knowing whatever I'm about to say won't be polite.

"Liam's interning for Lawrence at Bay State Investments," my mom says, as if that's supposed to impress me. "Small world, huh?" I narrow my eyes at her in warning. I can smell her intentions a mile away.

"Which is why I haven't had much time for socializing. But seeing as how I have *tonight* off, I could use one of those." Liam gives my empty glass a pointed look before plucking it from my grasp. "Can I get you another drink while I'm at it?"

I hesitate, eyeing him as if he's a stranger offering candy, but then I decide that I do, in fact, need another drink. And I do, in fact, want to get away from these people. I let him guide me away, and I almost change my mind on principle when I turn around to see my mother's triumphant smile. Then I see the barely concealed contempt in her eyes. She's upset with me. What else is new? I don't give it another thought, though. The best thing about being out on my own is that I don't have to overanalyze every little expression, every subtle shift in her mood or body language. I was so hypervigilant, so attuned to the minute changes in demeanor that I was damn near psychic. To say that I can read people well is an understatement.

"Sorry about him," Liam murmurs, his fingers grazing my lower back as he leads me toward one of the bars on the perimeter of the room. I reach behind me to swat his hand away. "You're not twenty-one yet," he states.

"And?" They don't exactly ask for IDs at these things. I've been sneaking drinks for years.

"I'll order for you."

"Not necessary," I say, but he's already walking up to the bar. As he talks to the bartender, I lift onto my tiptoes, still not tall enough even with my heels to see over the masses, scanning the room for Shayne once more. I don't see her, but I do catch a glimpse of my dad. His new fiancée is on his arm as they approach my mom and Lawrence. I watch as my mom looks around, no doubt seeking me out, so I take a subtle step to my left, concealing myself behind a big guy with a boisterous laugh. I've only been here for a handful of minutes, and I've already had enough.

"I'm glad I ran into you," Liam says as he hands me a new drink. It looks similar to the last one, except this one has an orange spiral instead of a lemon.

"That makes one of us."

"Come on, Valen. Are you really still mad at me?"

I blink at him. "I'm not mad at you. I don't feel anything for you."

He winces at my words. "And that's the crux of it all, isn't it?"

I mash my lips together, having no desire to continue this conversation. "It was great seeing you, Liam," I say, every word dripping with sarcasm. "Enjoy your night."

"Wait, Valen." He catches me by the elbow. "What I meant to say is I'm sorry."

I turn around to face him, raising a brow. "For cheating on me? Or for calling me a slut?"

"All of it. I just—I never knew where I stood with you."

"This doesn't sound like an apology."

"I'm getting there, I swear." When I don't walk away, he takes that as his cue to continue. "I was used to getting whatever I wanted. *Whoever* I wanted. Then you came along and made me work for it. But then, even when I had you, you were never fully in it."

"Once again. Not an apology."

"I was insecure as fuck," he spits out, surprising me. "You didn't *need* me."

I don't know why I'm entertaining him or this conversation. He's served his purpose of getting me away from my mom, but still, I find myself responding. "I liked you. Wasn't that enough?"

"I *loved* you," he counters. "When I left for school, you didn't even miss me. Tara was there, and she wanted me, and instead of talking to you about how I felt—"

"You decided to *feel* her instead," I finish for him.

He pinches the bridge of his nose and lets out a

self-deprecating chuckle. "I was an asshole, and you didn't deserve it. That's all I wanted to say."

"Thanks. I guess."

"Friends?" He flashes his million-dollar smile.

I shrug a shoulder. "Probably not." I finally spot Shayne. She's standing at the bottom of the grand staircase, staring at the phone in her hand, biting the thumbnail of her other hand, looking suspicious as hell. "I have to go."

"Still heartless, I see." His smile tells me that he's teasing, but I can feel the truth in his barb. "See you around, Valen."

I make my way across the room and over to Shayne. Her head snaps up when she senses my presence, sagging with relief when she sees that it's me.

"We've really got to work on your poker face," I tell her. She cracks a smile, so it must not be anything too bad, but then she notices my dress, and her mouth falls open.

"Holy shit." She laughs, looking me up and down. "You look insane. Even I want to marry you."

"So do you." Her dress is a gorgeous, formfitting wine colored mini dress held up by thin straps. "So, are we on a top-secret mission?"

"Thayer and Holden have been waiting for Samuel to leave their aunt's side for more than thirty seconds so they can question her about Christian, but I swear to God, the fucker knows that's what they want because he's been glued to her side all night."

"So why are you over here looking like you're about to shit your pants?" I ask, not connecting the dots.

"Because those two idiots decided to take this party as an opportunity to snoop around Danny's room."

That's it? "I know the guy's a douche, but he's still their uncle. How much trouble could they possibly get into?"

Shayne shakes her head. "You don't understand. At first, I thought he was just an asshole, but the way he looked at me... the things he said without caring that I was there to hear them?

He's *unhinged*, Valen. To the point where Christian told me himself that he was *dealing* with me so his father wouldn't take matters into his own hands."

I think back to when Shayne was on his shit list, all because he knew her presence would lead to the truth about Danny's death if Thayer and Holden stopped hating her long enough to compare notes and put two and two together. Christian lit her house on *fire*. If his father is the more rational of the two, I don't even want to think about what Samuel is capable of.

"I think they still underestimate him. Even knowing everything he did to Christian…"

"Sometimes it's hard to believe the worst about family, even when it's right there in front of you."

She nods, but then her expression changes into something sad. "Is it selfish of me? To wish they'd just let August deal with this like he insisted. I want Samuel and Christian to pay for their part in it as much as anyone, but not if it means putting themselves in danger."

"Not selfish at all," I tell her, my tone resolute, leaving no room for argument. "Here." I hold out my drink. "Want some?"

She takes it without hesitation, drinking half the glass in one go. "That's really good," she says, the last word ending on a burp that has us both laughing. Her phone lights up in her hand, drawing her attention to the screen. "Shit," she whispers, her eyes darting around the room.

"What now?"

"Holden has a death wish, that's what." She angles the phone toward me, and I lean in to see what has her so worried, ignoring the way my stomach dips at the mere mention of his name. What the *hell* is that about? I shake off the thought, focusing on the words on the screen.

> **Text me if you see my uncle anywhere near the stairs. James Bond over here thinks he can break into his office.**

"They were supposed to be in Christian's room looking for anything that could give them information on where he went. Now they're *breaking into Samuel's office*? With three hundred people wandering around?"

"I'm sure they'll be fine," I try to reassure her.

"The last time Holden tried to be incognito, he got drunk, left his blood at the scene of the crime, and then I almost hit him with my car," she reminds me.

There are so many things wrong with that sentence, but I choke back my laugh, knowing Shayne is legitimately concerned. "What he lacks in brain cells, he makes up for in guts. I'll give him that."

She smirks at me.

"Don't tell him I said that. He'll take it as a compliment."

She mimes zipping her lips. "Come on." She tugs on my arm. "I'm going to get one of those drinks, and then we're on lookout duty."

After Shayne gets her drink, we set our sights on the judge. The sunken room works to our advantage, the three steps allowing us a slightly higher viewpoint. We can see everything, but since we're on the perimeter of the room, we're mostly unnoticed. We spot him right away, making the rounds, Thayer and Holden's aunt on his arm, playing the part of the doting wife. Her smile seems forced, even from here. She moves like a zombie, her eyes glossy and dazed. She is one hundred percent *not* on this planet right now. No one notices. Or maybe they're just polite enough to pretend they don't.

"Is she always like that?" I ask.

Shayne shrugs. "I've only been around her a handful of times, so I can't say for sure, but I think she's always been kind of…checked out."

"That's one word for it," I mutter.

An older man with shock white hair and ice-blue eyes leans in close to whisper something to the judge.

"Who's that?"

"*That* is William Ames. Also known as Thayer's grandfather. Guy gives me the creeps," she says with an audible shudder.

"Yeah, no kidding. Are you sure he's not a vampire?"

"Not fully convinced, no."

Samuel nods at whatever the vampire says before he carefully deposits his wife at one of the nearby tables, leaving her to socialize with some of the other wives, from the looks of it. He glances around the room before he heads straight for the staircase on the opposite side of the room.

"Shit, shit, shit," Shayne says, fumbling for her phone. "He can't find them snooping around." She looks at me, eyes wide as saucers. I still think she's let her true crime consumption rot her brain, but better safe than sorry.

"Give me this," I say, plucking her drink from her hand since mine is mostly empty. "I'll handle him."

"Valen, no." She catches my wrist. "You do not want to be on his radar."

"I'm not on his radar. That's exactly why this will work. He has no idea who I am or that we even know each other."

She shakes her head, unconvinced, but I'm not worried. I know men like Samuel. I know how to *distract*.

I make my way across the room, planning to cut him off halfway. When I get close, I pull out my phone, pretending to be so preoccupied with it that I'm not watching where I'm going. Once he's within reach, I trip on nothing, catching myself on his bicep, sending my drink all over the front of his suit jacket. He swivels to face me fully, steadying me by my waist before I go down for real.

"I'm so, so sorry," I say, giving him my best deer-in-the-headlights expression. His grip lingers on my waist, squeezing, but I'm pretty sure it's out of anger. "Shoot, I got it all over your jacket. Here, let me."

He finally removes his hands, taking note of the wet spot on his lapel with a scowl. I pull out his pocket square and dab at his chest, and the irritation in his eyes morphs into appreciation as he zeroes in on the way my tits move as I do so. I barely contain my eye roll. Men are so easy. Even ones more than double my age with more money and power than most people can ever dream of.

"I wasn't watching where I was going. Totally my fault. I went to the bathroom, but then I couldn't find my way back to my friends. I mean, this place is huge, right?" I ramble on as I blot away at the wet patch.

His hand closes around mine, stopping my efforts, then directs my hand away. "Do I get to know the name of the young lady who spilled champagne on me in my own home?"

"Valentina," I say, opting to give him the name that feels less personal to me.

"Do you have a last name, Valentina?"

I hesitate for a fraction of a second as those hard eyes bore into mine. I see what Shayne meant. This guy oozes intimidation. "Solorio," I finally say.

A flash of recognition dawns in his eyes. "Claudia's daughter?"

"You know my mother?" I ask. Sawyer Point is a relatively small town, but I didn't think they knew each other. He must know her well enough, though, considering she no longer bears my father's last name.

"I know everyone in this town. Hazard of the trade." He lifts a brow before he looks me up and down. "Can't say I see the resemblance."

"I favor my father."

"Right." He shrugs out of his jacket and folds it over his forearm." Well, enjoy yourself, Valentina, and Happy New Year. Try not to spill your drink on any more unsuspecting victims." He winks, but it does nothing to soften the harsh delivery.

How can someone make wishing you a Happy New Year

sound like a death threat? Samuel starts to turn away, but out of the corner of my eye, I see Holden and Thayer walking down the stairs, casual as ever, as if they aren't on the verge of being caught.

"Wait!" I say a little too hastily. He gives a pointed look to his arm that I've latched onto.

"Yes?" he grinds out. He's quickly losing his patience with me now, no longer able to keep the polite mask in place. But I just need to keep him occupied for another ten seconds. I rack my brain for something to say. Anything at all. Bonus points if it leads to the answers Holden's looking for. Not because I care about Holden, but because I care about Shayne. The sooner this is put to rest, the sooner they can all move on.

"If this is your house, that means…" I let my words hang in the air, playing dumb. "You're Christian's dad, right? Judge Ames?"

Bad idea. Abort mission. If looks could kill, I'd be dead on the floor. I can see the moment suspicion sets in, his eyes narrowing into slits. I push on, pretending to be oblivious to his shift in demeanor.

"We went to SPH together. I haven't seen him since we graduated, though. How is he?"

It doesn't take much effort for Samuel to rein in his temper, easily slipping back into the role of the friendly neighborhood judge. "Excuse me. I need to run upstairs for a new jacket."

My eyes flit back to the staircase just long enough to see that the coast is clear. Out of the corner of my eye, I see Holden making a beeline straight for me, looking nothing short of furious. My eyes widen for a fraction of a second before I can school my expression. "Right. Of course," I say, keeping my tone light and airy. "Sorry, again."

I turn and walk away before he can say another word.

TWENTY-THREE

Holden

"HURRY THE FUCK UP," THAYER SAYS FROM THE doorway. He's keeping watch while I rifle through my uncle's desk drawers, looking for anything of significance. Christian's room wasn't fucking helpful at all. It looked the same it did before he disappeared. His bed was made. All his clothes were hanging in his closet. Not a single sock on the floor, nothing out of place. I don't even know what I was looking for. Signs that he's been here, something to tell me where the fuck he went, anything.

"We've been up here too long," Thayer says, rushing me. "We're not going to find anything without the password to his computer."

"Just give me a minute," I snap, slamming the top drawer before moving to the one below it. He's old school, still preferring filing cabinets and manilla folders to files on a computer. I flip through some folders I find, but they might as well be in another language. All legal jargon that makes zero sense to me. "Do you care?" I ask idly, still frowning at the paperwork.

"About what?" Thayer asks.

"Finding Christian. Making him and Samuel pay for what they did? About any of it?"

"The fuck is that supposed to mean?" He steps away from the door, coming closer to where I stand behind the desk.

"I get that you have Shayne and you're happy for once in your life, but—"

"But what?" He's already on the defense. "You think Shayne and I are just going to ride off into the fucking sunset, happily ever after? Well, I wish the fuck we could. Because we've been through enough. *You* have gone through enough."

"So, what, we just let them get away with it?" We've lost too many people due to our fucked-up family and their need to get rid of anyone who poses a threat.

"Dad said—"

"Since when do you listen to Dad?" I almost laugh. "It's been a year. And if we learned anything from Danny's death, we'll be waiting a lifetime if we sit around waiting for Dad to give us answers or make a move." If Shayne never came back into our lives, we'd still be sitting around wondering what the fuck happened to our brother.

I drop my attention back to the drawer, sifting through the contents. Thayer might be right. We should put all of this behind us. But it doesn't sit right with me, and I can't pinpoint why. Shayne would say it's because logically, I know Danny's death was an accident, and that deep down, I still love my cousin. I disagree. Thayer got to yell and scream and beat the shit out of Christian that night. I sat there, frozen in my shock at the betrayal of it all.

I don't remember what I said to him, if anything at all. After his confession, he promised to turn himself in the next morning, and lulled into a false sense of security thanks to the cold, hard proof we all had on our phones, Shayne and Thayer went to bed like nothing ever happened. Christian and his partner in crime friend left. The party ended. And it was just me. Me and the bottle of tequila left on the counter. Valen had just stormed off after her piece of shit boyfriend and my freshly wounded ego took a back seat to the grief that was suddenly threatening to swallow me whole.

I abandon the drawer, not finding anything helpful, and move to the computer on his desk instead. Racking my brain for possible passwords, I try the one for their Wi-Fi first. Doesn't work. His birthday doesn't work either. I type in 12345…nothing. I'm about to give up when I try one last possibility.

Bingo.

"Who the fuck sets their password as *password*?" I don't know what I'm looking for, but his email seems like a good place to start. He doesn't have much in his inbox other than court-related shit like scheduled hearings and upcoming cases. I check through his sent folder next. Nothing.

"Hold—"

"I'm almost done," I say, cutting him off, not wanting to hear whatever is about to come out of his mouth. A text message flashes in the upper right-hand corner of the screen from someone by the name of CJ. *"His phone is connected to his laptop."*

> **I appreciate your discretion. The wire transfers will now come from Providence Harbor Bank. They have a reputation for being discreet, and transferring across state lines will provide an additional layer of anonymity.**

"We gotta go now," Thayer says.

"Well, he's definitely up to some shady shit—"

"Samuel's with Valen."

That stops me in my tracks. My head snaps up to find him looking at his phone. *"What?"*

"Shayne said he's on his way up here, but Valen's buying us time. We need to go."

A cold sensation starts in my chest, spreading out through my body. My reaction doesn't make sense. It's not like he can hurt her with a house full of people, but the thought of my uncle even knowing Valen exists fills me with a foreboding sense of dread.

I slap his laptop shut and we're out of the office in two seconds flat. I have to force myself to take slow, measured steps even though my heart is threatening to pound out of my fucking chest. Thayer's right behind me, his steps unhurried. When

I finally find Valen, I stop short, causing Thayer to run into my back. My mouth goes fucking dry at the sight of her. She's wearing a silvery dress that clings to every curve, two slits clear up to her hips showing off those long legs I had wrapped around me the other night. Her dark hair is pulled up, and tied around it is a black ribbon. *Fuck me.* Valen always looks hot, but tonight, she's dressed to kill. If I didn't know better, I'd say she was doing it to torture me. Or tease me. Possibly both.

A shove to the back snaps me back to reality, and that's when I realize who she's talking to—who she's *smiling* at. It's a fake smile. I can tell that much even from here. I can only see the back of his head, but I know without having to see him that he's enjoying his fill of Valen. My uncle has never bothered to hide his interest in women, even when his wife is on his arm.

As if she can hear my thoughts, her eyes flit toward the staircase. It's only a fraction of a second. I can't even be sure she saw us. But when my uncle turns in our direction and Valen's hand snaps out to grab his bicep, I know she did. And that move right there is going to raise his hackles.

"Son of a bitch," I mutter, moving a little faster now. Without considering the consequences, I take the stairs two at a time before I shove my way through the throng of people. I'm five feet away when she spots me coming toward her, eyes wide and full of warning, and three feet away when Thayer's hand clamps down on the back of my neck, steering me to make a sharp right.

"Don't react. You'll only make him more suspicious. You don't want Valen to become a target." I shake him off me and straighten out my suit jacket, but I listen because I know he's right. A couple of years ago, I would have doubted it, but knowing what we know now, that's exactly what it would do.

I look over my shoulder, keeping my eyes glued to them as I blindly walk in the opposite direction. I stop far enough away that I'm not obvious, but not so far that I can't see what's going on. I can't tell what they're saying, but Valen doesn't look fazed in the slightest. She doesn't even flinch when my uncle's hand squeezes her hip. It only lingers for a second before he's dipping his head and turning to leave, but the fact that he touched her at all makes me want to punch a wall.

When I look up at Thayer, he's giving a pointed look at my fist that I didn't realize was clenched at my side. His gaze lifts to my face before he arches a brow.

"What?" I bark out, daring him to say anything about Valen and me again, but wisely, he stays silent.

"Nothin'." He flicks his head toward Shayne. "I'm going to talk to Shayne. Coming?"

When I look back up, Valen is nowhere to be found. "I'll meet back up with you guys in a minute."

"What the fuck are you up to?"

I hold my hands up. "Nothing. I swear. I just need a second to clear my head." I pat my chest where the pre-roll sits in the interior pocket.

He narrows his eyes, not believing me. "It's almost midnight."

"I'll be back before I turn into a pumpkin."

He rolls his eyes. "Don't do anything stupid."

"You mean like breaking into our uncle's office in the middle of his own party?"

"Yeah. Like that."

"You're welcome to join me," I offer, knowing he won't accept when it's this close to midnight, and his New Year's kiss is waiting on him.

As predicted, he declines and leaves in search of Shayne while I slip out to the terrace on the first floor, the length of it extending along one side of the room. It's dark out here except for the dim light that comes from a couple of the heat lamps. I'm surprised none of those old fucks snuck out for a smoke. Though, I guess the cold is probably too uncomfortable. Instead, they're probably in the warmth of my uncle's library, smoking their Cubans while they compare the size of their dicks, boats, and wallets.

Reaching inside my suit jacket, I pull out the joint I rolled earlier along with a lighter. I pinch the joint between my lips and light it, letting the smoke fill my lungs as I watch through the window. I have a perfect view of the party from out here, thanks to the sheer curtains and well-lit room. It must be closer to midnight than I thought because I watch as everyone starts to seek out their significant others, pairing off. I spot Thayer pull Shayne into a corner, away from the crowd. Instinctively, I search for Valen, jealousy already rearing its ugly head at the thought of someone else's lips on hers.

To my surprise, her bare back comes into view right in front of me, that fucking ribbon in her hair taunting me. She's followed by a tall, very familiar form and a couple of his friends. When he turns his head to smile down at her, my suspicions are confirmed. *Well, well, well, if it isn't fucking Liam himself.* The space fills in with more bodies as my uncle takes the floor, microphone in one hand, my aunt's hand in the other. An older couple moves in next to Valen, and the woman stops to fix a stray piece of her hair as she passes by, but Valen bats it away. I raise a brow. Her mother? She's taller, paler, her features more angular than Valen's round, but I suppose she bears a passing resemblance if I squint hard enough. The woman purses her lips, tugging the hand of the man behind her to move a little farther into the crowd and away from Valen.

I take another hit as the lights dim and the countdown starts. My eyes narrow as I watch Liam's arm go around Valen's shoulders, but she jerks away, sending him a scathing look. He's not even looking at her, laughing at something his friends must've said, undeterred by her rejection. I move slightly to the right so I can see more of her profile. Her eyes scan the room, as if she's looking for something.

Or some*one*.

Before hope can bloom that she's looking for me, she waves at Shayne from where she stands with Thayer's arms wrapped around her from behind. Valen smiles at her, but then it slips, her slender throat moving with a swallow as she pushes up onto her toes and continues to look around the room.

Six, five, four…

Everyone chants in unison, and I see Liam's intent before she does. He licks his lips, turning his back to his friends as he focuses on Valen.

Three, two…

Balloons start to fall from the ceiling as everyone cheers, couples turning toward each other, preparing for their first kiss of the new year. Valen's unconcerned with the festive display, though. She stares ahead, and if I'm not mistaken, she almost looks disappointed.

One.

Fuck it. I toss the joint behind me and twist the doorknob. I stick my arm through, my hand finding Valen's while Liam's attention is still on the balloons, and I pull her out to the patio, closing the door before he's even realized she's gone.

"What the hell!" Valen squeals as I press her up against the wall, caging her in. She clamps her mouth shut when she realizes it's me. Her chest heaves against mine and I duck down, bringing my face close to hers until our noses are almost touching. The muffled shouts of *Happy New Year* filter through the door and "Auld Lang Syne" starts to play as she stares up at me, her big brown eyes shining bright and alive.

She moves first, her lips crashing against mine. I groan when her tongue slides into my mouth. She tastes so fucking good and the fact that she's initiating only makes it sweeter. I kiss her back, my hands still planted on the wall on either side of her head, happily allowing her to take the lead. Her fingers curl into my chest as she fists my shirt to pull me closer. Bending my knees, I deepen the kiss, wedging my thigh between her legs. And not ten seconds after she pulled me closer, she pushes me away, ripping her mouth from mine.

"Are you crazy?" she hisses. "What the hell are you doing?"

"You're the one who kissed me," I point out.

"You're the one who dragged me out here!"

"You wanted me to!"

"I did not," she denies, indignant.

"Really?" I challenge. "So, you wanted *Liam's* tongue down your throat? Thought you'd ring in the new year with the guy who cheated on you?"

"Of course not," she says, folding her arms over her chest, which only emphasizes her tits.

"Or maybe you were looking for me, hoping I'd swoop in and take his place?" I take a step closer. "And maybe you wore this little fucking dress just for me, too."

"You're wrong about that one," she says, but I don't miss the fact that she doesn't bother to deny anything else. I'll take it as a win. "I wore this to piss my mom off."

I bite back my amusement. Okay. I'll buy that, but… "The ribbon."

"What about it?"

"I find the timing suspicious, is all. I tell you about my fantasy of tying you up with said ribbon, and then you show up wearing one, here in my uncle's house, where you know I'll be. But my fantasy has changed."

She cocks her head to the side, giving me a bored look that betrays whatever emotion she's actually feeling. "You got exactly what you wanted, then changed your mind? Color me surprised."

I finally allow myself to touch her and grip low on her hips. The material of her dress is so thin that I can feel the heat of her skin through it. My thumbs rub up and down, just inches away from her pussy, and I'm acutely aware of how easy it would be to slip my hand up her dress and make her come on my fingers. But I have bigger plans in mind.

"On the contrary, I got what I wanted and now I want more. My new fantasy still involves the ribbon, but now, I want it to happen right… *here.*" I flip her around so she can see inside the window. "I want you strung up and helpless while I eat your

pussy two feet from your idiot boyfriend while he tries to figure out where you disappeared to."

"He's not my boyfriend," she says, but the huskiness of
her voice tells me she wants this, too. If I wasn't so turned on
right now, the way Liam turns in a circle like a complete imbe-
cile would be comical.

I tug on the black satin, untying her hair, and her thick, dark
locks tumble out of the bow, her breath hitching with anticipation.

"Tell me I'm right. Tell me you were looking for me. Tell me
you wore this ribbon for me." I turn her back around, pressing
her back into the wall underneath a light fixture. Tell me you
hoped I'd finish what I started on the kitchen counter."

"I was looking for you."

It's not a full admission, but it's a start. And it's more than I
thought I'd get from her stubborn ass. "Does this mean you're
going to let me give you your New Year's kiss?"

"You already did."

I shake my head slowly. "Not here," I say, dragging my thumb
across her plump bottom lip before skimming down her body,
stopping between her thighs. "Here." Using my middle finger,
I trace her slit through her dress then draw light circles over
her little clit.

"Someone will see," she says, even as her hips arch off the
wall and into my touch. Her arms fall to her sides and her purse
slides off her arm, dropping to the ground.

"So tell me to stop."

"This is the last time."

"Sure it is." I pull my hand away, loving the way she practically growls in protest. "Patience, Sweet Valentine." Gathering her
wrists in one hand, I bring them both above her head. I quickly
tie them together with her ribbon before securing them to the
iron light fixture above her head. I step back to admire the view
and almost come in my fucking pants at the sight. Her hair is
wild, arms stretched over her head, full tits are close to spilling
out, and her dress has ridden up even higher, barely covering

her pussy now. She's forced onto her tiptoes, just barely able to reach the ground, even with the extra inches courtesy of those death traps she calls shoes.

"Holden, it's freezing out here," she says, snapping me out of my reverie. I want to take my time with her, but the reality is, we probably don't have long until someone either discovers us or realizes we're both missing from the party. Not to mention, it's now past midnight, which means there will be another hour or two of mingling and saying goodbyes before everyone makes their way home for the night.

Dropping to my knees in front of her, my fingers circle her right ankle before I widen her stance, making her open for me. She gasps, but she doesn't object. My hands skim up the outside of her smooth legs and underneath her dress before I curl my fingers into the thin straps of her underwear and tug them down, leaving them mid-thigh. Flattening my palms against the top of her thighs, I slide them up her body, bunching her dress up as I go.

"Fucking beautiful," I say, my greedy eyes roving her outstretched body, not knowing where to look first. But I don't let myself hesitate long, not wanting to make the same mistake I made last time. I'm not leaving here until my face is drenched with her cum. Her chest heaves, tits straining against her dress as I lean forward and part her lips with my tongue.

"Shit!" Her hips jerk away from the wall when my tongue hits her clit, and I take the opportunity to grab her ass cheeks, holding her in place as I bury my face between her legs. When I lick her with the flat of my tongue, her thighs tremble and she sucks in a sharp breath at the contact. I do it again and she fucking melts into me.

I don't care what she says. This is not the last time.

TWENTY-FOUR

Valen

"**O**H MY GOD." I CAN'T BELIEVE I'M LETTING THIS happen, here of all places, where anyone could catch us. More than that, I can't believe I'm *enjoying* it. Enjoying it is an understatement. My head falls back against the rough wall when Holden lifts my thigh and hitches it over his shoulder. My hands are itching to touch him, to tangle my fingers in his hair while he works his magic. For the first time in my life, I actually *want* to touch someone, and I can't. The cold wall bites into my back and my arms are already becoming sore in this position, but I'd rather die than stop whatever Holden's doing to me.

My head feels heavy when I look down to see Holden's head move between my thighs as he licks and sucks with reckless abandon, clearly unbothered by the risky location. He pulls back, keeping my thigh over his shoulder as he stares straight between my legs. I don't know why it's so unnerving when he does that, but I fight the urge to clench my thighs together.

"I love how wet you get for me." He wipes his face on the inside of my thigh, illustrating his point.

"Holden, please," I grind out between clenched teeth, and my hips push toward him of their own volition, chasing his mouth. He stills me, pinning me to the wall with a palm to my stomach.

"I need to see these," he says, fingering the neckline of my dress before peeling each side down, freeing one breast at a time. My nipples tighten to the point of pain against the cold, winter air, but the rest of me is on fire. He pinches one nipple and I jerk against the ribbon binding my hands. The material isn't especially thick and he didn't spend much time knotting it, so I think I could wriggle out of it if I tried.

Holden grips behind my knee, pushing it up and toward the wall before leaning back in to take a long, deliberate swipe. "Do you want your hands free?" he asks before doing it again. Each touch of his tongue sends me closer to the edge.

"Yes," I whisper, nodding frantically.

"If untie you, are you going to touch me?"

That gives me pause. "Do you want me to?"

"How about this?" he says, kissing my clit in between sentences. "If you stop touching me, I stop *this*."

I strain to look over my shoulder to see inside the window, but it's no use. "*Fine*. Just make me come."

His smile is nothing short of predatory. "Gladly." He stands, unhooking my hands from the light above my head, but not untying them. He lowers my arms, guiding my hands until I'm circling his neck, my arms stretched over his shoulders. Even with the platforms, he still has a few inches on me. He stares down at me, waiting for me to give him what he wants. I push my fingers through his hair at the base of his skull, and that's all it takes.

He clutches my jaw with one hand, his grip firm but somehow gentle as he angles my face upward. In the next instant, his tongue slips into my mouth. A moan slips free as his unoccupied hand slips between my legs. Two fingers push inside me, and he pulls back to watch them slide in and out.

Abruptly, his fingers are gone, and I'm left feeling empty.

"Stop playing with me!" I whisper-yell.

"I thought you wanted me to play with you," he taunts. "You're the one who broke the rules."

He reaches behind his head where my bound hands hang

slack around his neck, already having forgotten the terms of our agreement. He pulls on the ribbon, freeing my wrists, then stuffs it into his pants pocket. My hands fall to his shoulders, making sure to keep contact this time. But it feels all wrong. His suit is cold and stiff. I want his skin. He kisses me again, and before I've made the conscious decision to do so, I'm unbuttoning his shirt and shoving my hands inside.

He groans, never breaking the connection as he rips his shirt out of the waistband of his pants, giving me better access. I flatten my palms on his warm chest, sliding up and around his shoulders under his shirt. He abandons my lips as his own trail a path down my neck and chest, stopping to suck on each nipple before dropping to his knees again. I don't stop touching him for a second. He grabs two handfuls of my ass, pulling me to his mouth.

"Yes," I breathe, dragging my nails across his scalp as he feasts on me.

"That's it," Holden praises. "Fuck my face. Grind it against me." I freeze when I realize that's exactly what I'm doing.

"Nuh-uh," he scolds. "You're not getting shy on me now." Hands still on my ass, he guides my movements, encouraging me to continue. I start to rock against him, fingers tangling in his hair to keep him anchored to me. His arms hook around the back of my legs, his fingertips biting into my flesh on my inner thighs. My knees are bent, heels skidding against the ground. I'm so close. My legs start to shake, threatening to give out, and I think I forget to breathe as my orgasm builds. Sensing I'm close, Holden plunges his fingers inside me as he pulls my clit into his mouth, sucking hard.

I let out a guttural sound, something between a scream and a cry, doubling over as my legs finally do give out, but Holden keeps me upright, licking me through my orgasm.

"No more," I pant, trying to squeeze my legs shut.

He pulls back enough to look up at me from between my thighs, his mouth glistening. "Seems like you might be into getting your pussy licked after all." His fingers are still inside me, and I feel myself clench around them at his words. He raises an eyebrow, letting me know that he felt it, then slowly pulls them out of my body and holds them up, as if to show me the evidence of exactly how much I liked it shining on his fingers.

"It was all right, I guess." It might sound more convincing if I wasn't panting.

"All right?" he scoffs, standing up and unbuckling his belt with one hand.

I bite down on my lip, trying to hide my inexplicable excitement when I realize his intent. He unbuttons his pants, slides the zipper down, and I reach out and jerk him closer by his waistband, catching him by surprise. His stumbles into me, hands landing on the wall behind my head, to cage me in once again. I peer up at him as I reach into his pants and boxers, wrapping my fingers around him. His jaw is set, holding eye contact with me as I start to work him with my hand.

"Fuck, Valen," he whispers roughly as his head falls forward, eyes squeezed shut. He pushes into my hand that's trapped between us, fucking my fist. Lifting onto my tiptoes, I guide him toward my entrance, dragging the tip up and down the length of me. His eyes shoot open and he searches mine for something, his chest heaving against mine with his ragged breaths. The moment feels too intense, too intimate, like he's seeing something he shouldn't. The way he's looking at me almost hurts, and I can't make sense of why, but it does. When it becomes too much, I reach up to cup his face, pulling him down to kiss me. His hands finally come off the wall, one arm circling my lower back, and the other lifts my right thigh, opening me for him. He's still right there, poised at my entrance. I shift my hips, trying to wiggle my way onto his cock.

"Fuck me," I whisper, in case he's waiting for a verbal cue. He answers by slowly pushing into me, stretching me in the best way as he kisses down my neck.

"Jesus Christ—" a deep voice barks—one that doesn't belong

to Holden—and I slam back to reality, realizing our surroundings. Holden acts before I can make sense of what's happening, shielding me with the flap of his suit jacket. I duck down, hiding my face in his chest.

"Holden." The tone of the man's voice holds a sense of familiarity. Holden's still halfway inside me, his hand on the back of my head, holding me to his chest.

"Get the fuck out," he says, angling his body to block me from their view.

"Wrap it up. Party's almost over."

Wrap it up. He means our little rendezvous, but all I can think about is the fact that Holden did not, in fact, wrap it up. And he's currently inside me. *Oh my God*, what the hell are we doing?

As soon as I hear the door slide shut, I shove Holden off me.

"Are you ok—"

"I have to go," I say, pushing past him to grab my underwear off the ground. They're cold and damp, but my dress is too short to walk back through the house without them on.

"Relax, Valen. That was my dad. He's not going to say anything. Your dirty little secret is safe."

I whirl around on him, eyes wide. "Your dad!" I practically yell. As if it wasn't bad enough when I thought it was a random acquaintance. I straighten out my dress, tucking my boobs back in, then smooth out my hair as good as I can without a mirror. God knows what I look like right now, but I'm betting it's a lot different than how I walked out here.

Everyone will be too drunk to notice my disheveled appearance, I try to tell myself.

"He didn't see you," Holden insists.

I snatch my purse off the ground, shaking my head. That's not the point. What is it about Holden that makes me lose all rational thought?

TWENTY-FIVE

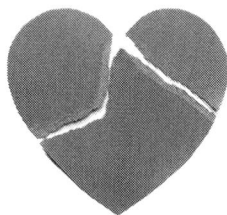

Holden

"FUCK ME," VALEN WHISPERS, AND I SWEAR TO ALL THAT IS fucking holy, it's the sweetest sound I've ever heard in my life. I sink into her warm, wet pussy, inch by inch, and she fucking melts into me. I love when she's hostile and slinging insults at me, but I love it even more when she lets her guard down and gets all soft for me like this.

Her head falls back against the wall and I take the opportunity to kiss her pretty neck, her pussy like a vise on my dick as I work my way in.

"Jesus Christ."

The voice belongs to the last person I want to hear as I'm trying to fuck my girl. I open the side of my jacket, shielding Valen from his view. He's facing me, still inside the house, so he can't see much of her, if at all, and I want to keep it that way.

Instead of leaving us to it, he spits out my name like an accusation.

"Get the fuck out!"

"Wrap it up. Party's almost over."

The second he's gone, Valen's pushing me away, scrambling to cover up and gather her things, saying she needs to leave. I tuck my dick back into my pants, which is a feat in itself with how hard I still am, even as I try to assure her that it's not as big of a deal as she's probably thinking.

"Relax, Valen. That was my dad. He's not going to say anything. Your dirty little secret is safe."

When she spins around, I can tell by the panicked look in her eyes that it was not the right thing to say. I'm pretty sure I just made it worse.

"Your dad?" she screeches.

"He didn't see you." I'm going to kill the bastard for interrupting and scaring Valen off. She shakes her head, not hearing me or not wanting to hear me, I can't be sure. She bends over to grab her purse, then shoves her arm through the strap, and she's gone.

"Fuck." I take a minute to zip my pants and button my shirt. I'm getting tired of getting interrupted. If I could take her ass back to the cabin right now, I would. I walk back inside to find my father waiting for me, eyebrow raised. In the center of the room, my uncle takes the floor once more, thanking people for coming, which is code for *I've got your money. Now get the fuck out.*

"What are you up to?" my father asks, suspicion clear in his tone. *Why does everyone keep asking me that?*

"I think you just had front-row seats to what I was up to," I say, walking past him. He falls into step next to me.

"Not that. What were you and your brother doing snooping around upstairs?"

I stop, facing him. "Finding answers, since evidently that's not something you can seem to accomplish on your own."

"I told you, I have it handled." His voice is low, but firm. Deadly. The voice he saves for rare occasions when he wants us to take him seriously.

"Yeah, well, I'm sick of waiting. You're okay with letting your nephew get away with murder?" I pause, then let out a bitter laugh when I realize the irony. Back when all signs pointed to Grey being the one to kill Danny, my dad covered for him, too. Seems it's becoming a pattern of his. "Of course, you're okay with it. You protected the guy who you thought killed your *own son,*" I spit. "Gotta preserve that family name at all costs, huh?"

"You don't know what the fuck you're talking about," he seethes, getting in my face before he considers our surroundings. He straightens, composing himself. "There are so many things you don't understand, and while you're over here playing detective, you're putting everything I've worked for at risk."

"At least I'm doing something."

"Yes, Holden. Sticking your dick into some run-of-the-mill whore at your uncle's house in between snooping around like you're in an episode of *Scooby Doo* is certainly something. You're really cracking the case."

My fingers curl into fists and my jaw pops from clenching so hard. I'm itching to hit him, but then I think better of it. Instead, I stride up to where my uncle stands, slinging an arm around his neck. He smiles at me, but I see the barely restrained anger behind his eyes. The silent warning in them.

"Thank you all for your generous contributions to—" I pause, stage whispering into my uncle's ear. "What's this for?"

There's a chorus of laughter and nervous chuckles.

"At-risk youth," he answers out of the corner of his mouth, not letting the smile slip. Mine only grows at the irony of it all.

"Right. At-risk youth. Which is especially important to us, with the passing of my brother, Daniel, and with my cousin, Christian, being a missing person for the past year."

A chorus of gasps and confused murmurs fill the room, and I can practically feel my uncle's blood boiling as he bristles next to me. I look him dead in the eye. "I can only hope that no other family will ever have to go through what we have ever again."

If I can't get answers, why not use the public to pressure him into giving them? I look around, taking in the various expressions in the room. Most people look shocked, and some don't so much as bother to hide their entertainment at this juicy little slab of information I just dropped. A bright flash, followed by the sound of a camera's shutter, breaks the silence. My father is furious if his red cheeks and clenched fists are anything to go by. Shayne looks horrified. Thayer is unreadable, as always, but if I'm not mistaken, he's trying to conceal a smirk. Well, at least there's one person I didn't piss off.

I search the room for Valen, wondering if she stuck around for my speech. I don't expect she did, but then I see a flash of her dark hair, sans the ribbon that's still tucked away in my pocket as she all but dashes from the room.

"You son of a bitch," my uncle mutters under his breath.

I waltz away, leaving him to do damage control.

TWENTY-SIX

Valen

"WAKEY WAKEY, EGGS AND BAKEY," SHAYNE sing-songs.

I pull up my sleep mask even though I've been awake for the past hour, contemplating my shitty life choices. Squinting one eye shut against the bright light, I look up at her. She's waving a brown paper bag with a grease stain on the bottom over my face. My stomach growls at the sight. "Nicky's?" I ask, sitting up in bed and reaching over the side to grab my lap desk from the floor to use as a table for our breakfast.

"Only the best for my girl," she says, plopping down onto my bed as she sets the bag onto the desk between us. "I don't think any of the campus cafes are open during break, so I figured I'd grab something." She divvies up the food, handing me an egg, bacon, and avocado croissant, followed by one for herself and a big fruit bowl to share.

"You're too good to me." I don't waste any time taking a huge bite out of it. Delicious. And still warm.

"Then you're really about to love me." She walks out into the kitchen before returning with two iced coffees from Dunkin.

"Marry me already," I mumble around a mouthful of food, causing her to snort out a laugh.

"You're missing an earring." She points to my right ear.

I feel my earlobe as an image of Holden's teeth tugging on

it enters my mind. "Must be in my sheets or something." I take out my other earring and drop it on my nightstand.

"I can't believe Holden did that last night."

I freeze, sandwich suspended mid-air in front of my mouth, thrown by the sudden shift in topic. "What do you mean?"

"You didn't see it? He basically called Judge Ames out and told everyone that Christian was a *missing person.*"

Oh, right. That part. "I caught the end of it as I was leaving. It could've been worse?"

"I don't know. August is livid," she continues before taking a bite.

"What happened after that?"

She shrugs. "Nothing, yet. Holden didn't go back to the house last night. I knocked on his door before I woke you up, but there was no answer. Thayer's checking his apartment right now."

A sinking feeling hits my gut. "Where do you think he went?"

"Who knows. I just hope he's okay. The last time he got shit-faced and took off, I found him with his pants down, chugging straight from the bottle as he was getting head from those two girls. In the *middle of the living room.*"

I drop my half-eaten sandwich, my appetite completely gone now. Shayne takes my reaction as being grossed out by Holden, but if I'm being honest with myself, it's more than that. The thought of him jumping from me to someone else in a matter of minutes…

"He's hurting, Valen. We all have our ways of coping," she says in way of defense.

"It's not that," I start before I realize what she said. "Wait, *was* he drunk?" He definitely didn't seem drunk with me. His breath smelled of weed and spearmint, but I didn't see him with a glass of anything. He's either really good at hiding it, or he works fast.

She gives me a weird look, cocking her head to the side in

thought. "It was New Year's. I just assumed, but I don't know for sure." Her phone vibrates on the bed, and she looks down to read the screen. "He's not at Thayer's apartment either."

"I'm sure he's fine. You know Holden."

"I don't want to know how Samuel's going to retaliate. I'll be at my dad's, so I won't even be here if shit hits the fan."

She's only just recently met her dad for the first time. Her mom kept him away, thanks to a nasty addiction to drugs and gambling, but from what she says, he's been sober for the past four years and wants to get to know his kid. "When do you leave?" I ask.

"Four days. Thayer's coming with me. You know, to make sure he's not secretly a creep."

"Good idea. What does your mom think about all of this?"

She lets out a heavy sigh. "She doesn't love it. But she supports whatever I want to do."

"I'm sure she just doesn't want you to get hurt."

"I know. Especially with everything with Grey going on. I think she's afraid I'm going to get attached and he'll let me down or something. But I don't even know this guy. If he disappeared tomorrow, I wouldn't give a single, solitary fuck."

That's my concern, too, but I don't voice it. Yet anyway. For as long as I've known her, Shayne's always wanted to know who her dad was, and why he wasn't a part of her life. *Of course*, she'd care, whether she'd admit it or not. "You'd totally care."

"Would not."

"Then why bother getting to know him at all?" I challenge.

"Let's talk about your dad instead," she suggests, putting the focus on me and my own fucked-up relationship with my father.

I take a huge bite of my breakfast sandwich, pointing to my mouth and mumbling incoherently.

"That's what I thought," she says smugly. "But seriously, how did it go?"

I roll my eyes, swallowing my food. "I barely saw him." I said hi to him and briefly exchanged pleasantries with his fiancée and her daughter after my run-in with the judge, but that was it. "He wants me to finish out the break with him."

Her eyebrows jump. "And?"

"I haven't spent more than two hours with him since I was fourteen years old. You couldn't *pay* me to stay with him while he's playing house with his new family."

She nods. "That would be pretty awkward."

"I told him I'd go to lunch before he goes home to hear him out, but it's not happening."

She shrugs a shoulder, holding her sandwich with both hands. "At least you'll get a good meal out of it. Maybe he'll buy you a whole new house to sweeten the deal."

TWENTY-SEVEN

Valen

WHAT DOES ONE WEAR TO DINNER WITH THEIR SEMI-estranged father? Jeans are too casual, but a dress is out of the question. It took me way too long to decide on an outfit that fits the occasion. I take one last look in the full-length mirror at my all-black ensemble. Comfy ribbed sweater, leather skirt, tights, oversized leather jacket, and knee-high boots all of the same color. Perfect reflection of my current mood.

I swipe my phone and my little purse—also black—off my bed and move a little faster once I see the time. "Dammit." I'm going to be late. I don't mind making my dad wait on me for a little while considering I've had a lifetime of waiting on him. However, I still have an hour drive ahead of me. More with evening rush hour traffic. I head out into the hall and lock my door, then toss my key card into my purse. I'm speed-walking down the hall and out the door with my head down, too busy making sure I have everything I need in my bag to watch where I'm going. Just as I rush out the double doors, I run right smack into a familiar muscular chest.

My purse falls to the ground, the contents spilling out onto the concrete steps. Key card, car keys, lip balm, sunglasses, driver's license, and a hair clip are scattered everywhere. "Shit!"

"Whoa," Ryan says, steadying me by the shoulders. "You good?"

"Sorry," I say, kneeling to the ground and tucking my hair behind my ear before I start to collect my things. Out of the corner of my eye, I see a man hold one of the doors open, then Ryan drops his bag at his feet and bends down to help me. He's sweating, wearing nothing but a t-shirt and basketball shorts despite the cold, so I assume he's just finished practice.

"Running away from Holden?" he asks, handing me my sunglasses and lip balm.

"He's here?" I can't help but glance back at their door behind me.

"I'm fucking with you." He laughs. "I have no idea."

I roll my eyes. "Sorry, I'm running late and wasn't paying attention."

"All good. See you around."

"Thanks," I say when he hands me the last of my stuff—a rogue hair tie—before we both stand and go our separate ways. I absently mutter a *thank you* to the man holding the door on the way out as I finish stuffing the rest of my things into my purse before zipping it. I check my phone one more time to see that I have forty-five minutes to get there. Yeah, I'm definitely late.

Surprisingly enough, there wasn't much traffic. I would've been on time if parking wasn't such a nightmare. Still, I'm only ten minutes late. Somewhere along the way, my nerves started to calm, and after talking on the phone with Shayne nearly the entire drive here, I feel…cautiously optimistic. My dad has always been a man full of false promises, but maybe the fact that I'm an adult and away from my mom changes things. *Maybe* it will be different this time.

I peer up at the restaurant my dad used to bring me to when I was little. I haven't thought about this place in years. I was a picky kid and wouldn't eat anything on the menu, so he'd would order a plate full of strawberries and pour a giant pile of sugar on my plate to dip them in. Naturally, my mom hated it and complained about the excess sugar. But it was our thing. Even as I got older, I never did end up liking the food, but I was happy to go for the strawberries alone. And the rare moments I got to spend with my dad.

Just as I'm about to walk inside, I spot my dad through the big, glass window. Any hope that he was genuinely interested in having a relationship with me evaporates at the sight of his fiancée and her daughter next to him. He said it would just be the two of us. I watch them from the outside looking in, smiling and conversing like the happy little family that they are. What would it be like to have this version of my dad? And why does his other family get this one?

When the server places their plates in front of them, I huff out a sardonic laugh. They didn't even wait for me before they ordered. I let my hand fall away from the door and walk right back to my car.

Welp. Can't say I didn't try.

I stop short of my bedroom door when I see that it's slightly ajar. I know I closed it before I left. "Shayne?" I call out. She doesn't respond, confirming what I already know. She's not home. She's been staying with Thayer over the break, and I haven't seen her since the other morning when she brought me breakfast.

I toe the door open, peeking into my room and immediately feel dumb for being so paranoid. No one's here. Nothing's out of place. Tossing my purse onto my bed, I send a text to Shayne to see when she'll be back before I set my phone on the table next to my bed.

I bend over to pull off my boots, and when I stand up, something shining on my nightstand catches my eye. My earrings.

Both of them. I pinch one between my thumb and finger as the little star dangles back and forth. This is the one I lost on New Year's. The other one is a moon. Shayne must've found it lying around somewhere.

"Hey!"

Shayne's voice makes me jump and drop my earring. I spin around to face her, hand on my chest.

"Jesus, why so jumpy?" She walks toward me and bends over to pluck the earring off the floor. "You found it. Cute," she says before holding it out and dropping it in my outstretched palm.

"You didn't leave this on my nightstand?"

"No." She frowns. "I just got here. Why?"

"I found it on my nightstand." I shake my head when it occurs to me. *Holden.* He must have noticed it after I ran off. It's just like him to sneak into my room to return my earring like nothing happened.

"Hmm." Shayne shrugs a shoulder. "Maybe it got tangled in your hair and fell out when you were getting into bed or something."

"Probably," I agree, even though I know better, dropping the earring inside the drawer of my nightstand before closing it.

"So, how'd it go with your dad?"

With a heavy sigh, I give her a look that tells her exactly how it went.

"That good, huh?"

"His *other* daughter and his fiancée crashed our dinner." I walk out of my room, into the kitchen area, and she follows.

"No! Tell me you're joking."

"I wish I were. Actually, I take that back. I think I was the one who crashed their dinner."

"What happened?"

I hand her the doggy bag of dessert I brought home for her. I didn't eat with my dad, but I did stop at a cute bakery on the way home. "I don't know." I shrug, pausing to take a drink from my water bottle, then set it back on the counter. "I never went inside. Saw them through the window and left before he even knew I was there."

Her face falls and she pulls me in for a hug. "Assholes," she says, her chin on my shoulder, her arm hooked around my neck. I scrunch my nose to stop the sting of tears threating to form. "If I were there, I'd have kicked all their asses."

I snort out a laugh at the seriousness of her tone, then shake my head. "This is actually a good thing. I feel better knowing where I stand."

She pins me with a skeptical look, but she doesn't call me on it. "He loves you. He just has a shit way of showing it."

"Either way, it goes without saying that I'm definitely not spending the rest of the break with him."

"Good. Maybe I should cancel on my sperm donor, too. We can make it a thing. Spend the rest of the break together, just you and me, and bitch about how fucked up the men who impregnated our mothers are."

"Nice try. You're going."

"But I'm nervous." She pouts. "What if he's still on drugs? What if he's a *murderer*?" She widens her eyes. I reach into the bag of desserts she's still clutching and pull out a cookie before stuffing it into her mouth to cut off her rambling.

"Yes, but you'll never stop wondering if you don't at least try to get to know him. Do it for you. Not for him. If he turns out to be a loser—which, let's be honest, is entirely possible— well, then you'll know. And then we can start our fatherless child club."

"Deal."

"Plus, you'll have Thayer. And hey, you never know, you just might secretly have a wicked stepsister, too."

It's her turn to reach into the bag and she throws a cookie at my face. "I have enough sibling drama as it is."

"That's an understatement." I see my phone light up from the corner of my eye. I assume it's going to be another message from my dad chewing me out about bailing on dinner, but it's

Holden's name that pops up onto my home screen. I quickly snatch my phone up.

> **Holden: Miss me?**
>
> **Me: Like a hole in the head.**
>
> **Holden: You sure you haven't been waiting for my call? That was a pretty quick response.**
>
> **Me: Don't flatter yourself. I'm with Shayne. I don't want her to see your text and get the wrong idea.**
>
> **Holden: Which would be…?**
>
> **Me: That there's something going on between us.**

The three dots pop up and disappear a couple of times before disappearing altogether.

"You're smiling at your phone," Shayne says it like an accusation. "So that rules out your dad."

"Am not."

> **Holden: Let me come over tonight.**
>
> **Me: I just said Shayne's here. Not happening.**
>
> **Holden: So if she wasn't, you'd let me?**

Shit.

> **Me: Go away.**
>
> **Holden: Come over here then. I want to talk to you about something.**

Here? Does that mean he *is* on campus?

> **Me: No.**
>
> **Holden: Suit yourself. I'll be over in 5. You know I have no issue with Shayne or anyone else hearing us.**
>
> **Me: Fine. I'll be there later. Ten o'clock.**
>
> **Holden: If you insist.**

God, he's infuriating. And relentless.

TWENTY-EIGHT

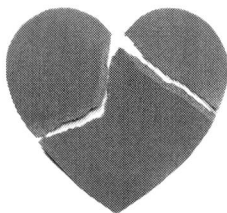

Valen

I T'S JUST AFTER TEN WHEN I QUIETLY WALK OUT INTO THE HALL, closing the door softly behind me. Shayne went to sleep early after I helped her pack while we watched a movie. I stand in front of Holden's door, making a mental list of all the things I'm going to say to him about how we can't keep doing this, but the words die on my tongue when his door swings open and he's wearing nothing but a towel. His hair is wet and hanging over his forehead. His forearms are braced against the top of the doorframe, bringing attention to his biceps. My eyes trail down his chest, not stopping until they take in the happy trail right above the knot in his towel. When I make it back up to his face, he's simply smirking, patiently waiting for me to finish taking my fill.

"Nope," is all I say before I do an about-face and march the three steps it takes to reach my door. Holden chuckles, his hand wrapping around my upper arm, and then I'm being pulled into his dorm.

"No?" he asks, shutting the door behind me. My back is against the wall with him towering over me—his favorite position, it seems.

I peer over his shoulder, looking for any traces of Ryan. His floor plan is a mirror image of ours, but the contents could not be more different. There are two black leather recliners in front of a mounted TV that's far too big for the space with three different gaming consoles stuffed into the stand underneath it. A matching loveseat off to the side, pushed against the far left wall. In front of the loveseat is a glass coffee table. Aside from a bong, a pizza box, a container of protein powder, and a couple of empty water bottles, it's surprisingly clean. It doesn't smell either. In fact, all I can smell is the fresh scent of body wash wafting from Holden.

"No one's here," Holden says, answering my unspoken question.

Oh, goody.

Needing to regain the upper hand, I place my palm against his warm, still-damp chest and push him backward before walking over to perch on the arm of one of the recliners. "You wanted to talk to me about something?"

He nods, moving toward me.

"Good. Me, too," I say, trying to keep my eyes trained on his instead of venturing south. I don't know what's gotten into me. I've never been so sex-crazed in my life.

"Ladies first."

"Don't you want to…get more comfortable first?"

"If you insist," he says as his hand unties the knot of his towel and releases it. "There. Much better. Proceed."

"That is not what I meant," I say, reaching a hand out to catch his towel before it falls to the floor between us. "More clothes. Not less."

"My bad." His hand replaces mine on the towel, and then he's walking into one of the bedrooms. "You can come in," he calls out after a couple of seconds. The last place I should be is in Holden Ames' bedroom. But curiosity gets the best of me, so I follow the sound of his voice. He's standing in a pair of gray sweats and nothing else, somehow managing to look even more indecent than he did with nothing but a towel on.

His bed takes up most of the small space with a desk in the opposite corner. I walk over to it, looking at the few pictures he has. One is of him and Danny playing basketball. Another is of him with Danny, Thayer, and Christian, all with their arms around each other at The Falls. This one I recognize from the slideshow they played the night of Danny's memorial.

"I saw what you did on New Year's Eve," I say, my back still to him. "How did he take it?"

"My uncle?" he asks. "He didn't like it. Even decided to come all the way here to tell me so himself."

"Did you find anything useful?"

"Not unless you count some sketchy texts from a guy by the name of CJ about discreet wire transfers."

"What do you think that's about?"

"Money laundering. Fraud. Who knows." He doesn't seem particularly disturbed by the possibility, like it's nothing out of the ordinary.

I turn around to face him. "Shayne seems to think he's dangerous."

He scoffs, "Must not think he's too dangerous seeing as how she let you play decoy."

"That was different. Publicly calling him out like that? That was beyond reckless."

He smirks, sauntering up to me until we're only inches apart. "Worried about me, Sweet Valentine?"

I roll my eyes. "Worried about your self-preservation instincts."

"I don't have those. Which explains why I'm still pursuing you."

"Hilarious," I say flatly.

"Jokes aside," he says, his tone becoming uncharacteristically serious. His palm cups my jaw, his long fingers curving around my neck, sliding into the back of my hair and gripping firmly. "I know what I'm getting myself into. But I don't want you near him again."

"Actually, I was just about to call him up and ask him out for coffee," I deadpan.

"I'm serious, Valen."

I look up into his eyes, noticing that there's something else beneath his usual playful demeanor. His eyes are rimmed with red with dark circles around them. He looks exhausted.

"Fine." I shrug, acutely aware of the fact that he's still cupping my face. "It's not like we'll ever be in the same room together again, anyway."

"Even if you are—"

"Jesus, Holden, okay. I will not ever speak to your uncle again. What's going on? And does it have anything to do with the fact that you look like a zombie?"

His hand falls from my face, taking his warmth with him as he takes a step back. "I haven't slept much," he admits, rubbing his eyes with the heels of his hands before running his fingers through his wet hair to push it off his forehead. "Which brings me to why you're here."

"You…want me to knock you out?" I'm not connecting the dots.

"I want you to sleep with me."

I arch an eyebrow. I mean, I figured that was what he wanted, but I didn't expect him to blurt it out so eloquently.

"I mean literally *sleep* with you. Next to you. I think we should sleep together."

"*Why*?"

"Because for some fucked-up reason, I haven't had a decent night's sleep since we were at the cabin, and I'm fucking desperate at this point." He sits on the edge of his bed with his elbows resting on his spread knees.

"You're serious," I say, the skepticism clear in my voice. "Just sleep?"

"No. I fully plan on fucking you again. And then we can sleep."

I shake my head. "You're unbelievable. If you remember correctly, we said last time was the last time."

"I'm honest," he corrects, "and if *you* remember correctly, we were interrupted before we got to *have* a last time."

"That's called divine intervention. Even the universe knows this is a bad idea."

"Fuck the universe. Tell me the truth."

"About what?"

"That you like how I fuck you." He reaches out to hook his finger into the waistband of my leggings, tugging me forward until I'm standing between his legs. His hands grip my hips as he looks up at me with heat in his eyes. "That you want to do it again. That we were both lying to ourselves if we thought for one second that once would be enough."

Technically twice. I open my mouth to tell him no, to tell him that it was a mistake and has the potential to blow up in our faces, but the words won't come out.

"That you haven't stopped thinking about it since," he continues, curling his fingers inside my leggings. He drags them down slowly, inch by inch, taking my underwear along with them. He stops once they're mid-thigh. The pulse in my clit throbs, my entire body buzzing with anticipation. Because he's right, and I hate that he is. "We both want this. Why should we stop?" His arms band around my thighs, holding them together as he jerks me forward. I steady myself with my hands in his hair, sliding my fingers through the wet strands.

"You have such a pretty pussy," he says before leaning forward. Just before his tongue can make contact, I tighten my grip in his hair and angle his head back. When he looks up at me, his eyes are blazing, thick with lust.

"I came here to end this."

"And yet here you are."

"Unfortunately for me, I have an itch that only you can seem to scratch."

His lips spread into a proud smile at my admission. It makes him look even more attractive, and I hate him for it a little. "I fail to see the problem here."

I swallow hard, knowing I'm about to agree to something that might be a really bad idea. "If we're going to do this, we need ground rules."

"I'm not much of a rule follower, but with your pussy two centimeters from my face, I think you could convince me to agree to just about anything."

I release my grip on his hair, biting back a laugh. "This stays between us."

"Fine," he agrees easily, leaning in to kiss the top of my thigh.

"This is strictly casual. No feelings."

"What's the matter? Afraid I'm going to break your little heart?"

"Please. You couldn't even give it a papercut."

He smirks. "Whatever you say." Another kiss, this time to the sensitive spot where my thigh meets my pelvis. "I'm not interested in breaking your heart, anyway. I'd much rather break your p—"

"Do not finish that sentence."

"No fucking anyone else," he says, adding in a stipulation of his own. I freeze and he feels it, looking up at my horrified expression. "You *don't* want to be exclusive?"

"God, no."

"So, if I were to hook up with someone else—"

"It'd be none of my business."

He narrows his eyes. "I don't want anyone else."

"Again. None of my business."

"Are you planning on fucking other people?"

"That would be none of *your* business." Am I planning on it? Negative. It's hard enough finding a guy I can stand to be in the same room with for more than five minutes, let alone finding someone bearable enough to get naked with. But everyone knows the moment you start expecting monogamy from your friend with benefits situation is the moment you set yourself up for disaster. I already know how this is going to go.

I'll let him fuck me until the thrill of it expires, which can't be too long considering his track record.

Holden holds my gaze as his tongue slips between my lips. His hands find my hips, using them to slide me across his tongue, back and forth. I gasp at the sensation, my fingers grasping his hair for support, or to pull him closer, or maybe both. All too soon, he pulls away.

"No fucking other people," he says again.

"Holden," I practically growl with frustration.

"As long as we're doing this, you're mine and only mine. Say it."

"Fine," I relent. "I'm yours." Before he can dive back in, I add, "But once Christmas break ends, so does this."

"I'll take it."

At first, he licks me soft and slow with the flat of his tongue, but soon he's burying his face between my legs, angling his head sideways to devour me, never breaking eye contact. His hands grip the thickest part of my thighs, right under my ass, keeping me in place as he sucks my clit into his mouth. My mouth falls open at the sensation, and when I finally give in to the need to grind against him, he growls his approval.

My knees buckle and I start to slide down into his lap, but he doesn't let up. Instead, he bends with me, keeping his mouth fused between my legs. "Holden, I can't," is all I manage to get out before he's throwing me onto his bed, ripping my pants off, and wrenching my legs apart. He dives back in, his mouth closing around my clit once more. I clutch at his blankets, head pressed back into his mattress as I come from his mouth for the second time in a matter of days.

I'm still trying to catch my breath when Holden hovers over me, lips swollen and glistening. His fingers stroke me softly, playing in the wet mess he created, and I jerk at the sensation, feeling raw in more ways than one. "I can't decide how I want you," he says, pushing my shirt up to my collarbone to expose my chest. "I want to see all of you—touch all of you at the same time." He dips down to suck my nipple into his mouth. A moan crawls its way up my throat at the same time his thick fingers push inside me—and just like that, I want more.

"I don't care how you do it. Just fuck me."

"I love when you get all bossy and horny." He scoops me up into his lap and sits on the edge of his bed, guiding my legs around him. With one arm around my waist, he reaches underneath me to tug his sweatpants down. His dick is hard, standing straight up. He's taking far too long, so I rise onto my knees, angling myself over him before I slide down in one quick motion.

"Holy fuck," Holden hisses at the same time I gasp, my head falling forward. It's so deep. Too deep. "Condom," he chokes out.

I still at his words. "Shit," I say, trying to slide off of him, but he holds me in place.

He flexes his hips, moving inside me. His eyes fall shut as if it's too much. "Are you on birth control?"

Heart pounding, it's all I can do to nod.

"You good with this?" he asks, his lips against my cheek as his hand slides into my hair at the nape of my neck.

I clamp down on my bottom lip, nodding again.

"Good. Because I need to fuck you now."

I roll my hips in response, sliding up and down his length. His hand on my lower back forces me closer, making it feel deeper than I thought possible. His hands move to grasp my hips, lifting, before slamming me back down onto him. I cry out, mouth falling open, and he takes the opportunity to slip his tongue inside and devour my mouth. He swallows my moans as he fucks up into me, and all I can do is cling to him and try to survive. His skin is damp with sweat as I kiss him back, our bodies grinding against each other, my hands clawing at the back of his neck. I feel my orgasm building, desperately chasing it as he breaks our kiss to look down between us.

He leans back, eyes zeroing in on where we're joined as he effortlessly lifts me up and down his length.

"Look at how well you take me," he says, staring, mesmerized. His bottom lip is trapped between his teeth, abs flexing with each movement, the veins in his neck more pronounced than usual.

"It feels so good," I say, closing my eyes, chin tipping toward the ceiling. I feel him shift again, and then his hot mouth is around my nipple sucking hard. "Oh God!"

"I can feel you squeezing me," he says before giving the other side the same attention.

Suddenly, it's all too much. My muscles tighten as the pressure builds, and I start to ride him hard and fast as he sucks on my nipples.

"Holden—" My legs no longer have enough strength left in them, but he takes over, pumping into me as I come. I think I scream, but I'm too far gone to know for sure as I contract around him, over and over. He follows me over the edge, his face in my neck as he fucks me through my orgasm, then suddenly, I'm being lifted off him, and I feel his cum paint my stomach and chest.

Cheeks burning, I look down between us, seeing his still-hard cock and the evidence left on my skin. Holden's eyes are glued to the same spot, chest heaving.

"This might be the prettiest sight I've ever seen."

I take us both by surprise when I let out a laugh. Holden smiles, lifting me by my waist and tossing me onto the bed.

"Stay there," he instructs. He stands, giving me a glimpse of his ass as he pulls his sweats up on his way out the door. He returns a second later with a towel in hand, then straddles my thighs. I try to take the towel from him, but he snatches it back, holding it out of reach.

"A gentleman always cleans up his ji—"

I snatch the pillow next to me and whack him in the face with it.

He begins to clean himself off me with the wet corner of the towel. It's warm against my skin, sending goosebumps across my flesh. He leans over me, his fist planted in the mattress beside my head before dipping down to swirl his tongue around my nipple. He takes it into his hot mouth, sucking gently before releasing it with a pop, then kisses the hardened tip, all while continuing to clean me up. His lips drag across my skin to the other side, giving it the same attention, and I have to squeeze my thighs together to stifle the ache between them because I already want more.

Fuck.

When he's done, he rolls off me, taking the pillow I threw at him with him. I clear my throat, sitting up abruptly. I reach for my shirt on the floor, but Holden hooks his forearm around my waist, dragging me backward. "Where do you think you're going?"

"Shayne's going to wonder where I am in the morning."

"That wasn't part of the deal. Now snuggle me and work your devil magic."

"My devil magic?" I ask, turning to face him.

"Mhm. Something about you puts me into a coma. This is me testing a theory."

I rear back to give him a dirty look. "Are you saying I'm boring?"

"You are so many things, Sweet Valentine," he says, hand curling around the curve of my butt before gripping a handful, "but never boring. I promise you that. Now relax. I'm not holding you hostage. I'm just…holding you."

My head is on his chest with his right arm underneath me, my bent arms between us with my hands balled into fists. I force my hands to relax, rolling my eyes. "I think this would qualify as both."

He pulls the blanket over us before his left hand slides underneath it, hooking around the back of my knee, positioning me so my thigh is draped across his lower stomach. The arm underneath me reaches out to turn the lamp on his night-stand off, leaving only the dim light from the other room to fil-ter through the opening. I'm still tense, not used to cuddling, especially when I'm completely naked with my best friend's brother for all intents and purposes. But then I feel the tips of his fingers on my back, trailing up and down my spine. The tension leaks out of me little by little at his touch, lulling me into a false sense of comfort.

His breathing starts to deepen, his fingers on my spine slowing down until his hand eventually comes to a stop, rest-ing at the curve of my hip. When the hand that's still latched to my thigh twitches, I know he's asleep. After a minute or two, I lift my head from his shoulder, looking down at his face. His eyebrows are pulled together, the space between them creased. I smooth it out with my thumb, then trace his eye-brows with tentative fingers. He really is beautiful when he isn't running his mouth.

Speaking of…

His mouth is my favorite feature. Even before he demon-strated his—ahem—*abilities* on New Year's and again tonight, I've found it hard to look away from his lips. They're full, al-most to the point of pouty, the top one slightly bigger than the bottom. It should be illegal for one person to have this face, this hair, and this body. No wonder he isn't used to not getting his way. I don't think he's been told no a day in his life.

Which is exactly how I ended up in his bed. And the sad part? I'm not even mad about it. I can't let myself stay the night, though. It feels too much like crossing some arbitrary line. Shayne also leaves tomorrow, and I want to be there be-fore she does. Not to mention the fact that I'd have to explain to her where I disappeared to in the middle of the night if she woke up and I wasn't there.

I lie here for another hour or so before I try to disentan-gle myself slowly and quietly, peeling my leg from where it has practically melded to his stomach. I feel sticky with sweat—mostly his—and wet between my legs. I'm going to need another shower already. Holden stirs a little, rolling onto his side when I finally free myself of his cocoon, but he doesn't wake. I quickly find my clothes and throw them on before making my way across the hall and back to my dorm.

I tiptoe into my room and slide into bed before checking the time on my phone I left forgotten on my nightstand. It's 1:45 A.M. Huh. It didn't feel like I was gone that long. Maybe I did doze off for a few. Right on time, my mind starts to race like it does every night before bed, reminding me of every stupid thing I've ever said or done. Tonight, I vacillate between replaying the scene with my dad and his family in the restaurant and feeling like the worst friend for lying by omission about sleeping with Holden. Eventually, my brain quiets enough for me to drift to sleep.

I don't know how much time has passed when I wake to being lifted from my bed. A scream works its way up my throat, but a warm palm is slapped over my mouth, muffling the sound. It's too dark to see anything, but his scent gives him away before panic can take hold. Holden.

"What the hell are you doing?" I whisper-yell.

He throws me over his shoulder and marches out of my room, making his way through the living room area and out into the hall.

"Holden, put me down!" Is he asleep? Maybe he's sleep-walking. Am *I* asleep? Maybe I'm dreaming.

He doesn't say a word. He simply carries me across the hall and to his bed before dumping me into it. "Stay," he sleepily orders before climbing in with me. This time, I'm on my back and Holden wraps his arm around my middle, using my stomach as his pillow.

"I'm not a dog, Holden."

"No, you're not," he agrees. "Dogs are much more obedient."

"Asshole." I try to free myself from his clutches, but he only tightens his hold on me, making it hard to breathe. I sigh and he relaxes his hold, sensing my surrender. I'm too tired to put up a real fight, so I reluctantly accept my fate as Holden's personal teddy bear for the night. He kisses my stomach where my shirt has ridden up, then mumbles something that sounds like *thank you* before promptly passing back out.

Insomnia, my ass.

TWENTY-NINE

Holden

I WAKE UP FEELING LIKE I'VE JUST HIBERNATED FOR AN ENTIRE winter, well rested and hungry as fuck. I came hard and slept even harder. That is, until I woke up from a shit dream to find Valen was gone. Luckily, I managed to wake up before it got too bad. Then I marched my ass over to her room and carried her back to my bed where she belongs.

Sometime between then and now, I must have loosened my death grip on Valen because she's now curled up on her left side, facing me with knees tucked to her chest, her head lying on my bicep. That explains the dead arm. I lift a piece of dark hair from her face, tucking it behind her ear. She frowns in her sleep, her lips pushing out into a pout as she makes an annoyed sound and wiggles in closer to me, wedging her knee between my legs. I'll take that as a good sign, conscious or not.

I didn't expect her to be here after having to drag her back to my bed last night. I thought she'd be gone at first light. To be fair, it's still early. Too fucking early to be awake, so I wrap my arm around her, pulling her in closer, and shut my eyes. Waking up to Valen in my bed feels equal parts foreign and… good. Right. The post-fuck regret is once again noticeably absent. The only thing that would make this better is if she was still naked. And sitting on my dick.

She stirs, her legs stretching before her eyelids flutter open. I see the moment the confusion clears, her eyes growing wide.

"Shit, what time is it?" She sits up impressively fast for just waking up.

"Good morning to you, too," I say, stretching out my dead arm and massaging my shoulder as I roll onto my back.

"For some more than others," she mutters, giving a pointed look at my dick. I laugh, rolling her underneath me, nestling between her warm thighs.

"It *is* a good morning. Because of you." She stares up at me, looking slightly bewildered. She probably expects me to go for round two, which I'm not opposed to. "Thank you," I add. Feeling weirdly exposed, I dip down to kiss the corner of her jaw and roll off her.

She doesn't say anything. Just clears her throat as she stands, taming her wild hair with her fingers. "I have to go."

I nod. I'd offer to walk her across the hall, but I don't think she'd appreciate Shayne seeing us doing the walk of shame. I do walk her to the door, though.

Just before she leaves, she pauses in the hall outside my door, turning to face me. "Where'd you find my earring, by the way?"

I frown, not knowing what the hell she's talking about. She notices my confusion and elaborates.

"My earring. It fell out on New Year's when we were—"

"Having hot secret sexy time?" I finish for her.

She rolls her eyes, but she can't hide the blush that blooms on her cheeks. "Yeah, that. Maybe next time don't sneak into my room to return it, though. Kinda creepy." The last part is laced with enough humor to let me know she's halfway joking, but I freeze when my mind finally catches up.

I didn't return her earring. I didn't even know it was missing. There's only one explanation. Rage bubbles up inside of me at the thought of him being in her room. Was she home at the time? Did he make his move the day he tried—and failed—to scare me into backing down? I don't know if he'd actually hurt her, or if it's one of his intimidation tactics, and to be honest, I don't give a fuck. I'm going to make sure he never tries it again.

"Holden?" Valen asks, concern etched in her pretty features.

I try to force a smile that probably looks more like a grimace. I don't want to scare her. Not until I know the facts. "I'll call you later," is all I can think to say before I shut the door on her stunned expression. I pace back and forth, fingers lacing together at the back of my neck as I try to figure out my next move. Thayer's taking Shayne to her dad's today, so I'll have to fill him in when he gets back. Instead, I pick up the phone and call the last person on this earth that would ever expect to hear from me.

"What do you want?" he asks, skipping the pleasantries. Fine with me.

"How would you like a chance to piss off your sperm donor and the judge at the same time?"

"Not interested in whatever fucked-up game you're playing with your family," he says in a bored tone of voice.

"It involves Shayne."

There's a pause followed by a curse, and I know I have his attention. "I'm listening."

"Meet me in the parking lot closest to Shayne's dorm."

A couple hours later, I'm approaching my uncle's house for the second time in a week's time with Grey charging up the steps right behind me.

"So, do you have a plan?" he asks, clearly not overly confident in me. "Or are we going in half-cocked and full of piss and vinegar?"

"Yeah. First, we fuck him up, then we threaten him with the video from the day at The Falls. We'll be back by dinner." The video that shows my brother's last moments alive. The video I had to delete from my phone because I watched it on repeat. Not that it helped. It still replays on a loop in my brain. Luckily, like Thayer, Grey is also a masochist and held on to it for safekeeping. Or, more likely, blackmail. Can't say I blame him, especially since he was our prime suspect until we found out the truth.

Grey shrugs a shoulder, as if it doesn't really matter to him either way. "Good enough for me." I knew he'd carry his fair share of residual hatred for my uncle, and my—our—dad. He doesn't like being related to us any more than we like being related to him, but more than that, he hates that we've claimed his baby sister as ours.

We come to a stop, looking up at the sprawling estate. I smile over at my temporary ally, already feeling the adrenaline in my veins. "Ready?"

He turns the handle in response and throws it open, sending the door flying into a potted plant next to it that shatters on impact. The sound echoes through the foyer, alerting everyone in a five-mile radius to our presence.

"Way to make an entrance." I look over at him, eyebrow raised, and he only shrugs, once again. The sound of high heels hurriedly clacking along the floor draws my attention to the other side of the foyer to find my aunt Rebecca staring at the pile of fractured porcelain and soil. Her hands cover her mouth in shock, but when she sees me, her shoulders sag with relief.

"Oh honey, step aside. You don't want to get all dirty. Or worse, hurt," she says as if I'm a kid who just spilled a glass of milk. "Let me get the broom."

Grey sends me an *is this bitch serious* look. Unfortunately, the answer is yes.

"Where is he?" I ask, stopping her from skittering out of the room. She swallows hard, clearly more unnerved than she was letting on, and motions toward the kitchen with a tilt of her head before making herself scarce.

We walk into the kitchen to find my uncle eating at the table. He doesn't so much as glance up from his plate when he hears us approach. He stabs a piece of meat with his fork and

214 | CHARLEIGH ROSE

happily plops it into his mouth. He isn't surprised by my presence. In fact, I'll bet he was counting on it.

"Well, you wanted me here. I'm here." That's why he left the earring, isn't it? He was sending a message. He had to know I'd show up.

He finally looks at me, holding up his index finger, signaling for me to wait while he finishes chewing. "Holden," he greets me with a fake-ass smile. "Good of you to stop by." His eyes travel past me, flashing with surprise when he realizes Grey is with me. That's one thing we both didn't see coming. "Traded out your usual sidekick, huh?"

I cross my arms over my chest, not responding to his goading. Grey is silent next to me, completely unreadable.

Samuel's gaze ping-pongs between us before accepting that he won't be getting anything in terms of a response. "I get it. Brothers can be tricky."

"You know what else must be tricky? Sneaking into little girls' dorm rooms without anyone noticing."

"On the contrary, you have no idea how easy it was." He stands from the table, smoothing out his tie. "Funny story. During the gala, a young girl approached me, not-so-subtly trying to pump me for information. In my own home, to boot. It didn't make sense to me then. I didn't recognize her." He smirks at me. "And believe me. A girl like that? I'd remember."

I clench my jaw so hard my ears ring.

"Quite the coincidence that she lives right across the hall from you." He rounds the table, coming closer to where we stand. "But I don't believe in those. What were you looking for in my office, Holden? If you have questions, all you have to do is ask. There's no need to drag innocent people into this. We don't want anyone else getting hurt, do we?"

I charge at him, pushing him back until he's against the wall behind him with my forearm at his throat. "Stay the fuck away from her. If you have a problem with me, take it up with me."

He tries to pry my arm away but fails, his face turning red.

I loosen my hold enough for him to get his words out. "I was simply returning something that belonged to her."

I've had enough of the cryptic games. I shove my forearm back against his windpipe, watching as he struggles to conceal any sign of panic or pain. "I'm sitting on something that can end your entire career, your entire fucking *life*. My patience is wearing thin. Stay away from Valen. Stay away from Shayne. Or say goodbye to everything you've worked for."

I step back, releasing him, gauging his reaction. I've always assumed that he knows about the video, but it's not until this moment that I know for sure. He doesn't seem fazed by my threat in the slightest. His answering smile is arrogant, and I know with that one look that he's about to drop a bomb.

"You mean the video my *own son* already turned in? Yeah, that won't be a problem."

I'm frozen in disbelief, his words echoing in my ears as my mind tries to make sense of what he just said. *Christian actually went through with it?* And Samuel simply…made it disappear? This entire time, we assumed Christian pussied out, all the while holding on to the video for a rainy day at my father's request.

"You're lying." He has to be. My family has a long history of using their money and influence to make things and *people* go away, but he's not untouchable.

"I assure you, I'm not."

"Then we take it to the news stations, pass it around social media. Do you think your new pal the governor would be cool with a judge covering up a crime?" After all, he's the one who has the power to appoint judges and remove them from office.

"You are so far out of your depth it's almost comical." He chuckles as if he's unbothered, but the way he speaks through gritted teeth says otherwise. "My sins are nothing compared to the people in power. This wouldn't even put a *dent* in my career, as far as scandals go. This is family business, and it should be dealt with between family. But since we're talking videos, I have one you might be interested in."

My chest feels tight, knowing I'm not going to like whatever he's about to show me. He fishes his phone out of his pants pocket, then holds it out for me to see. It's a still image of Valen and me on New Year's Eve. Her head is thrown back and I'm kneeling before her, face buried between her legs. The angle is too high and the patio too dark to see any details, but it does nothing to tamp down the rage I feel at him seeing her like this.

"After I got word that you and your brother were sticking your noses where they don't belong, I thought it would be a good idea to check my security cameras. You should think twice next time you decide to fuck your bitch in public. Not that I blame you. I watched the whole thing, and a pussy like that could make a man do anything. I might try it out myself. When you're done with her, of course." He winks.

That's all it takes for me to charge him again, but this time, he's ready for me. My sole focus is on his phone, which allows him the chance to hit me square in the mouth. I wipe my lips with the back of my hand, leaving a streak of blood on my sleeve, then spit a bloody mouthful right at his face. "I'm not your fuckin' kid. I hit back."

I pull back my fist and swing, sending it right into his jaw, making him stagger back. Suddenly, Grey appears to my right, and he doesn't give Samuel any time to recover. He hits him again, this time laying him out. Jesus Christ. I didn't know Grey had it in him. He holds Samuel in place with a knee on his chest and a hand at his throat.

"I've wanted to do that for two years," Grey explains casually, as if discussing the weather.

I retrieve Samuel's phone from the floor, chest heaving. I delete the video from both the security app and his phone before walking over to the counter. I hold his phone face-down on the edge of the counter with one hand. Using the other hand, I send the butt of my palm into it, snapping it in half until the screen shatters and the back detaches. Once I'm satisfied that it's completely unsalvageable, I walk back over and squat down next to his head.

"You do realize that's not the only copy I have?" He coughs, gripping at Grey's forearm. "I can enjoy it any time I want."

I raise an eyebrow, surprised he's dumb enough to taunt me with the information, given his current position. My uncle has trouble with anything more advanced than sending an email. I highly doubt he had the knowledge or the foresight to back it up. No, he just wants to shut me up by whatever means necessary. "I'm starting to believe you have a death wish."

I stand, dropping the bent piece metal on his face, and Grey takes that as his cue to stand. Wordlessly, we walk away as my uncle pulls himself to a sitting position.

"I'll be sure to let your father know you paid me a visit!"

THIRTY

Holden

"YOU AND VALEN, HUH?"

We're back on campus, and apart from declining my offer to smoke, those are the first words out of Grey's mouth. I guess neither of us was in a talking mood, too busy trying to make sense of tonight's revelations. I'm a little surprised by his question, considering there are more pressing matters to discuss, but Valen is a safer subject. One that doesn't feel so fucking heavy.

Inhaling, I hold the smoke in my lungs and look at him out of the corner of my eye while trying to figure out how to respond. Today we might have called some sort of unspoken truce, but it doesn't mean I'm ready to trade secrets and braid each other's hair.

"It's complicated. Shayne doesn't know." It's risky throwing it out there like that. Who's to say he won't run to his sister the second I leave just to spite me?

"None of my business," he says. "Just trying to gauge whether my sister is going to be his target again. Even if he's set his sights on Valen, my sister *lives* with her. She's bound to get caught up in the crossfire. Hasn't she dealt with enough from your family?"

So much for sticking to a safe subject.

"And *I* live right across the hall."

"And yet, he still managed to waltz into their dorm without anyone noticing."

Feeling my anger rise, I shake my head. I take another hit, waiting a beat before I speak again. "I wouldn't let anything happen to her, you know? She's my sister, too. I love her."

Grey works his jaw, staring straight ahead. "Yeah. I know."

Wanting to break the tension, I decide to give him shit. "And not in the way Thayer loves her. With his penis."

He punches me on the arm.

"Ow, motherfucker!"

He snatches the joint from between my pinched fingers, then takes a drag. I laugh, rubbing at my arm. "In fact, she might even be more my sister than yours now."

"What the fuck does that even mean?" he asks on a cough, his voice hoarse. Fucking baby lungs.

"Well, if Thayer keeps fucking her, technically, she'll be my sister-*in-law*, too." We both know it's far past just *fucking*. Honestly, I'm surprised Thayer hasn't already talked her into marriage. They practically lived together before school started, and if it wasn't for the fact that living on campus is mandatory for freshmen, they still would.

Grey takes another hit before passing the joint back. "She's still my *blood*, idiot. That trumps everything."

I raise both eyebrows at his insinuation as if to say *you sure about that?* Technically, he and I are blood, too. Something I don't think either one of us is ready to admit.

"Maybe not everything."

"Dick." I laugh.

"Runs in the family, apparently."

I check my phone for the time, ignoring the stab of disappointment I feel when I don't see Valen's name in my notifications. She hasn't texted me once today. Not that I expected her to. Knowing her, she's still in the denial stage, too busy pretending she doesn't like our little secret as much as I do. It's already ten o'clock, which means I've officially spent my entire day on this bullshit. All I want to do is crawl into my bed and pass out while using Valen's thighs for pillows. And now, thanks to our temporary arrangement, I can do just that.

I pass the joint back to Grey. "Parting gift," I explain.

He shakes his head, stubbing it out on the lid of a water bottle that sits inside the cupholder. "Gotta drive." Instead, he drops it into the chest pocket of his t-shirt for later and gives it a pat. We both step out into the night air and Grey's shoulders hike up to his ears as he stuffs his hands into his pants pocket, but I welcome the cold.

"Thanks," is all I say.

"Don't mention it."

The parking lot is the closest one to our dorms, but it's still a fucking trek back to the room with the campus being the size of a small city. When I finally get to our hall, I hesitate between both doors, hand hovering over my door handle. I don't know what I look like. I don't know what I *smell* like. I should at the very least shower and change my clothes. A nice guy would probably send a courtesy text before showing up in her room late at night. Too bad I'm not a nice guy.

Fuck it. I'm already reaching for her door before I've made the conscious decision to do so. The fact that it hasn't even been a full day and I'm this desperate for her should probably concern me, but I can't seem to find it in me to give a shit. I want to see her now.

I knock, shoving my hands into my pockets, feeling weirdly nervous and on edge as I wait for her to come to the door. There's loud music coming from a few dorm rooms down, so I knock again when she doesn't answer. Still nothing. A feeling of dread snakes its way up my spine. I have the fleeting, irrational fear that my uncle could have come back for her in the name of revenge for my visit, but there's no way he could've pulled himself together in time to beat me back here.

I shake off the thought and reach out to try the handle, finding it locked. Thank fuck. She left it unlocked after she left my bed last night, so I'm relieved. The relief doesn't last long, though. It's still relatively early. Even if she was asleep, she'd hear me knocking. Maybe my uncle sent someone here. He's exactly the type of spineless pussy to have someone else do his dirty work.

My heart kicks in my chest, my palms starting to feel clammy as my brain convinces me that something is wrong in record time. Walking into my dorm, I consider my options. I could sweet talk the RA into letting me in. She tried coming to bed with me after we had some people over a few months ago, so I'm pretty sure she'd be willing. I grab the baseball bat that Ryan left in the living area. I could bust her door down. Extreme? Yes. Effective? Also yes. And quicker than waiting for the RA.

Walking back over, bat in hand, I pound with the side of my fist three times. A few people who decided to stay on campus over break pop their heads out of their rooms to see what the commotion is all about. Some look horrified. Some look amused. I look down at myself, realizing how I must look pounding on someone's door with a baseball bat in hand. The tangy taste in my mouth tells me I still have blood on my lip, which I'm sure just ties it all together. I look like a goddamn psychopath.

"Holden?"

Her sleepy, raspy voice has my head whipping back around. She stands in front of me with one earbud in her ear, the other in her hand, staring up at me with confusion. I let my eyes rove over her, realizing that she's safe and in one piece. And highly annoyed by the looks of it.

Okay, so that might have been a bit of an overreaction.

"What are you *doing?*" she asks when I still don't say anything, leaning her head out into the hall and seeing that we have an audience. It's then that I notice her flushed cheeks, her disheveled hair, and the fact that she's wearing nothing but a t-shirt that barely reaches the tops of her thighs.

I bend my knees, reaching down to scoop her up with one hand around the back of her bare thigh. She squeaks out a surprised sound, dropping the earbud to the floor. When her legs wrap around my waist and her warm pussy presses up against my stomach through my shirt, my suspicions are confirmed. No underwear. And wet as fuck. The kind of wet that makes me think she was playing with herself before she fell asleep. I'm instantly hard, my dick straining against my jeans.

"She likes to role play," I say to the nosy fucks still watching. I walk her back into her dorm, hearing their laughter as I close the door behind us.

"Explain," she demands, trying to slide down, but I tighten my hold, keeping her where I want her.

"I came to see you," is all I say.

"And the bat?" She arches a brow, holding on to my shoulders.

"It's...a present," I say, instead of admitting it was to beat the shit out of a non-existent threat because I was feeling a little paranoid. I prop it up against the wall behind her door. Just in case.

"Uh-huh," she says, not sounding convinced at all. "Are you going to tell me why you're bleeding? Or am I just supposed to ignore that part, too?"

I bring my other hand to cup her pussy from behind, sliding my fingers through her slippery flesh. She gasps when I push two fingers inside. "Are you going to tell me why you're getting yourself off instead of calling me? Or am I just supposed to ignore that?"

She moans when I pump them in and out, laying her head on my shoulder, pushing her ass back against my fingers as I walk us to her room. "You weren't here."

She doesn't even bother to deny it. Fuck, I love when she's so turned on that she drops her guard and forgets to pretend to hate me. "Were you at least thinking of me?"

"Maybe."

I take my fingers away, using my other hand to slide into the hair at the nape of her neck, tugging backward until she's forced to look at me. Her mouth parts on a gasp, her big brown eyes looking up at me, somehow both defiant and needy at the same time. I lean down to kiss her, gliding my tongue along her lip before pushing into her mouth. I swallow her moans as her tongue slides against mine. I fuck her mouth with my tongue and Valen kisses me just as hard, dragging her pussy up and down my stomach, desperate for friction. I pull back abruptly, stopping it just as quickly as it began. I'm panting, my dick so hard that it's *painful*.

"Yes, I was thinking of you." Her eyes are glossy and dazed with lust.

I quickly undo my belt and unbutton my jeans, pulling them down enough to free my dick from my pants. This isn't what I came here for, but fear mixes with adrenaline and the need to protect, the desperation to make her mine. "That's my girl. Now, lift."

Arms around my neck, she raises that perfect ass. I line myself up with her pussy until I'm notched right against her entrance, then my hands find her hips and slam her down onto me. I fill her in one swift movement, my knees almost giving out at how fucking perfect she feels around me.

"Oh my fucking God," she groans, clinging to me. I step into her room, backing her up against the nearest wall, then tug her shirt off. She unzips my jacket, pushing it off my shoulders, then her fingers curl underneath the hem of my shirt before she pulls it up and over my head.

Gripping underneath her knees, I spread her wide open, pinning them back against the wall. And then I begin to fuck her into it.

"Yes," she says between clenched teeth, eyes squeezing shut.

I make the mistake of looking down between us, seeing her pretty tits bounce, her pussy swollen and stretched tight around me. If I'm not careful, this might end a lot sooner than I want it to.

"You're so fucking perfect." Every time we're together like this, Valen seems to think it'll be the last time. That it'll get old, and I'll get sick of her and move on to the next one. What she doesn't know is that every time I have her only makes me want more. More of this. More of her. In any way she's willing to give it to me.

Not wanting this to be over yet, I pull out abruptly.

"Holden!" Her protest is cut off when I shove her up the wall. Her hands fly to my head, holding on for dear life as I bury my face between her legs. I lick up her center from ass to clit with the flat of my tongue, applying more pressure with each pass. I can see everything in this position. Her pussy pink and wet, her swollen clit, her perfect little asshole. Fuck, I want every part of her. I tilt my head to the side to look up at her, letting my tongue travel farther back. She jerks when she feels my tongue there, swirling around the tight ring.

"Do you like that?" I ask between licks. She doesn't answer out loud, but her pussy clenches around nothing, telling me all I need to know. "Say it."

"Yes," she breathes, fingers sliding through my hair and gripping tight. I take one last lick before I move back to her clit, sucking it into my mouth. Her legs start to tremble, her tell-tale sign that she's close to coming. I release her clit to rub my tongue against it, over and over. "Please, please, please," she chants. She doesn't have to beg me to give her what she wants, but I'll never get tired of hearing the sound.

Valen's whole body tenses, and I'm pretty sure she stops breathing as I continue my assault on her clit, and then she screams out her release, her knees clamping shut around my head. I lick her softly as I carry her away from the wall, lowering her spent form to her mattress. And then I lick her some more, intent on getting every last drop until she's pushing my head away and bringing her knees together.

"I can't," she says, breathless, staring up at the ceiling, her chest rising and falling.

I pry her legs apart, then rub my fingers through her wetness as I lick her gently. "One more, baby," I say against her clit. "And then I'm going to fuck you."

She brings her knees up, planting her feet on the mattress in response. God, I love fucking this girl. I'm pretty sure she was made for me. I dip two fingers in and out of her pussy until she's rocking against my hand, wanting more. I pull them from her before finding her even tighter hole. She doesn't object when my middle finger swirls around the outside, applying the faintest of pressure.

"You want more?" I press into her, dipping just the tip inside. She nods frantically, wordlessly, and I slowly work my finger into her ass as my tongue laves her tight bundle of nerves. "You're doing so good," I praise, picking up the pace when she starts to push back against my finger.

Her back arches off the mattress, fingers pushing through my hair to keep my head firmly between her legs as her white-tipped toes curl into the sheets. I finger her faster, flicking her clit with my tongue as she comes in my mouth. Her ass contracts around my finger and her knees pull up into her chest as she rolls onto her side. Her cheeks are red, a strand of hair stuck to her parted lips.

"One more, Sweet Valentine." I roll her boneless body onto her stomach, and even though she's exhausted, she pushes her ass into the air in offering, her left cheek pressed against the sheets. My dick twitches at the sight. I smooth my palm down her spine before covering her back with my front, bringing my lips to her ear. "Are you sure you can take it?" I brush her hair away from her cheek, tucking it behind her ear. She blinks up at me, her eyes full of lust.

"I want it."

She traps her bottom lip between her teeth in an uncharacteristically shy gesture, and I drag my thumb down her chin until she releases it. "Tell me."

"I want you inside me." She presses her ass back into me to illustrate her point.

I sit back on my knees, then angle her hips upward with her chest pressed to the mattress. I give her ass a smack, causing her to jerk forward in surprise.

"Hold yourself open for me." Reaching back with both hands, she spreads herself open, her pussy and ass on full display.

"Fuck." I stroke myself, almost coming from the sight alone. I lean in for a taste, eating her pussy before showing attention to her other hole, making sure she's nice and wet. Unable to wait any longer, I guide myself to her entrance and slide into her until her ass is flush with my stomach.

Valen groans, still holding herself open. I gather both of her wrists in one hand, holding them at the small of her back as I start to fuck her hard and fast. I won't last long. It's a miracle I haven't come as it is. I release her hands and they fall limply at her sides. I spit on my fingers before sliding my hand between us, curling my middle finger into her back entrance as I pump into her.

"God, yes," Valen breathes.

I add my index finger and she freezes as I work two fingers into her, stretching her slowly.

"Play with your clit," I instruct. She complies instantly, rubbing herself with her fingers. "You're so perfect." Once my fingers can slide in and out with ease, I start to move again.

"It's so much," she mumbles into the sheets. "I'm so full."

That's all it takes. My orgasm hits before I know it's coming and I jerk, spilling inside as she reaches her third climax, fluttering around me. I roll her onto her back, sitting back to see my cum spill out of her. I position myself back at her entrance and scoop it up with my tip before pushing my half-hard dick inside her.

"There is no way I can go again," she says, looking up at me, mildly alarmed. I crawl up her body, pressing open-mouth kisses to her stomach, to the swell of her breasts, then finally each nipple on my way up, and she shivers, contracting around me. I plant one hand on the mattress next to her head, then use my other hand to push her hair off her forehead.

"I just want to stay inside you for a little while." I don't know what the fuck is wrong with me, or why I would confess such a thing *out loud*. Valen's eyebrows knit together, looking up at me with something I can't place. I bury my face in her neck, inhaling her scent, feeling her heart pound against mine. Her fingertips trace my spine, sending goosebumps across my skin.

Not too long ago, she was practically allergic to affection, and now I'm inside her, and she's touching me because she wants to. I don't know if she's aware she's doing it. This thing between us isn't supposed to mean anything, but with Valen, it always feels like more. And now she's a target because of me and my impulsive bullshit.

The thought is a cold dose of reality, reminding me why I'm here. Valen must sense the shift in my demeanor. Her touch disappears, her legs falling limply to the side, releasing me. I pull back, meeting her gaze. "I have to tell you something."

THIRTY-ONE

Valen

"**I** HAVE TO TELL YOU SOMETHING."
Holden's words set me on edge, but I school my expression, reverting back to my carefully constructed blank mask that gives nothing away. He rolls off me, sitting on the edge of my bed. His elbows rest on his knees, head bowed, his dark hair hanging in front of his eyes, damp with sweat. I scoot back toward my headboard, bringing my blanket with me, ignoring the soreness between my legs.

"Don't tell me you cheated on me," I say, trying to lighten the mood.

His head swivels around to look at me. "What? No. Wait, are you saying you want to be exclusive?"

"I was joking!" My cheeks burn and I stand on shaky legs, dropping my blanket. His eyes shamelessly wander over my naked body. "Can whatever it is wait five minutes? I could really use a shower." And a minute to collect myself in private. Sex with Holden tonight felt more intense than before. More intense than anything I've *ever* experienced. I need to remind myself that it's just sex. It can't go anywhere, for so many reasons, and I need to remember that.

He nods, but I'm already walking away, grabbing my towel off the hook on the back of my door on the way out. I don't bother putting it around me for the short walk to the bathroom since Shayne's still gone. I step inside, closing the door behind me, my back pressed up against it as I close my eyes, exhaling a sigh. When I open my eyes, I'm shocked at my appearance. I step forward to inspect myself more closely. My cheeks are pink, eyes shining brightly, my hair a wild mess, my skin peppered with red marks. I look down at myself, feeling raw but sated. His cum leaking down my inner thighs reminds me that we didn't use a condom. Again. Thank God for birth control.

When the door opens behind me, I jump, whirling around on Holden, my arms covering my chest by instinct. "Can I help you?"

"I just had two fingers buried in your ass. It's a little late for modesty, don't you think?" He gives a pointed look at my chest. I roll my eyes, dropping my arms to my side. "I could use a shower, too," he explains.

I shake my head, bewildered.

"What?"

"You! That's what. One minute you're all *I have to tell you something,*" I mimic his voice and the serious tone. "And then the next, you're all…" I trail off, gesturing toward him. "Holden."

"I'm all *Holden?* Is that a new adjective? Is it synonymous with sexy?" He lazily scratches his lower stomach, drawing my attention to his V, then even lower, where he hangs heavy between his legs. It's disgusting how perfect he is.

"It's synonymous with *perv.*"

"Look," he says, catching me staring, but not calling me on it as he reaches over to the shower knobs, turning on the faucet. "We do need to talk. But I've had a long ass day, I need to shower, and I like seeing you naked, so might as well kill two birds with one stone, right?" He steps into the shower, holding his hand out for me.

His demeanor is playful, but I'm starting to realize that turning everything into a joke or sexual innuendo is Holden's way of coping when shit gets too real.

"Fine. But I get the front." His lips tug into a smile as I take his hand and step inside with him.

"Whatever you say, Sweet Valentine." He steps behind me, letting me stand under the stream of hot water. The shower is barely big enough for a single person, let alone two, and the water pressure sucks, but it still feels good. I shudder under the hot water, tilting my head back and closing my eyes as I run my hands through my hair. "The view's better back here, anyway."

I snort out a laugh, spinning around to smack his shoulder. He swallows hard, his heated gaze landing on my chest. "Nope. This view is definitely better." His hands reach out to cup each one, brushing his thumbs against the hardened peaks. I shiver at his touch, watching as he slides one hand down my wet stomach, my breath hitching as he stops between my thighs. When he feels the evidence of our combined orgasms, he crouches down until his face is level with my pelvis.

"Let me see it," he instructs. I hold on to the bar of the soap holder to keep my balance as his hand circles my ankle, bringing my foot to rest against his shoulder.

"Holden," I say, my tone holding a hint of warning. "I'm sore." I'm sore *everywhere* down there, but even so, I feel my body tingling, the pulse in my clit starting to throb.

"I know." He turns his head to kiss the arch of my foot. "I'll be gentle."

I'm wide open, completely exposed to him under the bright, florescent lighting. I should feel vulnerable as he inspects me, scooping up his cum before stretching it between two fingers, but the look in his eyes tells me I have nothing to be insecure about. "I've never…" he trails off, using his thumbs to part my lips. "Fuck, that's hot."

He leans forward, his slick tongue so soft and gentle as it ghosts along my clit, barely making contact. Something between a moan and whimper slips free as my other hand pushes into his hair.

"Why can't I get enough of you?" he asks, sounding equal

parts angry and mystified, spinning me around until my back hits the cold tiles. He grips the back of my thigh, pushing it higher as his mouth covers my clit. His lips are pliant as he alternates between sucking softly and licking me with the flat of his tongue, gently coaxing another orgasm from my spent body. This time when I come against his mouth, it's not as violent, but no less intense.

"I think you're going to kill me," I say, breathless, as I start to slide down the wall. Holden stands, catching me by the waist. I throw my arms around his neck, feeling him hard and thick against my stomach. He moves us back under the spray of the showerhead, keeping me upright as I rest my head on his chest. I feel him shifting around, reaching for something behind me. "Soft vanilla, fresh orange, and toasted coconut," he reads out loud. *The description of my body wash?*

"Hmm?"

"This is why you smell like a fucking Creamsicle." He wags the bottle of body wash in my periphery before pumping some onto a loofah. He gathers my hair, bringing it to one shoulder before he washes my back. When he's done, he drops the loofah, using his bare hands on my skin. I moan, sagging against him even more. "That feels so good."

His dick twitches against me, begging for attention as his hands curl around the curve of my ass, kneading. I've had four orgasms in the span of an hour, and he's only had one. Dropping one hand between us, I wrap it around his length, slowly sliding up and down. He shudders, flexing into my grip, his palms slapping against the tiles behind me to steady himself.

I've never had the desire to get on my knees for any man, but right now, I want to make Holden feel as good as he makes me feel. I sink down to my knees, one hand braced on his thick, tattooed thigh, the other still wrapped around his cock. I look up at him, his palms flat against the wall, his head bent under the showerhead, blocking the water from hitting me. Rivulets of water stream down the side of his face, down his chest and the hard lines of his stomach. His wet hair hangs in front of his eyes, appearing almost black. I slide my hand up and down his length and his lips part, eyes falling shut.

When I lick up the underside of the head, his eyes shoot open. He looks down at me, watching with heavy-lidded eyes as I take him into my mouth. I barely get to taste him before he pulls away and grasps my chin with his fingers, his thumb tracing my lips. "As much as I want to see those lips wrapped around me, I know I'll end up needing to fuck you again, and I think that pretty pussy of yours needs a break."

The look on my face must say *and that's a problem because…?* Holden smiles at me, his hands lifting me by my armpits. "Now who's the perv?"

THIRTY-TWO

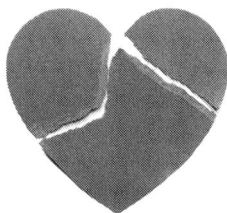

Valen

I QUICKLY WASHED MY HAIR AND THE REST OF MY BODY, WONDERING what Holden could possibly have to tell me and if it has anything to do with why he was at my door with a baseball bat. Now, he's sitting on my bed after running across the hall to grab a pair of clean black sweatpants. I threw on a fitted, white long-sleeve top and blue and white striped sleep shorts. I walk over toward Holden, drying my hair off with a towel. He fingers the hem of my shorts before tugging me closer, looking up at me.

"First, I need you to know that you're not in any danger."

I tense, not expecting those words. They're meant to reassure and comfort, but they do the opposite. "Okay."

"I wasn't the one who returned your earring."

I narrow my eyes, once again not expecting the conversation to go in this direction. "So who did? Shayne said it wasn't her."

He shakes his head. "It was Samuel."

"Samuel was in our dorm?" I back up, leaning my butt against the top of my desk. "In *my room*?"

He nods.

"Why? How did he know where I was? How did he even know it was mine?"

Holden works his jaw, anger filling his eyes. I can sense his hesitation, like there's more he's not saying.

"What else? I know there's something else because this doesn't make any sense."

"He knew Thayer and me were in his office, so he checked his security cameras and saw us together."

I lift a shoulder, shrugging. "So he knows we know each other now. Big deal."

Holden stands, frustrated. "He knows you were distracting him for us. The earring was his way of taunting me. Letting me know how easily he could get to you and Shayne."

How would he get into our dorm without us noticing? I only left it unlocked last night because I was half-asleep. Shayne has hammered the importance of locking our doors into my brain for as long as I've known her.

"Wait," I say, grabbing my purse from my desk behind me as something suddenly occurs to me. I unzip it, dumping the contents onto the bed next to where Holden sits, rifling through it all just to be sure. "I couldn't find my key card when I got home. I bumped into Ryan—"

"When?"

"Two nights ago. I was in a hurry to meet my dad for dinner, not watching where I was going. Ryan was coming in as I was leaving, we collided, I dropped my purse, and my stuff went everywhere. I thought I got everything, but when I came home, I could only find the key card for the building, not my dorm key. The door was unlocked, and my bedroom door was open. At first, I thought it was Shayne. Then, you."

"What time was that?" Holden asks.

"Around five? I was home by eight. But how—" I break off mid-sentence, thinking back to when it happened. "There was a man holding the door while Ryan helped me pick up my stuff, but his back was to me. I never got a look at him, but it was Samuel. It had to be."

"So he swiped your key and went for you instead of me," Holden says, echoing my thoughts. "My guess is that he had your earring after watching the security footage. We've got to work on your situational awareness."

I roll my eyes. "Don't we have security cameras in the hall?"

"Doesn't matter," he says cryptically. "We know it was him. I knew it was him the second you thanked me for returning it earlier. I called Grey—"

"Wait, you called *Grey*?" I interrupt. That is, perhaps, the most surprising part of this story so far.

"He hates Samuel just as much as I do, maybe even more. I didn't want to call Thayer and ruin Shayne's trip, but I needed backup in case things went south."

Makes sense. I nod for him to continue.

"We drove over to rough him up a little. Told him to stay the fuck away from you. And then I threatened to turn in the video from the night Danny died."

That explains the bloody lip. It looks a lot better after a shower. Swollen, with a small cut in the middle, but much less noticeable. "You should," I agree. "I don't know why you guys haven't already, to be honest."

"And tarnish the Ames family name?" he asks bitterly. "My dad said he'd handle it. But turns out, it doesn't fucking matter anyway. It never did." His expression matches the defeated tone of his voice.

"What do you mean? Why do you keep saying it doesn't matter?"

"Christian kept his word, after all." Holden stands, closing the space between us, looking down at me as he squeezes my hip. "But there's something you're not getting."

"What?" I ask nervously.

"When I say he saw us together, I mean he saw us *together*," he stresses the word, making his meaning clear. "On the patio."

"What?" My heart pounds harder as I try to make sense of everything that he's telling me.

"He had the video on his phone. I erased it from the security app and his phone, then I broke his phone just in case. It's blurry and pixelated and you can't even tell it's you." He's quick to assure. "If I wouldn't have called him out like that, if I hadn't been digging through his shit, he would've never checked those cameras. I'm so fucking sorry."

I push him back, shaking my head. I feel violated and disgusted, but mostly, I'm fucking angry. Another man in power thinking he can control everyone around him. If there's one thing I can't stand, it's a man who thinks his checkbook or his status can get him out of anything. "So, what, he's threatening to post the video if you turn him in or something?"

He shakes his head. "The cops have already seen the video of the night Danny died. Christian did what he promised. He turned Samuel in, and then he disappeared. My uncle has more pull than we ever thought."

"Then what's the point?"

"Another one of his little games to show he has the upper hand. To bait me into going over there. Fuck, I don't know."

The idea of him seeing us like that makes me sick to my stomach. The thought of him in our dorm makes it even worse.

"We have to tell Shayne and Thayer he was here. If he decides to pull something else, they can't be blindsided."

He nods. "I know."

"And then you guys have to find Christian."

Another nod.

I my grab my laptop off my desk before I turn off the lights and crawl into bed.

Holden walks over to the side of my bed and tucks my hair behind my ear before tilting my chin up with his fingers. Weirdly, it feels more intimate than everything else we've done tonight. "I'll fix this," he promises. "We'll call the housing office to get your key deactivated tomorrow." Before I realize his intent, he holds my chin in place as he leans down and kisses me. It's gentle but possessive and he pulls away before I can overanalyze it. Without another word, he turns to leave.

"Where are you going?" I raise a brow.

He turns back to look at me, surprise written all over his face. "You want me to stay?"

"Your creepy uncle has the key to my room. You're not leaving me here alone." I lift the corner of the blanket in invitation. "Besides, it's not like you won't just drag me to your bed later, anyway."

"It's cute that you'd think I'd actually leave. I was just going to take the couch."

THIRTY-THREE

Valen

WHEN I BLINK AWAKE, I CAN TELL HOLDEN'S ALREADY been up for a while. He doesn't notice me watching him at first, apparently lost in his thoughts, staring at the ceiling with his hands folded behind his head. Whatever he's thinking about has his eyebrows pulled together in a frown and his jaw set hard.

I climb on top of him, straddling his stomach. My hair falls forward, brushing his chest. His hands immediately leave their position under his head to slide beneath the hem of my shorts, grabbing two handfuls. His frown melts away instantly, and the knowledge that I could be the reason sets off the butterflies in my stomach.

"Your hands are so warm," I say, flattening my palms against his chest. His hands move from my butt to the tops of my thighs, rubbing up and down. "What?" I ask when I notice the smirk on his face.

"Are you cuddling with me, Sweet Valentine?"

"Never," I scoff, leaning forward until our chests are pressed together, my face in the crook of his neck. "I'm stealing your warmth."

"I like it when you touch me." His hands slip underneath the back of my shirt, one curling around my shoulder, the other one at the small of my back.

"Don't tell anyone," I mumble into his neck. "You'll ruin my ice princess reputation."

"Well, what does the ice princess want to do today?" he surprises me by asking.

"Unless you can teleport us to a beach somewhere tropical, I'm not leaving this bed. It's too cold to be alive."

"As much as I'd like to spend all day in this bed and in *you*, I have a better idea."

I pull back, looking down at him and raise a brow, feigning offense. "Better?"

"Okay, not better." He slaps my ass, rolling me off him.

"Where are you going?"

"Be ready in an hour."

I puff out a breath, blowing a lock of hair from my face. I hear my door close a second later. "What the hell am I doing?" I ask myself, pressing my palms into my eyes. I don't know what Holden has up his sleeve, and I can guarantee that spending time with him *outside* of the bedroom and in the light of day is a bad idea. Curiosity overrides my better judgment, and I force myself to leave the warmth of my bed and get ready for whatever the hell he has planned

Once I've brushed my teeth, put on some makeup, and thrown my hair into a ponytail, I stand in front of my pathetic excuse for a closet, which is really just a rolling garment rack with a couple of fabric drawers on one side, not having any idea what to wear without knowing what we're doing. Aiming for comfort, I settle on a pair of loose-fitting jeans and throw a thick, light gray zip-up jacket over a tight white seamless tank that doubles as a bra.

My phone lights up on my desk with a picture of Shayne's smiling face and I answer it quickly, wanting to know how it's going with her dad.

"You're alive," I say, sitting on the edge of my bed. "So is it safe to assume he isn't an axe murderer?"

"Jury's still out," she says quietly. I can see that she's outside, but her face takes up most of the screen.

"Well? How's it going?"

"It's fine. He's fine."

Thayer's face pops in front of hers. "She's lying," he says before Shayne shushes him, slapping her hand over his mouth.

"He can probably hear you," she whisper-yells. "He's trying," she explains. "It's just…"

"A little weird?" I guess.

"Yeah. I mean, we're practically strangers, but I thought there'd be some…built-in connection or bond or something."

"I'm sure he's just nervous." I try to assure her.

"What are you up to today?" She changes the subject. "I feel like we haven't talked in forever."

"I know." I flop backward, collapsing onto my mattress, holding the phone above my face. "Come home already." She's only been gone for a couple days, but so much has happened.

"Soon," she promises. "Is everything okay?" Her best friend senses must be tingling. When it comes to my own problems, I'm a professional at keeping things to myself. But this involves her, and I feel guilty. Guilty that her privacy was invaded because of me. Guilty for keeping things from her.

"Yeah, I'm good." I try to sound convincing. I don't want to lie to her, but I also don't want her to worry about Samuel right now. She has enough to deal with.

We talk for a few more minutes about nothing and everything, but my heart stops when I hear Holden come back in. He's changed into his usual uniform of a black hoodie and gray sweats, his hair covered by a backward hat. I hold up a finger, not wanting to explain what he's doing here. He hears Shayne's voice and smirks, clearly not feeling conflicted in the slightest, walking over to the bed. Shayne continues talking about her new schedule when classes start back up in a few days as Holden bends over, pushing my jacket up and kissing his way up my stomach. I shove my free hand into his hair, knocking his hat off in the process, to stop him from venturing any farther. Not that he lets it deter him.

"Why is your face so red right now?"

Holden squeeze my sides, making me laugh. "It's not."

"Oh my God, you're not alone!" Shayne squeals. "Why didn't you tell me?"

"I—"

"I'll see you tomorrow," she says, cutting me off. "Have fun! But not too much fun. Use a condom and all that."

"Jesus Christ." I roll my eyes, feeling Holden's laughter against my stomach. *Too late for that.* "Goodbye."

"Love you, bye!"

She disappears from my screen, and I drop my phone to my mattress. "I'm going to kill you."

Holden pulls me up to stand in front of him before putting his hat back on. "Kill me later. We've got shit to do."

We've been walking through campus for a good twenty minutes, and I still don't know where he's taking me. The sun is finally out, but the snow still stubbornly clings to the tree branches and sidewalks. Holden grabs my hand, and against my better judgment, I let him. Campus is still pretty dead with four days of break left, so there's not much risk of anyone seeing us. It's weird to see it like this when it's normally so crowded.

"Almost there," he says, which only confuses me more, because there's nothing around except for a closed dining hall and the health center. A minute later, we come to a big white building shrouded in the trees with vines crawling up the walls and glass ceilings. Holden opens the door, pulling me inside.

"What is this place?" I ask, following him through a room full of potted plants and flowers.

"Hadley Conservatory," he says, leading me into a connected room. The next door leads to what can only be described as a jungle. Almost every surface is covered in greenery. I duck under a large leaf, stepping inside. "It's so warm," I say. It's probably twenty degrees outside, but in here, it must be almost eighty. The air is humid, and the glass of the greenhouse allows the sun to illuminate everything.

"You wanted tropical. This is the best I could do within an hour."

I spin around, taking everything in, those stupid butterflies taking flight again.

"Come on," Holden says, leading me across a small, wooden foot bridge with a pond underneath. *A pond.* I look over the edge, surprised to see the biggest, brightest goldfish I've ever seen swimming around.

"I didn't know this place existed," I say. "Is this where you take all the girls?" I tease.

"Just you," he says, unfazed by my comment. "Sometimes I come here between classes when I don't feel like walking back to Hawthorne. Or when I feel like being alone."

"I can see why."

I follow him to the other side of the bridge and come to a stop when I see what's laid out in front of me. There's a circular, concrete clearing in the middle of all the trees and greenery with a few benches on the perimeter, and in the middle, there's a blanket spread out with an obscene amount of food. "You did all this?" I ask.

He scratches the back of his neck. "I was aiming for a beach picnic vibe, but I didn't know what you liked, so I bought a little of everything."

"Is that…You got me coffee?"

"You're the only psychopath I know who drinks iced coffee in January."

I can't help but wonder why he went through all this trouble, especially when he already got what he wanted from me. Several times. He must sense my inner turmoil because he looks over at me, frowning. "What?"

"Why?" The word comes out clipped, sounding harsher than I meant it to.

"You don't like it?" He seems almost nervous about my reaction. Holden doesn't get nervous. "I'm not good at this shit—"

"No, it's not that," I interrupt quickly. "It's just... I mean, clearly, you're not doing this to get in my pants."

"Who says I'm not?" he teases.

I roll my eyes. "Seems a lot like a date."

"A date?" he spits out the word *date* as if it's a dirty word. "Never."

"Good."

"Can we eat now that we've cleared that up?" he asks. "I'm fucking starved."

I follow him over to the blanket, sitting cross-legged on one end. Holden sits next to me, handing me a sandwich wrapped in white deli paper.

"You had turkey on Christmas, so I figured it was a safe bet," he explains.

I don't know what to say, feeling weirdly touched by the fact that he's remembered so much about my preferences, down to my coffee order. My own parents wouldn't know what to order for me if they had a gun to their heads.

Holden starts taking the lids off of the plastic containers of every kind of fruit the store had to offer by the looks of it. Strawberries, cherries, blueberries, apple slices, grapes, pineapple, even kiwi.

"This is pretty romantic for a not-date," I tease. Not to mention excessive. There's no way we'll be able to put a dent in this much food.

He plucks a blueberry out of one of the containers and flicks it at my face in response. I laugh, popping it into my mouth. We don't talk after that, both of us content to sit and eat in comfortable silence.

Once I'm finished eating, I pop the button on my jeans, earning an amused look from Holden. "I'm stuffed," I groan.

"Leave me alone." I was wrong because we did, in fact, put a dent in the food. The food, along with the warm temperature and the humid air, has me feeling sleepy and sated. In fact, it's too warm for my jacket, so I unzip that next, letting it fall off my shoulders, leaving me in nothing but my tank top. Leaning back on my palms, I stretch my legs out in front of me. I close my eyes, tilting my face toward the glass ceilings of the green-house, fantasizing about summertime and beach days as the sun beats down on me.

After a few minutes, I feel the weight of Holden's stare on me before I open my eyes. When I finally do, my gut feeling proves to be right. His gaze is set on my chest at first before drop-ping to where my pants are unbuttoned. Over the past couple of weeks, I've come to recognize that look. I have a feeling it mirrors my own. My breathing quickens along with the pulse between my thighs. When I squeeze them together, his eyes la-zily flick up to mine and his gaze darkens knowingly.

I rise onto my knees and climb onto his lap, my arms cir-cling his neck. "Thank you. No one's ever done anything like this for me before."

Holden tugs on my ponytail, kissing his way up my neck. "Anything for you, Sweet Valentine." He lays me flat on the blanket, his body covering mine. He kisses me, coaxing my lips to open for him. His tongue slides against mine, and I squirm, waiting impatiently for him to make his move as the kiss deep-ens, but he never takes it any farther.

"Holden." My voice comes out needy and pleading against his lips. I take his hand, guiding him inside my unbuttoned pants until I feel his fingers where I need them. He rubs me through the thin material of my underwear, his finger pressing into my clit. When his teeth scrape against my hard nipple through my bra, I arch up into him.

"Harder," I tell him. He doesn't disappoint, biting my nipple and tugging on it just enough to add a hint of pain to the plea-sure. He does it to the other side, and my thighs tighten around his wrist, needing more. I snake a hand between us, slipping into the waistband of his sweatpants. He's hard and hot in my hand, his hips flexing forward when I stroke him.

"I thought you were sore." His finger traces a line up my slit.

"I don't care. I need you." I don't know what it is about Holden that makes me this crazed and desperate and needy. Maybe it's our impending end making me feel this way. Maybe it's just Holden. Either way, I'll hate myself for letting him know I want him this much later, but right now, I'm not above begging. "Please?"

"Fuck," he grits out. "You want me to fuck you right here in the open? Where anyone could come in?"

"Yes," I answer without hesitation. Because in this moment, I don't care. It's a risk I'm willing to take.

"Turn over," he says harshly, flipping me around. My hands slap against the concrete as he roughly tugs my jeans down to the middle of my thighs, then pushes inside me, filling me in one thrust. I gasp at the initial bite of pain, but it's quickly replaced with pleasure. I drop to my elbows, my cheek pressed against the concrete, pushing my ass back into him. I spread my legs as much as I can within the confines of my jeans as deft fingers slip between my thighs. He parts my lips, circling my clit as he fucks me from behind.

Now that I know what I've been missing, I don't know how I'm going to give it up.

THIRTY-FOUR

Holden

"**W**HAT THE HELL IS HE DOING HERE?" THAYER JERKS his chin toward Grey who's helping himself to a beer from Shayne and Valen's fridge. After almost a week of having Valen all to myself—most of it spent in the conservatory—the gang's all fucking here. Grey included. If the reason for this little family meeting wasn't a serious one, their confusion would be comical.

"What's the matter, you're not happy to see me? I'm crushed." Grey clutches his chest.

"I asked him to come," I interject before they really piss each other off and end up beating the shit out of each other. Again. Maybe we should've picked somewhere neutral. And somewhere bigger than a shoebox.

"What's going on?" Shayne frowns, looking to me for answers.

"This have anything to do with why Dad has called me no less than five times in the last few days?" Thayer asks, arms folded across his chest.

I scratch behind my ear. "That's probably a safe bet." He's called me, too, but he hasn't left a voicemail, and I haven't been in the mood to get my ass chewed out, so his calls remain unanswered.

"Samuel knows you guys were snooping around on New

Year's." Valen surprises everyone, me included, by coming right out with it. Leave it to her to not beat around the bush. "And he knows I was attempting to stall him."

"I knew that was a bad idea." Shayne points a finger at Valen. "What did he do? Are you okay?"

Valen looks to me, for reassurance? For backup? I nod for her to continue.

"Remember when I thought you returned my earring that I lost on New Year's?"

"Yeah," Shayne drawls out, seemingly confused on how this ties into the current topic.

"Apparently, creepy Uncle Sam brought it upon himself to return it. Without either of us knowing."

"He was here?" Thayer raises his voice, directing the question at me. "When?"

"Day before you guys left," I say.

"And you didn't fucking think to mention that before now?"

"Wait, he was here? In our dorm?" Shayne asks, looking horrified.

"Again, why the fuck are we just now hearing about it?"

I open my mouth to answer, but Valen beats me to it. "Because I told him not to. We didn't realize what happened until you guys had already left, and it's not like Shayne was in any danger."

"But you were!" Shayne yells.

"It was an intimidation tactic. A head game," Valen says, sounding unaffected. "Nothing happened."

"It doesn't make any sense. Why Valen?" Shayne muses aloud.

"Same reason he had Christian target you," Grey says with a shrug. I tense at the implication. Shayne was Thayer's weakness. Our show on the patio made Valen mine.

But Shayne doesn't know that. She shakes her head. "No. I posed a threat because he knew if we stopped hating each other for five seconds, we'd communicate and find out the truth about what happened the day Danny died. Valen was just...a decoy as far as he knows. She could be irrelevant to us."

Valen's eyes flick up to mine, guilt shining back at me, before she looks away again.

"The point is, historically, he preys on women," Grey says. "He goes for what he deems the weaker target."

"You're calling me weak?" Valen asks, raising a brow.

"I'm saying *he* deems women weak," Grey corrects. "Plus, he knows you two don't give a fuck about yourselves." He gestures to Thayer and me. "Threatening you does nothing. Threatening the people you care about might get you to back off, though. I'm sure he's done enough digging to know Valen's in your inner circle."

"You're not staying here," Thayer tells Shayne. "You stay at my apartment most of the time, anyway."

"Uh, yes, I am. I'm not leaving Valen alone."

"No one has to go anywhere. Valen already had residential services deactivate her key, and I'm right across the hall," I cut in.

"Lot of good that fucking did," Thayer scoffs.

"That's what I said," Grey mumbles his agreement.

"No one's talking to you," Thayer spits back, earning a middle finger from Grey.

"No offense, Grey, because I'm glad you're here, but where do you come in?" Shayne asks.

"Oh, Holden called me to help him fuck up the judge, and you know I'm always down to put an Ames in their place." His words are said with a smirk, his tone light and casual, meant to piss us off. It works.

"Aren't you technically an Ames?" Valen asks.

"No!" all four of us answer in unison, some of us sounding more defensive than others.

Valen holds up her hands in mock surrender, but I don't miss the amused smile she's trying to smother. *Brat.*

"Wait, back up. You beat him up?"

I blow out a breath, pinching the bridge of my nose. "He

was in your dorm," I remind her. "He wanted a reaction, and he got one. He's lucky that's all I did." I look over at Valen for that last part, making sure she knows it's directed at her. I don't mention the security camera footage out loud. Just like I didn't tell Valen about the thinly veiled threats he made against her. But I should have done worse. Much worse than a broken phone and a bloody face.

"What else?" Thayer asks, instinctively knowing there's more than what I'm saying. If everyone would shut the fuck up, I could get to the point sooner.

"Christian turned over the video like he said he would. Samuel found out about it, used his connections to bury it, and then Christian disappeared."

Arms crossed over his chest, Thayer drops his head back, looking up at the ceiling. "Fuck."

"You know that for a fact?" Shayne asks, biting on the tip of her thumb.

I shrug. "If Samuel's to be believed. He was gloating about getting away with it, letting us know that if we push any further, there'll be hell to pay, etcetera, etcetera. Typical super villain shit."

"This isn't a fucking joke," Thayer says.

"I seem to remember you being amused during my speech on New Year's."

"If that's true," Shayne cuts in, her voice soft and hesitant. "Then there's no chance Christian ran away?"

For the first time since we've started this conversation, no one has anything to say. Silence falls over the room, the air thick with the fear no one wants to voice, the obvious conclusion no one wants to jump to. The very thing I haven't let myself consider because I don't know how or *if* it changes anything.

We knew there was a chance that our uncle did something to Samuel, but until now, I didn't actually believe it. Never thought he'd go that far, especially when he went through all the trouble to protect Christian the night that Danny died. But it wasn't really about Christian at all, was it? It was about the family name. It was about *his* name.

"It's possible that Christian turned him in and then disappeared before Samuel even knew what was happening," Valen chimes in, breaking the silence. We all nod, as if it's an acceptable theory, but I don't think anyone truly believes it. Not even Valen.

Thayer does that thing he does when he's thinking hard, biting down on the piercings at the corner of his lip before he looks to me. "You up for a drive to the city tomorrow?"

"You really want to bring Dad into it? We don't know what he knows or what he's in on. Maybe that's why he's been so insistent that we let him handle it." Call me naïve, but it's only just occurred to me. We don't know who to trust or how deep this shit runs.

He shrugs. "Then it's time we find out what he knows."

I nod, glad to be on the same page for once. I'm sick of being in the dark.

"I can stay here with the girls," Grey offers.

My lips twitch when both Valen and Shayne cut him dirty looks, offended by the idea.

"It's not a bad idea," Thayer concedes. He might not like the guy who shares half of our DNA, but he knows he'll protect Shayne more than anyone.

"Okay, that's enough," Shayne says, both her and Valen rising from the couch at the same time.

"Get out." Valen points to the door.

Thayer looks to Shayne, eyebrows raised.

"Shoo," she says, gesturing with her hands. "All of you out."

"Why me?" I ask. "I didn't even say anything!"

"You would've if we gave you the chance," Shayne says.

"Guilty by association." This comes from Valen. "Go be big, strong heroes across the hall and leave us *weak targets* in peace."

"If my services aren't needed, I'm out," Grey says, walking over to Shayne. "You guys can always come stay with me, if it comes down to it."

"In your smelly dorm with your roommate? No thanks. You're all overreacting." She laughs, hugging Grey. Her voice is too quiet to make out the rest of what she's saying, but it sounds like she's thanking him for something. He nods, his chin on the top of her head. When she pulls back, he ruffles her hair.

"Later, fuckers," Grey says to the room, and a second later, he's gone. Shayne follows Thayer to the door before they both step out into the hall for a heated discussion, leaving only Valen and me on opposite sides of the living area.

"What do you think they're talking about?" Valen asks.

"Probably something along the lines of *me Tarzan, you Jane. Must keep you safe*. I'm pretty sure the lightning incident fried both of their brains."

Valen's soft laughter goes straight to my dick. "It's called being *in love*," she says, mocking, her eyes widening.

"And what do you know about the subject?" I ask, crossing the room. A crease forms between her eyebrows, and I immediately regret putting it there.

"Not a thing," she says, folding her arms across her chest in a defensive stance as I eat up the distance between us.

I pull her arms down before rubbing the pad of my thumb across her nipple until it hardens beneath her shirt. "So you don't love it when I do this?" I ask, pinching lightly, earning a soft gasp from her pretty lips, her eyes darting toward the door before flicking back to meet mine. Moving lower, I trace the outline of her pussy lips through her thin leggings, running my middle finger up the center until it brushes against her clit. "What about when I'm on my knees with my tongue in your pussy? You don't love that?"

"Not as much as you do," she says, trying to sound unaffected, but she can't hide the lust in her voice.

I laugh, dropping my hand from between her legs. "You're probably right about that." I never cared much for eating pussy before Valen came along. If I could survive off her cum alone, I would. I pull her into my chest, wrapping my arms around her.

Her hands rest on my waist and she tips her chin up to look at me. I hold her face in my hands, wishing I didn't have to deal with this shit so I could hang out with her instead.

"Too bad our time has come to an end."

That wipes the smile off my face.

"Classes start Monday," she reminds me, keeping her face perfectly blank. *Classes*. And a new semester, which means I'll officially be a full-time student and practicing with the team.

"And what if I don't want it to end?"

Her mouth parts in surprise, but the door swings open, making both of us spring apart.

"Please don't do anything stupid," Shayne says, oblivious to the tension in the room.

Too late. I'm fucking your best friend and I'd rather saw off my shooting hand than stop.

"Me? Never."

"Super reassuring."

THIRTY-FIVE

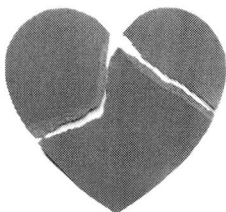

Valen

HOLDEN DIDN'T COME BACK LAST NIGHT AFTER HE DROPPED that bomb. I half-expected to wake up to being carried to his bed or find him in mine. I woke up feeling more disappointed than I'd like to admit, and even more so when I checked my phone and found nothing from him. Not a goodbye. Not even a dirty joke or a request for nudes.

Shayne and I stayed up way too late, watching movies, catching up, and making plans for today. We decided to drive over to the next town to do some shopping for our dorm and make a day of it. Between finals, the holidays, and break, it still looks like we just moved in. We're three stores in, having picked out towels and décor for our bathroom, new sheets for me, and an actual table to eat at, when we decide to get lunch.

"I need sustenance," she groans, swinging an oversized shopping bag into the back of her car.

"Where to?"

There are dozens of little restaurants within walking distance. "Flour?" I ask, spotting the restaurant that's famous for its delicious sourdough bread bowls and soup.

"Hell yes."

"So," Shayne says, pushing her bowl of the soup to the side before leaning forward, resting her elbows on top of the table, her chin propped on her folded hands. I already know what's coming from the tone of her voice and the look in her eye. "You hooked up with someone."

"It was nothing serious." I pinch off a piece of bread bowl before stuffing it into my mouth.

"That hickey looks pretty serious." She flashes a bright smile, leaning forward even more, flicking her blonde hair behind her shoulder. "Did you at least get an orgasm out of the deal?"

I roll my eyes, pulling the collar of my crewneck sweatshirt up to cover said hickey. I'm going to kick Holden's ass for that one. "One or two." I shrug.

Her eyebrows shoot up, impressed.

"Or six?" Six in one day, but I leave that part out. I've lost count of how many times Holden's made me come.

"Six!" she shouts with a smack to the tabletop before remembering our surroundings, glancing around at the heads that have turned in our direction. "Six?" she repeats, her voice a whisper this time.

Her phone lights up on the table, temporarily saving me from having to answer. "Last party of winter break," she says, flashing the text from Christina, one of her volleyball friends.

"I heard about that one." The cheer group chat has been talking about it all morning.

"Are we going?"

I feel like I've been cooped up since my injury, whether in the cabin or in the dorms. I've been in this sex-induced Holden haze and today's the first time I've come up for air. It hasn't stopped me from thinking about him, though. With every twinge of soreness between my legs, with each brush of my shirt against my raw nipples—I shake away my thoughts. The sooner I get back to the real world, the sooner I can stop thinking about Holden.

"I'm down if you are."

"Dunkin on the way home?"

"Obviously."

We both throw down a few bills for a tip before standing to leave. Shayne walks out first, holding the door open for me with her back. "Six orgasms also sound pretty serious, by the way."

I glare at her.

"What? You said no one has ever been able to. Now you found someone you like enough to give you six?" She pauses to think. "Or do you like him *because* he gave you six of them? Honestly, either way is a win."

"I don't like him," I say quickly before amending. "Not like that." What was once the truth now feels like acid on my tongue. After spending these past few weeks together, I don't know how I feel anymore. I definitely don't *dislike* Holden. I was disappointed when we didn't get to have a proper goodbye fuck last night. Then this morning, I woke up missing his warmth, his touch, his *scent*, and just…him.

Fuck. I *like* Holden Ames.

The realization has my heart beating faster, panic suddenly and inexplicably blooming in my chest.

"So, it's just sex?" Shayne asks, oblivious to my impending internal meltdown.

"Just sex," I confirm, my tone resolute. "Temporary sex."

She stops short on the sidewalk, giving me a weird look.

"What?"

"It's okay to like someone, you know. Or want someone. It doesn't make you weak or embarrassing. It makes you human."

"I know," I say lightly, but it doesn't sound convincing even to my own ears.

"And so we're clear, casual hookups are cool, too, if that's your choice. I know you're allergic to talking about your feelings, so that's all I'm going to say on the subject."

I press my lips together, suppressing a smile. "Okay." I knock my shoulder into hers. "Thanks, weirdo."

But the truth is, having feelings for Holden doesn't feel okay at all.

THIRTY-SIX

Holden

"GOOD EVENING, GENTLEMEN. HOW MAY I ASSIST YOU?" The woman at the front desk is all teeth, her ruby lips stretched into a permanent smile as she greets us.

"We're here to see our father," I say.

"Of course. Is he a guest at our hotel or a resident?"

"Resident."

"Unit number?"

I look over to Thayer who shrugs. "Fuck if I know. I've never been here before."

That makes two of us. "Not sure," I tell her.

Her smile slips a little, either pitying us or finding us suspicious, I'm not sure. I'd guess most people probably know exactly where their parents live. "What's his name?"

"August Ames."

Recognition flashes in her wide eyes. At least I know we're in the right place. "May I please see some identification?"

I reach for my pocket for my wallet, but Thayer beats me to it, slapping his driver's license onto the marble counter. She verifies that we are who we say we are before sliding it back to him. "I can't let you up there without his permission, but I can call him if you'd like?"

"Please do," Thayer says, losing his patience. Not at the lady who's doing her job, but at the situation at hand. You'd think we'd be on some type of approved visitors list. This lady didn't even seem to know we existed.

She types something into her computer and then dials his unit number before holding the phone up to her ear. I can hear it ringing from the other side of the desk. And ringing. And ringing. Just when I'm sure he isn't going to answer, I hear his muffled voice come through the speaker.

"Sorry to bother you, Mr. Ames, but your sons are here to see you?" She sounds unsure, as if she isn't convinced that we are who we say we are. "Do I have permission to go ahead and send them up?"

There's a beat of silence before he responds, but his voice is too muffled to make out what he says.

"Great, I'll send them on their way. Enjoy the rest of your evening." She hangs up the phone, her smile back in place. "The residential elevators are just over to the right of the lobby." She hands us a plastic key card with a gold logo on the front. "This will give you access to the elevator. Take that all the way up to the top floor, and he's in unit 5802."

I take the key card, thanking her, and we're on our way. We head straight for the elevators, not bothering to look around the place that my dad calls his second home. Once the elevator door glides open, we step inside. I lean back, bracing my hands against the rectangular handrail, the cool, hard metal edges biting into my palms as Thayer hits the floor number.

"What's your plan?" I ask. Thayer stayed on my couch last night so we could leave first thing in the morning, and I lay in bed, awake all night. All I wanted was to go across the hall and climb into Valen's bed, but I didn't want to risk getting caught. Personally, I don't give a fuck who knows about our...situation. But she does. By the time I finally started to doze off, Thayer was knocking on my door, telling me it was time to leave. I managed to sleep for a while in the car, but that means we didn't get to talk strategy.

"Get answers," is all he says, making me laugh at the irony.

"This coming from you? The one who always gives me shit for being impulsive and reckless?"

"Hardly the same thing," he deadpans.

The elevator dings, reaching the top sooner than I thought possible. We step out into the hall, the thick, plush carpet absorbing our heavy footsteps.

"Right here," I say, pointing to the door plate listed as number 5802. My dad takes his sweet ass time coming to the door, and when he finally answers, he doesn't look particularly happy to see us.

"Boys," he greets us, swinging the door open wide. He looks slightly sweaty, and his belt is undone, like he got dressed in a rush. "What'd you do this time?"

"Oh, ye of little faith," I say, walking inside his apartment. I let out a low whistle, taking the place in. It's huge. Open floor plan. All sleek and modern, the complete opposite of our Heartbreak Hill home. I make my way over to the floor-to-ceiling windows with a view of the whole city. We're quite literally above the clouds up here. "I see why you never come home these days."

"I have a lot of meetings," he says. "We're working on expanding our routes."

"Clearly," Thayer says drily.

I turn around to see what he means to find a bra dangling from his outstretched hand. My dad snatches it from him with an exasperated expression. I raise a brow, looking at Thayer to see if he's thinking the same thing. Dear old Dad got some afternoon delight, and I'd bet the *delight* is still here. Walking down the hallway to my right, I make an educated guess as to where his bedroom is. The door is slightly ajar, so I nudge it open with the toe of my shoe.

A startled blonde, early thirties from the looks of it, is in the middle of shoving her arm through the sleeve of her button-up cream-colored blouse. Her hands fly to conceal her chest and I close my eyes, turning back for the hall. Jesus Christ.

"Sorry to interrupt," I say over my shoulder. "We have some family business to discuss. You understand."

She doesn't respond verbally, but after a second or two, I hear her heels clacking against the floor behind me. Red in the cheeks, she hurries over to my dad, who holds out her bra, appearing unfazed if not mildly annoyed. She stuffs it in her purse as my dad gives her an apologetic yet impersonal pat to the shoulder. "I'll call you later, Haley."

She nods, not bothering to acknowledge either of us before she strides out of the apartment.

I fold my arms across my chest, slightly amused but mostly grossed out. "Well, she seems nice," I say with false cheerfulness once the door slams shut.

He clears his throat, walking over to the bar area, picking up a bottle of whiskey and a glass tumbler. "As always, your timing is impeccable. Turnabout's fair play, I suppose."

Thayer sends me a *what the fuck is he talking about* look and I shrug my shoulders, playing dumb. He doesn't need to know our dad caught me seconds from being inside Valen on our uncle's patio.

"I thought I told you to be on your best behavior," my dad says, switching gears, as if the last sixty seconds never happened.

"I have been on my best behavior. Talk to your brother about *behaving*."

"Your best behavior involves coming to blows with your uncle after I specifically asked you to let me handle it?"

"That was *after* he showed up in Shayne's dorm."

That gets his attention. Figures Samuel conveniently left that part out. My dad tolerates most people at best, but he seems to have a soft spot for Shayne, probably due to his lingering feelings for her and Grey's mom. Something she'd never agree with. He's well aware of everything that went down last year when Samuel told Christian to make sure Shayne didn't become a problem.

He didn't consider her a legitimate threat, though. Not really. Us finding out the truth about Danny's death was an inconvenience at most. He counted on the fact that we were family, and that my dad would be able to shut us up easily enough. And he was fucking right. Until now.

Now that I have his attention, I explain everything. I tell him about Valen covering for us, about Samuel showing up to the dorm she shares with Shayne. I tell him about Christian turning in the video from that night, and how he gloated about having it buried. Against my better judgment, I leave out the part about the security cameras. My dad witnessed what transpired on that balcony with Valen and me, but he never saw her face.

He blows out a breath before pouring himself a glass of whiskey and taking a swig. At eleven A.M. "I don't think you'll have to worry about him anymore," he says after a minute of thinking.

"Oh okay. That's reassuring," Thayer says, heavy on the sarcasm. "We'll just go home now then."

"He's currently preoccupied," he explains. "Your brother's little speech put eyes on Samuel. It took a few days for news to spread, but the media's been calling him, asking about Christian. Inevitably, they'll start looking in other places. Starting with his questionable rulings." He takes another drink. "Which, you can imagine, is not ideal for him. He's under a microscope right now and has been working overtime to maintain his image and talking with his lawyers for the past few days. Your grandfather said he's talking about hiring a crisis management team should things continue to escalate. I guarantee he'll be too busy and too careful to risk doing anything stupid right now. Especially to his own family."

Damn. I hoped my public callout would force his hand and he'd have to explain where Christian went, but I didn't consider the ripple effect it might have. Even better.

"Shayne and Valen aren't his family," Thayer reminds him. "And we've seen how he treats his own flesh and blood, so forgive me if I don't feel reassured by the sentiment," I add. "If anything, now he has more of a reason to fuck with us."

"I've asked you both multiple times to stand down and let me handle this. If only you had this much interest in the family business."

He's baiting us into changing the subject. He counted on Danny to take over AmesAir as the oldest and most business-minded, but then he died and responsibility fell to us. Unfortunately for him, Thayer has zero interest, and as far as my dad's concerned, I'm too much of a fuck up. A loose cannon and last resort. Fine with me.

"You've had a year to handle it. If you want us to sit back and do nothing, you're going to have to give us something here." I try to reason with him.

"He indirectly went after Shayne once," Thayer says. "If you think I'll stand by—"

"There is a plan in place," he interrupts through gritted teeth, clearly losing his patience with us. "But if he knows people are looking into him, he's going to cover his tracks before I have a chance to get what I need. You can see how your latest stunt might pose a problem. It might be too late as it is."

Thayer and I exchange looks. I didn't see that coming, and judging by the look on his face, neither did he. My dad is working *against* his own brother? Well, color me surprised. I didn't think he had it in him.

"What exactly are you planning?" I ask, still unconvinced. Who's to say this isn't simply lip service to shut us up? "And what about William?" My dad taking down Samuel is enough of a stretch, but my grandfather? I have a hard time believing that. Then again, William Ames is nothing if not mercenary.

"That's not for you to worry about. But if you have incriminating evidence—I'm talking hard evidence, not this circumstantial shit—you send it to me. Other than that, if you have even a lick of sense, you won't speak a word of this to anyone else. You want to keep Shayne and her friend safe? Then keep them out of it, too."

"You mean like video evidence of him covering up a crime?" I ask pointedly. "Because we've had that in our pockets for a year now."

"And look what good turning it in did. We need to be smart about this. All of our futures depend on it."

"Answer me one thing," I say, dread crawling up my spine.

He dips his chin, gesturing with his hand for me to get on with it.

"Do you know what happened to Christian?"

"No." His answer comes without hesitation.

I work my jaw, glancing over at Thayer before looking back to my dad. "Do you think he hurt him?"

He sighs, his gaze flicking back and forth between us. "I don't know," he says, but the haunted look in his eyes makes me think otherwise. "We'll find out. I can promise you that as long as you—"

"Let you handle it," Thayer finishes for him. "I think we've got it."

"Good." He walks over to the door, a clear indication that our visit is over.

Knowing that we won't get anything more out of him to-night, we allow him to kick us out, following behind him.

"Oh, and boys?" he says as we're leaving. "Next time you want to stop by, call first."

THIRTY-SEVEN

Holden

"Y̲O̲U̲ S̲T̲A̲Y̲I̲N̲G̲ A̲T̲ S̲H̲A̲Y̲N̲E̲'̲S̲ T̲O̲N̲I̲G̲H̲T̲?" I A̲S̲K̲ M̲Y̲ brother. We're walking back to Hawthorne Hall after being stuck in the car all day.

"Yeah, probably. Fuckin' sick of driving."

Getting back from Boston took a lot longer than it took to get there. Traffic in the city is bad on any given day, but throw in a Celtics game and you're fucked. I can tell he's anxious to get back to Shayne, especially after tonight's revelations. Something that feels a lot like jealousy twists inside my stomach. How would it feel to have that? To have Valen every night, not only to sleep with, but to *talk* to. To touch. To call mine. *What the fuck is wrong with me?* Of all my fucked-up fantasies, the one about having a girlfriend has to be the most demented.

"You think Dad's full of shit, or do you think he actually plans on doing something about Samuel?" Thayer asks, pulling me from my thoughts.

"Hard to tell. Usually, I'd say that the best predictor of future behavior is past behavior. But if what he says is true and they're digging into Samuel, he'll want to separate himself to save his own ass."

He nods. "That's what I was thinking. I'm guessing he

and William are trying to figure out how to deal with the business. Buy out his share of the company or something."

I shake my head. "He'll never sell. If they so much as tried to buy him out, he'd know they were up to something."

"They'll figure something out. No way in hell they're going down with him."

That's one thing we can agree on. I check my phone for the time and see a text from Ryan on the screen.

Where u at?

There's a party tonight, and since Hadley won their game, everyone's going to be there to celebrate it along with making the most of the last weekend before break ends. I told Ryan I'd think about it before I left, but after today, there's nothing I'd rather do less.

Nah, just getting back into town. Gonna call it a night.

He responds almost instantly.

So you won't mind if I keep your girl company tonight then?

What the fuck is he talking about? Before I get the chance to ask, another text comes in.

Scratch that. Looks like someone beat me to it.

Attached is a video of Valen at said party. I squint at the screen as if that will help me see more clearly through the drunk bodies and flashing lights. I don't have to have a clear picture to know she looks good. He zooms in on Valen and Shayne dancing just in time to see some guy move in behind Valen. The video cuts off before I can see what happens next.

"Change of plans. We're going to a frat party." I show Thayer the still of the video.

He shrugs. "Contrary to what you seem to believe, we do things separate sometimes. I'm not going to a fucking frat—"

I hit play on the video. He takes one look at the guy trying to grind on Shayne and Valen, his mouth snaps shut, and we both head back for the car.

Me: On my way. Let anyone touch her and I'll kill you.

Ryan: Thought so.

THIRTY-EIGHT

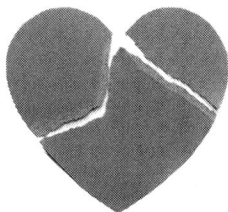

Holden

THE AIR IS THICK WITH THE SCENT OF SWEATY BODIES AND beer. We push through the crowd and I spot Shayne and Valen surrounded by people in the kitchen. Instead of yelling over the music, I jerk my chin in their direction to let Thayer know where they are.

"Ames!" Clay, a guy on the basketball team, shouts, stepping in front of me, effectively blocking my path to Valen. "You ready to play next season?"

"That's the plan," I say, clapping him on the shoulder. "Congrats on the win."

He gives me an animated play-by-play of the game over the sound of the music blaring from the speakers, gesticulating wildly with a beer in hand. When I look back at Valen, the guy from the video is lifting a red cup to her lips. She jerks back, shaking her head. He doesn't take the fucking hint and tries again, this time shoving it past her lips.

I move Clay to the side, quickly walking toward her with Thayer hot on my heels. Valen handles her own, though, slapping the cup from his hand. It sloshes all over him before falling to the floor. I can't tell what she's saying, but I can tell that it isn't pleasant by the fierce look on her face and the finger she stabs into his chest.

My dick twitches in my pants and I look over to find Thayer

watching the scene with amusement written all over his face. If it was Shayne, it'd be another story entirely. I reel in my temper, knowing Valen has it handled. I'm not exactly playing it cool, but Thayer hasn't called me on it, so I must not be as transparent as I feel.

I can tell Shayne shouts something along the lines of "get the fuck out of here," and the guy runs off with his tail between his legs, soaked and humiliated, finally leaving their friend group alone. Cheerleaders. They're not in uniform, but the hair and the temporary tattoo of Hadley's seal on their cheeks gives it away.

The handsy fuck shouts at people to move out of his way. I know Valen already handled it. She doesn't need a knight in shining armor to defend her honor or a protective boyfriend who punches holes in the drywall in his spare time, so I should leave well enough alone. But when he tries to pass me, my foot darts out in front of him, causing him to trip and fall on his face.

He starts to yell, pushing himself up off the ground with his hands, but I stop him with a foot between his shoulder blades, keeping him pinned to the floor. When he stops struggling, I remove my weight and squat down next to him. He rolls onto his back, glaring up at me as he gasps for air, but he must be smarter than he looks because he doesn't say a word.

"No means no," I say, giving him a slap much too hard to be considered a friendly pat to the cheek. I lean in a little closer, keeping my voice low enough so Thayer doesn't overhear. "If you so much as look in her direction again, I'll rip your fucking nuts off and feed them to you."

He nods, red-faced and seething, and I stand. The crowd of bodies parts to let us through now that we've gained their attention. I can feel Thayer's eyes burning into my side profile as we head over to Shayne and Valen.

"What?" I ask. "Foot slipped."

He arches a disbelieving brow that I ignore. Valen's back is to us, so Shayne spots us first, breaking away from the group and making her way toward us.

"How'd it go?" she shouts, looking between us expectantly.

"Tell you later," Thayer says back, pulling her in for a hug.

Shayne shakes her head, pulling away. "Tell me now. Let's go out back so I can hear you."

"I gotta piss." The excuse easily rolls off my tongue as I take a couple backward steps, pointing toward the hall. "Meet you out back in a few."

Shayne nods before leading Thayer to the backyard. When she passes Valen, she motions with her hand that she's going out back. Valen nods in understanding, and I don't miss the way her eyes scan the room. She can deny her feelings all she wants, but she's always looking for me. My feet are propelling me toward her before I've made the conscious decision to do so, like some kind of invisible string pulling us together.

"You look lonely," I hear the flirtatious voice a second before the person it belongs to intercepts me on my way to Valen. I vaguely recognize the blonde standing in front of me, but I couldn't tell you her name if my life depended on it.

"I won't be in about two seconds if you'll excuse me," I say, moving around her. Her palm lands in the center of my chest, stopping me. I give her hand a pointed look, then meet her eyes with what I know is an impatient expression.

Undeterred by my disinterest, she looks up at me through hooded eyes. "I could help you with that?"

Pre-Valen, I might've taken her up on the offer. Post-Valen me isn't even slightly tempted. I should be concerned about the revelation, but I can't find it in me to give a fuck right now. She takes my silence as acquiesce, running her finger down my chest.

"Not interested." I seek out Valen again, but I'm surprised to find her already looking at me. More specifically, at the finger still trailing down my chest. She's so focused on that pink fingernail that she doesn't notice me watching her, her eyebrows pulled together, lips pursed. Oh, she's jealous. And I couldn't feel more satisfied by that fact.

Ryan suddenly appears, pulling my attention away from

Valen. He hooks an arm around the girl's shoulders, the beers he's double fisting sloshing over the side of the cups with the movement. "Holden can't help you tonight, baby. But I can."

She laughs, leaning into his side. "Hi, Ryan."

He flashes his megawatt smile at me. "It's about time you showed your ugly mug."

"Thought I told you not to let anyone touch her?"

He frowns, confused, handing me one of the cups. "I watched her until I saw you walk in, then I grabbed us beers. Did something happen?" He looks over at Valen and I follow suit. Her expression turns from burning hot jealousy to blank and vacant in two seconds flat. I almost wonder if I imagined the reaction, but her stiff posture tells me I didn't. She pins me with those emotionless eyes for a second longer before she breaks contact. The ice princess is trying to take over, but it's too late. I already saw what I needed to see.

"Nothing she couldn't handle."

"No harm, no foul then. It's not like she's your girlfriend, anyway, right?" he taunts.

Blondie presses up on her toes to whisper something in Ryan's ear and I take the opportunity to gulp down my beer, blocking out whatever the fuck they're saying. No, she's not my girlfriend. But the idea doesn't bother me like it would with anyone else. By the time I look over to where Valen is again, she's gone.

I barely notice when a few more of our friends and some girls I don't know join our group. I'm on autopilot, giving one-word responses, too busy trying to catch a glimpse of Valen. Maybe she went outside to find Shayne. Maybe she left.

Finally, I catch sight of her near the stairs, being approached by yet another guy I don't recognize. Her back is to me, so I have a prime view when he bends over to hug her, his hands lingering on her lower back a little too long for my liking. She must know him because she doesn't scowl or kick him in the balls for daring to touch her. Valen doesn't like anyone. So who the fuck is this douche in boat shoes who can walk up to her and hug her with the familiarity of an old friend? Or lover?

Lover? Who the fuck talks like that? What is she doing to me?

"Jesus Christ, it's worse than I thought," Ryan says, following my line of sight. "You're so fucked."

I don't bother denying it. I pull out my phone, sending her a text.

> **Me: You can do better than this guy. He's wearing boat shoes, Valen.**
>
> **Me: ...in January.**

She glances down at her phone in her hand, but I can't see her face from this angle, so I have no way of judging her reaction.

> **Valen: Stop stalking me. And he's nice.**
>
> **Me: You'd get bored with a nice boy.**
>
> **Valen: You're nice to me. Are you calling yourself boring?**
>
> **Me: I'm nice to you in ways that end with orgasms. There's a difference.**
>
> **Valen: You looked pretty cozy with Quinn a minute ago. Go be nice to her.**

Quinn. So that's her name.

> **Me: Are you jealous?**
>
> **Valen: Please.**
>
> **Me: Please what? Be specific. You know I love it when you beg.**

To that, she doesn't respond, deciding to pay attention to the *nice guy* in front of her instead. Luckily, she doesn't keep the conversation going much longer, giving him a friendly squeeze to his upper arm before she walks away.

272 | CHARLEIGH ROSE

"Ouch," Ryan says, apparently still watching. "Friend-zoned for sure."

"He's right," Quinn agrees. "The body language tells it all."

Ryan scoops her up into his arms with his free hand and she squeals in surprise as she winds her arms around his neck. "What's my body language telling you?"

Annnd that's my cue to leave.

I ditch the rest of my drink on the fireplace before I set off in search of Valen, keeping my gaze straight ahead. I avoid eye contact, not wanting to get held up by anyone else. I catch up to her upstairs in the hallway, heading for the line of people waiting for the bathroom. Before she sees me coming, I grab a hold of her hand and yank her into the nearest bedroom. She yelps, caught off guard as I close the door behind her.

"Running from me, Sweet Valentine?"

The room is dark, and I don't hear any moans coming from the bed behind me, so I'm fairly confident that we're alone in here. Thank fuck.

"You should get back to Quinn," she says, her breathy voice sounding more than a little bitter.

I smile, crowding her space until she backs up against the wall. "Did it bother you? Seeing me with her? Seeing her touch me?"

"Why should it?" she asks, but I can hear the forced ambivalence in her tone. "You can do whatever you want, remember? And if she's what you want—"

"She's not my type," I cut her off.

"She's everyone's type," she counters. "She's cool, too. You should go for it."

She's so full of shit.

"I'm sure she's great, but you should know by now that my type is bratty brunettes who are too ashamed to be seen in public with me." I twirl a stand of her hair around my finger before giving it a sharp tug. "Now stop pretending like you haven't missed me."

"You're the one stalking me," she says into the dark. "If anyone's missing someone, it's you."

I slide my hand along the side of her neck, my thumb grazing her cheek. I can't see her expression, but I can feel the pulse jumping in her neck.

"I did miss you," I say bluntly, deciding to lay it all out there. "I missed falling asleep with you. I missed waking up and smelling Creamsicles in my bed before I even open my eyes. I missed touching you—"

Valen interrupts by linking her fingers behind my neck, pulling me down to kiss me. I lift her by the backs of her thighs, and she moans into my mouth, telling me everything with this kiss that she won't let herself say out loud. This girl is like a drug to me, seeping into my bloodstream, making me more addicted with each taste of her tongue. Too soon, she pulls back, breathless.

"I'll take that as a yes," I say, breaking the silence.

She slides down my body, and I reluctantly let her go. "We can't do this here," she says.

As much as I hate to admit it, she's right. Shayne and Thayer are probably already looking for us. I pull my phone out of my pocket, and as I suspected, there's a text from Thayer asking where I went.

Valen reaches for the doorknob, bathing the room in light. I squint against it and go to follow her out, but she whirls around on me. "Get back in there!" she whisper-yells, shoving me back. "I'll go first. Wait two minutes and then you can leave."

"You're starting to give me a complex, you know that?"

"It's good for your ego," she quips, right before she slams the door in my face.

Valen is drunk.

I don't know how it happened, but what I thought was going

to be a quick stop turned into hanging out for two hours. At first, it was all fun and games as Thayer and I watched from the perimeter of the room with amusement as Valen and Shayne danced, together. If you can call it that. Valen's hands were on Shayne's shoulders, her long hair bouncing behind her as they laughed and screamed the words to every song at the top of their lungs.

Things took a turn when we tried to tell them to rethink the last two shots of fuck knows what kind of cheap ass liquor, knowing it would send them past the point of no return. Shayne laughed in Thayer's face, throwing the shot back before he could finish his sentence. Valen followed suit, and then they both ran off like a couple of bank robbers. That was about ten minutes ago.

"Guess we should go find them," Thayer says.

"We?" I ask, raising a brow. "That's boyfriend duty. I'm just the brother," I joke, not wanting to seem too eager to help. Thayer already suspects something's going on between Valen and me. I need to reel it in.

"The sooner we find them, the sooner we can get out of here."

"Good point." This is the last place I want to be after today.

I follow him upstairs, pushing through the clusters of drunken bodies. There's a line like earlier, but this time, a couple of girls are pounding their fists against the door, yelling at whoever's in there to hurry while another girl crosses her ankles, hands clutching her crotch as she bounces around like she's trying not to piss herself.

"Ah fuck," I mutter, knowing that's exactly where they are. The girls at the door move aside when we get there. I raise my fist, knocking hard, yelling for them to open up. I put my ear to the door, listening for any indication that it is, in fact, Shayne and Valen. Nothing.

The door is locked when I jiggle the handle, but it's one of those janky ass locks that can be opened by sticking a coin in the slot. I turn around, eyeing the girls lined up behind me. "You," I say, pointing at one of them with long fake nails. "Come here."

She steps forward with a confused frown, but she doesn't argue as I take a hold of her wrist and use her thumbnail to turn the lock. "Thanks," I say, pushing the door open. Thayer and I both pause in the doorway, taking in the scene in front of us.

"Jesus Christ," he mutters. Shayne's made friends with the toilet bowl, her face way too close to the seat to be deemed safe in a frat house. Valen appears to be wetting a washcloth for her at the sink. Shayne reaches over, trying to pull herself up by the waistband of Valen's jeans, except instead of pulling herself up, she ends up pulling Valen's pants *down,* exposing her black thong. They both fall to the floor, cackling.

I stifle a laugh, looking over at Thayer who does the same.

"I'm going to pee my pants," a desperate voice says behind me, snapping us into motion.

Bending over, I work Valen's pants back up over her ass and hips, willing my dick not to react. "Upsy-daisy," I say, scooping her up into my arms as Thayer peels Shayne off the floor and tosses her over his shoulder.

"All yours," Thayer says to the girl who doesn't wait for us to close the door before pulling her dress up and sitting her ass on the toilet.

Twenty minutes later, we're pulling into the student parking lot with two bags of mostly uneaten fast food that Shayne insisted on stopping for before promptly passing out in the back seat of Thayer's Hellcat. When we open the back door, they're both asleep. Shayne's slumped against Valen with a lap full of French fries, while Valen's head rests on top of Shayne's.

"Like herding fucking cats," I say.

"Wake up, baby," Thayer says, pulling Shayne upright. "Where the hell are your shoes?"

"I don't want to go home," Shayne groans, without opening her eyes or answering his question.

"We're already here. Let's go inside."

She shakes her head. "I was having fun."

"We can still have fun," he says. "If you come inside, we can watch *Criminal Minds*."

She peels one eye open, squinting up at him. "Really?"

He nods.

"Can you take off my makeup, too?"

Valen, who has apparently woken from her slumber, laughs at that.

"Deal," he says, bending down to lift her out of the car.

Bracing my hand on the roof of the car, I lean down to look at Valen. The strap of her shirt hangs off her shoulder, her hair is wild, eyes glassy, nose red from the cold, and she's still the most beautiful fucking thing I've ever seen. "Do you need to be carried, too?"

"I can walk," she says, scooting toward the edge of the seat instead of opening the door she's closest to. She takes the hand I hold out for her, letting me help her out of the car. She gets a few wobbly steps in before tripping over her own feet. I catch her before she goes down, steadying her at the waist. She lets me help her to her room, which is a testament to how drunk she is because accepting help is not something Valen knows how to do.

Thayer's helping Shayne into the bathroom when we catch up to them, and a second later, I hear the shower turn on. Once we're in Valen's room, she plops down on her bed before tearing her shirt off. "It's really fucking hot in here."

I kneel in front of her to help her out of her shoes and jeans, leaving her in nothing but the tiniest black thong I've ever seen and a matching bra. I leave those on, but apparently, she has other plans. She stands, hooking her thumbs into the sides of her underwear before pulling them down her legs, leaving her bare pussy centimeters from my face. She reaches for her bra next as I hold on to her hips to keep her steady. Once she's fully, torturously naked, she slides her fingers into my hair, sending goosebumps down my spine as she looks down at me.

Jesus, fuck, she's going to be the death of me.

I lean forward, pressing a kiss to her hipbone before I stand and walk over to her dresser, pulling out one of her baggy shirts she likes to sleep in. She takes it, giving me a look I can't decipher as she pulls it over her head.

"I hate it when you're nice to me," she grumbles.

I snort out a laugh. "I know."

"So why do you keep doing it?"

Because I like you and I'm secretly waiting for you to realize that you like me, too.

"Because I'm a masochist."

THIRTY-NINE

Valen

I FEEL LIKE SHIT. I DIDN'T PLAN ON GETTING DRUNK LAST NIGHT. Shayne and I usually have strict rules about how much we drink when we're out, always making sure at least one of us is sober enough to drive and make decisions. But then Thayer and Holden showed up, and we couldn't pass up the golden opportunity to let our guards down at the same time. It didn't help that I was already on the verge of spiraling due to the horrifying realization that I might have *actual* feelings for Holden. Suffice it to say, waking up this morning was rough.

It would have been worse if Holden didn't make me chug a bottle of water after taking two Ibuprofen. I expected him to stay with me even though I tried to break things off, but annoyingly, he was the perfect gentleman and left after tucking me in. Probably a good thing, considering the fact that both Shayne and Thayer stayed here last night.

"Ready," I mumble to Shayne, still half-asleep as I grab my keys off the counter and trudge toward the door. It's too early to be alive, but Shayne always wakes up at the crack of dawn after drinking. Thayer's still passed out in her bed, so she bribed me with the promise of another breakfast bagel from Nicky's and an iced coffee in exchange for taking her to pick up her car before the sun has fully risen. We're both wearing Hadley crewnecks, baggy sweats, unwashed hair thrown up, and oversized sunglasses. All that to say, we look about as good as we feel. At least Shayne is wearing real shoes. I couldn't be bothered to put on anything other than my fleece-lined slippers.

"God, I don't even know if my stomach can handle food right now," Shayne groans, opening the door and stepping out into the hall. I open my mouth to respond, but the door across from ours swings open at the same time, and the words die on my tongue at the sight in front of me.

"Valen!" Quinn chirps, entirely too bright-eyed and enthusiastic for six in the morning, but my attention is locked on to the person behind her. Holden looks at me, bare-chested and eyes wide with panic. Quinn is still in her dress from last night, looking just as perfect as she did before we left. Even her sex hair looks good. I want to hate her, and in this moment, I do a little. But she doesn't deserve my anger. She did nothing wrong. Technically, neither did he. We're not together. So why do I have a lump in my throat and an ache in my chest? And why do I have the sudden urge to claw her eyes out? Technically, our arrangement is over. I just didn't expect Holden to find a replacement so soon.

"Last night was crazy," she says, filling the awkward silence. When I still don't speak, she continues. "How's your ankle, by the way?" I tell myself to say something, but I'm stunned silent. I can feel Shayne looking at me with concern and that's what snaps me out of my frozen state.

"Feels brand new," I say, pasting on a counterfeit smile in record time. "If it were up to me, I'd be back already."

"Oh, good. Hopefully I'll see you at practice soon. Are you at least coming for media day?"

I nod. "I should be back by then."

"Thank God. Between you and me, Lilah can't tumble for shit, and Jada's making everyone want to quit."

She leaves me with that bit of information, then turns around to hug Holden before she walks off with a wave. Shayne asks Holden something about their visit to their dad last night, but I don't catch it, too busy trying to make sense of the inexplicable hurt I'm feeling. I've been cheated on. *Publicly*. By my actual boyfriend of a year. I've watched my dad abandon me for a new family. I've had my mom choose men over me, time and time again. Why do I give a shit that Holden did exactly what Holden does? Why is this what finally penetrates my numb exterior?

After a minute or two, they finish their conversation, and we walk out to my car. I can feel Holden's eyes on my back the whole way, but I don't turn around.

"Are you okay?" Shayne asks once we're outside. "What was that about?"

"My stomach is still messed up," I say, telling a half-truth. "I thought I might throw up."

"Do you want to go lie down? If you give me your keys, I can go grab our food and coffee."

I shake my head. "No, it's fine. I think the fresh air will help."

After we got back, we spent the rest of the day ordering groceries for the week, comparing classes so we could plan our study schedule together, then we lay around on the couch, alternating between taking cat naps and scrolling on our phones while movies played in the background that neither one of us really paid attention to. Sometimes you just need a day to do nothing but rot on the couch with your best friend.

Thayer came back after being gone for most of the day and caught us up on the conversation they had with their dad and assured us that we wouldn't have to worry about Samuel. It might've been more of a relief if he seemed like he actually believed that, but I'm not too worried about it.

Now that I'm in bed, I open my texts, allowing myself to read the string of messages Holden sent earlier.

Holden: I realize what that looked like, but I didn't fuck her.

Holden: Answer me so I know that you don't think I hooked up with someone else.

Holden: Nothing happened.

Holden: Don't make me come over there.

After rational thought kicked in earlier, I realized pretty quickly that it was entirely likely that Quinn could've been there for Ryan. The *problem* is the way I felt when I thought Holden slept with her. I'm not supposed to like him. I've never truly liked anyone. I've spent so many years trying to conjure up feelings for boys who wanted me, and when that didn't work, I pretended. For a long time, I assumed everyone else was a pretender, too.

Now, the only thing I'm pretending is that I don't have feelings for him. As I drift to sleep, I do so wondering if Holden might make good on his threat of coming over and sneaking into my bed later.

He never comes.

I toss my backpack into one of the few empty booths in the corner and open my laptop to read an article on the impact of social media on journalism for my introduction to journalism course. I read it three times, but I don't retain any of it, barely able to focus on the words on the screen. I haven't been here for more than ten minutes before I'm interrupted.

Walking into the bustling student union a few days later, I head for a small booth right next to the big glass window where the sun beats down after the first day of spring semester. The place is packed, and I can't help but miss how quiet campus was when everyone was gone over break. On the flip side, I'm glad the dining halls are open again.

I toss my backpack into one of the few empty booths in the corner and open my laptop to read an article on the impact of social media on journalism for my introduction to journalism course. I read it three times, but I don't retain any of it, barely able to focus on the words on the screen. I haven't been here for more than ten minutes before I'm interrupted.

"You're avoiding me," Holden says in way of a greeting.

He's wearing that stupid backward hat again and a stupid plain white t-shirt that showcases his stupid biceps even though it's twenty-five degrees outside.

"When am I not avoiding you?" I tease, trying to keep things light. He slides into the booth across from me because it would be very un-Holden like to wait for an invitation. "Help yourself," I say sarcastically.

"I swear I didn't fuck her," he starts without preamble.

I blink at him before taking stock of our surroundings. He wants to do this *here*? In front of the whole damn campus? "You don't owe me an explanation."

"After I put you to bed, I went back to my room. Twenty minutes later, Ryan showed up with Quinn. I walked her out in the morning because I don't fucking sleep on a normal night—but throw in all the moaning and skin slapping going on—"

"Holden." I hold up a hand to stop him, my cheeks tingling with embarrassment at the mention of him putting my drunk ass to bed. "I believe you."

His eyebrows shoot up. "You do." It's a question, but his skeptical tone makes it sound more like statement.

"Unless I shouldn't." I laugh, second-guessing myself.

"No, you should. I mean…" He pauses, frowning in an adorable way. "If you believe me, then why the fuck are you avoiding me?"

I shrug, aiming for unaffected. "I'm not avoiding you." Lie. "The break ended. That was the deal."

"Fuck the deal." His voice rises in volume, earning some curious looks. "We both know that's not what this is."

"Can you lower your voice?"

Leaning back in the booth, he crosses his arms over his chest and rolls his tongue along the inside of his cheek, assessing. "What's this really about?"

I fix my eyes on the screen of my laptop, avoiding his probing stare. I hate when he sees more than he's supposed to. "I don't know what you want from me."

"I think you know exactly what I want from you," he counters without hesitation. "The question is, why are you so fucking scared to admit that you want it, too?"

I shake my head, snapping my laptop shut and shoving it into my backpack. "I have to go."

FORTY

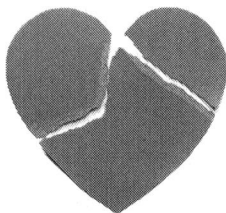

Holden

"REMIND ME HOW YOU MADE THE TEAM," Ryan says after my third shot in a row bounces off the rim. We've been at it for an hour, and I'm off my game. I haven't had a decent night's sleep in over a week. Valen's still avoiding me. Practice and classes starting back up have kept us both busy, but it's more than that. I'm not even convinced it's about the whole Quinn misunderstanding. The only good thing is that my dad seems to have been right about my uncle. He's too busy doing damage control and covering his tracks to worry about fucking with us. But we're no closer to finding Christian, and it's weighing on me more than I'd like to admit.

"Wasn't the whole point of sitting the first semester out to get *better*?"

He's giving me shit, but he's right. If I don't get it together before I meet with the coaching staff to evaluate my progress next week, I risk losing my spot on the team permanently. I slacked over break, opting to spend all my time with Valen instead of in the gym or on the court where I should've been.

"Fuck off." My gaze drifts over to the other side of the gym where some cheerleaders are practicing on the mats, but I don't see any sign of Valen.

"Should've known it had something to do with her," Ryan says, smirking. "Trouble in paradise?"

"Something like that."

"You fell for the situationship?" He lets out a low whistle that echoes across the court.

I think about denying it, but I don't bother. Instead, the word vomit pours out of me, unable to keep it in any longer. "I don't know what the hell happened. I'm horny for her *all the time*, but not just for sex. It's like I'm horny for her company. For her mind. For watching movies and…cuddling."

His eyebrows shoot up. "I think that's just called being in love."

I pin him with a glare. "Once again. Fuck off."

"Fine. You *like* the girl," he says with a shrug, simplifying it for my benefit. "What's the problem? She doesn't like you?"

"She likes me. She just doesn't want to admit it." I doubted it for a minute with the way she cut me off so quickly, as if it was easy for her. We said no feelings, but it was more for me. I felt it. I refuse to believe she didn't feel it, too.

"If you believe that, then why have you been in our dorm room being a crybaby bitch for the past week instead of across the hall with your girl?"

I bend over to pick up the ball, throwing it hard into his chest, but he sees it coming and catches it easily with a cocky smile. I lift the bottom of my shirt, using it to wipe the sweat off my brow before walking off the court.

"Don't hate me because I'm right!" he shouts after me.

I grab my phone and hoodie near the wall on my way out, sending a text to Valen.

Me: I'm coming over tonight.

FORTY-ONE

Valen

MY WET HAIR DRIPS ONTO THE FLOOR AT MY FEET AS I WRAP my towel around myself and lean over the sink, reading my earlier texts with Holden to see if he's said anything else.

> **Holden: I'm coming over tonight.**
>
> **Me: I can't.**
>
> **Holden: Too bad. I want to see you.**
>
> **Me: I'm on my period.**

It's not a lie. I'm not usually so blunt, but I'm close to cracking, and it's a guaranteed way to scare him off. I was right because that was hours ago, and he hasn't responded since. I didn't expect to miss seeing Holden this much. He wormed his way into my bed, into my life, and made me like him. The fact that he's ruined my vibrator for me only makes me resent him more.

I wipe the steam off the tiny bathroom mirror above the sink with my hand, then brush my hair before grabbing my phone and heading back to my room. I push open my door, stopping short with a shocked gasp when I find Holden sitting on the edge of my bed.

"What are you *doing* here?" I whisper-yell, quickly shutting the door behind me.

"I told you I was coming," is all he says.

"And *I* told *you* I'm on my period." I walk over to my desk and lean up against it, keeping a safe distance.

"Three things," he starts. "Number one, the fact that you think I don't want to see you if sex isn't involved is bullshit and quite frankly, insulting. Number two, I come bearing gifts." He gestures behind him at a shit ton of candy and chips and beer, and...is that a heated blanket? What did he do? Rob a Costco before coming over?

I swallow hard, not knowing how to feel. "And number three?" I ask, crossing my arms. His answering smirk tells me I should be scared of whatever's about to come out of his mouth next.

"What's the point of having a sword if you never get it bloody?"

I blink at him in surprise. "Oh my God." I didn't think I was capable of being shocked by anything that comes out of Holden's mouth anymore, but I stand corrected.

He doesn't laugh like I expect him to, his gaze filling with heat at it drifts down my towel-clad body. "If you think I'm scared of a little blood, then you severely underestimate the way I feel about you. There's nothing I wouldn't do to you. *With* you."

My heartbeat kicks up a notch when I realize he might be serious. He stands and closes the distance between us. I tilt my head to peer up at him, feigning nonchalance. "Doesn't number three contradict number one?"

He shakes his head, his fingers teasing the opening of my towel near my thighs. "I said there doesn't have to be sex involved, and I meant it. We can lie here and watch a movie and eat snacks if that's what you want."

"And if I don't want to?"

He lifts me by my waist and plops me down onto the top of my desk. I lean back, my palms resting on the solid oak.

"Then I can eat you first and have the snacks second." One

hand grips the base of my neck as he brings his mouth to mine, kissing me, slowly, deliberately, while the other hand trails up the inside of my thigh. God, I've missed this so much. I melt into his kiss, feeling my pulse between my legs as his hand moves higher while his tongue coaxes my lips to part. I don't stop him when he slips a finger inside me. He swallows the desperate sounds clawing their way up my throat, my legs parting slightly, hips shifting forward of their own volition.

"Already so wet," he says against my lips. "Open your legs for me."

I do as he says, because even though I'm slightly humiliated, I've never been more turned on in my life. He adds another finger, eyes glued to where he pumps them in and out. His hand stays anchored on the back of my neck, holding me in place as he fucks me with his fingers.

"Tell me you need this as much as I do," he says, dipping down to pull one of my nipples into his mouth before releasing it with a pop. "Tell me you'll stop avoiding me and I can have this pretty pussy whenever I want it."

I don't respond, but I clench around his fingers, giving away exactly how I feel, his dirty, blunt words sending a bolt of lust straight to my core.

He removes his fingers, leaving me feeling empty. "Say it."

"It's not just you." I grip his wrist, pulling it back where it belongs between my thighs. "I need you so much it makes me feel fucking crazy." The admission shocks both of us. Suddenly, Holden drops to his knees, flipping up one side of my towel.

"Holden." I try to close my thighs, but he wrenches them apart, fitting his shoulders between them. I push my fingers into his hair, holding his head back. "I've never—" Having sex on my period for the first time is one thing, but having his face so up close and personal is another thing entirely.

"Even better. It'll be a first for both of us." His hand circles my ankle and brings my foot up to rest on the edge of the desk before doing the same with the other. I'm spread wide open, completely on display for him.

Am I really doing this? I swallow hard, heart pounding as he spreads me apart with his thumbs, the cool air hitting my over-sensitive clit. He hesitates, waiting for permission, and I release my grip on his hair, leaning back on my hands once again in silent offering. Hungry eyes devour the sight before him, and then he's kissing his way up my inner thigh. With the first swipe of his tongue, my hips fly off the desk. *Oh my God*. His hands move to my thighs, fingertips biting into my flesh as he keeps me anchored to the desk, then he dives back in for more. My head falls back, high off the feeling of his hot tongue swirling around my clit. Everything feels heightened and just *more*. When he sucks my clit into his mouth, my arms slip out from under me, sending my textbooks and makeup mirror crashing to the floor as I collapse onto the desk.

Holden doesn't stop for a second, licking and sucking as I lie here, back arched, gripping the edge of my desk for dear life. Within seconds, I shatter under his mouth, slumping against the hard surface. I pull myself upright as Holden stands, his gaze burning into mine as he wipes his mouth with the back of his wrist, chest heaving.

"Off," I say, gesturing to his shirt as I hop down from the desk on shaky legs. He's not moving fast enough so I pull his shirt up, standing on my tiptoes to get it over his head. He shoves his pants down his thighs, his thick length already hard and bobbing between us. I barely let him get his pants off before I'm pushing his chest, making him fall onto my bed.

I undo the knot of my towel, letting it drop to the floor.

"You're too fucking perfect to be real," he says with awe in his voice. He grips the base of his dick, giving it a couple of strokes. "Come sit on me, baby."

I don't hesitate, climbing onto his lap to straddle him. I don't take him inside me yet, and I can feel how hard he is between my legs. He captures my mouth in a kiss, his tongue desperate and demanding. When I feel him twitch against me, I push on his shoulders until he's lying flat.

I have a moment of uncertainty, nervous about a potential mess, but Holden's hand slides up the outside of my thigh before settling on my hip, guiding me until I'm hovering over his length. Slowly, I lower myself onto him, both of us groaning at the feeling. Once I'm completely full of him, I rise onto my knees, then slide back down again, this time hard.

"Fuck, Valen," Holden says, his big hand covering the top of my thigh, squeezing.

Leaning forward, I flatten my palms against his chest, letting my head hang while I adjust to the sensation. I start to grind on him, rotating my hips in circles, my clit rubbing against his pelvic bone.

"It's so fucking wet," Holden says, both hands grabbing my ass to help my movements. It feels different, and not just because of the added lubrication. It's more intense, everything nerve ending hypersensitive. I start to move faster, nothing but the sounds of our desperate gasps and moans fill the air, but a knock on the door has me freezing.

"Valen?" Shayne calls from the other side of the door. I didn't even hear her come in.

"Shit," I whisper, starting to pull myself off Holden. The door isn't locked. I'm lucky I remembered to close it.

"Don't stop," Holden warns, his voice low as he clamps down on my hips to keep himself buried inside me. I cover his mouth with both of my hands.

"Yeah?" I call back.

"I'm home. Everything okay?"

Holden tilts his hips up, making me take him deeper. With both hands over his mouth, I start to ride him slowly, unable to help myself.

"I'm good," I squeak out. "Cramps."

"Okay, let me know if you need anything. I'm going to bed."

"Night!"

If she responds, I don't hear her because Holden's flipping me around, never breaking our connection, then he's the one holding his hand over my mouth to muffle the sounds trying to escape as he fucks me into the mattress. The fingers of his other hand find my clit, stroking over the bundle of nerves, playing my body like an instrument he knows by heart.

He must feel me spasm around him because he asks, "Are you gonna come all over me, Valen?"

I look up at him, nodding frantically, unable to speak with his hand still over my mouth. His breathing is ragged, sweat dripping down his temples as he slides in and out, hips moving in tandem with the hand between my legs. My orgasm rips through me violently, my back bowing off the bed, toes curling. My fingers clawing into his shoulders, head thrown back into the mattress as I struggle to get enough air into my lungs.

"You're so pretty when you come."

I know he follows me over the edge when he lets out a curse followed by the feeling of him pulsing inside me. His movements slow, kissing my neck and collarbone before he slides out of me and pulls back to inspect the damage. I follow his gaze, expecting the worst. His still hard cock bobs between us, streaked with red. There's some on his pelvis and smeared on my inner thighs, but it's nowhere near as bad as I feared.

"Sorry," I say, then mentally chastise myself for apologizing when he quite literally signed up for this. "I'll get a towel."

When I start to sit up, his palm wraps around my throat, gently pressing me back into the mattress. "I told you," he says before leaning down to press a kiss against my lips. "A little blood doesn't scare me."

"So, are you going to tell me the real reason you've been avoiding me now?" Holden asks as I'm in the middle of pulling a big sleep shirt over my head. We gave it a few minutes, hoping

Shayne would be fast asleep, before quietly sneaking into the bathroom to clean up. Now Holden's lying in my bed like he owns it, asking questions I don't know how to answer.

"I told you." I slide my arms through the sleeves and pull the hem down past my butt. "Our time was up. If one of us didn't cut it off, we would have never stopped."

"And that's a problem?"

"Yes," I say without elaborating, my voice flat.

"Why?" He sits up, pulling me into the space between his legs, his hands on my waist. "What if I don't want to stop?" It's the second time he's said something along those lines.

I sigh. "We can't."

"Is it because of Quinn? You know I didn't touch her."

I shake my head. "Even if you did, I'm not your girlfriend, Holden. We said no feelings, no commitments."

"You're telling me you wouldn't care at all if I fucked someone else?"

"Nope," I lie through my teeth.

"You're a shit liar."

I roll my eyes, knowing he can see through me. "Fine. It bothered me. Which is exactly why *this* is a problem."

Understanding flashes in his eyes.

I sigh, dropping my head back. "Sex is one thing. But the picnic and the conservatory and the heated blanket and the candy and the sleepovers and the cuddling," I ramble. "It's making things all…muddled." My heart pounds in my chest and my face feels hot with the admission. It's the most honest and vulnerable I've allowed myself to be with him, and I hate the way it makes me feel. Holden, on the other hand, is biting back a smile.

"What is so funny?" I snap.

"Nothing. It's adorable that you're in love with me, that's all."

I bat his hands away, giving him a horrified look. "Who said anything about *love*?"

He laughs, grabbing me by the waist and tossing me onto

the bed. "You don't have to be embarrassed. You're practically obsessed with me."

"In your dreams."

His hands are braced on either side of my head, his hips fitting in between my parted thighs. "We don't have to complicate things. We can keep doing exactly what we're doing. If you truly want to end it here and now, I'll walk away. But only if that's what you actually want."

The thought of giving up nights like these and never having Holden sneak into my bed scares me more than the thought of falling for him and having it end in disaster. So, I guess I have my answer. "I don't want to stop either."

"Good, because I wasn't really going to let you." He drops a kiss to my lips. I return the kiss before pushing back on his shoulders.

"But it can't be more than this."

"Yeah, yeah. No feelings. No commitments. This means nothing."

"Exactly."

But as I curl up next to him under the heated blanket he bought me, eating the chocolate he picked out for me, with my head using his arm for a pillow while his fingers absently twirl the ends of my hair, I know we're both liars.

FORTY-TWO

Valen

I T'S BEEN A FEW WEEKS SINCE HOLDEN AND I AGREED TO KEEP
seeing each other, and the more time I spend with him, the
more attached I feel myself get, despite my efforts to keep
things surface level. Something in him has shifted, though. He
seems exhausted, and not just because he's practicing with
his team almost every day now. I think not knowing what
happened to Christian is fucking with his head more than
he'll admit. He hasn't said it outright, but I know both him
and Thayer are assuming the worst. That Samuel killed their
cousin for turning him in to the police.

He's not the only one fucked in the head. He consumes
my thoughts far too often for something that's supposed to be
casual. Like right now, for example. My mother roped me into
coming home for a *family dinner*, and all I can think about is what
Holden's doing back in Sawyer Point. He didn't even tell me he
was going home. Shayne mentioned it in passing when I told
her I was going to my mom's for the weekend.

"You grace us with your presence once a month if that,"
my mother starts, pulling me from my thoughts. "The least you
could do is engage us in conversation when you're here." The
vibes are off tonight, and I felt it the moment I walked through
the door. She's already blitzed out of her mind, and Lawrence
is particularly reserved. They must be fighting.

I feel a stab of guilt at her statement, passive-aggressive as it is. I want to look forward to seeing her. I *want* to love her like a child should. But every time I try, it just feels…fake. I sigh, dropping my fork to my plate and fold my hands on top of the table. "What would you like to talk about, Mother?"

"Anything. Have you given any thought about declaring a major? The clock is ticking," she sing-songs.

"I have plenty of time," I remind her.

"A semester has already passed. Don't take too much longer."

"I know." I pick up my fork and push the food around on my plate, mostly so I don't have to look at her. I don't consider telling her that I'm leaning toward a journalism major. The less information she has, the less ammunition she has to use against me and talk me out of it.

"Something wrong with your food?" she asks, pointing a fork toward my untouched plate. "I ordered from Gordon's specifically for you. You used to love going with me when you were little."

"Actually, *you* used to love it. I always asked for pizza."

It's her turn to drop her fork. It clangs loudly against her plate. "Could you grab my phone from my purse, sweetheart?" she says to Lawrence who doesn't move to follow her orders. His eyes flash to me before cutting back to my mom. "Valentina wants pizza, and God forbid, she doesn't get what she wants."

At that, I can't help but laugh, and for some inexplicable reason, it's what finally makes me snap. "That's a joke, right? When have you ever cared about what I wanted?"

"Since always." She has the nerve to look offended.

"Settle down, Claudia," Lawrence says.

"Like that time you signed me up for pageants when I was seven even though I begged you not to, then made me continue even after I puked on the stage from being so anxious? Or when you did the same thing with cheer, gymnastics, piano lessons…" I list off.

"You love cheer. You should be thankful I pushed you so hard. You have no idea what it took to support your lifestyle."

"*My* lifestyle?" My laugh is an incredulous one. "I didn't care about any of that. You were the one concerned with keeping up with appearances. All I wanted—all I *ever* wanted—was for my parents to give a shit about me."

"Well, your father didn't want us, Valentina," she says, still sounding bored. Apathetic. Like I'm some silly girl throwing a tantrum at the dinner table. "There's nothing I could do about that."

"No," I say through clenched teeth. "He never wanted *you*, and you only wanted me because you wanted control. And I'm sure the monthly check was a nice perk."

She stands from the table, her cool and collected mask starting to crack. "*I* was there. Not him. I gave up everything for you." Her words are said through gritted teeth and full of disdain. "Why do you hate me? Why are you so *angry* with me all the time? Tell me what I ever did that was *so* terrible?"

This is it. I feel the words clawing their way up my throat, and I can't stuff them back down now if I tried. "Well, I have so many things to choose from, but I'd say letting your boyfriend get away with crawling into my bed tops the list."

I look over to Lawrence who looks like he might become physically ill. "She didn't mention that? I'm not surprised." I look back at my mom who's visibly seething now. The sad part is, she's probably more upset about Lawrence thinking she's a bad mother than actually being a bad mother.

"What on earth are you talking about?"

"I was fourteen, Mom. I was so scared to tell you, and when I finally worked up the courage, you believed *him*. Over your own daughter. You kept dating him for months after that." I don't realize I'm crying until I taste my salty tears on my lips. "You made *me* apologize!"

"Here we go again with the theatrics," she says, throwing her napkin down before standing. "You have no idea what

I protected you from. If that's the worst thing you've been through, I think I've done a pretty good job. Did you know he offered me money to let him have you? A lot of money in a time where we really could have used it."

The admission cuts through me like a knife to my stomach, and by the look on her face, she doesn't realize the implications of what she just said. My eyes dart back over to Lawrence. Why, I'm not sure. Maybe to gauge his reaction, to see if I heard her correctly. I try to keep my face expressionless, but fat, hot tears roll down my cheeks. All this time, I let myself think she didn't believe me. I held on to it like a lifeline, the last thing keeping me tethered to her, and with a single sentence, I feel that tether snap.

"He was willing to pay for access to your *daughter*, and you still didn't believe me?" Her eyes widen as her mouth snaps shut as it finally clicks for her that she just told on herself. "Or you knew, and you didn't care. Which one is it?" She treated me like the competition. Like some slutty little seductress who tried to tempt her boyfriend. "Am I supposed to thank you?" I give an incredulous laugh, batting my tears away. "Wow, you're right, Mom. Thank you *so* much for your sacrifice. I know that must've been a hard decision to make."

I can't be here. I rush out of the dining room, grabbing only my keys off the entryway table on my way out of the house. She doesn't chase after me to apologize. Instead, she runs over to a horrified looking Lawrence to plead her case, caring more about the men in her life than her own flesh and blood.

At least she's consistent.

I take a second to collect myself on Holden's front steps, dabbing my eyes with my sleeves and taking deep, calming breaths. I haven't been here since the night I stood in this same spot, arguing with Liam after he showed up uninvited. The same night

Holden found out Christian was the one to kill Danny. God, it seems like a lifetime ago now.

I didn't make a conscious decision to drive to Heartbreak Hill, but deep down, I know there's nowhere else I'd rather be right now. When I finally get it together, I step forward, ringing the doorbell. Holden told me that his dad spends most of his time in his condo in the city, and I'm hoping that's still the case for my sake. When he still doesn't come to the door, I turn around, scanning the property for his car, but I don't see it anywhere.

"So stupid," I say to myself, angrily batting at my tears as I start down the steps to head back to my car.

"Valen?"

I whirl around to find him standing in his doorway in nothing but his boxers with a concerned look in his eyes. His hair is mussed, like he was asleep, but his eyes seem wide awake.

"Hi," is all I can think to say.

"What happened?" he demands.

My chin wobbles, my nose stinging with the threat of more tears. I shake my head as a single rogue tear rolls down my cheek, but Holden's thumb brushes it away with a tenderness I didn't know he possessed. "I know I said no feelings and I know we're supposed to keep it casual, but can we just pretend for one night? Can we pretend we're a real couple and that you love me?"

My face is hot with embarrassment at how pathetic that sounded out loud, the tips of my ears burning. I almost turn to leave again, but Holden simply nods before pulling me inside. "I can do that."

FORTY-THREE

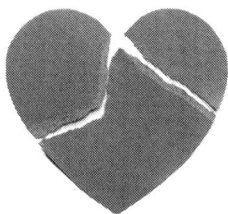

Holden

VALEN WAS THE LAST PERSON I EXPECTED TO SEE AT MY FRONT door on the security cameras. I had to squint and enlarge the screen to do a double take, but sure enough, there she was, standing on my snow-covered steps in nothing but a skintight dark brown shirt, a short black skirt, and those combat boots that give her an extra few inches of height, looking like she came straight out of a wet dream. It wasn't until I noticed that she wasn't wearing a jacket that alarm bells went off in my head. Valen's always cold, and I know the thin tights on her legs do nothing to keep her warm. Wherever she came from, she left in a hurry.

I dropped my phone to my mattress and took off down the stairs wearing nothing but my fucking boxers, wondering what could've happened in the timespan of leaving campus and now. I half-expected it to have something to do with my uncle. I was already planning his funeral. What I didn't expect was for Valen to be standing in front of me with tears in her eyes, asking me to love her.

The second the words leave her lips, her eyes grow wide, as if she didn't mean to let them out.

"I can do that." I tug her inside, closing the door behind her. She pushes up on her tiptoes to kiss along my jaw, her hands sliding up my abs. No longer feeling cold, I'm instantly thick and

hard at her touch. Rough and needy, she reaches into my boxers, her palm wrapping around my dick as her teeth tug at the
lobe of my ear, sending goosebumps down my arm.

My mouth falls open as her hand works my dick and she
licks along my bottom lip before sliding her tongue into my
mouth. I snap into motion, banding an arm around her waist
to pull her closer. The taste of salt from her tears on her lips reminds me what she asked for and has me pulling away.

"Stop." My fingers circle her wrist, making her release her
grip on me.

"Why?" she asks, sounding slightly wounded.

"As much as I'd like to fuck you right here in the foyer, you
asked me to love you tonight," I remind her, dipping down to lift
her by the backs of her thighs. "So let me love you." The word
love rolls off my tongue a little too easily. This is dangerous territory, especially when it feels like part of me has just been waiting for Valen to realize that she cares for me more than she'd
like to admit. That this is more. That *we* are more.

She holds on to my shoulders, her legs circling my waist
as I walk us up the stairs. I take her to my room, setting her on
the edge of my bed. She looks around, reminding me of the
fact that she's never been in here before, no matter how many
times I've imagined having her in my bed. There's not much to
see here. A king-sized bed against one wall, a dresser, and a TV
on the opposite one. It's mostly empty now. A single box inside
my closet that holds all my memories and the shit that used to
decorate my walls are all that remains. When I left for Hadley,
I didn't bring anything except for clothes and a few pictures of
my brothers.

Kneeling in front of her, I peel off her boots before sliding
my palms up the outsides of her thighs. I pull her tights down
her legs, letting them fall to the floor.

Valen leans back on her hands, watching me intently as my
lips burn a path from the inside of her knee to her upper thigh,
kissing and biting. When I dip my head, disappearing under

her skirt, her breath hitches, her soft thighs spreading wider to accommodate me. I lick her through the thin material of her underwear and her hands slide along my blanket, making her slip backward.

"Lie back and let me kiss your pussy, baby."

She falls flat to the bed, bringing her heels up to rest on the edge of the mattress. I can see her perfect pussy, wet and waiting, thanks to the see-through material of her underwear. I hook a finger into them and pull them to the side, then dive back in, parting her lips with my tongue.

"Yes," she gasps, rolling her hips, pressing herself into my mouth.

"Is this what you need?"

I can feel more than see her nod, her little fingers fisted in my blankets at her sides. I lick up the length of her, loving the way she tastes on my tongue. Her moan sounds desperate, her thighs tensing up when I suck her clit into my mouth.

"I need you inside me."

"Patience," I mumble into her. I'm just getting started.

Her fingers wind through my hair, tugging my head back. "Please?" Her eyebrows draw together, brown eyes pleading, her lips pouty. How can I deny her when she asks so prettily?

I rid myself of my boxers and crawl onto the bed between her legs. She scoots backward until her head is on my pillow. Her stomach rises and falls with each shaky breath as I undo the buttons of her shirt one by one, letting it fall open. I peel one cup of her black lacy bra down, then swirl my tongue around her tight nipple, lightly rolling the other one between two fingers. Valen arches into my mouth with a moan, her hands reaching underneath her back to unclasp her bra. She pulls it off, along with her shirt, and drops them to the floor beside my bed. My mouth never breaks contact with her pebbled flesh until I feel her trying to wiggle out of her skirt. I sit back, pulling her skirt off before I lean forward to grab a pillow.

"Lift your hips."

She does as I say, looking like a fucking angel with her dark hair fanned out across my pillow, her naked body on display for me. Sometimes it's hard to believe she's real. I slide the pillow underneath her, then take my place between her spread legs. Her knees cradle my hips, welcoming me. Hands braced on either side of her head, I hold her gaze, notched against her hot entrance.

"You're so beautiful it hurts."

She swallows hard, her wide eyes looking up at me with an emotion I can't place as I start to push inside her. Her bottom lip is trapped between her teeth, eyes squeezing shut as her pussy stretches to accommodate me in this position. I lace our fingers together, pressing the back of her hands against the mattress as I start to move. It's different this time, and I know she feels it, too. Like our walls are down and she's finally letting me see the pieces of herself she keeps hidden. The pieces I've only seen glimpses of before. I want her to let me in fully, and when she does, I want to embed myself so deep inside her that she'll never be able to get me out.

I start to fuck her faster, holding back the urge to come already with how deep I'm buried inside her in this position. Sitting back on my heels, I grip her hips, pulling her toward me until her ass is resting on my thighs. I take a minute to simply look at her. The sight alone almost makes me come undone. Her hips are tilted up, her pussy gripping me tight. My hands circle her waist, guiding her movements. Her breasts bounce with each thrust, her head thrown back.

"You feel so fucking good." I gather her in my arms, pulling her upright onto my lap without breaking our connection. She gasps at the new angle, spreading her thighs wider to take me even deeper. "It's never enough with you," I tell her.

She rolls her hips, and I taker her nipple into my mouth, sucking on her. She clings to me, her elbows resting on my shoulders, her hands in my hair. Releasing her nipple, I move one hand to the top of her thigh and bring the other to the small of her back, keeping her anchored to me as she grinds into me. We're both coated in a light layer of sweat, our foreheads pressed together, faces so close that we're sharing the same breath. I bring my lips to hers, and she opens for me, her tongue sweeping into my mouth to dance with mine.

I've never had this connection with anyone. This all-consuming need to be in Valen's presence. And when I'm inside her, all the bullshit in my head ceases to exist. I feel comfort and need and peace, but underneath that, more than anything, is the fear that I'll lose her and never find this feeling again.

Breaking our kiss, Valen rises onto her knees to take control, her movements becoming more desperate and frantic as she rides me hard. She's so wet that I can hear it with every shift of her hips. "Please, please, please," she chants with her lips against my ear. Her pussy tightens around me and I know I can't hold back any longer.

I bring a hand between us and use two fingers, rubbing her slippery clit to help her along. Her thighs tense, mouth falling open. Her movements stop, so I take over, fucking up into her. She screams out her orgasm as her pussy spasms around me, squeezing so damn tight. I come on the next thrust, my fingers biting into the soft flesh of her thighs as I empty myself inside her.

She's trembling, both of us still shaking with aftershocks as I hold her in my arms. She tucks her face into my neck, her boneless body melting into me. I move her sweat-slicked hair to one shoulder, and she shivers at my touch, nuzzling deeper into me. I trace her spine with my fingertips as we catch our breath, content to stay like this for as long as she wants.

After a few minutes of silence, Valen shifts in my lap. I lay her back down, holding her knees apart to appreciate the view as I slide out of her. My half-hard dick twitches back to life when I see my cum pooling at her entrance before it spills out. I'll never get used to the sight.

My head snaps up when Valen lets out a throaty laugh. Her

hair is wild, cheeks flushing. "What?" I say, unable to stop myself from smiling back at her.

"Always admiring your handiwork. You're obsessed."

"Obsessed with *you*." I tug her back onto my lap, giving her ass a hard smack before I stand, carrying her to the hall bathroom. "Now let's go get cleaned up and then you can tell me what the hell happened."

FORTY-FOUR

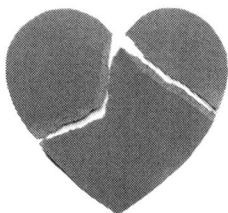

Holden

I SUSPECTED VALEN WAS STALLING WHEN SHE INSISTED ON STAYING in the shower until the water turned cold, then again when she said she was hungry. After ordering pizza and watching a movie in my room, my suspicions were confirmed. Valen's not one to open up and show emotion, and if I push her too hard, she'll shut down completely, and I'll be back to square one.

Then again, she did come to me. For the first time, she sought me out for comfort. That has to mean something.

"Just ask," she says, her voice sounding resigned, her cheek pressed to my chest, eyes fixed on the screen. I don't know how she knew what I was thinking, but I take the in without question.

"What happened tonight?"

"You want the long version or the short version?"

"I want whatever you're willing to give."

Picking up on the double meaning, she lifts her head from my chest, studying me intently. After a few seconds, she seems to come to a decision and sits up, putting some distance between us. She sits crisscrossed on my bed, her long legs on display, wearing nothing but my t-shirt.

"I got into an argument with my mom at dinner. Which is nothing new." She picks at her black nail polish. "I don't even know why I care."

"What about?"

She rolls her eyes, then inhales deeply. "After my parents divorced, my mom had a revolving door of boyfriends and even another husband. Some lasted longer than others, but they were always wealthy. Always assholes. And she *always* put up with whatever bullshit they came with because they funded her lifestyle. There was one guy, though, that was worse than the rest. He drank too much and stared too long, but it wasn't anything that I couldn't handle. Until one night, he came into my room when I was asleep."

My stomach turns to lead, my heart starting to race. "Did he hurt you?"

"No," she says quickly, shaking her head. "I screamed. He jumped up, claimed he was drunk and got the wrong room." She gives a bitter laugh. "Her room was on the opposite side of the house."

"Did you tell her?"

"Not that time. I convinced myself that I was making a big deal about nothing. That she'd only blame me or call me dramatic. Then a couple weeks later, it happened again. Only this time, I woke up to his hand up my shirt."

I clench my jaw, trying to keep my reaction under control until she gets through her story.

"That time, I kneed him in the balls." Her lips pull into a small smile. "Hard."

"What's his name?"

She shakes her head. "It doesn't matter now."

"The fuck it doesn't. Tell me."

"Cameron," she relents. "Some attorney with a god complex because he owns a detention facility."

I commit the name to memory, making a mental note to look him up as soon as possible.

"The second time, I did tell my mom. He had the same story about being drunk and confused. She called me a liar. Gave me the silent treatment for weeks. She looked at me like…she resented me. Like it was my fault."

I reach over to cover her fidgeting hands with one of mine. She holds on to my fingers instead of her own, her thumb rubbing across my knuckles.

"All this time, I thought she didn't believe me, and I was so mad at her for it," she continues. "But tonight, she had one too many glasses of wine and let it slip that she knew all along. She fucking *knew*. And she still kept him around. And God, that's so much worse than not believing me."

The sadness in her voice, in her eyes, is almost too much to bear, so I try to keep my anger in check, offering up some kind of explanation that might take away an ounce of her hurt. "Maybe she was in denial. Maybe she—"

"He offered her money to let him fuck me, Holden. I was fourteen years old." Her tone is harsh, eyes turning hard with the blunt truth. "Then she acted like Mother Teresa for not allowing it. Didn't stop her from seeing him, though."

What the fuck? I grind my teeth together, my entire body radiating with red-hot rage. At her poor excuse for a mother for letting this man around her daughter, at the man himself for thinking he could touch a hair on her head, at her father for not being there. They all fucking failed her.

"Where was your dad in all this?"

She lifts a shoulder, trying to appear unaffected. "He tried to see me for a while after they split, but I think my mom made the back and forth so miserable and impossible that it eventually just…wasn't worth the fight anymore."

I hear what she's not saying. That *she* wasn't worth the fight. It couldn't be farther from the truth.

"I think a part of me was afraid to tell him. My mom didn't care when I tried to tell her. If he didn't care either," she stops, shaking her head as she bats a tear away as if she's angry at it for falling.

"It was safer to keep it to yourself than to risk the pain of not being believed again," I finish for her. Her answering nod is almost imperceptible.

"Or worse, if he believed me and didn't care enough to do anything about it. It's funny," she muses. "I always thought he was the bad guy for leaving me. Even when my mom treated me horribly, I loved her *so* much. I defended her. Because she was *there*. Then, as I got older, I realized the way she acted, the things she said, the things she did. None of it was normal. It wasn't love. It was…control."

The more Valen opens up to me, the more I realize how similar we really are underneath it all. We both know what it's like to be discarded by the people who are supposed to love us most. We just cope in different ways.

She swipes her tears away and takes a fortifying breath. "Anyway, thanks for letting me come over. I should probably—"

I cut her off before she can finish that sentence. I can tell from the look in her eyes alone that she's ready to bolt. "You're not going anywhere. If I have to tie you to this bed, I will."

"Holden, I can't stay here, and all my stuff's still at my mom's, anyway."

"Why the fuck not? No one else is here. We'll get some sleep, then in the morning, I'll go with you to get your shit."

"I don't think that's a good idea."

"I think it's a great idea," I counter. I tug her down to lie next to me. She doesn't resist when I wrap an arm around her waist, pulling her closer until her back is pressed firmly against my chest. At first, neither one of us speaks. I know Valen enough to know that opening up to people isn't something she does often, and for some reason, it makes me want do the same. The only problem is, I'm not exactly used to talking about my feelings either. I don't know where to start, so I opt for the obvious.

"My mom left, too. I've always had trouble sleeping, even before then. For as long as I can remember. According to my her, I'd wake up the whole house with my crying. At first, she thought I was awake because my eyes were open, and I'd be standing in the corner of my room, screaming at the top of my lungs. Scared her so bad she took me to the pediatrician. They said it was normal. Just night terrors that are common for that age and that I'd grow out of them. It got better as I got older, but after my mom left, my sleep got worse again." Her hand squeezes mine, letting me know she's listening.

"Danny used to calm me down in the middle of the night. He taught me to change the channel in my mind, like a TV. He said whenever I was having a bad dream, I could switch to the next channel and watch something else."

"Did it work?"

"Sometimes. I think it helped me fall asleep knowing I could try, more than anything else. Trying to control my dreams became a game to me, and eventually, they tapered off altogether. Then Danny died and they came back with a vengeance."

"And now?"

"They come and go. Sometimes, I'll go months without a single dream, good or bad. Then something will happen to trigger one. Sometimes it's obvious. Sometimes it's something that I didn't even realize affected me."

"Like this thing with your uncle? It's understandable, you know. For all of this to stir up feelings about Danny. Not having closure with Christian. It's fucked up."

I nod in the dark, even though she can't see me.

She fidgets with my fingers on the hand splayed across her stomach. "That thing you said about changing the channel. It reminded me of something my psychology professor said. He said animals don't suffer from PTSD like humans do."

I tense up at the direction this conversation seems to be heading, but if she notices, she doesn't let on.

"In the wild, animals deal with stress and fear every day. They feel it, process it, release it, and move on. If they didn't, they wouldn't survive long. Humans…we stifle our emotions. Then we wonder why we're condemned to reliving shit in our dreams."

"Yeah, well, lucky for me, your pussy seems to be the cure for nightmares," I say, bringing my hand to cup between her thighs. She lets out a raspy laugh, sending an elbow into my chest, but then her fingers curl around my forearm, allowing my hand to stay where it's nice and warm.

"There he is. You were *almost* civilized for an entire evening."

"There was nothing civilized about what we just did," I say to add some much-needed levity.

"As I was saying," she says, ignoring my attempt at derailing the conversation. "I think…" she trails off, hesitating for a second before deciding to continue. "I think whatever you avoid in your life manifests as nightmares. Have you ever really processed Danny's death? And Christian was like your brother, too. You lost both of them. You're allowed to miss him, even if you hate him for what he did."

My lips skim across her bare shoulder as I think back to the night Christian finally confessed. How I stood there, frozen in my shock. Thayer got to yell. Thayer got to hurt him. Then he disappeared upstairs with Shayne, Valen left with her douchebag boyfriend, and I was left alone to try to make sense of it all. When I thought Christian ran, it was easy to hate him. Part of me still hates him, not only for what he did, but for keeping it from us as long as he did. But now, knowing something might have happened to him and we sat here doing nothing for an entire year? The guilt has been slowly chipping away at me and burning a hole in my resolve to hate him.

"Anyway, all of that to say if changing the channel ever isn't enough…you can always talk to me. If you think it would help, I mean."

I press a kiss to her shoulder, unable to find the words.

We're both quiet, and I can only assume she's lost in her thoughts like I am. I don't know what's going to happen with Valen and me, but the longer this goes on, the harder it's going to be to let her go. I don't know how much time has passed when her breathing starts to deepen, telling me she's falling asleep. I close my eyes, my limbs feeling heavy as sleep starts to pull me under.

"Thank you," she whispers into the dark, sounding like she's on the brink of sleep.

"For what?"

"For pretending to love me."

I lift my head off the pillow to look down at her. The TV gives off just enough light to see that her eyes are closed. I take a minute to study her pretty features. Her long, dark lashes fanned out across the top of her cheeks, the shape of her pillowy lips. The tiny beauty mark on the side of her neck. The ice princess is beautiful, but when she's like this, in my bed and in my arms, she feels like mine. Whether she realizes it or not, she is.

"Who's pretending?"

FORTY-FIVE

Valen

"**A**PPARENTLY, *NO ONE SPENDS ANY TIME HERE, ANYMORE,*" Holden says, closing the empty refrigerator. "Guess we'll eat on the road."

I shrug. "Good with me." It feels a little surreal being here. This house that was once full of life and parties and drama is now lifeless and stale only a year later.

Holden rounds the kitchen counter and lifts me by my waist before plopping me on top of it. I squeal when the cold granite hits the back of my thighs, and he steps between them, bringing my arms up to circle his neck. "What are the chances you'll let me have my favorite meal before we go?" His hands slide down my sides before settling on the outsides of my upper thighs.

"Slim to none," I say, as tempting as it sounds. I'm not looking forward to facing my mom after last night, and while I'd usually welcome the distraction and the chance to take the edge off, I'd rather just get this over with.

"Tonight then."

He starts to back away, but I pull him down by the back of his neck, pressing my lips against his. I slide my tongue along the seam of his lips, seeking entrance, and he opens for me, groaning when my tongue glides against his. I don't know how to tell him thank you for last night, for making me feel cared for and valued and safe for the first time in a very long time, so I try to show him instead.

By the time we break the kiss, we're both breathless, and I can feel how hard Holden is between my legs. He looks at me, eyes searching mine, and I suddenly feel exposed. Like he knows exactly what I was trying to convey with that kiss.

"Is this your way of finally admitting that you like me?"

I shove him away. "Shut up."

He laughs, backing away. "I'm going to grab my stuff, then we can go."

I nod and he takes off for the stairs, but I hear footsteps approach not ten seconds later. "The answer is still no—" I start to say but stop short when I see that it's Samuel who enters the kitchen. I hop down off the counter, hating the way his eyes zero in between my legs as I pull my skirt back into place.

"Well, hello again. Valentina, was it?" His eyes are bloodshot, his clothes rumpled, like maybe he slept in them. It's a far cry from his usually polished appearance.

He walks closer in a clear attempt to intimidate me. I cross my arms over my chest and straighten my spine, refusing to shrink under his stare. I might be more afraid if Holden wasn't right upstairs, but right now all I'm feeling is anger. This man is responsible for nearly every bad thing that has happened to Shayne and Holden in the past couple of years, and that's just the stuff we're aware of. With men like Samuel, men who live their whole lives doing whatever the fuck they want because they've never had to face any real repercussions for their actions, what you see is always just the tip of the iceberg.

"What do you want?"

He blinks in surprise at my brusque tone, but it's quickly replaced with amusement. "Feisty. I like it. I get what my nephew sees in you." His lecherous gaze travels over my body from head to toe, making me shudder with disgust. "Not that I didn't before. After I witnessed the little show you put on out on my patio, I had to talk myself out of experiencing it firsthand. Maybe now is my chance. Do you believe in serendipity?"

He watches me carefully for a reaction, but I don't give him one. I know he's referring to the video from New Year's. *Where the hell is Holden?* "No, but I believe in karma, you sick fuck," I say, deciding to move past him and toward the foyer. I give him a wide berth, but his hand shoots out from his pants pocket, grabbing my upper arm.

"Watch how you talk to me." His fingertips dig into my flesh as he squeezes.

"Or what? You're gonna kill me, too?" I raise a brow, staring him down.

"Is that the story my nephew is spinning these days?" His eyes harden as he leans in so close that I can smell the liquor on his breath. *Oh yeah, he's spiraling.* "He won't be happy until he's taken everything from me. It's only fair I take something from him, too."

"Let go of the girl, Sammy," a masculine, bored sounding voice says from the foyer. I glance in the direction to find Holden's dad, August, approaching. "That's no way to treat a guest."

I jerk my arm out of Samuel's bruising grip and he reluctantly releases me, face red and eyes narrowed into slits. He's practically shaking with his rage. He didn't like being told what to do one bit.

"I assume my son is around here somewhere?" August asks me, apparently unfazed by his brother's actions.

"He's just grabbing his stuff," I mutter, pointing to the ceiling as I move toward him, putting distance between Samuel and me. I should feel embarrassed to face Holden's dad, considering the circumstances of the last time he saw me, but I'm too busy shooting daggers at the judge to give a shit.

Holden appears at the top of the staircase, backpack slung over his shoulder, frowning when he sees his father standing in the foyer. From his angle, he can't see Samuel, so I tilt my head in his direction in an attempt to silently communicate, but he's too focused on August to notice. When he gets to the bottom of the stairs, he stands next to me, still oblivious of his uncle's presence in the kitchen behind him.

"Go wait outside for me," he murmurs before kissing my temple.

"Well, isn't that cute," Samuel says.

Holden bristles at the sound of Samuel's voice before he spins around, stepping in front of me to shield me from his view. "What the fuck are you doing here?"

"Is that any way to greet your uncle?" His demeanor is deceptively calm. "Especially after I gave you the courtesy of not having you arrested for assault?"

Holden gives a small shrug. "I don't think it would be the smartest move involving the police, considering your current predicament."

Samuel's smile slips a little, his lip twitching, but he fights to keep it in place. "What predicament might that be? Are you implying something?"

Holden shrugs. "Just that you have eyes on you from what I hear. Might want to tread carefully."

"That's enough," Holden's dad says, his voice authoritarian and commanding, yet calm. "We have business to discuss." He walks up to Holden, giving his shoulder a threatening squeeze. "You look like you're on your way out."

Holden hesitates, and I think he might not walk away, but then he tears his gaze away from his uncle, giving his dad a nod. "Yeah."

"I'll walk you out." He looks over to his brother before addressing him. "Dad should be right behind me. I'll meet you in the upstairs office."

Holden surprises me by taking my hand as we follow his dad outside. I have the urge to spit at Samuel, or at the very least flip him off, but I let Holden lead me to the car instead.

"Did he say anything to you? Did he touch you?" Holden asks the second we're outside.

"Don't antagonize him," August says to him before I can respond. "You came close to saying too much, and he's unstable at best right now."

"Valen?" Holden prompts, ignoring his dad.

"No, I'm fine," I say without hesitation.

August's eyes flick to mine, flashing with surprise. He saw Samuel grab me, and I wouldn't be surprised if he heard our exchange. I don't need Holden running back in there and picking a fight, especially if it's going to ruin whatever plans August has for taking him down.

"He came to me, not the other way around," Holden says. "Handle it before someone gets hurt."

August nods. "Why do you think he's here right now? Trust me."

FORTY-SIX

Valen

"**I** CHANGE MY MIND," I DECLARE, MY NAILS BITING INTO THE leather steering wheel. Holden insisted on coming with me to get my stuff before heading back to campus. I agreed at the time, but now the thought of having Holden and my mom in the same room seems like the worst possible idea. I can usually predict how she'll react in any given situation, but after last night, I don't know what we're about to walk into.

If I had to guess, I'd put my money on her acting like nothing happened. Or maybe she'll give me the silent treatment. Fingers crossed for the latter.

"Okay."

"Okay?"

Holden nods. "Yeah. You stay here, and I'll go get your things."

He's out of the car before I can say another word, marching toward my front door without a backward glance. At first, I think he's bluffing, but when I see him raise his fist to knock, I realize he's one hundred percent serious.

"Shit." I scramble to unbuckle and get out of the car, running up to the house. "You are insane." Luckily, no one has come to the door yet. I punch the combination into the electronic lock, but it gives me a red X, indicating an incorrect code. I try it again. Same thing. "She changed the fucking code." I laugh incredulously, shaking my head. I shouldn't be surprised, but somehow, I am.

Holden reaches across me to ring the doorbell, his finger pressing the button in quick succession.

"Stop it," I hiss, hitting his arm away. "She's not here. Let's go."

"Give it a sec—"

The door swings open, and both of our heads snap around to find my mother. And boy is she in rare form. Her blonde hair is pulled back into a sleek ponytail. She's wearing a black formfitting dress with a long camel-colored cashmere coat that cost more than most people's cars. Oversized, black cat eye sunglasses with a gold YSL emblem on the temples complete the look. I'm suddenly acutely aware of the fact that I'm wearing last night's clothes—minus the tights—my hair wild and untamed from sleeping on it wet.

"Oh," she says, sounding startled as if the twenty-seven doorbell rings didn't tip her off to our presence. "I was just on my way out." She pulls her sunglasses down her nose enough to take in my appearance. Never one to be able to hide how she feels, her nose scrunches up and her eyes flash with disapproval. But I don't miss the fact that even though she's wearing a face full of makeup, her eyes are bare and rimmed with redness. Has she been crying? I don't remember a time my mother cried without an audience. I'm not delusional enough to let myself believe she suddenly sprouted a conscience overnight.

Must be allergies. In the dead of winter.

"It's not a good time, darling," she says, glancing over her shoulder behind her.

"You changed the code," I say, shouldering past her. Holden follows me in without hesitation like he owns the place.

"Which I would have mentioned last night if you didn't storm off like an insolent child."

So that's how she's going to play it? We both know she

changed the locks to spite me, and she knows I don't believe that she changed them before I left for even a second. It doesn't matter how well I think I know her games. She changes the rules every time. She's an expert at making herself the victim in every situation. It's an art form, honestly.

"I'm sure," I say, my tone thick with sarcasm. "We just came to get my stuff and then I'll be out of your way."

"We?" she asks, following me toward the staircase. "Are you going to introduce me to your little friend?"

I almost laugh. One thing Holden's never been accused of is *little*. In any sense of the word.

"This is Holden. Holden, this is Lilith, the she-demon herself."

"Nice to meet you, Lilith," Holden says, playing into it, holding out his hand. He says it so innocently that I almost laugh.

"My name is Claudia. That's Valentina's idea of a joke. She gets her sense of humor from her father, I'm afraid. What did you say your last name was?"

"He didn't—"

"Ames," he answers at the same time. Her eyes light up at the mention of his family name, and I can practically see the dollar signs flashing behind her sunglasses.

"As in AmesAir?" Her voice rises an octave. "You must be August's son then?" she surmises.

Everyone knows that Judge Ames only has one son who happens to be MIA at the moment, and August has several, including one who passed. It's not hard to guess which one Holden belongs to.

"Come on," I say, tugging on the sleeve of his sweatshirt. He follows me up the steps and into the hall, staring a little too closely at all my pageant pictures lining the walls from the ages of four to fourteen.

"Don't say a fucking word," I warn.

"Wouldn't dream of it, beauty queen." I can hear the smile in his voice.

I remember thinking my mom was so proud of me for those stupid sashes and tiaras. She *must* be proud if she had me plastered all over the walls. But eventually, I realized that I was simply a reflection of her. And when anyone ever called me beautiful, it was only because she made me so.

"I just need to grab a couple of things," I say, walking into my room.

Holden looks around before sitting on the edge of my bed. "Do you know how many times I wished I could be here in high school?"

I huff out a quiet laugh, half-amused and half-flattered. "And I wished I were anywhere *but* here."

I hear my mom's heels click-clacking on the stairs, and I start to shove my clothes into my bag a little faster. Luckily, I didn't have time to unpack my toiletries, so once I grab my laptop, phone charger, and trusty heating pad, I'm done. "Okay, let's go," I say, swinging my backpack over my shoulder.

"That was fast." Holden snatches the strap, taking it from me.

"I can carry my own bag."

His only response is a smack to my ass. In doing so, his fingers make contact with my bare skin under my skirt. His eyebrows pull together in confusion as he lifts the hem, craning his neck to take a peek and confirm his suspicions. I bat his hand away, knowing my mom is going to appear in my doorway any second.

Holden groans, lowering my bag to cover his crotch. "Evil woman."

"It's not my fault. I wasn't going to wear dirty underwear." I walk over to my dresser and snatch the first pair of underwear I touch from the top drawer. Holden watches as I quickly pull them up my legs and right my skirt.

When we make it out into the hall, my mother is at the top of the stairs. But it's not me who has her attention. It's Lawrence who's clear on the opposite side of the hall, holding a big cardboard box. Is he—is he moving out? I feel Holden's presence like a sentry at my back as he moves closer to me, sensing the rising tension.

Lawrence ignores my mother altogether, coming to a stop in front of me, setting the box down at his feet. "I'm sorry, Valen," he says, his tone solemn. "I know how your mom can be, but I didn't think—I didn't know—" He stumbles over his words.

I shake my head. "I didn't want this to happen."

Lawrence stops me before I can finish my sentence. "This is not your fault," he insists. Tears prick the back of my eyes and I nod, clenching my jaw, willing them not to fall. "If you need anything, you have my number." He gives my shoulder a squeeze before bending down to retrieve his box of belongings.

"Thanks, Lawrence." I try to give him a smile, but I think it comes out wobbly.

I watch him make his way down the stairs, walking past my mother without a word, without so much as sparing her a glance. Her spine straightens, chin jutting out, refusing to show any signs of weakness, but I can tell by the way her throat bobs on a swallow and her fingers curl into fists that she's barely containing her reaction.

Guilt snakes its way up my spine, even though logically, I know it's misplaced.

Lawrence disappears from view seconds before the front door slams behind him. My mom flinches at the sound, then turns her attention on me. I don't realize that I'm fidgeting with the hem of my skirt until Holden's hand stills my movements, then settles on my lower back, warm and steady. It's embarrassing having him here to witness this, but there's also a comfort in his presence and his silent support.

"Well," my mother starts, coming to a stop in front of me, "you must be very pleased with yourself."

"Yes, because this was my master plan. You caught me."

"I'm sure it's an added bonus."

"Would it kill you to take an ounce of responsibility for your actions?" I step forward until there are only inches between us. "You are the most selfish, manipulative person I've ever known. I never understood why you insisted on clinging to me when you clearly hate me so much, but I think I've finally figured it out."

A single brow arches above her dark frames, daring me to continue.

"It's because deep down, you know that at the end of the day, no one sticks around for long, and once I'm gone, you'll be all alone forever."

Her lips purse, her hand poised to slap me, but Holden intercepts it before she can make contact with my face. He holds her bony wrist, not releasing her when she tries to jerk it away.

My mother just tried to hit me. *My own mother just tried to hit me.* My laugh is a derisive sound as it bubbles up my throat and past my lips. "Goodbye, Mom." I walk past her, trying to appear unfazed as I make my way down the stairs.

"Let go of me," she says to Holden.

"You're lucky your daughter is a better person than me, because if I were her, I'd throw you over this railing right now."

I don't look back, but I hear her bracelets clink together, so I assume he's released her. I don't stop to wait for him, needing to get out of here. I pull the door open none too gently, not stopping until I'm at my car. When I turn to look for Holden, I find him in the doorway.

"Nice to meet you, by the way!" Holden tosses over his shoulder before closing the door behind him, making me snort out a laugh. He jogs over, dropping my bag at our feet before taking my face in his hands. "Are you good?"

I nod up at him. "I'm fine. Sorry you had to see that." I look away, peeling his hands from my cheeks, then turn away, reaching for my door handle. Holden slaps a palm against the car door, stopping me from getting inside. "Don't."

I spin around, my back pressed against the car door. "Don't what?"

"Don't try to shut me out. Stop hiding from me."

"I'm not hiding. You're just ruining my dramatic exit."

He smirks, not buying the lie. "No, you're trying to act like none of that bothered you."

I don't deny it, knowing it's no use with Holden. "And?"

"And it should fucking bother you. I'm not exactly an expert on love, but I'm pretty sure that when you love someone, your first instinct is to protect them."

Like you protect me?

"I'm *fine*," I say again, feeling farther and farther from fine the longer we continue this conversation.

"I'm sorry she didn't protect you. You deserve so much more than—"

"Holden, please don't be nice to me right now. You're going to make me cry and I really fucking hate crying." I rest my forehead against his chest. His palm smooths down the back of my head before he leans down to kiss the top of it.

"Fine. You want me to be mean to you?"

"That would be great."

"You snore like a bear and your tits aren't even that great."

I laugh into his shirt.

"Tell me what you want to do," he says softly.

"I want to go back to campus." I almost say home, because as pathetic as it is, the dorms really do feel like home now. *Holden* feels like home.

"Then let's go." He reaches around my back to open my car door. "You want to drive, or do you want me to?"

I lift my head to look at him. "What about your car?"

He shrugs. "Leave it. I'll come back for it another time."

I nod. Part of me wants time alone to lick my wounds in peace, but a bigger part of me is glad Holden's coming back with me. "I'll drive," I say, sliding into the driver's seat. He closes my door, then bends down to pick up my bag. I pop the trunk as he rounds the car and tosses it in the back before taking his seat next to me.

"What?" he asks, looking over at me when I can't hold in my laughter.

"You make this car look like a clown car."

"This *is* a clown car," he corrects, reaching below the seat to try to scoot it backward. It only moves a couple inches, not making much of a difference. "And not very practical for New England winters."

"But it's pretty," I tease. "You sure you don't want me to take you to get your car?"

"Positive." He pulls the hood of his sweatshirt over his head, settling back into his seat.

I hit the start button on my car, and Holden's hand squeezes my thigh as I look behind me to back out of the driveway. His fingers are dangerously high on the inside of my leg, but they don't travel any farther, apparently content to use my thighs as a hand warmer.

"I was lying about your tits not being great, by the way."

FORTY-SEVEN

Holden

I'M THREE HOURS INTO PRACTICE WHEN VALEN'S CHEER TEAM infiltrates the gym, followed by a whole crew of people carrying cameras and various equipment. It's been four days since she showed up at my door asking me to love her. She hasn't gone back to cheering as far as I know, so I'm surprised when I see her walk through the double doors. I smirk when I see that she's wearing one of my hoodies, the sleeves hanging past her hands, two blue pom-poms sticking out at the end. It's a plain black hoodie—nothing that anyone would recognize as mine—but it tells me she's one step closer to staking her claim on me. Publicly. That torturous ribbon is tied around her ponytail that swings with each step she takes, and my dick strains against the thin fabric of my shorts when I remember the last night she wore one.

"Since it's getting too cold, we'll get the rest of our shots in the gym," the woman with the camera says, leading them to the opposite side of the court. "I think we have enough team shots, so let's work on solos."

I tear my eyes away from Valen when it's my turn to shoot. It's the end of practice where everyone's shooting and fucking around for the most part, but one of the coaches still makes the rounds, making sure we're not slacking off completely. The second I take my shot, I find myself seeking her out again.

Two guys have a black backdrop set up in seconds, and music starts playing from the portable speaker they rolled in. Coach throws up his hands, exasperated. "It's not like we're practicing over here or anything," he grumbles, his gruff voice carrying across the gym. Ryan lets out a laugh that he tries to disguise with a cough when Coach cuts him a glare. Everyone else smothers their amusement, trying to refocus their attention on practice.

Valen pulls my hoodie over her head and drops it to the floor. *Holy fuck.* They must've gotten new uniforms because I've never seen her wear this one. It's white, short as hell, and tight, so fucking tight, with a thick blue stripe down the sides and a little slit at the top of her thigh on one side.

"If you're ready, we can start with you," the photographer says to Valen. She bends over to pick up her pom-poms, giving me a prime view of her ass as she does so. She hasn't so much as looked in my direction, completely oblivious to my presence.

The second she's in front of the camera, she effortlessly turns it on, hitting several different poses in a matter of seconds. First, she has one hand behind her head, her left leg popped out, toes pointed. Then, she takes her pom-poms and shakes them together, her pretty face breaking into a smile. The next second, the photographer directs two people to spray fog spray—whatever the fuck that is—behind Valen while she brings her left leg straight up in the air, revealing the white underwear that goes under her uniform. She holds on to one foot while the other one stays firmly planted on the ground like it's the easiest thing in the world. Her team hypes her up, cheering while the camera flashes. And I've never been more turned on in my life.

I don't think a single player is actually practicing anymore, much to Coach's dismay. All eyes are on the cheerleaders, particularly Valen. The photographer gives her instructions that I can't hear from here. I raise a brow, watching the scene play out in front of me as Valen does some kind of backward cartwheel looking thing. She does a few more stunts that I can't begin to name, and then the photographer looks over her shoulder, sizing our team up.

"Can I borrow one of your players?" she asks. Coach barks out a sarcastic *why the hell not,* but my eyes are locked onto Valen's, because she's finally realized I'm here. I lift a brow, not hiding the way I look her up and down appreciatively. She rolls her eyes, but a hint of a smile plays on her lips, and she gives me the smallest wave of her pom-pom.

"I volunteer!" Isaac says, already making his way over to the cheerleaders. He might be the tallest motherfucker on the team, but he's a stiff. He pushes his blond hair off his forehead as he approaches with a cocky smile, eagerly waiting for directions.

"Feel like lifting a bunch of girls for the next thirty minutes or so?" the photographer asks.

"Gladly," he says, walking up to Valen where she stands in front of the backdrop.

Ryan comes up next to me, shaking his head at the sight. "This can't be good."

"Let's get one of you on his back," the photographer says, and I let out a groan that Ryan apparently finds hilarious.

Isaac squats as low as a six-foot-nine guy can, and Valen jumps on his back, pom-poms in hand. The next pose involves her sitting on his right shoulder, his hand gripping her upper thigh.

"Do I at least get your number for acting as your personal chair?" Isaac asks, looking up at her.

"Nope," she says without so much as looking at him or breaking her smile, still posing for the camera.

"Come on, let's finish shooting," Ryan says.

"Fuck that."

"Coach is still here," he explains. "Don't get kicked off the team before you've even had a chance to play."

Instead of listening to him, I'm walking toward Valen, dribbling my ball. You know, just in case. Her eyes flash toward mine for a second before she looks back at the camera, pasting on her pageant smile.

"Okay," the photographer announces. "I think we're good. Who's next?"

Isaac lifts Valen off his shoulder, his freakishly big hands circling her waist as he slowly lowers her to the ground, her body sliding against his on the way down. Red-hot jealousy burns through me at the sight. One minute the ball is in my hand, the next it's being throttled at Isaac's head. A chorus of gasps and *oh shits* echo throughout the gym as the ball nails him in the side of the head with a loud thump. He jerks forward with the impact, cradling his head.

"What the fuck, man?"

"Sorry, Lurch. Ball got away from me," I say in a tone that makes it clear that I'm not sorry at all. He moves for me quicker than I thought him capable of, but before it can escalate, Coach blows his whistle.

"On the line!" he shouts. "All of you! Now!"

Everyone groans, knowing damn well that means the whole team will be running suicides for the next twenty minutes. *Worth it.* I take one last glance at Valen as we jog over to the baseline to find her standing there with her arms crossed over her chest, looking unimpressed.

Too bad it only turns me on.

FORTY-EIGHT

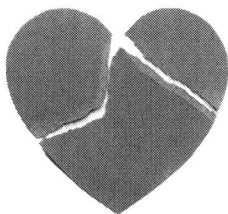

Valen

After Holden made a scene in the gym earlier, his team was forced to do running drills for nearly half an hour before they all filtered out of the gym, panting and sweating. Our media day ran a little longer, and by the time we're done, it's almost nine o'clock. I push through the double doors, stepping out into the snow. Shivering, I pull my phone out of my duffel and see a text from Holden.

> **Meet me in the conservatory. Don't change out of your uniform.**

My stomach dips, my body already buzzing with anticipation. We've gotten pretty good at sneaking around in the dorms, but if he's asking me to meet in the conservatory, wearing my uniform no less, I know he's planning something that requires more…privacy.

I fold my arms over my chest to keep warm, following the path that leads to the conservatory. The sky is dark, the falling snow dancing in the glow of the lampposts that line the sidewalk. My bare legs are freezing with nothing but Holden's hoodie to keep me warm. When I approach the conservatory, it's pitch-black. I glance around, making sure the coast is clear before I slip my cheer briefs down my legs and stuff them into my bag.

I open the door, walking through the first room with the

rows of tables with potted plants, following the dim glow that shines through the glass door across the room. I step inside what Holden and I have started referring to as the tropical room, the humidity instantly warming my skin. Before I can take another step, Holden strides over to me, backing me up against the door.

His palm wraps around the front of my throat, angling my head upward as he dives down to capture my lips. I groan when his tongue licks into my mouth. He kisses me so hard I can feel it between my legs, and when he pulls back, I'm practically panting.

"My team couldn't stop staring you in that uniform," he says, his hand finding its way under my skirt. "I wanted to rip their fucking eyes out just for looking at you."

"You're insane."

His fingers rub me through my underwear, and I moan, opening my legs for him. "You *make me* insane." He takes his touch away too soon, leading me toward the back of the room. He sits on one of the benches, leaving me standing there in front of him. "Take off the sweatshirt."

Heart racing and skin tingling, I start to pull it off.

"Slowly," he instructs, leaning back, resting his arms along the top of the bench.

I let my arms fall to my sides, the tips of my fingers trailing up my thighs, slowly bringing the hem of my sweatshirt up. Holden swallows hard, watching me intently. When I finally pull it over my head, I drop it to the ground next to me.

"What now?" I whisper.

"Come here."

I take a step toward him, and he leans forward, one arm curling around the back of my thighs. "I've tried giving you time. I've been patient." I tense, his words setting me on edge, not knowing where he's going with this. He drags his lips up my thigh, kissing and nibbling. "I want everyone to know you're mine."

"That wasn't part of the deal."

"Are you really going to act like this still means nothing

to you?" When I don't answer, he shakes his head, as if disappointed in me. "I forgot. The ice princess doesn't have feelings." His words feel like a punch to the stomach, especially coming from him. "Tell me how much you don't need me. Tell me how little I mean to you. I dare you."

"Fuck you."

"I'm in love with you." His response comes without hesitation, shocking me into silence.

My mouth falls open, then snaps shut. "No. You're not."

"Yes, I am." He stands, towering over me, forcing me to tip my chin up in order to hold his gaze. "And for some fucked-up reason, you seem to think you're unlovable, but I've been here loving you all along."

"Well." I swallow past the lump in my throat, looking up into his dark eyes. My heart races so fast and hard I think it might beat out of my chest. "I don't love you." The lie tastes like acid on my tongue. *Why can't I just be normal and say how I feel?*

He narrows his eyes, assessing. "Lie." I scoff, turning to walk away, but he catches my arm, stopping me. "I know you love me, Valen. Why the fuck is it so hard for you to say it?"

"Because I'm scared!" I yell, shocking both of us. Tears sting the back of my eyes, adrenaline coursing through me. "You turned me into this pathetic version of myself. You made me need you. You made me love you. I hate this feeling." I bat my tears away, angry at them for falling.

The only people I've ever loved—the two people who were supposed to love me unconditionally—they never really cared about me. They tolerated me.

"Do you think I like it?" he shouts. "I've lost three of the six people on this fucking earth that I give a shit about. That's fifty percent. Every fucking day I'm afraid I'll lose you, too. That one day you'll cut this off and walk away for good. But you know what I realized?"

"What?"

"It doesn't matter if we don't say it out loud, and it doesn't fucking matter if we don't put a label on it. If you ended this right now, it would hurt all the same. We're in too deep to walk away unscathed." He takes my face in his hands, bending down to kiss my tear-soaked lips. "Tell me you're mine."

I clench his shirt in my fists as I bring my lips to his. My tongue slips inside his mouth and he groans, pulling me in closer. Soft, yet possessive quickly turns into desperate and demanding, and I don't know who is claiming who in this moment. His hand wraps around my ponytail, holding me in place as his lips trail down my cheeks, neck, and collarbone, kissing my stream of tears away. "I'm yours," I whisper, finally giving in.

"You have no idea how long I've waited for you to say that." His teeth scrape against my throat before he sucks the skin into his mouth and releases it. I'm breathing hard, already wet, and he's barely touched me. I tug at his shirt, wanting it off, and he takes the hint, pulling it off. He straightens, standing to his full height before taking his seat on the bench. He leans back, pinning me with his heated gaze.

"Lift your skirt."

The tone of his voice makes goosebumps break out across my skin. I do as he says, curling my fingers underneath the hem of my skirt before slowly raising it. He raises a brow when he sees that I've ditched my briefs, wearing nothing but a white thong underneath. Then he's leaning forward, resting his elbows on his thighs, his eyes locked on the space between my legs.

"Now show me what's mine."

My heart pounds as I reach down to pull my thong to the side, baring myself to him. His teeth scrape over his bottom lip, watching me, his face mere inches from my pussy.

"Bring it here."

I shift forward, bringing my pussy to his mouth. The tip of his tongue traces my slit, one of his hands holding me in place by the back of my thigh.

"I knew you'd be wet. Keep holding that skirt up for me," he instructs before diving in to kiss and bite and suck at my flesh.

"Holden." His name on my lips is somewhere between a moan and a plea as I rock my hips, his tongue sliding across my clit. He hooks his fingers into the strings of my underwear at my sides and tugs them down my legs.

"That move you did earlier," he stays, pocketing my underwear. "I want to see it again."

I know which move he's referring to. My pulse hammers in my ears at what I'm about to do, equal parts turned on and embarrassed by the idea. "This one?" I ask, my voice coming out breathier than I mean it to. I lift my left leg, toes pointed, and grab the bottom of my cheer shoe. Holden watches with barely restrained lust in his eyes as I bring my leg straight up in the air, pulling it close to my body.

"Fuck, your pussy is so pretty," he says, dipping his middle finger inside me. "So wet and hot inside." His mouth closes over me as he sucks my clit, my lips parting on a gasp. I can't take more than ten or fifteen seconds before my leg starts to shake, my muscles straining to hold this position.

His hand slides along my extended leg from the back of my thigh, all the way to my ankle. His fingers circle my ankle, and then he's slowly lowering my leg to the bench, his mouth never leaving its target. Needing more, I drop my knee to the bench, bringing my other leg up to straddle his lap. Holden quickly lifts his hips, pulling his shorts and boxers down just low enough to free himself.

"Put me inside you."

I don't hesitate to reach behind me, wrapping my fingers around his hard length, and then I line him up with my entrance and sink down onto him in one swift motion. His mouth falls open as I cry out, unprepared for how deep it would feel. I pull off my shirt, letting it fall to the floor behind me, leaving me in nothing but my skirt and cheer shoes. Holden's mouth immediately latches on to my nipple, sucking hard.

"Yes," I breathe. I start to ride him faster, feeling this inexplicable urge to show him without words how much I need him.

My arms circle his neck, holding him tight. His hands splay across my back, and I bury my face in his neck as I fuck him. I keep him deep inside me, my clit rubbing against his lower stomach with each roll of my hips.

"You're going to tell me you could give this up?" Holden asks, his voice harsh, his hand sliding through my hair to grip my ponytail.

I shake my head in response, feeling my orgasm building.

"Then be with me," he says. "I want everyone to know you're mine. I want to kiss you in public and fill this pussy with my cum in private. Every night. And I know you feel the same, even if you're too fucking stubborn to admit it."

"Please," I say, feeling myself clench around him at his words. We're both sweating, our bodies sliding together, my hair damp and sticking to the side of my face.

"And if for some reason I'm wrong about that, I'll teach myself to live with however much of yourself you're willing to give. If that makes me pathetic, then so be it." His voice is strained, our bodies grinding against each other.

"Holden," I start to cry, overwhelmed physically and emotionally, the heart I didn't even know I had breaking and mending simultaneously at his words.

"I'm in love with you, Valentina." *Valentina*. Not Valen. Not Sweet Valentine.

My head falls back, and I look up at the drops of condensation streaming down the glass ceiling as tears stream freely down my face. He slips a hand between our bodies and under my skirt, his fingers finding my clit, making me feel so good.

"That's it, baby."

My eyes squeeze shut, thigh muscles burning, and I break apart, coming harder than I ever have. "I love you," I say, my lips against his ear.

Holden cradles the back of my head as he stands before lowering me to the cement floor, never leaving my body for a second. He pounds into me, ruthless and desperate between my spread thighs. *"Say it again,"* he begs.

"I love you, Holden."

His eyes close, lips parting, as he fucks me harder. His body tenses, and then he spills inside me with a groan.

He rolls us over until I'm on top, never breaking our connection. His breathing is ragged, chest heaving beneath me as his fingers trail up and down my spine. Suddenly, it's all too much. I hide my face in his neck, feeling raw and stripped bare.

Holden seems to understand that I need a minute to collect myself. I'm grateful for the fact that he holds me without asking questions.

"Ever since Danny died, I've felt like I was drowning, too." His deep voice finally breaks the silence, the tips of his fingers ghosting across my shoulder blade. *"Over and over again. In my dreams. When I'm awake. I forgot what it was like to breathe until you moved in across the hall. You breathed the life back into me."*

Holden

I lay there on the concrete floor of the conservatory for as long as I could with Valen on top of me. Eventually, my body couldn't take it. I was too tired, my muscles sore and stiff from practice. I might have had to fuck the truth out of her, but she finally opened up to me. Finally let me in. I can still hear her voice in my ear, her breaths coming out in little pants as she told me she loved me. It's enough to get my dick hard all over again.

We parted ways once we got to the dorms. Valen might've told me she loved me, but I don't think walking in together looking freshly fucked with her limp ponytail and smeared mascara is the way she wants to announce it. I went to my room for a quick shower, and once I was out, I got a text from my dad that had me walking right back across the hall.

Thayer's the one to answer the door when I knock. We filled them in on what happened with both Valen's mom and Samuel when we got back the other day, and as far as they know, Valen came over in the morning after a fight with her mom when Samuel and my dad showed up.

Valen's sitting cross-legged on one of the barstools eating a bowl of cereal. She's still in my hoodie, her ponytail still slightly off-kilter.

"Did Dad text you?" I ask Thayer, holding my phone up.

"I was about to check it when you knocked. What is it?"

"The governor just withdrew his nomination." I walk inside, closing the door behind me and read it out loud for everyone. "In light of recent controversy and concerns, Governor Greg Thomas has made the difficult decision to withdraw his nomination of Judge Samuel Ames to Associate Justice of the Massachusetts Supreme Judicial Court."

The entire release is about four paragraphs long, explaining the vetting process, the importance of transparency, and his commitment to ensuring that all individuals in positions of public trust are held to the highest standards.

"Holy shit," Valen says.

"They have something on him if the governor is trying to cover his own ass," Thayer points out.

"It this good or bad?" Shayne asks, walking over to take my phone and reading it for herself. "I thought your dad didn't want him to know he was being investigated."

"Well, the cat's out of the fucking bag now either way," Thayer says.

I nod, suddenly feeling conflicted. I should be relieved. This is what I wanted all along. For Christian to pay for Danny's death. For our uncle to pay for the part he played. So why do I feel this sense of unease settling like a brick in my stomach? "Something tells me that Samuel isn't going to take this lying down."

FORTY-NINE

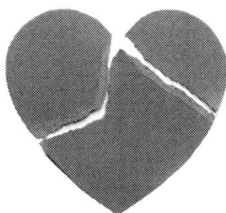

Valen

I'T'S BEEN RADIO SILENCE IN THE FEW DAYS FOLLOWING THE NEWS about Samuel. He hasn't so much as released a statement, and Holden's dad assures him that he's too busy dealing with lawyers, trying to keep his current position to even think about retaliating. Holden's been on edge, though he won't say it out loud. And for the first time since we've been together, I witnessed one of his nightmares. He woke up sweating and gasping for breath next to me in the middle of the night. I could *feel* his fear and guilt and grief like they were my own.

Feeling helpless, I pull out my phone and search Samuel's name for updates, for anything that might point to what happened to Christian, like I've done the past couple of nights. I don't know what exactly I'm searching for at this point since the details are still scarce, but I read everything I can find, scour every social media mention, every tagged photo while Holden sits on the floor in front of the couch between my legs. He's oblivious to my scrolling as he plays video games, his arm hooked around my leg that dangles off the couch.

I'm twelve pages deep in my image search when I see something that has my blood running cold. Or rather, some-*one*. Holden must feel the way my body goes rigid because he drops his controller to the floor, before standing. "What is it?"

I rise from the couch, showing him the photo of his uncle

at an event, shaking hands and laughing with the man I haven't set eyes on in years. Holden's eyebrows cinch together, not following. "What am I looking at?"

"That's Cameron," I say, pointing at the picture. "My mom's ex-boyfriend."

Recognition flashes in his eyes and he grabs my phone, zooming in on the image. He says something about putting a face to the name of the guy he's going to kill, but I don't fully hear him, my mind too busy trying to connect the dots.

Samuel knows Cameron. Is maybe even friends with him. Samuel knew my mother's name. Does he know they dated? Does he know about Cameron's proclivity for young girls and his willingness to pay for them?

I take my phone from Holden's hand, searching for a post I read earlier. It was a mother claiming that her fourteen-year-old son was sent to a juvenile detention facility for nine months for getting caught with weed. I scan the article for the name of the place, my stomach dropping when my suspicions are confirmed.

Hillside Youth Center. The same one owned by Cameron James.

"Valen," Holden says, sounding alarmed. "What's wrong?"

I tune him out, on the brink of putting it all together. Holden's speech from the night of the gala pops into my mind.

"*Thank you for your generous contributions to…*" He turned to Samuel. "*What's this for?*"

"*At-risk youth,*" Samuel said, trying to conceal his anger.

"*Right. At-risk youth…*"

Then I remember the message about a wire transfer that Holden intercepted. The one from someone saved in his phone as CJ. Cameron James.

"I think I know where Christian is."

"Explain," Thayer says half an hour later when we're all gathered in my dorm. I sent Shayne a text immediately after telling Holden, asking her to bring Thayer and meet me at home.

"Cameron is my mom's ex," I start.

"The one who—" Shayne breaks off mid-sentence, not wanting to say it out loud. I don't think I've ever seen her so angry as when I told her. I don't know who she hates more—him or my mom.

I nod. "He owns a private juvenile detention facility."

"What does that have to do with Christian?" Thayer asks.

"My guess is that Cameron has been bribing Samuel to send kids to his facility in exchange for money." I explain everything, from the photo of the two of them together, the charity gala for at-risk youth, the articles accusing Samuel of subjecting kids to overly harsh punishments for minor crimes and mistakes to the text about the wire transfer from CJ. All of it.

"And you think Christian's there? Can they do that even though he's over eighteen now?" Shayne asks.

"Clearly, this guy isn't concerned about legalities," Holden says. "And there's no telling how much Cameron makes in kickbacks from Samuel. I'm sure he'd have no problem keeping Christian there as a favor."

"Fuck." Thayer blows out a breath and scrubs a hand over his face. "It makes too much sense."

"I have no idea if Christian's there, but it's worth checking out," I say. I don't want to give false hope that Christian's alive, but my gut tells me he's there.

"Only one way to find out," Thayer says, fishing his phone out of his pocket.

FIFTY

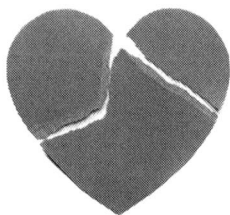

Valen

I HAVE A DEATH GRIP ON MY STEERING WHEEL, MY EYES STRAINING to see through the thick snow. I'm on my way back from my last appointment with my physical therapist where I got the green light to go back to cheer. Her office is a good thirty minutes away, and by the time I got out, it was already dark out. I don't know why I feel so anxious. You don't live in Sawyer Point, Massachusetts your whole life and *not* know how to drive in snow, but tonight, the combination of icy roads and white-out conditions have me on edge. *Five more minutes until I'm back at Hadley.*

Thayer called his dad and told him about my theory about Christian last night. They expected to hear the same old recycled response of, "I'll handle it," to placate them, but to their surprise, he told them that accepting bribes was one of the many things he's suspected of doing. He promised to check it out, but Thayer and Holden didn't have much faith and tried to call the facility themselves. Of course, they didn't get anywhere due to privacy policies. I had to talk Holden out of tracking Cameron down himself, knowing that won't end well for anyone.

A dark SUV appears in the distance behind me, pulling me from my thoughts. It speeds up, approaching too fast to be considered sane, especially in this weather. I assume he'll pass me, but instead, he rides my ass, flashing his bright lights.

"What the fuck." I squint involuntarily, trying to adjust to the sudden brightness. "Go around, asshole!"

He doesn't. Instead, he accelerates, getting even closer. I swallow hard, speeding up to switch to the left lane before he can make contact with my bumper, only he follows me there, too.

Shit, shit, shit. This guy is going to hit me. When he tries to hit me again, I swerve back into the right lane again, hoping by some miracle that he'll speed off ahead of me, but I hit a patch of ice and fishtail for a few scary seconds. There's nowhere to turn for another mile or so and nowhere to pull over. Not that pulling over anywhere near this psychopath would be a good idea. There's nothing but woods to my left and an embankment that leads to the river on my right. If I can just make it to the next stoplight, I'll be in a more populated area.

Suddenly, the car slows down, almost to a full stop, and I breathe a sigh of relief watching their headlights get smaller in my rearview mirror until I see nothing at all. I press a hand to my racing heart, trying to calm myself down. I'm almost to the light when I hear the car again, but this time, I can't see him. Or her. I look out my side mirror, barely making out the form of the SUV speeding toward me without their lights on, but it's too late.

Everything happens within a matter of seconds. I jerk forward with the impact, then I'm skidding off the road. I let out a scream as I hurdle down the embankment, toward the river. My car hits the frozen water, my face bouncing off my steering wheel, then everything goes eerily silent. I'm hyperventilating, struggling to make sense of what happened. I try to force myself to take deep breaths and gauge my surroundings, trying to figure out the best way out of this. I can't see anything outside my windows. I'm dizzy and disoriented and I know I need to act fast, but my thoughts are in slow motion. The sound of rushing water draws my attention to the floor of the car, and only then do I realize my feet are submerged, and the car is filling with water.

Help. I need to call for help. I look around for my purse, finding it on the floor of the front passenger seat. I unbuckle my seatbelt, carefully leaning forward to reach for it. Finally, my fingers make contact with the thin, wet leather strap, and I pull it onto the seat next to me. My hands are shaking so badly that I can barely get my purse unzipped.

I finally get my hands to cooperate, pulling out my phone, only to find it at one percent battery. I squeeze my eyes shut, banging the back of my head against the seat, sending out a silent wish that it will stay on long enough to call for help. If I'm lucky, I can make one phone call, so I have to make it count. I close my eyes, hitting the name of the person I trust more than anyone else.

Holden

I frown at my phone, my hackles rising when I see Valen's name flash across my screen. She knows I'm with Shayne and Thayer. The only reason she'd call is a butt dial or an emergency. I walk into the bathroom to take the call, telling myself I'm being paranoid for nothing.

"It's a little early for a booty call, isn't it?"

"Holden?"

The tone of her voice is one I've never heard before. Vulnerable, scared, laced with a hint of panic. It instantly sends chills up my spine.

"What's wrong?"

She starts rambling, her words too fast and jumbled for me to make out much other than *accident* and *river* and something about being stuck in her car.

"Valen, breathe," I tell her. I hear her take a shaky breath. "Tell me where you are."

"In the river. Right before the light on University."

"You're in the water now?" I clarify.

"Yes," she breathes. "The water is starting to get inside and I'm afraid to move." I hear movement in the background, as if she's shifting around. "I don't think I'm far from the embankment. It feels like I'm tilting forward, like the back end of my car is stuck on something."

"Listen to me," I say, trying to sound calm when I'm feeling anything but. "I need you to roll your window down before the water gets any higher, okay?" I throw the bathroom door open, earning curious looks from my brother and Shayne. "It's going to rush in, so I need you to move fast."

"My car's dead. The windows won't go down."

Fuck.

"Did you call for help yet?"

Shayne frowns at my words, looking over to Thayer who shrugs his shoulders.

"No. My phone is dying and I called you—"

"Call 911," I shout, pointing at Shayne as I run for the door. "Valen's trapped in her car in the river right before the light on University."

"What?" Shayne shrieks, bolting up from the couch. "How do you know that?"

"Just call!"

I run out into the hall and burst through the double doors, almost taking out a guy trying to enter at the same time in the process. I hesitate for a fraction of a second to consider taking my car, but I could make it to Valen on foot in less time than it would take to get to the student parking lot and drive over, and I don't know how much time she has.

"I'm coming," I tell Valen, my feet pounding against the snow-covered sidewalk as I cut through campus. "Tell me what's happening."

"The water's coming in," she says. She's trying to keep her composure, but I can hear the underlying panic.

"How much water?"

"Just hurry."

"Valen," I say, coming up on the busy main road. From here, it's just a little over a mile. "How much?"

"It's past my waist," she finally says.

Shit. It's worse than I thought. Not wanting to waste another second, I dart out into the street, taking my chances with four lanes of traffic. A car swerves into the next lane to avoid hitting me, and another one honks their horn, but I make it across in one piece. "I'll be there in just a couple minutes," I tell her, picking up the pace. "Do you have anything in your car that you can use to break your window if you need to?"

"Um…I don't think so."

"Okay." I rack my brain, trying to think of something that could help. "What about your headrest? Is it detachable?"

"Hang on," she says. I hear shuffling again, and the sound of rushing water. "Yes. I got it."

"Good. You're doing good. If for some reason your car goes under completely, use the metal ends to break the window."

"I could really use that tropical vacation about now," she tries to joke, but it falls flat.

"I'll take you anywhere you want this summer," I promise. "The Bahamas, Maldives, Costa Rica. Wherever you want to go."

"Don't be nice to me. It makes me feel like I really am going to die."

An image of Valen, blue and lifeless and limp just like Danny, pops into my mind, unbidden. Panic claws its way up my throat, but I shove it down, needing to stay calm for her. "I'm always nice to you, remember?" I clear the worry from my voice. "And after tonight, you're going to owe me at least a month of sleeping in my bed, so don't think you're getting off easy."

"There's a joke about getting off easy in there somewhere."

I try to force out a laugh, but the only sound that comes out is my harsh breathing. I might be in good shape, but it's no easy feat to carry on a conversation when I'm running full speed.

"Valen?" She's been silent for a minute. I need to hear that she's okay.

"I'm here," she says, and I can hear her teeth chattering. "Are you close?"

"I'm not far now. Shayne called for help, too. It's going to be okay. You're going to be okay."

"Good, because it's almost to my chest."

I never truly understood the expression about blood running cold until this very moment, but that's exactly what happens. The coldness seeps from my chest, spreading out to my limbs, followed by complete numbness. And pure terror.

"Remember what I told you. Break the window if you have to." I push myself to run faster.

"Okay," she says, her voice trembling. "Holden, I don't want to die."

"You're not going to die. Even if the car goes under, you will not die. This is just a backup plan, okay?"

The line suddenly goes quiet. Too quiet. "Valen?" I say, pulling my phone away from my ear to see that the call ended. *No.* I call her back and it goes straight to voicemail.

"FUCK."

I see the intersection up ahead, and everything else goes blank. My adrenaline takes over, not letting myself think about anything other than getting there, knowing Valen is just past that light. After mere minutes that feel like hours, I make it. I see the tire marks in the snow from where she swerved off the road and run toward them. I jump over the guardrail and weave through the trees above the embankment before skidding down the steep hill.

I don't want to die.

And that's when I see it. Her car is only a few feet out into the water, just like she said. The back end is still just above water, but the front end is submerged. I scan the ground, looking for a rock to break the window. I grab one with a sharp point quickly, and then I drop my phone to the frozen soil and run into the water, holding on to the cold, jagged rock like a lifeline.

Please, baby, please be okay. Please be okay.

The water is so fucking cold it takes my breath away, but even knowing that, it barely registers. I wade out into it, moving as fast as I can against the current. By the time I'm close to Valen's car, I'm nearly up to my chest in water. I try to spot her through the windows. When I see a flash of white glowing from the back seat of the car, I realize it's her ribbon, and I could fucking die of relief.

She's okay. She's safe.

"Valen!" I bang my fist on the window behind the driver's side.

She says something that I can't hear, looking up at me with panic in her big brown eyes. She has the headrest in both hands suspended above her head. I hold up the rock so she can see my plan and she nods in rapid succession.

"Turn around, baby," I shout. I don't want the glass shattering in her face. She does as she's instructed and then I hit the window one, two, three times before it splinters. I use my hand to knock out any remaining shards so that she doesn't get cut on her way out, then hold out my arms, motioning for her to climb through.

Vaguely, I'm aware of the sound of sirens in the distance as I reach for her. I grab her under the arms, pulling her out of the window. She slams into my chest, her body melting into mine as we cling to each other. She doesn't say a single word, burying her face into my chest as her whole body shakes with silent sobs, her fingers clutching my shirt. "You're safe. It's okay. You're safe." I keep her anchored to me, one arm banding around her waist, one hand on the back of her head.

Her hair is soaked, and she feels like ice in my arms. I need to get her out of here. She needs to get out of these wet clothes and get warm. I trudge through the water, making my way toward the riverbank. Once we're out of the water, I lower her to her feet, taking her face in my hands, searching for injuries. I notice blood under her nose and a gash on her forehead, but there's not enough light down here to make out much else.

"Are you okay?" She hasn't said a single word yet, and it's freaking me out. She nods, looking up at me with wide eyes, still not speaking.

"Words, Valen. I need words."

"I'm okay," she says, but the way she's violently shivering says otherwise.

We both look over at her car just in time to see it slip beneath the inky black water, the bubbles breaking through the surface the only evidence that it ever happened.

If I got here seconds later…

"Holden!" I hear Shayne's voice from the road above us as a flashlight shines down in our direction. "Is she okay?" Before I can answer, she's running down the side of the embankment with Thayer right behind her.

She crashes into Valen, throwing her arms around her neck. I take a step back, keeping my arm around her waist to steady her just in case. "What the hell happened? Are you hurt?" She pulls back, inspecting her like I did seconds before with glassy eyes, rubbing Valen's arms with the palms of her hands.

Valen shakes her head dismissively. "I'm fine. I'm just really tired. Can we go home?"

Shayne's eyes flick to mine and then Thayer's, concerned written all over her face that I'm sure mirrors my own.

"She needs to get warm," I say before turning back to Valen. "Can you walk?" The sirens are louder now, their flashing lights coming into view near the road.

"Yeah," she says, but her foot slips in the mud and starts to slide down the embankment when she tries, so I dip down, sliding my arms behind her knees and back to scoop her up, holding her close to my chest. I can tell she doesn't think it's necessary, especially given our audience, but her arms wrap around my neck anyway.

"Can you grab my phone? I dropped it somewhere over there." I gesture to the ground with my chin.

"Got it," Thayer says.

"I swear I'm fine," Valen says, tensing up as we get closer to the top of the steep hill. "I just want to go home."

"You should get checked out," Shayne says.

"She's right," Thayer agrees.

Once we get near the top, Ryan is there, reaching out a hand, pulling me up over the edge with Valen still clinging to me.

"Where the hell did you come from?"

"I heard you yelling across the hall. Came out just in time to see them," he explains. "You didn't think to put on any shoes before you took off for a mile and a half long rescue mission?" he asks, shining the flashlight of his phone on my feet. I look down, finding my formerly white socks now a soggy mixture of blood and dirt and leaves.

"You *ran* here?" Valen asks, wriggling out of my grasp until I set her down.

I shrug. "It was faster."

"With no shoes," she deadpans.

I suppress a smirk at the attitude in her tone because it means she's snapping out of her shock. "I forgot."

"Jesus, Holden, your hand!" Shayne gasps.

I hold it out in front of me, noticing the damage for the first time. "It's a couple of scrapes. Relax, little sister."

Shayne rolls her eyes. "Both of you are stubborn assholes."

The sirens are so loud they drown everything else out as the fire truck comes to a screeching halt a few feet away. Three men hop out before it's even stopped completely, one of them making his way toward us.

"Everyone okay?"

Valen nods yes at the same time I tell them no. "She was in the water for at least fifteen minutes."

"Let's get you checked out and warmed up. The ambulance is en route."

"I will if he does," she says, gesturing toward my hand.

I don't bother arguing if that's what it takes. We follow him over, Valen leaning on me for support, as if it takes too much strength to hold herself upright.

"I need you to take your clothes off," the fireman says, pulling out a blanket that looks more like tin foil.

"I'm not doing that here," Valen says, and I can tell by her stubborn tone that she means it.

"Miss, your privacy is not my priority. Your safety is."

"Ryan," I shout. He jogs over quickly. He's the only one with a dry, long-sleeved shirt. "Your shirt." He reaches behind his neck, pulling it off with zero hesitation. "Thanks, man."

I turn my attention to the firefighter. "Hold the blanket up," I tell him.

He looks impatient, but he nods and does it anyway, shielding Valen from view.

"Put your hands on my shoulders," I tell her gently, dropping to my knees in front of her, throwing Ryan's shirt onto the edge of the truck behind her. She acted like modesty was her concern, but I know her well enough to know it was a front. If I had to guess, I'd say she wasn't confident in her ability to physically remove her clothes and didn't want to appear weak or vulnerable. As if being involved in a car accident is somehow embarrassing to her. Once she braces her hands on my shoulder and steadies herself, I unbutton her jeans, working the wet denim down her thighs along with her underwear. Her shoes and socks are next, then I stand, pulling her sweatshirt off.

"Thank you," she whispers as I reach behind her to unclasp her bra. With the bright lights from the inside of the fire truck, I can now see just how pale she is. Her lips hold a blue tint and the relief I felt for a brief moment is replaced with fear once again.

I reach around her for Ryan's shirt, then pull it down over her head, careful to keep the neck hole stretched away from the cuts on her face as I lower it. She slides her arms into the sleeves that hang past her hands as I bend over, gathering her wet clothes.

Apparently, fresh out of patience, the firefighter drops the blanket, then wraps it around Valen's shoulders. "Let's take your temperature," he tells her, motioning for her to sit on the back of the truck. I look over, finding Shayne studying me with frown.

Somehow, I know that tonight will change everything.

FIFTY-ONE

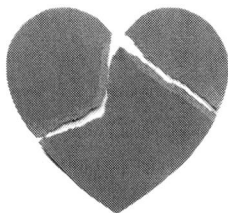

Valen

EIGHT MINUTES AND FORTY-EIGHT SECONDS. THAT'S HOW LONG it took Holden to get to me. He made it before the fire truck, before the ambulance, before Thayer's car. I needed him, and he was there. He literally ran to my rescue.

Shortly after they took my vitals and determined my temperature indicated possible hypothermia, the police showed up, followed by the ambulance that whisked me away in a rather dramatic fashion. Holden ended up riding in the ambulance with me, stripped down to his boxers, donning a matching silver blanket. Once we got to the hospital, he insisted on staying in my room until they were ready to treat the cuts on his hand. The nurse was nice enough to let him and Shayne both stay, but Ryan and Thayer were relegated to the waiting room.

"You should go home and get some sleep. I don't even know why *I* have to stay the night," I tell Shayne. They finally called for Holden a while ago, so it's just us now. I can see the questions in her eyes, but she's letting me off the hook. For now. "We've been here for two hours and all they've done is give me broth and hot chocolate."

"I'm staying. And as soon as I know you're okay, prepare for an interrogation."

I'm surprised she hasn't said anything until now. "Don't hate me."

She opens her mouth to respond, but a knock on the door interrupts her. We both turn to see two men in uniform standing in the doorway.

"Valentina?" one of them asks.

I nod.

"I'm Officer Davis and this is Detective Rodriguez. I apologize about the late visit, but we wanted to ask you some questions about the incident while it's fresh in your mind, if that's okay with you."

"Okay," I say, agreeing. I'd rather have this happen while Holden is out of the room anyway.

"Great. Can you tell me what happened?"

"I was driving back to campus when a car sped up behind me. I thought he wanted to pass, so I switched lanes, but he just followed me. At one point, he backed off, then stopped completely, but then he sped up again, and that time, he hit me from behind."

"Did you notice what kind of vehicle it was, or a license plate number?"

"It was dark and he had his high beams on. Black, maybe? An SUV." I close my eyes, searching my mind for anything else, but come up short.

When I open my eyes, I catch Shayne's worried expression, the fear in her eyes, and I know she's come to the same conclusion as me.

"You said *he*," the detective chimes in, bringing my attention back to them. "It was a man then?"

I shake my head. "No, I just assumed."

He jots something down onto a notepad. "Can you think of anyone who might want to hurt you?"

I open my mouth to tell them about Samuel, but I hesitate, seeing Holden approaching behind them, his right hand and arm wrapped in gauze. "Uh, no. Not that I can think of."

Holden walks over to my side, crossing his arms over his chest.

"The tire marks indicate that this wasn't an accident," the officer says. I feel Holden tense up beside me. "Can you think of anything else that might be helpful other than the fact that it might've been a dark colored SUV?"

Holden and Shayne exchange a look that all but confirms my suspicions. I don't know what kind of vehicle he drives, but from their reaction, my money's on an SUV.

"It was dark," I say again. "It happened fast."

"I understand. If you think of anything else, give me a call." He holds up a business card before walking over to the bedside table where my cup of forgotten hot chocolate sits, leaving the card there.

"Don't," I tell Holden. "We don't know for sure."

He scrubs a hand through his hair, blowing out a breath.

There's another knock at the door before he can respond. Another interruption. This time it's the nurse. "Just a heads-up, visiting hours were over a long time ago, but I'll give you a few more minutes with your friends as long as you're all quiet. We'll monitor you for a few more hours, then you can most likely leave first thing in the morning."

"Okay. Thank you," I say, even though I want nothing more than a shower and to sleep in my own bed.

"Are you sure you don't have any family members you'd like me to call?"

"God, no."

"We are her family," Shayne says.

The nurse gives me a sad smile, patting my leg. "If you need anything at all, let me know."

Shayne rises from the chair when the nurse heads for the door, coming to stand next to the bed. "I'm going to run back to campus and get some clean clothes for when you leave." She looks over to Holden, who's wearing a pair of hospital provided scrubs that barely reach his ankles and hospital socks. "And some shoes for Holden. Do you need anything else?"

I shake my head. I don't plan on being here any longer than

I have to. She kisses my cheek goodbye, and when Holden starts to follow her out, my anxiety spikes at the thought of being left here alone. That only makes me even more anxious, because I used to thrive on solitude before Holden barged his way back into my life and made me need him.

"I'm just going to walk her out," he says, reading my mind. Like always. "I'll be right back."

FIFTY-TWO

Holden

"Where's Ryan?" I ask Thayer. He's in the mostly empty waiting room, but Ryan isn't with him.

"Told him to go home," he explains. "He passed out in the chair."

I nod. There was a game tonight and we both have practice early tomorrow. There's no reason for him to stick around. "Valen said the car that hit her was a black SUV. You know who just bought a brand new, black BMW SUV?"

"Samuel," Thayer says without hesitation. "Along with the rest of the world. Yourself included."

"It had to be him." And if my suspicions turn out to be right, I'll put a bullet in him myself.

"Think about it," Shayne says. "The governor just withdrew his nomination, people are coming out of the woodwork accusing him of shit, and he feels like he's losing everything. He's unraveling."

"I know Samuel is a sadistic fuck, but why Valen? Why not one of us?" Thayer asks me.

"Because I'm the one who put this whole thing in motion. I'm the one who called him out in front of an audience on New Year's." He didn't know that my dad had been planning his downfall prior to that. As far as he's concerned, this extra scrutiny, his entire downfall, is because of me and me alone. "And he knows the best way to hurt me is to hurt her."

"How would he know that?" Shayne asks. Thayer pins me with a glare, and I know with that one look that he's known about Valen and me for longer than he's let on. He warned me to stay away from her months ago.

"He saw Valen and me…together. On his patio on New Year's. The day Grey and I went to pay him a visit, he had the video on his phone."

"For the love of fuck, Holden. All this is because you couldn't keep your goddamn dick in your pants?" Thayer shakes his head.

"Fuck you. It wasn't like that." I'm well aware that this is all my fault.

"You love her," Shayne says. It's not a question.

"More than I've ever loved anything in my life."

Her eyes soften and she nods in understanding. "Just don't hurt her. You're my brother and I love you, Holden, but she's my sister. Don't make me choose." I hear the unspoken part of her warning loud and clear. *Don't make me choose, because it won't be you.* I'm not surprised or offended. I'm glad her allegiance is with Valen. But it doesn't give me the warm and fuzzies hearing it out loud.

"Understood."

Valen doesn't notice me at first. She's staring out the window, her gaze fixed on a snow-covered lamppost outside, seemingly lost in thought. The nurse must have come back because the lights are dim now. Even still, I can see the bruises starting to form under her eyes. My fingers curl into fists at my sides thinking about how close she came to dying. If she would have hit one of those trees on the way down, if her phone wouldn't have had enough battery left to call me, if I would have gotten there just a few seconds later…

I shake the thoughts away, unable to let my mind go there, making my way over to her. Now that the adrenaline has worn off, I can feel the cuts and bruises on my feet with each step, but it's nothing compared to what Valen must be feeling. Her head whips around when she hears me, alarmed, but she relaxes the second she realizes it's me. She looks exhausted, her eyes glassy and unfocused. I go to run the backs of my knuckles down her cheek but think better of it, not wanting to hurt her. Instead, I tuck her hair behind her ear.

"What's wrong? Besides the obvious."

"It's like my body is tired, but my mind won't shut off. The nurse just gave me pain meds. She said they'd help me sleep, too, but I just…" she trails off, shaking her head and rolling her eyes at herself. "I don't want to close my eyes."

I know the feeling. "Figures you'd be too stubborn to let the medication work."

Wordlessly, I toss my phone onto the metal rolling table next to the bed, then reach behind my neck with my good arm, pulling the scrub shirt over my head and toss it to the chair next to the window. I sit on the edge of the bed and Valen lifts the blankets, scooting over to make room for me. I lie back, careful not to hurt her, and she curls up on her side, her thigh draped over my stomach, her head resting against my chest. She still feels cold and clammy, even with the warm blankets. I wrap my arm around her, pulling her in closer.

"Change the channel," I tell her, knowing she'll understand my meaning. "When you close your eyes and see something you don't want to see, replace it with a happy memory instead."

She's quiet for a minute, and just when I think she's fallen asleep, she speaks again. "The conservatory."

"Hmm?"

"My happy place."

"Mine, too." Anywhere with her is my happy place, whether it's on the cabin floor without heat and electricity or a shitty twin bed in her dorm or this hospital bed.

"Will you stay with me?" she asks, sounding like she's on the brink of sleep already. The medication must be kicking in because she'd rather die than risk sounding like she needed someone under normal circumstances.

"For as long as they let me." The fingertips of my bandaged hand glide up and down her arm. It doesn't take long for her to fall asleep. In a matter of seconds, her breathing evens out. I should feel some semblance of peace knowing that she's okay, but every time I close my eyes, I see the gruesome image my mind conjured up of Valen limp and lifeless in the frozen water. It's burned into my brain, and no amount of changing the channel will help.

I don't know how long I lie like this, staring up at the brown watermark on one of the ceiling tiles. Shayne comes back at one point, just long enough to drop off a bag of clothes and my shoes. She takes one look at us and leaves without a word. The nurse comes in, too, giving me a disapproving look, and tells me I have five more minutes, but she never comes back. So I never leave.

Whether it's the pain pills or just exhaustion from today's events, Valen sleeps harder than ever. Her breathing is slow and deep, her little puffs of breath hitting my chest with each exhale. She looks serene, her heartbeat steady and strong against my chest. It's the complete opposite of how I feel.

My phone buzzes from the table and I reach over Valen's sleeping form to grab it. I clench my jaw so hard my ears pop when I see that it's a text from my uncle.

> **Ran into Valentina tonight but didn't get to say hello before she disappeared. Send her my best.**

I stiffen at the words on the screen, knowing he chose them carefully. *Ran into* Valentina. It might as well be a confession. As carefully as I can, I extract my arm from underneath Valen. I don't want to leave her, especially like this. He's baiting me with that text. He knows exactly what my next move will be. He'll be waiting for me to show up. Even with that knowledge, I can't stop myself from doing exactly that.

FIFTY-THREE

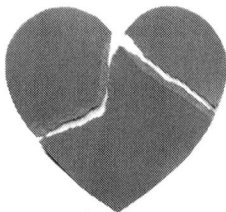

Valen

I DON'T KNOW WHAT PULLS ME FROM SLEEP, BUT THE SECOND I'M awake, I know something is wrong. Holden's no longer in bed with me. I can sense that much before I've even opened my eyes. I rub my tired eyes, squinting up at the glowing clock on the wall. It reads 2:46 A.M.

Slight movement draws my attention to the left, and I find Holden looking out my window with his hands clasped behind his head. For a brief second, I'm relieved that he's still here, but there's something about his silence, his body language, the fact that he's not in bed with me…all of it screams wrong.

He doesn't react when I climb out of the hospital bed, or when my bare feet slap against the cold floor. It's not until I wrap my arms around his waist that he startles and tenses, blinking rapidly like he's been pulled from his thoughts.

"What's wrong?" I lean my cheek against his back.

"It was Samuel," he says, his voice flat.

I nod, even though he can't see me. "I know." At least, I assumed. It's not like it was hard to put two and two together.

He spins around abruptly, knocking me off balance, then steadies me by my elbows. "Did you hear what I said?" He raises his voice. "He tried to kill you, Valen."

"I know," I say again. "But he didn't. I'm fine."

"He tried to kill you. Because of me. You could have died. You *almost* died."

"But I didn't. You can say it as many different ways as you want, but it doesn't change the outcome. You saved me." He's always saving me. More than anyone else, in so many little ways, every single fucking day.

He shakes his head. "What about next time? I can't—" he stops himself, directing me back to the bed. "I can't do this."

I throw his hands off me. "Do *what*?"

He shoves his hand through his hair, his jaw clenched tight, and pins me with a look that says everything he's not saying out loud. He's leaving me.

"Don't."

"I have to."

"No, you don't," I argue. "You have to stay. With me. I need you to stay." I hate how pathetic I sound begging for him to stay.

He turns away, his silhouette moving farther away from me with each step.

"You did this to me."

He flinches at my words, twisting back around to face me.

"I was fine before you. I didn't need anyone. But you made me need you. You made me fall in love with you." My voice breaks on the last sentence, tears streaming down my face. Holden's throat bobs on a swallow, his empty gaze fixed on a spot on the wall over my head. "And if you're going to leave me now because of your own misplaced guilt or self-loathing or whatever the fuck this is, then you're the coward."

Not a flicker of emotion crosses his features, and I'm reminded of the night outside of his house. The night he found out Christian killed Danny.

"Well, you were right about one thing. You said you'd break my heart into a million little pieces, and you just succeeded. Congratulations."

Still nothing. Just a dead, hollow stare. "I'm sorry. I should have never touched you."

FIFTY-FOUR

Valen

"RISE AND SHINE, PRINCESS." SHAYNE'S VOICE BRINGS ME from sleep, and I crack open my eyes to find her standing above me, shaking an iced coffee. The pain meds are the only reason I've been able to sleep since Holden left. "The nurse said you can have caffeine now."

"I feel like I got hit by a train."

"Well, you did crash into a frozen river."

"There is that." I pull myself into a sitting position, scanning the room for Holden. He wasn't here an hour ago when a new nurse took my vitals again, and I try to hide my disappointment at the fact that he's not here now. After he left, I went to call Shayne, but then I remembered I didn't have a phone. It's probably at the bottom of the river. Or inside my car, wherever the fuck that is. God, I'm dreading dealing with that whole situation. I know I'll have to tell my parents at some point, but I can't find it in me to care about any of it.

"The nurse said Holden stayed most of the night," Shayne says. "What happened?"

A knock saves me from trying to explain and has us both turning for the door. It's halfway open and standing on the other side is the last person I expected to see. *Spoke too soon.*

"What are you doing here?" I ask my father. I told the nurse I didn't want my family called. He ignores my question, his expression unreadable as he walks into the room like he owns the place.

"Are you okay?" He eyes my face, then scans the rest of me, as if checking to make sure I'm in one piece.

"I'm fine," I say, my tone clipped. "How did you know I was here?"

"Good news," the morning nurse says brightly, walking in behind him with a small packet of paperwork in hand. "I've got your discharge papers. Once you sign these, you're free to go."

I quickly sign the papers as she recites the discharge information and instructions about my medication, but I don't really hear anything she's saying. The whole process only takes a minute, and then I quickly use the bathroom to change into the clothes Shayne brought. I dig through my cheer bag full of stuff, finding a brush and a hairclip on top. I don't bother taming my hair, knowing it's going to take some serious conditioning later. I throw it up into a clip, then pull out the clothes she picked out. She brought my most comfortable leggings, an oversized, long-sleeved Hadley shirt, and some thick white socks. She even brought my favorite slippers.

It takes me a while to get dressed, my body still stiff and sore, but once I do, I swear I feel almost human again.

"So much better," I say, walking out of the bathroom. "All I need now is a shower."

"I got a hotel near campus. You should stay with me until you're feeling better," my dad says. Shayne and I both exchange bewildered looks.

"Why?"

"I think it would be a good idea, considering the circumstances."

"Since when do you act like a parent?" I eye him skeptically. What does he know?

"Since I got a call at four o'clock this morning from your boyfriend telling me that you were run off the road, and if I was a halfway decent father, I'd come take care of you."

I couldn't look more shocked if he slapped me across the face. Holden called him? Why? How did he even get his number? That's fucking rich. "Why isn't he here himself if he's so concerned?"

"That I don't know."

"I'll be fine at the dorms," I say, trying to sound grateful, because I am. It's just…a little weird. And a little late. I stand on my tiptoes to give him a peck on the cheek. "Thanks for checking on me."

He looks like he wants to fight me on this, but what can he do? I'm not a minor. It's not like he can force me. "I'll deal with your car and get that sorted out. In the meantime, I'll be at the Inn on Northampton."

"Where's Holden?" I ask Shayne once we're outside the hospital doors. "I have a really bad feeling."

She stops short. "I was going to ask you that question."

My heart dips into my stomach. "You mean you haven't seen him?"

Shayne shakes her head. "Not since last night, no. I've called him like a thousand times. Why?"

"We have to go to Sawyer Point. Now."

"You need to rest. What the hell happened, Valen?"

"Where are you parked?" I say, hurrying my steps.

She points in the direction, and I spot her white car not too far from the entrance.

"Call Thayer. Tell him to meet us in Sawyer Point."

"Explain first," she says, opening the front door and sliding inside. "You're scaring me."

I lower myself into the passenger seat and close the door. "One minute, he was holding me in the hospital bed, and then when I woke up in the middle of the night, he was all freaked out, telling me that Samuel was the one who ran me off the road, and saying he couldn't do this. I thought he was breaking up with me."

Shayne frowns. "He just told me he was in love with you. He wouldn't leave you."

"He's going after Samuel." And he called my dad to make sure someone was taking care of me.

Her face drains of color. "Fuck."

"And we have no idea when he left if no one's talked to him. Call Thayer. Call August, too." It was nearly three in the morning when he left. I check the clock on Shayne's dash. It's almost seven now.

"I'm calling Thayer, but we've tried calling his dad all night and morning. He's not answering."

Shit. "Something's wrong." I just hope we're not too late.

FIFTY-FIVE

Valen

"**H**E'S NOT HERE," THAYER SAYS AS WE RUSH OUT OF Shayne's car, coming to a stop near the fountain in front of their Heartbreak Hill house. We tried Samuel's house first, thinking he'd go there, but it was completely empty. Not even his wife was there.

"Where the hell is everyone?" I ask. "Have you gotten a hold of your dad?"

Thayer shakes his head. "Crickets." The word barely has time to leave his lips when Thayer and Shayne both get a text at the same time. My heart stops, dread crawling up my spine as they pull their phones out. I lean in close to Shayne to see her screen. It's a message from Holden.

"Oh thank God," I say, heaving a sigh of relief.

Shayne shakes her head, her eyes filling with tears as she angles the screen toward me. "Samuel has Holden. They're at The Falls."

My heart takes a nosedive, blood rushing in my ears. Holden's on his knees near the edge of the cliff with his hands tied behind his back, staring blankly at the camera. *No.* My head swims as panic sets in. *He wouldn't.* That's too far, even for someone as morally corrupt as Samuel is.

Thayer reacts quicker than any of us, his expression contorting into a mixture of fear and rage. "Stay here," he orders, jumping into his Hellcat before we can object. It roars to life, and he takes off like a rocket as Shayne runs after him, screaming at him to stop. I don't waste any time jumping into the driver's seat of her idling car.

"Get in!" I yell. She runs back to the car, and I lay on the gas, speeding down the long driveway.

I come to a skidding halt at The Falls and throw the car in park before flinging the door open. Samuel stands feet away from where Holden is kneeling in the snow, with a gun pointed in Thayer's direction. Holden's eyes widen with terror when he sees me. He lunges, but Samuel swings the gun back in his direction. Holden freezes, nostrils flaring, jaw clenched hard. Shayne runs over to Thayer's side, but he positions her behind his back, putting himself between her and Samuel.

"You'd think he'd have learned his lesson by now," Samuel says, chuckling. "But he keeps falling for it. Every time."

"Leave, Valen," Holden says, his tone low, his eyes begging me to listen.

I shake my head. "I'm not going anywhere." I walk over to where Shayne and Thayer are, and Thayer pulls me to stand behind him, too. "You don't really think you can get away with this, do you?"

The deranged smile slips from Samuel's face. "That's the whole point," he says. "He took everything from me." He jabs the gun in Holden's direction, making me flinch. "There's no going back. So, I figured we could all go out with a bang." He wiggles the gun a little. "Literally."

My heart starts to pound even harder when I realize what he's saying. He's not planning to walk away from this.

"Do you like the location? I thought it was kind of poetic," he says proudly.

"Fuck you," Holden spits.

Samuel tightens his grip on the gun, extending his arm, and I don't think. I just run.

"No!" The scream that rips from Holden's throat is deep and guttural, but I don't stop until I'm covering his body with mine. My arms circle his neck, my back to Samuel as I squeeze my eyes shut. "Valen, you have to leave," Holden whispers harshly, his lips against my ear. "It'll be okay, I promise. But you have to leave."

I shake my head. "I can't," I say, my entire body trembling against his.

"Now," he says, his voice pleading.

"Two for the price of one bullet. Even better," Samuel says, taunting.

Taking a fortifying breath, I stand in front of Holden to face Samuel. Holden gets to his feet behind me with his hands still tied behind his back, and then he's stepping in front of me.

"One more move and I'll shoot you both," Samuel says, prowling toward us.

"Stay the fuck away from her," Holden warns, trying to keep me back with his tied hands. As surreptitiously as I can, I reach down, trying to untie the cord around his wrists without attracting any attention. Samuel's eyes narrow as continues to walk toward us, tilting his head to the side to see behind Holden. I try to move faster, loosening the cord as much as I can before he comes to a stop in front of us.

Fuck.

His hand shoots out to grip me by the upper arm, jerking me forward.

"Don't fucking touch her!" Holden yells.

Samuel simply arches a brow and pulls me to stand in front of Holden, but out of his reach. "Just for that, you get to watch her die first."

He raises his arm, the gun aimed at my chest. I start to hyperventilate, and Shayne lets out a bloodcurdling scream that rips me apart as Thayer wraps his arms around her middle. She fights against his hold, trying to get to me. I can sense Holden behind me, and I know he's coming for me, too. Just before he reaches me, Samuel gives me a menacing smile, his finger hovering over the trigger.

A deafening gunshot echoes through the woods, and I can't hear anything other than muffled screams. Blood coats my chest and face, and then I'm being tackled from behind and shielded with Holden's body. Thayer runs toward Samuel, who's standing there with blood pouring from his right shoulder. Thayer easily wrestles the gun from his hand before Samuel clutches his shoulder and drops to his knees, revealing the person standing behind him.

Christian.

"You're okay," Holden says, pulling me into his arms, the cord hanging from one wrist as he wipes the blood from my cheeks. "I'm so sorry, baby."

Shayne runs over, throwing her arms around me from behind, and Holden wraps his arms around her, too, as she sobs into my hair. I hear footsteps crunching in the snow, and I lift my head to find Christian approaching. I tense as Holden stands, walking with Thayer to meet Christian halfway. I hear sirens in the distance, and my eyes follow the sound, noticing August standing off to the side with Christian's mom. Tears stream down her face, her hand covering her mouth as she watches.

When the hell did they get here?

As soon as Christian's within arm's reach, Holden pulls back his fist and sends it right into his face. "Took you long enough."

FIFTY-SIX

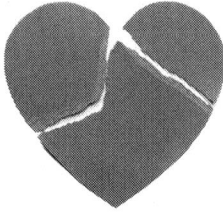

Valen

A N HOUR OF QUESTIONING LATER, AUGUST USED THAT FAMOUS Ames' privilege to talk the police into letting us go home. Samuel was rushed to the hospital where he'll stay until he's stable. Christian turned himself in and was taken away in handcuffs, but August assured us he'd be let off after everything comes to light. Apparently, shortly after Holden got the text from Samuel, he got another one from August. Turns out, I was right about where he was. August picked up Rebecca and drove the two-hundred miles to bust Christian out of Hillside Youth Center before concocting a plan to take Samuel down for good. I don't know all the details, but I'll hear the full story another day. If my brain tries to process anything else tonight, I think it might break.

Now, we're all gathered at Holden's house, grouped off in different parts of the house. I'm with Shayne in Thayer's old bed, both of us curled on our sides facing each other, still stunned and reeling from everything that happened.

"Are you okay?" she asks.

I snort out a laugh at the absurdity of her question. "Just peachy. Are you okay?"

She nods, her cheek rubbing against the pillow. "Relieved that it's over."

"Same. I'm sorry I didn't tell you about Holden."

She shrugs a shoulder. "You're allowed to protect the things that make you happy."

"It was supposed to be a one-time thing. I really thought he'd get what he wanted and move on to the next girl. But he didn't. And then it turned into a two-time thing, and a three-time thing—"

"I get it." She holds up a hand, stopping me.

"I didn't want to say anything because I didn't want to mess with the dynamic for something that was supposed to be temporary. But he was really good to me. It started to feel…real. I know it sounds crazy because it's Holden, but he's different with me. I've never felt like this about anyone."

"And that freaked you out?" she guesses, knowing me all too well.

"Yep," I say. "Because I'm an idiot."

"You're not an idiot, Valen. You had an emotionally unavailable, narcissistic mother who was jealous of her own daughter and a flaky father who was only present intermittently at best and overcompensates for his absence by buying you expensive things. *Of course*, having genuine feelings for someone is scary."

My mouth falls open at her casual delivery and the brutally accurate assessment. I half-laugh, pulling myself up into a sitting position, ignoring the twinge of pain. "Wow, that psych major kicked in hard and fast."

"You've never considered that your upbringing might be the reason you're kind of…" she hesitates, choosing her next words carefully. "Closed off?"

I shrug. "Not really. I thought it was just because I'm a Scorpio."

The door opens behind us, and I look over my shoulder to find Holden in the doorway. "Why are you in my brother's bed instead of mine?" he asks, walking over to us. He bends down to scoop me up, carrying me out of the room like a baby. Shayne shakes her head, but there's a smile on her face, so I know she's fine.

"I really need a shower," I tell him. I still haven't showered since before the accident. I was able to change my clothes and wash Samuel's blood off my skin, but it's not enough. It's the only thing I want to do before crawling into bed and sleeping for two days straight.

"I can arrange that."

Holden

I turn the shower on, making sure the water's hot before helping Valen undress. She has a bruise from her seatbelt across her chest, a few small cuts on her face, and the guilt for what happened to her hits me all over again. I thought I might lose her twice in a twenty-four-hour span. Once in the river, and again when I thought Christian wasn't going to make it in time. If he had been half a second later...

"Don't," she tells me, reading my mind, stopping that train of thought.

I nod, helping her into the shower. I undress quickly before following her in and standing under the spray of water. She crosses her arms, pushing those pretty little tits up, water cascading down her body as she gives me a look I can't quite decipher. "You left me."

I shake my head, pulling her in by her waist. "I'm sorry. I didn't want to. He would've never stopped if I didn't end it for good."

"I thought you were breaking up with me."

"Never." I take her face in my hands, kissing her wet lips. "Leaving you in that hospital was the hardest thing I've ever had to do. I'm in love with you, remember?" And I am. So fucking much. And if I had any doubt before tonight that she loved me, too, I sure as shit don't now after watching her use herself as a human shield to protect *me*.

She nods, her face still in my hands. I reach for the body wash behind her and she leans into me, closing her eyes as I start to wash her body.

"I knew if I told you I was going after him that you'd try to stop me."

"Obviously," she mumbles against my chest. "Because it was a stupid fucking idea."

"Agree to disagree."

"Don't ever do it again," she warns.

"Done," I say. "Anything else?"

"Take me to bed."

"Gladly."

EPILOGUE

Valen

Six months later

I F YOU WOULD'VE TOLD ME A YEAR AGO THAT I'D BE AT MY father's wedding with Holden as my date, I'd have laughed in your face. But here I am, slow dancing to a song called "Daylight" with the boy who took my frozen heart and made it burn for him.

After my dad came to the hospital, he did exactly as he said he would and took care of my car—and by that, I mean he bought me a new one. Along with a phone. I finally came clean about the night I stood him up and how I saw his fiancée and her daughter at the table. He asked for a do-over, and I agreed. Holden urged me to open up to my dad about the things my mother had said and done over the years, and against my better judgment, I agreed to that, too.

Needless to say, he was angry, with both my mother and himself for letting me down, with the half-truths and outright lies my mother fed me. All of it. I haven't talked to my mother since the day I walked out her door. I've heard through the grapevine that she's telling an entirely different version of events, but I can't be bothered to care.

As for Samuel, the stuff with Hillside was only the tip of the iceberg. He ended up getting twenty years for a laundry list of crimes, including money laundering, racketeering, fraud, extortion, bribery, and more than I can even begin to remember. Cameron James went down with him and is now currently serving time for his part in it. He's also serving time for a video that was found on his computer of him with a teenage girl. Sick fuck.

On a more positive note, once Holden and Thayer have forgiven Christian for his part in Danny's death. I don't know if things will ever be like they were before, but they all seem happier than they've been in a long time. Even Grey comes around more often now, and Shayne loves it. Until they all team up against her.

They might not be my blood, but they've become my family all the same, and I wouldn't trade our dysfunctional group for anything in the world.

"Summer's almost over and I still owe you that tropical vacation," Holden says. "Have you made up your mind?"

I shrug, looking up into his light brown eyes, my arms around his waist, my chin resting on his chest. "I was thinking we'd just hang out in the conservatory. Or maybe the cabin in Vermont."

He arches a brow. "When are you thinking?"

"Now's good."

His eyes darken, picking up on my meaning. "Are you trying to get fucked, Sweet Valentine?" he asks, lowering his voice as he gives my ponytail a sharp tug. "Is that why you wore this ribbon in your hair for me?"

I nod, feeling him grow hard against my stomach already.

"Lead the way."

ACKNOWLEDGEMENTS

First and foremost, thank you to my readers. I'm so beyond grateful for you. This book almost didn't happen, and without getting all sappy, I just want you to know that you're the reason it did. Well, that and because Bebe Reid bullied me into it.

Thank you to Stacey Blake for your beautiful formatting (and for always fitting me in last minute), to everyone at Grey's Promo who made this process so easy, and to Paige, my amazing editor who still puts up with me. I don't deserve you. Thank you will never be enough.

Mary Elizabeth, here's your credit for that one sentence you helped me with. Love you for that.

If you haven't read Shayne and Thayer's story,
here's an excerpt from

TELL ME
PRETTY
LIES

PROLOGUE

Shayne

I CLING TO MY BROTHER'S ARM AS HE LEADS ME UP THE RAIN-slicked steps and through the door to Whittemore, thankful for the support. My shaky legs have threatened to go limp beneath me more times than I can count today, between the wet, soft ground at the cemetery that tried to swallow my heels and the fact that I've never been good in anything other than sneakers to begin with. As soon as we enter the foyer, the smell of one thousand casseroles hits my nostrils. Why do people think food makes everything better? *Sorry your loved one died. Here, have some fucking potato casserole. Hope that helps!*

"I'm going upstairs," Grey says flatly, unlatching my grip on his arm. His eyes are bloodshot, and I'm pretty sure he's still in a state of shock. And probably a little high.

"You okay?" I ask. Stupid question, considering. But it's more than Danny's funeral. He seems distracted and distressed.

"I'm fine." He gives me a perfunctory kiss on the top of my head, and I spot Thayer over his shoulder, casually swiping a bottle of brown liquor from the bar. Grey heads for the stairs and I glance around, wondering if I'm the only one seeing this. Holden and their cousin Christian sit on the white sofa, glassy-eyed and ties loosened, elbows resting on their knees. I look to my left as Greyson's intercepted by Mom and her fiancé August—Thayer and Holden's dad—before he can make his escape. Mom pulls him in for a hug, and August claps him on the shoulder, and Grey tenses. Dozens of people I've never even met before are gathered in the house we've called home for the past two years, mingling and remarking on what a tragedy it is to lose someone so young.

I want to throw something.

A crashing sound brings my attention back toward the bar where a glass has now shattered on the hardwood. Thayer steadies himself on the edge of the bar cabinet, staring blankly at the broken glass. His grandfather appears, pulling him upright, and Thayer tries to shake him off.

"Man up," he orders in that quiet-but-deadly tone that brooks no argument. "Your family needs you." His hands tighten around Thayer's upper arms, shaking him a little.

"Move," Thayer says through clenched teeth. Instinctively, I hurry over to him, trying to attract as little attention as possible, ready to intervene. I know two things for certain by the look on Thayer's face. One, he's two seconds from punching his own grandfather at his brother's funeral, and two, nothing is going to stop him from leaving right now.

"I'm so sorry for your loss," I rattle off the cliché line, stepping between them, even though it's the last thing I want to do. William Ames is as powerful as he is old, and not nearly as nice. He eyes me like I'm a nuisance, but he brings me in for a polite hug and a kiss on the cheek, knowing people are most likely watching. I fight the urge to wipe my cheek.

"Thank you, Shayne," he says as if it pains him to play nice, his hands still holding my forearms. When he tries to release me and walk away, I tighten my grip on his arms, sidestepping with him in an effort to buy Thayer more time.

"Is there anything I can do to help?" I ask innocently. His

piercing blue eyes bore into me, and his wiry, white eyebrows are set in two permanent, angry slashes, giving him a villain-ous appearance.

Thayer takes advantage of his distraction and prowls for the door without looking back, and I let out a relieved sigh once he's out of sight. Crisis averted. For now.

"I think we have it covered," William says shortly, bringing my attention back to him. I let go quickly, taking a step back. His nostrils flare and he makes like he's going to go after Thayer.

"Let him go," I say, my voice firm even though this man scares the shit out of me. I've never been this assertive with him. I don't know where this is coming from, and judging by the unimpressed look on his face, he doesn't either. "He'll only cause a scene if he stays here," I say, trying another tactic. No one wants that, least of all William. His family acquired this estate in the early 1800s, making the Ames family one of the first, and he won't let you forget it. Owning the oldest and most trusted cargo airline turned passenger airline makes for a very rich man, and being a rich man means people are always watch-ing, waiting for you to fall from grace. To a man like William, appearances are everything.

He scoffs, walking away, and I don't waste any time hurry-ing for the door in search of Thayer.

"Thayer?" I call out, closing the front door behind me, but I don't see him anywhere. Thunder rumbles in the distance, the weather mimicking the somber day, and I scan the front yard, knowing in my gut he isn't here. My eyes lift, gazing out at the trees surrounding the property. These woods are massive, but I know exactly where he went. Without thinking of the conse-quences, I hurry down the steps and take off in a sprint, but I don't get far before my shoes trip me up. I pull them off, brac-ing one hand against a tree for balance, before tossing them into a pile of leaves.

The wet ground seeps through my knee-high tights, but I don't care. I push through, running as fast as I can. My hair whips in the wind, and I don't realize I'm crying until the cold air hits my tear-streaked cheeks. Raindrops fall slowly at first, but by the time I get to the old barn, my clothes and hair are more than a little damp. When I see that the barn door is slightly ajar, I slow my steps and breathe a sigh of relief, knowing he's here.

"Thayer?" I say softly, pushing on the old weathered wood. The door opens with a creak, like something out of a horror movie, but this barn could never scare me. This barn is my sanctuary, in all its leaky-roof, spider-having glory.

It's dark, but the sliver of daylight remaining allows me to see his shadowed form on the couch, bottle of liquor in his left hand. I bend down, reaching for the lantern we left here last night, and turn it on, closing the distance between us. I don't ask if he's okay. I'm not even *okay*. I set the lantern down at his feet, then climb onto the couch next to him, tucking my legs underneath me as I lace my fingers with his. Our arms rest between us, but his hand is limp, not squeezing back.

"Go." His voice is flat—lifeless—and he stares straight ahead, avoiding eye contact.

"No." I'm not leaving him. Not like this.

He takes a swig straight from the bottle, wiping his mouth with the back of his hand. "I mean it, Shayne. Give me some fucking space. I need to be alone."

His brusque tone makes me flinch, but I take the bottle from him anyway, tears welling in my eyes. "Then let's be alone together." I bring it to my lips, letting the liquid burn my throat, unable to keep from sputtering and coughing on the bitter taste.

His jaw locks, and I can tell he's holding back unshed tears. He didn't cry at the funeral either. Setting the bottle down, I pull his head into my chest, his wet hair chilling my already icy skin. I kiss the top of his head, my fingers curving around the nape of his neck, holding him close. He takes a shuddering breath, sagging into me, and I swallow hard, trying to keep it together. I've never seen Thayer Ames show emotion. Before now, I wasn't sure he was capable of it. Seeing him like this is enough to break me.

After long seconds, his hands find my hips and his lips find my chest when he turns into me, pressing a kiss to my bare skin. A shiver rolls through me, and he does it again, this time a little lower. Dark eyes look up at me as he peels the low-cut fabric of my dress away from my body and kisses the swell of my breast. My eyes fall shut, heart pounding, and then he's gripping my waist and pulling me onto his lap.

I cradle his cheeks in the palms of my hands and lean in, pressing my lips to his jaw. Hands squeeze my hips enough to leave a mark as I do it again, this time on each of his closed eyelids, then finally, his lips. As soon as my mouth brushes his, he snaps into motion. His tongue slips into my mouth as one of his hands snakes up my spine and grips the nape of my neck. He shifts his hips upward, causing a moan to slip free, and then he's unbuckling his belt, lifting his hips to shove his dress pants down just far enough. Rough hands bunch my dress up my thighs, and then he's flipping me over, settling between my legs.

My body's buzzing with barely contained lust in record time, and when he grinds into me, I lose all rational thought. I lock my legs around his waist, and he dips his head down, kissing me again. I flick my tongue across the two lip rings curved around his full bottom lip, and he groans, yanking the top of my dress open. I arch up into him as he swipes his tongue across my nipple. My clumsy fingers fumble to the buttons of his dress shirt, pushing them through, one by one. Thayer pulls back just long enough to tear his shirt off, and then he's back between my legs.

"Touch me," I beg, wanting more.

He snakes his hand between our bodies, using his fingers to rub the damp spot on my underwear. "I need you."

My legs fall open, drunk on the feeling. We haven't ever gone this far—never been this desperate for each other—and somewhere beyond the haze of lust, I know this is wrong. Not the fact that we're together, but it shouldn't happen like this.

Not when we're sad and he's drunk and we're on the verge of catching fucking pneumonia in this cold, wet barn. Most people would frown upon losing your virginity this way. Most people would also frown upon losing it to your stepbrother.

Thayer jerks my underwear down my hips, and I capture his jaw in my palms, bringing my lips to his. My eyes fall shut as his tongue slips inside my mouth to dance with mine. He pours everything into the kiss. I feel his pain, his heartache, his need, his love. I recognize it because it matches everything I'm feeling inside.

"I love you," I whisper against his lips, and I feel him tense at the words. When he doesn't speak, I lift my eyes to his. His eyes are squeezed shut, brows pinched together in pain, jaw clenched tight. Dread unfurls inside me as he pulls away, sitting back on his heels.

"Get out."

"What?" I bring my arms up to cover my chest. Thayer's eyes look almost black with only the light of the lantern, his cold expression sending a chill through me. Thunder cracks outside, making me jump, but Thayer remains unmoved, a blank expression on his face. It's as if a switch flipped.

I right my dress, then pull my underwear back into place. Thayer stands, his open belt hanging loosely from his unzipped pants. He pushes a hand through his hair before pulling a pack of cigarettes out of his back pocket. Lighting one, he brings it to his mouth and inhales before he makes his way to the door. He pushes it open, the sound of the storm getting louder, and props one hand against the frame. Rain falls in sheets in front of him as he continues to smoke as if I'm not even here.

I bite down on my lip to keep it from trembling as I stand, straightening out my dress. My tights are askew and still soaked, my dress is stretched out at the chest, but I don't care. I don't care about the fact that I don't have shoes, or that it's storming. All I care about is getting out of this barn. When I pass him, Thayer catches my wrist, stopping me. I turn to face him, but he says nothing, his eyes zeroing in on the state of my dress at my chest. I jerk my wrist from his grasp and run out into the rain.

It's coming down much harder than before, and I'm instantly soaked from head to toe. The sky is dark grey and angry, barely visible above the trees. Thunder booms again, followed by a flash of light that illuminates the forest for a fraction of a second.

"Shayne!" Thayer's voice breaks through the heavy rain. I cross my arms and continue toward my house.

Thunder rolls and lightning follows again, much sooner this time, telling me the storm is moving closer. I push wet hair out of my face, squinting to see through the rain.

"What the fuck, Shayne," Thayer booms, running up behind me. I turn to face him, his dark, wet hair falling in front of his eyes. "Are you crazy?"

"You told me to leave!"

"Well, now I'm telling you to get your ass back inside the barn!"

I shake my head as the thunder booms once more. I know I'm being unreasonable. Now is not the time to hold anything against him. But I can't help it. I turn back around, heading for the house. We're only slightly closer to the barn anyway, and I'd rather get somewhere warm. But then Thayer's hand is gripping mine, pulling me back toward him.

A loud crack splits my ears as another flash of light appears, interrupting us. Both Thayer and I look over to see a bolt of lightning hit a tree only feet away. It blazes down the tree in a straight line, chunks of bark flying off. I stand there, wide-eyed, staring at the smoke that follows.

"We need to leave." Thayer grabs my hand again, jerking me out of my stunned state. When we touch, I feel a jolt shoot through my thumb and down my wrist, and I drop his hand like it's on fire.

"What was that?" It doesn't exactly hurt, but I definitely felt something.

Made in the USA
Coppell, TX
31 October 2023